Faith

Anj

Yellow Rose Books
a Division of
RENAISSANCE ALLIANCE PUBLISHING, INC.

Nederland, Texas

Copyright © 2002 by Anj

ISBN 1-930928-79-3

First Printing 2002

9 8 7 6 5 4 3 2 1

Cover design by Talaran

Published by:

Renaissance Alliance Publishing, Inc.
PMB 238, 8691 9th Avenue
Port Arthur, Texas 77642-8025

Find us on the World Wide Web at
http://www.rapbooks.biz

Printed in the United States of America

Acknowledgements

First, I'd like to thank all the people at RAP that were in any way involved in the coming together of this novel. A special thanks to Day, Stacia, and Lori; you guys made the experience far more pleasant than I ever dreamed it would be.

Next, I'd like to acknowledge and thank "the gang" for their unwavering belief, constant support, and steady stream of encouragement. Debbie, Tania, Mo, Myra, Dawne, Brenda, Nancy, Greer, Rita and Linda, thanks, girls, I appreciate it.

A special thank you to Rita for letting me know about RAP taking submissions, as well as her friendship, support, counseling and encouragement over the last twenty-five years. If you were my therapist, sweetie, I'd owe you a fortune.

To Greer, who took it upon herself to read *Faith* in raw form—when I had put it aside as not good enough—and see "potential." Thanks for all the encouraging chats and laughter, bud.

To Bragg, my partner and financial supporter for the past twenty years...just thanks for everything!

And last, but not least, a special thank you to Reed—an invaluable friend made via the Internet and another short story of mine posted online—who spent countless hours, via the phone lines, encouraging, prodding, joking and counseling. This would not be the story it is now, nor would I have overcome my fears of submitting, were it not for you.

And let me not forget to thank all those readers online for taking the time to let me know that this story was a worthwhile venture. Each and every one of you played a unique role in making this book possible, for which I'll always be grateful.

— Anj

This book is dedicated to the memory of my mother,
Dorothy Chapman: 1928-1998.

Miss you and wish you coulda seen this, Mama.

Chapter
1

Voices drifted into my consciousness.

"Marion?" a man's voice called.

Who's calling my mother? I wondered, not recognizing the voice. I tried to open my eyes, but nothing happened.

"Marion?" the voice called again, a bit more insistently.

"I thought she was going to wake up." This came from an equally unfamiliar feminine voice. "But...guess I was mistaken."

Why can't you wake her? I wondered. *All you have to do is tap her on the shoulder,* I attempted to say, but no words came out. My mouth and eyes felt like they were glued shut. *Could this be a dream?* I wondered. Was it one of those weird nightmares where you believe you're trying to wake up, trying to open your eyes and speak, but nothing works properly? *Has to be,* I reasoned and ceased my struggle, for I had always found fighting against a scenario of this kind futile, at best. The dreamscape would give you up when it was good and ready, and not before.

"Well, at least she moved," the same female voice insisted, invading my thoughts again. "That's a good sign."

"Perhaps," said the man, "but I have seen many of these cases. And movement does not mean they're out of the coma. It could have been an involuntary response."

Coma? I thought, *Oh Lord, this is a nightmare. My mother is in a coma? I have to wake up!*

I heard footsteps receding away from me and strained to open my eyes. They fluttered open briefly, and bright light filtered through momentarily. *Where am I?* I wondered, my eyes closing of their own volition.

"Wait!" the woman cried out. "Her eyes...she opened them."

I tried once again to force my lids apart and succeeded,

although the bright light blinded me, making it nearly impossible to focus.

"Marion?" the man called again, as footsteps drew closer.

I tried to lift my hand in order to clear my vision and block some of the bright light, but my arm felt like it weighed a ton, and it pained me to even attempt movement.

My lips finally came unglued, however. "L...lu...light," I managed to say.

"Cut that light out!" the man demanded.

The light dimmed with the flick of a switch. The world swam into view quite slowly, consisting of little more than a single face: pudgy, rosy cheeks, and gray eyes peering down at me from behind the bifocal lenses of a pair of half glasses, perched upon a small nose. My first impression was that this was the actor, Danny DeVito.

"Marion, can you hear me?"

I knew the face belonged to the male voice, because I had seen his lips move in time with the words. *Danny DeVito with a Southern accent? Must be a dream,* I deduced. *But why is he looking at me and calling my mother's name?* I wondered. Just then another face came into view over his shoulder. My mind latched onto two features: blue eyes and blonde hair.

"Mu...Mother?" I murmured, as my vision blurred and my heavy eyelids closed again.

"I...I'm sorry, Marion," the woman apologized. Soft hands touched my right arm. "But I'm not your mother."

She called **me** *Marion,* I thought. *So, she's not talking about my mother, she's talking* **to** *me. Now why would she call me... Of course, my first name and my mother's are the same.* This woman obviously thought I was called Marion. *But who is she, and where am I? This has to be a dream! There's no other explanation!*

I resigned myself to playing my part. I'd surely wake up soon. *In the meantime, might as well set this dream straight,* I decided. "Fai...Faith," I struggled to say, my voice so hoarse I barely recognized it as my own.

Managing to get my eyes open again, I saw the blonde when she mouthed the word "Faith?" and turned her head in a quizzical manner.

"Faith is her middle name," confirmed a deep male voice that sounded a lot like my father's.

"Fa...Father..."

"No, Faith, I'm your uncle, Brandon," answered the man who appeared on the other side of me, looking like an older version of my father, minus the moustache. The thinning dark hair on top of his head and gray streaks around his temples made it quite plain he was *not* my father. I'd been told I had an uncle named Brandon, but had never met him. "Can you see me, Faith?" he inquired.

"Y-yes," I replied. "But...wh-where am I, and..." I paused and swallowed. *God in heaven, that hurt! For a dream, the pain's certainly real enough!* "...where's my...father and mother?" I finished, the last word hardly above a whisper.

He looked up at the other man and then glanced over at the woman; both were still peering down at me. I heard whispers and saw lips moving, but couldn't make out what they were saying.

"You don't know where you are, do you, Faith?" my uncle asked.

"No. Where's...Mother?" I inquired, a bit more demandingly, even though it hurt to do so. I was getting tired of this dream.

"She's...she's not here, right now," he replied.

My eyes slowly scanned the faces in front of me and came to rest on the blonde, who wore a pained look on her rather attractive visage. "Where...is she?" I demanded.

The woman lowered her eyes, sadness contorting her features. One light brown eyebrow arched slightly and her lips parted, as if she were about to deliver bad news.

"She...she's here...in the hospital," Uncle Brandon answered.

At this, the woman looked over at him and her expression changed dramatically to one of sheer surprise. Her eyes flitted from the older man beside her to me. The expression on her face changed to polite professionalism, as her gaze dropped to the bed. It was then that I realized these two were dressed in white. *A doctor and a nurse? I'm in a hospital? This dream is getting worse by the minute!*

My eyes strayed back to my uncle, who was wearing a gray three-piece suit. Memories of a businessman I had seen in an airport flashed through my mind. *When was that?* I wondered. *What am I doing in a hospital? What's that sighing noise near my right ear?* I cut my eyes in that direction and caught a glimpse of a tall machine with tubes running from it. Following their course with my eyes, I found they traveled in my direction. All at once, I got the sinking feeling that this was no dream, and closed my eyes on purpose.

If this is reality, I want no part of it! I thought. *It can't be reality! It's just a dream. Just a dream! You'll wake up any minute now!*

"Faith, are you experiencing any pain?" the doctor asked.

Yes! I'm in lots of pain! I wanted to scream. *This is a nightmare and I want to wake up!*

"Faith...can you hear me?" he prodded, lifting one of my eye-lids.

"No...pain," I finally answered, realizing this dream was not about to let me go until it was finished. Yearning for the comfort, safety, and security of my family, I asked again, "Father...where is he?"

The doctor cleared his throat. "You shouldn't talk too much right now," he admonished.

"Faith, Dr. Rosemund is going to take real good care of you," Uncle Brandon's voice added.

I opened my eyes and looked in his direction. "Where...is he?"

He merely smiled and reached down, placing his hand over mine as if to soothe me. His dark eyes betrayed him, however, when they strayed from mine to the doctor's. *If he's looking to him for answers*, I thought, *I will too*. I fixed the doctor with my gaze and he immediately looked away, the dim overhead light gleaming orange off his shiny, balding pate, the unnatural dark brown color of his sideburns taking on a red hue.

"You had us worried for quite a while there," Dr. Rosemund began. "You've been... unconscious for nearly two weeks."

"Two...weeks!" I shrieked. *Oh, sweet Jesus, that hurt!* "Wh-What hap-pened?"

The doctor glanced over at my uncle before answering. "You were in a very bad accident."

"Ac-ci-dent?" I mouthed the word slowly, my eyes closing involuntarily. And as they did, I felt as if I were sinking into the bed, propelled backwards through a gray, hazy, spinning vortex. Memories began playing out before my mind's eye: not in flashes, but in full, real-time, vivid detail. I was reliving the past, complete with thoughts, emotions, and sensations.

Two weeks before

"Faith...Faith...get up, sweetheart," prodded the same sweet voice that had awakened me countless mornings over the years, its slight lilting British accent making her words sound like music to my ears. She brushed my hair back from my face. "Faith...remem-ber we're going on 'oliday with your father, and we really need to be underway."

I could lie here forever, I thought. My mind drifted back in time to when I was a little girl and she used to read me bedtime stories or sing me to sleep when I'd had a scary dream. How wonderful I'd always thought her voice sounded. I suppose if both my parents had had the same accent, then I would have found it commonplace. But my father's deep voice had a pronounced Southern accent; the same one that I myself possessed, for I was surrounded by it in my hometown of Jackson Falls, Tennessee.

"I know very well you are listening, sweetheart," she was saying, as I drifted back to reality. She then caressed my cheek one last time before rising to leave. "All right...I suppose I'll be forced to walk about Hollywood by myself. We'll take lots of pictures for you to look at when we return."

Hollywood! I had completely forgotten that this was not just another one of my father's short trips to Memphis to autograph his latest book. This time, instead of just promoting his new novel, he was flying to Hollywood to sign a movie deal. They were actually going to make a movie of my father's newest novel!

"Hollywood!" I said, enthusiastically hopping out of bed. "Swimming pools...movie stars!" I added, reciting the theme from an old sitcom.

My mother laughed as I pretended to dance a little jig like one of the characters. "I thought that would lift your spirits," she snickered. "I just wasn't aware how high."

"Isn't it exciting?" I reached out, and taking both of her hands in mine, began imitating a square dance I had seen on TV. "I wonder if movie stars are any different from the rest of us? Surely they are," I continued, letting go of her and spinning around by myself. "Should I be more dressed up than this?" I motioned to the off-white polyester blouse and beige gabardine slacks I had previously laid out to wear.

"I'm quite sure whatever you choose, you will look lovely," she answered with a smile.

"Oh, Mother, you're no help," I mumbled, sitting down on the stool before the simple brass vanity they had given me on my fifteenth birthday. Unlike most girls, I seldom used it for more than a mirror. Of course, I did enjoy being able to spin around on the stool at a moment's notice.

"As you've told me before, you're quite old enough to make your own decisions," she remarked, moving up behind me, her voice dropping an octave in the process, taking on a more serious tone.

I had always loved the way it did that, as if her voice followed her emotions. It betrayed her at certain times, however, when she'd rather hide those feelings.

"You have turned into a beautiful young woman." Her voice became low and raspy, as she gently placed her hands on my shoulders. "I just wish…"

I looked up at her reflection in the mirror, finding her blue eyes quickly taking on a misty appearance. "Well, just hurry along now." She patted my shoulder. "Breakfast will be ready shortly." With that, she slowly turned and walked toward the door.

I watched her seemingly glide across the room, her stride so short and light that it appeared her feet barely touched the floor. *She's a beautiful person*, I thought, watching her shiny blonde hair sway gently as she moved. Some people were merely beautiful on the outside, living up to the old saying "Beauty is only skin deep." However, there were rare exceptions whose beauty was internal, as well, their very existence making a complete mockery of that old saying. My mother was one of the latter: kind in thought and deed, with a heart of pure gold.

Needless to say, I had not inherited this from her; nor was it the only thing I had not been so blessed with. I had neither her external beauty nor her grace and style. Of course, I had been told that I favored her quite a bit: endowed with the same basic oval-shaped face; unmistakable deep-set blue eyes, of the same ilk as the sea blue ones I had always associated with love, warmth and security; and hair of the same soft, fine texture. In my opinion, however, this is where the similarities ended. Where her hair was blonde, mine was dark brown like my father's. Her nose was dainty and slightly upturned, while mine was larger and rounded on the end—compliments of my father's gene pool. My lips were fuller, although they retained the same basic bow-shape; my bone structure heavier, making me, at twenty-one, two sizes larger than her well-maintained size eight. Swapping clothes, to her dismay— since she always wanted me to share her taste in apparel—had ended at age sixteen.

That had not been as hard for me, however, because as with most everything else, I hadn't inherited her sense of style. I was strictly a jeans and T-shirt kind of gal and truthfully, always had been. For years I'd humored her rather than see the sad look that came over her face when she knew I didn't want to wear a particular outfit she'd picked out for me. After I had entered college and been on my own, however, she seldom broached the issue of clothing.

While staring into the mirror, assessing our similarities and differences, I couldn't help but recall how her eyes had become misty only moments before. I knew at the time, what she'd been referring to when she said, "I only wish…" She'd been thinking about my younger brother, Jonathan David Neilson, Jr., who died at the very tender age of six. Even though it had been over twelve years since that sad, tragic day, I remembered it clearly, as if it happened only yesterday.

It had all come about because of one of my father's business trips on which we sometimes accompanied him. This particular excursion had been to New York City, the Big Apple as they called it. My father had gone there to sign with another publisher, who wanted to distribute his newest adventure novel. Why he had changed publishers, I didn't know—I was only nine at the time. I just remember my mother saying that the former distributor had not promoted his books adequately. Even though she never failed to have faith in my father and his talent, her belief in herself wavered from time to time. And that particular day in New York, her confidence wavered considerably.

She blamed herself for my brother David's death. Many's the time I'd heard her say, "If only I had held on tighter to his hand." And my father would try to soothe her with, "It wasn't your fault, darling. It was no one's fault." His words were meant to relieve her guilt, but they never seemed to penetrate deeply enough. I could understand that, for I had my own share of guilt.

David lived in my memory as an especially innocent child: always loving, happy, and bursting with a tremendous amount of enthusiasm for life. And it may well have been the latter of the three that caused his death. Intent on seeing the "horsies," as he called them, David bolted from my mother's grasp while we were crossing a busy intersection in downtown New York. He darted into the path of oncoming traffic so fast; it was all over in a matter of moments. Mere moments that, when played out by my brain in slow motion, seemed to last for hours.

A tear fell onto my cheek as I wondered what would have happened had we never gone to New York City. *Would David still be alive to enjoy this trip to California? Or would fate have played out a different scenario in order to take him? Was it destiny, or was it merely an accident? What if we had never crossed that particular street at that particular time? What if Mother had held onto his hand a little tighter? If only the horses had not been there, would he have bolted away?*

Wiping away the tear meandering down my cheek, I tried to clear my head by thinking of other things. This wondering "what if" and "if only" could go on forever, and as my father always pointed out when mother brought this up, "It doesn't change the reality of the here and now." And my reality was that I needed a shower.

He's a pretty smart man, I conceded, thinking about my father as I blow-dried my hair. I hadn't always felt this way, however. It was only within the last year or so, after being away at college, that I began to acknowledge my parents as actually being human, rather than the heartless overlords I had thought them to be in years past. Although not a truly rebellious teenager, I had butted heads with both parents, especially my father, over what I considered to be strict rules. After being on my own and hearing the tales of classmates left to their own devices with no close relationship with their parents, it hadn't taken long to discern that my parents' rules were born of love and concern for my well-being. Considering them—specifically, my father—from this new perspective, I could now appreciate their advice, rather than resenting it as an attempt to run my life.

Looking back, it seemed there was never a problem too big or too small for my father to handle, except of course, when it came to his writing talent. From time to time, he doubted his ability to produce that next novel. Many nights I had been lulled to sleep by the rhythmic tap, tap, tap of his typewriter, only to awake the next morning to the same staccato rhythm. And somehow, after spending those long, grueling hours agonizing over it, he always came up with that next book.

Yet no matter how engrossed or involved he was in his writing, he always had time for even the slightest predicament I might have. Of course, when I was younger, my mother quite often ran interference for him. She'd hear my latest quandary, and if she couldn't offer a satisfactory solution, then she'd permit me to interrupt him. As I grew older, I was able to weigh the importance of the problems myself.

"The solutions to all your problems are within you," he'd once told me.

Wise advice, I surmised, while dressing in the outfit I had previously laid out.

When I reached the dining room, my mother and father were already there.

"Good morning," he said, with a serious look on his face. "Are you all ready for the trip to...Memphis?"

For a moment, he almost had me believing that my mother and I had been mistaken. However, as I sat down at the table and watched him out of the corner of my eye, I noticed that all too familiar silly grin on his face. The one that always gave him away, because he looked like the cat that had swallowed the canary. I saw his thick, dark brown eyebrows twitch involuntarily, as well as the very tip of his equally dark moustache.

"Well," I hesitated, reaching over and picking up the bowl of scrambled eggs in front of me, "I don't know about the two of you, but..." I paused, dumping a spoonful in my plate, "I'm packed and going to California. Swimming pools...movie stars." I stressed the latter four words by drawling them out in an exaggerated Southern accent.

My parents looked at each other and then started laughing. I could tell they were as excited as I was.

The breakfast chatter centered around everything we planned to see while there. Of course, a tour of the stars' homes was near the top of the list, battling it out with Grumman's Chinese Theatre as the main attractions. Everything else would be taken care of as we came to it, and if Father's schedule allowed. I could tell from the animated expressions that flitted over his face that he was just brimming over with pride at the thought of having a movie made about one of his books.

"I've always maintained that you are talented," my mother said, as she reached over and squeezed his hand.

"Yes, you always said just have faith and my dreams would come true," he remarked, winking at her.

"Yeah, well, I can't take all the credit," I interjected, without cracking a smile.

Both of them looked over at me and burst out laughing.

I could tell they were still very much in love. I wondered if I'd ever meet a man like my father, whom I could love as much as my mother obviously loved him. So far, there had been only a few boys who'd even piqued my interest. I had learned quite early in high school that most of the handsome boys had only one thing on their mind, and that one thing was something I wasn't the least bit interested in.

I'd seen too many young girls who had "lost their virtue," as my mother would say, at a young age and then been forced to drop out of school to become unwed mothers. I had plans for a career in psychology, and that meant many more years of college ahead. Of course, there were birth control measures, but no pill could keep you from falling in love. My mother was living testimony to that fact. She had been preparing herself for the same profession I was pursuing, but after only two years in college, she'd met my father; and her career was history, as they say.

I'd heard the story a thousand times, but always enjoyed listening to her tell it again and again; and as I helped her clear the table, I asked her to do so.

"What brought this on?" she asked, her soft tone revealing the way she felt about what I assumed were sweet memories.

"Oh, I just noticed the two of you at the table. I can tell you're still very much in love."

"Does it show?" she queried, her voice revealing surprise and a note of embarrassment.

"Yes, to me, at least," I answered, separating the silverware in order to put it into the dishwasher. "How'd you know that he was the one? I mean..."

"You'll know," she replied softly. "Some say you will hear bells, but I say that your heart will tell you."

"But...how did you...how do you keep it..." I stammered, searching for the right words. "I mean, so many of my friends' parents are divorced," I added, voicing my doubts about the endurance of marriages in general.

Not only did I fear falling in love and dropping out of college, but I feared my husband might then divorce me and there I'd be, with nothing.

"To that I say: let no one fool you. Marriage is not a bed of roses," she replied, her voice dropping an octave to a more serious tone. "There will be hard times in the best of marriages. You have to work through them together."

"Did you and Father have hard times before... Well, in the beginning?"

"Yes," she confessed with a sigh, a note of sadness creeping into her voice.

"Tell me the story again, Mother, please," I pleaded. Although I'd brought up the subject of hard times, I really wasn't in the mood to hear anything sad. I wanted to hear the romantic story of when they'd first met.

"If you insist," she relented with a sigh. "Well, as you know I was attending college in London at the time. One day I was walking across the campus lawn, trying to study for an exam by reading as I walked."

"What were you reading?" I interrupted, not wanting her to leave out my favorite part, which made it all seem so romantic.

"*Romeo and Juliet*," she obliged demurely, before continuing with her story. "I obviously wasn't paying attention to where I was walking and...ran right into your father, who was doing the same thing I was, believe it or not. He literally knocked me down," she added, her eyes taking on a familiar faraway look, which made it seem as though she were reliving it all in her mind. "I remember I hit the ground, quite hard as I recall, and your father...he was very apologetic. I was so embarrassed I could hardly even bring myself to look at him, even after he helped me to my feet. But he was so sincere with his apologies that he piqued my curiosity. So I looked over at him, and...fell in love with those dark brown eyes right there on the spot.

"Well, he felt so very awful about knocking me down that he offered to walk me to my next class and carry my books. I thanked him but declined his offer because I needed to study. It turned out he was majoring in English Lit and as he walked me to class, we discussed *Romeo and Juliet*. But before he returned my books, he asked me to promise that I would consider going out on a date with him, so that he could make proper amends for knocking me down. And from there...well, you know the rest."

"Tell me again about Shady Grove," I prodded.

"Oh my, look at the time," she said excitedly. "We have to get moving. Where are your bags?"

"In my room."

"Well, hurry along and bring them down, sweetheart. We should leave for the airport soon. I wonder if John remembered to pack the..." Her voice trailed off, as she left the room.

I knew we had plenty of time, because my mother always made allowances for the unexpected. As a matter of fact, we were always early, no matter where we went. I knew she had just used the time as an excuse, to avoid discussing a part of her past that, for some reason, had not been pleasant.

She had already told me how, after she and my father were married, they moved to his ancestral home, which had once been a large plantation on the outskirts of Atlanta, Georgia. The way she described Shady Grove it sounded like Tara in *Gone With The Wind*. I had wondered many times why they had left, since she and Father had their own wing to themselves. Of course, she explained that Father found it hard to work in those environs, since he hadn't spent much time there as a child. He and his brother Brandon had been raised in boarding schools, because their parents had passed on, as they say, when my father was only a year old and Brandon, seven.

"Passed on" in this case was more of an assumption than a known fact, because the couple had actually disappeared from their yacht, somewhere off the coast of Florida. The story itself had always intrigued my ever-curious mind, for I'd known for quite some time that their yacht had been found adrift on the ocean. When I was a child, I used to imagine them turning up one day with tales of having been kidnapped by pirates. This was just one of many theories expressed by their father's cousin, Raymond Graham, who—via their father's will—was left with the running of the company and the guardianship of the children. Later, my more mature, analytical mind dismissed the pirate theory, as well as the notion that either of them might show up again. But the unresolved question of what had actually happened to them was a mystery I would try to solve late at night, when I needed a diversion in order to fall asleep.

We left ahead of schedule for Nashville, a two-hour drive from our home. As we wound our way up the two-lane highway leading out of Jackson Falls, I glanced back at my sleepy little hometown, nestled in the shadow of two mountains. The sun was just about to peek its head over the eastern mountain range, the pale morning light bestowing an almost surreal appearance upon the landscape. I wondered if it would seem different to me when we returned from California.

I remembered gazing at much the same view when leaving for my first year away at college. Appraising it from a more mature vantage point upon my return from Nashville, I had been surprised at the way so many things I once perceived as sizeable, or at least adequate, diminished in proportion as my horizons broadened.

Once we were off the winding two-lane and on a major thoroughfare, I pondered what lay ahead. Would I like California? Was it possible that I could be visiting my future home? I had always known that I would leave Jackson Falls once I graduated and started my career, because there just weren't many jobs in the field of psychology around the area. Not that there weren't people in need of such services; I am sure there were. "But most folks have a hard enough time holding body and soul together. They can't be paying someone to probe around in their heads," or so old Doc Brown claimed, when I inquired about setting up practice in my hometown.

I wondered if California—all those stars with their egos, diverse hang-ups, and money to burn—needed another psychologist. Could this trip possibly be a glimpse of the course my destiny would take?

We arrived at the airport early and had at least twenty minutes to kill before our flight to L.A.—by way of Atlanta—began boarding. I went to the bathroom first, to get that out of the way, and then took a seat by my mother in one of those hard plastic chairs. While watching the people go by, I pondered what they might be like and where they were going.

I could pick out the businessmen easily enough in their three-piece suits and briefcases; the tourists, already decked out for the weather they hoped to find in Florida, I assumed, or maybe even California; and of course, the soldiers, with their unmistakable haircuts and posture: backs straight, heads held high.

These weren't the passengers that intrigued me, however. It was the ordinary people, like us, that aroused my curiosity. Like the woman with two small children—dressed in a blouse and slacks, her hair neatly pulled back in a bun at the back of her head. Where was she going? To visit her parents, perhaps? To meet her husband somewhere? Or was she recently divorced?

And how about the elderly couple—both as nervous as two cats on a hot tin roof? He was constantly checking the tickets, while she fidgeted with the carry-on luggage. What were they so nervous about? Was it their first flight? Or was there a more ominous reason for their nervous activity? Was someone in the family sick? Or perhaps even dying?

And what about the dark-skinned, mustachioed man with the black bag and dark suit, who kept looking up at the clock on the wall and then checking his watch, while his right leg pumped up and down to some indiscernible rhythm? Just as I was about to start speculating about him, our flight to Atlanta was called over the loudspeaker.

HotLanta, I murmured, repeating an expression I'd heard in reference to the city. Rising from my seat, I massaged my right hip, which had almost gone numb. *How come the very places you have to wait the longest always have the hardest, most uncomfortable chairs?* I wondered.

When my father went to the restroom, I tried yet again to get my mother to tell me about Shady Grove, but he returned too quickly. I knew it was a dead subject now, for she never spoke of that time in their lives in his presence. Although I never truly understood why, I had the vague feeling it had something to do with my Uncle Brandon, who ran Neilson Enterprises. His name was rarely mentioned in our house except on Christmas and birthdays, when we'd receive a card from his family. And even then, my father, who seemed not to want any contact with his family, quickly dismissed the subject. My mother just grew sad and often looked at me oddly. I had even noticed tears in her eyes, once or twice. And whenever I inquired as to why we didn't visit, so that I might meet my only two cousins, my father would reply, "Perhaps one day."

So far, that day had yet to arrive. I was even more curious about my cousins now than ever before and often wondered if Jason was anything like David, but was especially curious about Ashley, who was six years older than me. *Are we at all alike?* I wondered. And then of course there was Shady Grove, which in itself was enough to tantalize my insatiably curious mind. *I bet it looks like Tara,* I speculated, standing in line to board the plane.

Our flight departed on schedule. Once in the air, I settled back and amused myself by watching the miniature world passing

below our plane. It wasn't long, however, before a mass of omi-
nously dark clouds obscured the view. The air grew more turbulent beneath the small craft. Lightning flashed around us and
thunder reverberated off the walls. The pilot's voice then came
over the intercom.

"This is Captain Murphy. We are experiencing a bit of turbulence at the moment, but there's no need for alarm. We do ask,
however, that you remain seated and fasten your seatbelts. Due to
the current weather conditions, we will be diverting our course
slightly, but should arrive in Atlanta in plenty of time for those
making connecting flights."

My mother fidgeted in her seat, checking the time and departure schedule for our next flight. Father patted her hand reassur-
ingly. "Don't worry, Marion, I've seen this happen before. It'll be
fine." He then looked over at me and smiled.

We seemed to fly out of the worst of the storm, for a while at
least, until we neared Atlanta. When lightning flashed once again
and the lights inside the plane flickered, people murmured
amongst themselves. As the turbulence increased, so did the
uneasy swell of voices inside the cabin. My mother's hand latched
on to my left arm. The plane dipped and bobbed, like a toy boat
loosed upon the waters of a gurgling stream. Fingers tightened
around my arm in a death grip. The plane took a sudden plunge
and so did my stomach, seemingly ending up somewhere around
my knees. A tremendous jolt shook the plane. Screams rang out.
Nails dug into my flesh. A deafeningly loud crack resounded in
my ears and then...darkness.

The same spinning vortex that had pulled me back into my
past suddenly delivered me onto the shores of reality as carelessly
as a battered and broken shell was tossed upon the sand. My eyes
flew open; the same concerned faces surrounded me: Uncle Brandon, Dr. Rosemund, and the blonde with the bright blue eyes.

The realization that we had crashed hit me like the jolt that
shook the plane right before everything went black. "Mo...ther!" I
screamed, bolting upright. A sharp pain sliced through my head,
and everything swam away into darkness once again.

Chapter
2

When my eyes fluttered opened the next time, they focused better, yet my thoughts were still fuzzy. The blonde—presumably a nurse—was leaning over the hospital bed, adjusting the covers. Busy with her task, she didn't immediately notice I was awake. The scent of her perfume drifted up to me as she moved about. A strand of hair, which had crept out of the smooth, tightly wrapped hairstyle designed to contain it, dangled loosely by her cheek. From this vantage point, she reminded me of my mother, and a lump formed in my throat.

"Well, hello again," she said with a smile, noticing I was awake. "We thought you might sleep the day away."

"Wh-Where's...my mother?" I questioned, in a voice barely above a whisper.

"Excuse me?" she asked, drawing closer.

I cleared my throat, which was a painful experience, then tried again. "Where's my mother?" I repeated.

She backed away, a sympathetic look on her face.

"Good!" barked another voice from the open door, causing me to flinch. "You're awake. Nurse, would you please get the doctor?" Uncle Brandon quickly moved up on my left side. "We've been worried about you." He gently touched my arm.

I attempted to shift my position before repeating my previous question, directing it at him.

"Now, now, you need to lie still," he admonished, placing one strong hand on my shoulder. "Remember what happened last time you did that? You've been through quite an ordeal. Just try and rest, all right? You do remember me, don't you?" he queried, his Southern accent not nearly as pronounced as my father's. "I'm your uncle, Brandon. And trust me, I intend to see that you have the best care money can buy."

I was just about to voice my question, but was once again interrupted.

"How's our patient today?" Dr. Rosemund asked, as he and the nurse strode into the room.

Not very patient at the moment, I wanted to say.

"Trying to get up again," Uncle Brandon interjected.

"Oh now, you mustn't do that," the doctor cautioned, nearing the bed. "No, you must understand that you were in a pretty bad accident, sustaining trauma to both your head and lower back. It's best if you don't try to sit up just now. If you need anything, I'm sure Miss Bennington, your nurse, will be happy to get it for you."

If someone would just answer my question about my mother and father, I wouldn't need to try and get up, I wanted to say. I fidgeted a little, feeling uncomfortable surrounded by strangers. I felt like a kid again, and wanted to kick out at something in my frustration.

"My legs!" I exclaimed, the sudden realization that I couldn't even feel them, much less move them, sending me spiraling toward the brink of panic.

"Just lie still," Dr. Rosemund calmly admonished, placing one hand on my shoulder. "Remember I said you've suffered injuries to your lower back?" He paused, his gray eyes peeking over the half glasses and searching mine before continuing. "This is why you can't move your legs right now." There was another pause as his gaze traveled upward. "Now, the external head injury is a fairly straightforward contusion; however, your brain was badly bruised." His gaze shifted back to meet mine. "We will want to run some basic neurological tests in the next few days, but since you seem lucid and alert and all your encephalograms are showing good brain activity, I'm not truly worried about long-term damage." He glanced over at my uncle as if speaking to both of us. "As for your spinal injuries, I'm cautiously optimistic. The good news is that we've already given you a full x-ray and MRI battery and as far as we can tell, your spinal column is intact, with no severances or otherwise permanent damage.

"From the standard pain stimulus response tests we've been administering, however, we can tell you have little or no feeling below the waist. Our best guess is that inflammation in your lower back is compressing the nerve endings along your spine, causing a loss of mobility and sensation. It's very possible this is a temporary condition." He paused and looked down at me. "We'll be able to tell more once we can perform some additional tests. For now, all you need worry about is getting enough rest."

*Little or no feeling below the waist...In other words, I'm par-
alyzed,* I thought, and purposefully shut my eyes. *Dear God, let
this be a dream! Let me wake up! When I open my eyes again, I'll
be back home! Yes, back home, safe and sound. Back in my own
bed with...*

"Faith?" the doctor asked.

You're not real! I wanted to scream. *Go away! Leave me
alone!*

"I know it's hard for you to talk right now, but do you...or
your uncle have any questions you'd like to ask?"

"Yes," I answered, in as loud a voice as I could muster without too much pain. "My...parents..." I rasped, my voice breaking
up like a bad cell phone connection. "How bad...they hur..."

"Now, now." Uncle Brandon intervened before I could get an
answer. "Your mother and father are...in good hands. You should
rest, like the doctor says. Perhaps we'll discuss this further tomorrow."

"I...want...know now!" I demanded, irritation apparent in my
voice.

Since I obviously wasn't going to get an answer from my
uncle, I glanced from the doctor to the nurse; both of them were
looking at Brandon. Miss Bennington's face bore a decided frown,
which quickly dissipated once she realized I was watching her,
and returned to the sympathetic expression she'd worn each time
I'd inquired about my parents. I knew in my heart they were hiding something from me.

"As I told you, they're in good hands," my uncle repeated, his
tone suggesting he would not be offering any further details. I felt
trapped. I couldn't even get out of bed in order to find out about
my parents. *Dear God, let me wake up!* I closed my eyes again.
Take this dream away! It's not real. It can't be!

And yet I could hear the doctor and Uncle Brandon whispering as they moved toward the end of the bed. I slowly opened my
eyes and focused on Miss Bennington. Having seen the way her
expressions changed previously, I reasoned she would be my best
hope of getting to the truth. Despite my difficulties communicating, I persevered and repeated what was to me the most important
question of the moment. "Are my parents...badly hurt?" I struggled to say.

"Shh," she said softly, putting her finger to her lips and glancing toward the two men who were moving toward the door, still
talking in hushed tones. "Doctor's orders. Try not to strain your
vocal chords; they were also bruised in the accident. You'll have
difficulty speaking for a while." She flashed a brief smile. I

searched her face and eyes for any telltale sign that she might be lying. "Yeah, I know...how are you going to ask all those questions that I'm sure you have rumbling around up there if you can't talk, right?"

I attempted to nod my head, but found it quite painful. Obviously noticing my dilemma, she added, "And that's not a good idea, either. So, until your throat heals, let's make a deal, shall we?" She paused, letting down the guardrail. "When you want something, you can point to it or...make a fist like this. Once for yes." Her hand demonstrated the movements as she described them. "And twice for no, okay?"

Again, my first instinct was to nod. Painfully realizing my error, I clenched my hand into a fist once.

"Good," she acknowledged with a smile, dimples forming at the corners of her mouth. "Your lips look a bit dry to me, are you thirsty?" I made a fist once. "Okay, now we're getting somewhere, hmm?" I made another fist. Her smiled broadened, tiny lines forming at the corners of her eyes.

Watching as she reached over to the nightstand and retrieved a pitcher, I realized she probably wasn't as old as I'd first assumed. As a matter of fact, she didn't appear to be over thirty, at most. And even though she was a complete stranger to me, somehow I felt that I could trust her. There was just something about the warmth in her vibrantly blue eyes that made me feel she wouldn't be just a nurse, but a friend.

"It's not going to be easy to swallow for a while, but of course you know that already, don't you?" She glanced up at me, while removing a piece of ice from the pitcher. "So we'll start off slowly, with an ice chip, and just wet your lips, hmm?"

Perching herself on the side of the bed, she placed the melting ice to my lips and moved it over them gently. The frozen water felt good against the hot, dry tissues. I felt comfortable allowing her to take care of me—as if I were a child and she were my mother, nursing me through one of many childhood illnesses.

When I finally swallowed, it did indeed hurt like a bitch. "That bad, huh?" she commented sympathetically, removing the ice from my lips. I cut my eyes over at her. "Dumb question on my part," she acknowledged with a bit of a rueful smile. "More?" I started to shake my head, and then remembered to make a fist twice. "Okay, maybe that's enough for now."

Hearing noises beyond the door, I looked in that direction while she took care of the ice. "Lunch," she confirmed, glancing at her watch and returning to her previous position by my side. "Now, let's see if I can answer some of your questions without you having to ask, hmm? First off, did you understand what the doctor told you?" Her gaze dropped to my right hand, waiting for a reply.

I made a fist once, paused, then clenched a second time.

She frowned and looked over at my face. One light brown eyebrow arched skyward; bright blue eyes searched mine in puzzlement. I glanced down at my hand and repeated the previous gesture.

"Oh, oh...I think I get it now." She let out a soft laugh as her right hand patted mine. It was quite warm; there was a gentleness to her touch as her fingers tightened around mine, careful to avoid the IV. "Yes and no, right?" I squeezed her fingers once. She quickly glanced up at me, a smile on her face. "And that would make conversing easier, now wouldn't it?" she queried, evidently referring to the squeezing of her fingers, rather than me just making a fist. I squeezed once.

"Okay, so let's see...Where should I begin?" Her gaze shifted briefly to the wall above my head. "They did a lot of tests while you were unconscious, and everything they found seems to indicate that your injuries are temporary. Their tentative prognosis, at this point, is for a full recovery."

That sounds good, I thought.

"Now, how long your recovery takes is up to your body's ability to heal itself and how hard you're willing to work. Both are going to take time." She pointedly looked down at me. "When you're strong enough, we'll be starting physical therapy to keep those legs in shape." She grinned and glanced up at the wall again. "As for the head injury, there was no brain damage apparent in..." She paused as I squeezed her hand. "Hmm?" she queried, both eyebrows arching.

I moved my index finger and pointed at her. Her gaze shifted to my hand. She shook her head and frowned. "Y-you," I murmured.

"Me?" she questioned, seemingly taken aback. "What about... Oh, you want to know about me?" I squeezed her hand. "Oh well, of course, my bad there. I'm sorry. I suppose I should've started off with an introduction, hmm? That would be the natural place to begin, now wouldn't it?" Her lips turned down in a smirk. "Okay, well, my name is Sara Bennington, and yes, you can call me Sara. I'm a private duty nurse slash therapist." Two fingers of her left hand made quotation marks in the air. "Your uncle retained my services about a week ago because he wanted someone here at all times to monitor your condition. And that's not a reflection on the hospital staff; you really are in good hands, believe me. No, I think your uncle mainly wanted someone in the room, so that when you came around you wouldn't be alone." She glanced away again briefly.

"So if you need anything, anything at all, I'll be happy to get it for you. That's what I'm here for, after all. If you're in any pain, please don't hesitate to let me know. I'll get one of the hospital staff to administer some medication."

Hospital staff? Why can't you do that? I wondered.

Obviously reading my questioning look she added, "This is something they won't allow me to do while you're here, due to issues of liability."

I wondered if other private duty nurses were watching over my parents, as well. *What condition are they in?* I assumed it wasn't good, since no one wanted to answer my questions. Least of all, Miss Bennington, or rather Sara, whose facial expressions as my gaze pinned hers—eyes searching questioningly—were enough to warn me away from inquiring about it for the moment.

"I hope I have covered all your questions about your condition," she said, although it sounded more like a question. I lightly squeezed once. "And unless you'd like some more ice for those lips..." Two squeezes. "Then I should let you rest. It really is the most important thing right now." She patted my hand as she got to her feet. "If you need anything, I'll be right over there." She nodded toward the right side of the room, where a large, high-backed vinyl chair sat near the window. "You should be feeling stronger tomorrow," she concluded with a smile.

Stronger tomorrow? I thought. *But not strong enough to get up and go see about my parents for myself.* Watching her walk away, I remembered my mother telling me that after I was born, I spent a month in the hospital because I was an underweight baby. Yet this had not affected me at all as I was growing up; I was as healthy as a horse. I was always into some sort of sports activity, because I just loved to compete. I loved a challenge of any kind, usually, but the one I was faced with now would be the biggest challenge I'd ever undertaken. And one tinged with anger, because I'd had no say-so in the matter.

Feeling quite frustrated with the whole situation, I tried to reason with myself about my parents. *Uncle Brandon said they were in good hands. They're probably hurt like me...*

"*Or worse,*" a little voice inside my head whispered.

No, no, don't think like that! Just focus on the fact that they're being taken care of. "In good hands," he'd said. *Focus on that.*

As I lay there, my eyes growing exceedingly heavy, I had one thought: *They're in good hands.* I repeated it over and over like a mantra, until my thoughts grew fuzzy and the need for rest claimed my body.

I awoke sometime during the middle of the night, and it took me a while to realize I wasn't at home, in my own bed. Once the full weight of past events settled over me, a flood of emotions, which had heretofore somehow been kept in check, coursed through me like a tidal wave. Tears flowed from my eyes and streamed down my cheeks. Reaching up to wipe them away, I felt something foreign above my eyebrows. My right hand traced its path up and over my head. I gasped when I realized it was a bandage that covered my entire head. I had seen movies about people with head injuries, and couldn't help but wonder if I had any hair underneath.

I felt around the sides of the cloth, tracing its full breadth. It covered my forehead completely, went around the side and over my right ear, where I felt the beginnings of closely cropped stubble. I knew then that the chances of me having any hair left beneath were slim. Tracing the bandage on around the circumference of my head, I found my left ear completely covered.

After that brief journey of discovery, tears flowed like water from a faucet again. *How bad are my injuries? What do I look like?*

I attempted to reach up with both hands this time and wipe the tears away, but my left hand was slow to respond, and a sharp pain shot up my arm as it neared my face. I stopped the progress of both hands before they reached their destination and, blinking in disbelief, took in their condition. My right hand, which still contained the IV needle, was slightly bruised and scratched. Several more bruises and scratches dotted my lower arm, alongside what appeared to be multiple needle marks. My left hand, however, was swollen all out of proportion. The diamond pinky ring my mother had given me for my birthday the previous July was missing; there was a bandage around my forearm, and one that ran from my shoulder to my elbow. *No wonder it hurt to raise it,* I thought.

While surveying all the damage, I remembered that my mother had been sitting on my left side in the plane, my father sitting beside her. If my arm and head were in such bad shape, what might have happened to them?

"Oh good God in heaven, this can't be happening," I muttered unintelligibly, and broke down again.

Sara must have noticed, because I heard the squeak of springs and then the soft patter of bare feet on the tile floor as they neared the bed. The guardrail went down with a clank, the bed gave when she sat down, and then her hand touched my face.

I wanted desperately to be held at that moment, by someone, anyone. I didn't care who; I merely needed the comfort of arms around me. Despite the pain, I attempted to raise up, reaching out for her. A dull throbbing started in my head, sharp pains shot up my left arm, and the blackness overtook me once again.

The next time I drifted back to consciousness, it was morning. Sara was busy removing the cot she'd slept on the night before.

"Good morning," she said warmly when she glanced my way and realized I was awake. "Think you might be up to eating something this morning?"

I started to tell her I was famished, but thought better of that idea and merely raised my right hand and made a fist, once.

"Good," she said, with a broad smile. "But first, let's see if we can raise the head of this bed just a little. That'll make it easier for you to drink from the straw and swallow." She pressed one of the buttons on the remote control attached to the guardrail. "Let me know if you feel any discomfort, okay?"

The top of the bed slowly started to rise; my head began to feel heavy, my stomach quite unsettled. I motioned for her to stop. She reached over and took my hand in hers.

"Pain?" she queried. My reply was negative. "Dizzy?" I answered affirmatively. "Okay, let's just leave you there for a moment and we'll see if it goes away, hmm?"

I closed my eyes and tried to will the dizziness away. "Better?" she inquired, when I reopened my lids. I answered "yes." "Think we can go just a bit further?" I signaled "yes" once again, and this time didn't suffer from the dizziness or queasiness. "All right, everything okay?" I squeezed once. "Good, then I'll go see about getting you something to eat."

She came back a little while later with some type of white liquid that tasted awful. She snickered as I made a face following the first sip. Then she wiped my chin where some liquid had dribbled out the side of my mouth.

"I don't blame you a bit," she said, smiling. "I hated this stuff myself."

My eyes grew wide at the thought of her being in my predicament.

"Oh yes," she confirmed, understanding my expression. "I was right where you are. As a matter of fact, my injuries were worse. Except for the paralysis, of course." She twirled the straw around in the liquid and then looked over at me. "I lay in a hospital bed for several months." She paused, watching my expression.

"You want to know what happened, hmm? Well...I was in a car accident, and I wasn't wearing a seat belt. My head went through the windshield, and I broke my left arm and leg. So I know something about what you're going through." She turned her attention to the straw in the drink. "It's one reason I chose to become a private nurse and a therapist—so I can help other accident victims. Here, take another sip," she said, offering me the straw. "I know it tastes god-awful, but you want to get out of here, don't you?" Her eyes twinkled as she smiled. " Well, humor me, hmm?"

Knowing that she had been in a somewhat similar situation encouraged me to accept the proffered drink. Encouragement, however, did not change the god-awful taste one iota.

"I can tell you're gonna be an excellent patient," she remarked as I grimaced once again. "I'm sure you'll make wonderful progress in no time."

I could only hope she was right. But my thoughts were no longer on myself at the moment; they were already straying to my parents.

"Good morning," boomed a deep, masculine voice from the doorway. Again I flinched. "Remember me?" my uncle asked.

I squeezed Sara's hand once. "She remembers you, Mr. Neilson," she conveyed.

He eyed her rather strangely for a moment, as if wondering why she was answering for me. Then his eyebrows shot up. "Oh yes, I forgot. We're not supposed to talk, are we? I see you're looking better this morning." He flashed a winning smile as he approached the left side of the bed.

I tried to return the gesture, but it never reached my lips, because the liquid had left me with a pasty, bitter taste in my mouth.

"Why the frown?" he asked, his tone of voice revealing concern. He moved as if to take my hand, then seemed to have second thoughts as his eyes traveled over it and up my arm to my head.

"It's the drink, I'm afraid," Sara offered. "It doesn't have a very pleasant taste."

I made a face, as if to say *that's an understatement.* She merely grinned, then lowered her eyes.

"Oh well, I'm sure you'll be eating real food soon," he offered, patting my leg.

It was strange, being unable to feel this simple gesture of comfort. As if realizing his mistake, he cleared his throat and asked,

"Has the doctor been in yet?"

"No, it's a bit early for that," Sara answered, getting up from the bed. "We were just having breakfast."

"Oh, I won't stay long then. I just wanted to see how my girl was doing." He smiled again.

My girl? I thought. *Where'd he get the idea I'm his girl?* Was he just trying to be affectionate to his brother's daughter, or was there some other reason for his comment? I could not say why, but for some reason, when I looked into those dark brown eyes—not so unlike my father's—I had the distinct feeling there was something missing from their depths. Or was I just prejudging him on account of his previous comment, because I was still my father's girl, unless...

"I can't get over how much you look like your mother," he said softly, his eyes turning misty. "Yes, well..." He paused, cleared his throat again, and glanced down at my left hand. "I...I must get to the office now, but I'll be back this afternoon to check on you." He bent over and gently lifted my hand to his lips, placing a kiss upon my misshapen fingers. "You have a good day now." He slowly placed my hand back on the bed and winked. "Miss Bennington, may I see you outside for a moment?" he asked, his voice changing from the soft tone he had used with me to an imperious one.

"Of course," she replied.

I wanted to inquire about my parents again, but knew it would be a waste of breath, for my uncle and the nurse were both headed for the door. *They're waiting until you're strong enough to hear about it,* I reasoned. *The stronger and calmer you appear, the sooner they'll tell you.*

He closed the door behind them and I was unable to hear what was said, but I could tell by the way she acted, as well as the unnatural smile plastered on her face for several moments after her return, that their conversation had not been cheerful. I couldn't imagine what she had done wrong.

Her mood seemed to lift rather quickly, however, and she then informed me that she was going to give me a light wipe-off, since I couldn't get up to bathe. I was a little embarrassed to have anyone other than my mother do this, but after all, things had to be done. As she moved the warm washcloth over my body, I closed my eyes and tried not to think about it. I did look, however, when she removed the sheet from my legs.

I was surprised to find they had suffered very little visible damage. There were a few scratches, and a bruise or two, but nothing like the rest of me. It appeared the parts that had incurred the most harm were from my waist up. And the worst injuries, I had already seen or felt. *Hadn't I? What's beneath the bandages?* I wondered. *If they're keeping the condition of my parents from me, what else might they be hiding?*

I again closed my eyes when I noticed her moving toward my most private part. Even though I wasn't experiencing any physical sensations, I still felt awkward about it. I also felt rather peculiar about the tubes that were running from this part of my anatomy to the side of the bed. I knew what they were immediately. *At least I don't have to worry about making a mess,* I thought.

After my bath, I dozed off again. The doctor came in later and was pleased to see I was sitting up. He said he hoped that tomorrow I'd be strong enough for him to perform a few tests. And perhaps I could have soft food by that afternoon, if my throat was not too sore. After he left, my eyes grew heavy and I was gone again.

When I awoke, it was late afternoon and Sara was in the high-backed chair, reading a book by my favorite author, D.J. Fleming. It was the new one, whose publication in paperback I'd been eagerly awaiting. Oh, how I wanted my mother to be there in that chair, safe and sound, reading to me as she had when I was a child.

"Hungry?" Sara asked, stuffing a bookmark in the novel.

I made a fist for "yes," then made a face about the taste.

"Perhaps tomorrow we'll get some real food into you." She stood up, placing the book on the long heating/cooling unit located beneath the window.

I stared at the novel while she stretched and yawned. I wanted to be able to walk over, pick it up, and read the jacket cover.

"You like to read?" she asked, obviously following my gaze.

I made a fist. She reached down and retrieved the book, then placed it in my right hand on her way out the door. "I'll be back soon," she called.

I was only able to read for a minute or two before my eyes began to feel quite tired and sore. When she returned, she must have noticed the way I was rubbing them.

"Too soon, huh? Perhaps I'll read to you after supper. That is, if you want me to." She reached over to retrieve the book, and as she took it from me, I squeezed her hand rather hard for emphasis. "Oh, you like that idea, hmm? You're pretty strong, too," she remarked, looking down at my hand on hers. I glanced over at my left one and grimaced. "It'll get better," she offered. "You'll see."

After I downed as much as I could stomach of the awful liquid, she pulled her chair up beside the bed and began to read. No sooner had she started than the door opened and Uncle Brandon walked in. He gave no warning whatsoever of his arrival, but gave Sara a sharp glance as her voice trailed off.

"How's my girl?" he asked with a broad smile. This time the return gesture did make it to my lips, because he looked and sounded so much like my father at that moment, I could hardly resist. "Feeling better, I should think. Yes, I see that beautiful smile. This is indeed good," he remarked, walking up to the right side of the bed this time and taking my hand in his.

"I was quite worried about you there for a while. But, now I'm sure with all this great care you're receiving..." He paused and glanced down at Sara, who was still occupying the chair beside the bed. She seemed to take the hint and got up. "...why, you'll be out of here in no time at all." He paused again as he released my hand, sat down in the chair, and then reclaimed my hand through the guardrail. "I knew you had that Neilson spirit. I could tell the moment I saw you that..." He cleared his throat, as if he had almost said something he shouldn't. "Well, I could just tell you were a fighter. Especially when you kept insisting..." He bit his lip and turned away.

I knew he was once again attempting to sidestep the issue of my parents, even though he was the one that had raised it. I wanted to scream out: *Are they close by? Are they badly hurt? Just tell me, please, and stop this anguish!* But I held my tongue. I knew my mother and father would want me to obey the doctor's orders and get better as fast as I could, so I could come visit them. At least this is what I told myself in order to remain calm and appear strong enough to handle hearing a report on whatever condition they might be in. *They're in good hands,* I told myself. *Just keep telling yourself that. They're in good hands.*

"Your cousin Jason sends his regards," he conveyed, changing the subject. "Oh, that's right; you haven't met Jason, have you? You'd like him. He's a fine young man; top of his class at school this year. Yes, he makes me very proud. A true Neilson, through and through; never gives up, no matter what." He patted my hand. "He'll come see you when you're stronger. He's probably out riding his favorite horse right now. Oh wait; you've never even seen Shady Grove, have you? You'll love it; Jason does. You can go horseback riding, swimming, play tennis... You do play, don't you?" he asked, as if there were nothing wrong with me that a few days' rest wouldn't cure.

I squeezed his hand to say I knew how to play tennis.

He merely looked at me quizzically. "Is there something wrong?" he asked, concern in his voice. I squeezed his hand twice.

"Nurse, there's...there's something's wrong, she's squeezing my hand!" he added excitedly.

"She's answering your question," Sara stated, glancing over at him from her seated position on the heating/cooling unit. He merely stared at her. "She squeezes once for 'yes' and twice for 'no.' It's just our way of communicating until her throat gets better."

He continued to stare a moment longer, his expression one of envy. When he turned back to me, however, there was a quaint smile on his face. "Like I said, you'll love it. Your mother did. We had some rousing good tennis matches in our day. She almost beat me several times." He laughed heartily, his eyes taking on a softer appearance, as if reliving a memory. "Yes, your mother was one special lady."

Was! Had he just slipped up and revealed something I should know, or was he merely speaking of her in the past tense because his memories were of the past? I glanced over at Sara and found her watching him intently. The moment our eyes met, she looked away.

"Oh yes, I brought you something," he said, "I left it in the hall. I'll be right back."

He came back in with an oversized brown teddy bear, a big red heart between its paws that read *I Need A Hug* in big gold letters. It was a beautiful bear, but I was no longer a child who could be placated by a stuffed animal.

He brought it over to the bed, grinning from ear to ear. His smile was contagious, and I couldn't bring myself to hurt his feelings, especially when it was the thought that counted. I gave him a smile in return and reached out with my right arm for the large bear. I held onto it as tightly as I could, for it was the first thing I had been able to put my arm around. At the moment, I thought not of Uncle Brandon's feelings, but of my own. *I* needed a hug. And I needed my parents. Or at least I needed to know how badly they were hurt.

"Get well soon, Princess." He leaned over and lightly kissed my cheek, then quickly turned and left.

Princess? I thought. *What is this with the pet names?* First it was *my girl* and now *Princess*. Was it just his way of showing concern and affection for his niece? I could only assume so.

I wondered if he had been to see my mother and father. *If so, why aren't they asking about me? Why didn't he say anything about them? Could they both be in a coma like I was? Are they even worse off than I was? On the verge of death, even?* A lump formed in my throat. Tears threatened once again. *Stop this!* I admonished myself. *They're in good hands!*

Sara read to me that night until I fell asleep.

The next morning I felt stronger and was even able to move my head a bit without feeling any pain or dizziness. Sara thought that was definitely a good sign. One of my legs even twitched, although I didn't feel it. She claimed that was especially promising.

Uncle Brandon arrived before the doctor and stayed until the tests were completed. I'd never had so many tests in my life. They poked, prodded, examined, and x-rayed me from head to toe, or so it seemed. When they finally wheeled me back to my room on the gurney, I was exhausted. Back in my own bed, I went right to sleep.

When I awoke later, no one was in the room, but I could hear voices outside the door: my uncle's and Sara's.

"Yes," said Uncle Brandon's baritone. "It has all been arranged. Yes, most assuredly."

"What about..." Sara's voice softened, and I couldn't make out all her words. "Well, I don't agree," I heard her say, quite loudly.

He said something I didn't understand and they resumed their normal volume, which was too muffled for me to make out.

"But the longer you wait, the harder it'll be," she said a few moments later. Her tone was no longer angry, but pleading.

"In the end, it's my job," he said. "I'll make that decision. I think I know what's best for her. She's *my* niece."

Although I hadn't understood all of the conversation, I had a good idea what it was about: my parents. *They're in good hands,* I reminded myself.

A few moments later, Sara walked into the room, her face a sad, tortured visage. "Oh, you're up," she said, surprise coloring her voice.

Dr. Rosemund and Brandon then came through the door with smiles plastered on their faces.

"Hello, Faith," Dr. Rosemund said in greeting. "I believe I have some good news for you. We found nothing to indicate our first diagnosis was incorrect. Your spinal column still looks good on the x-rays. Even though any spinal injury is serious, we see no reason why, with time and physical therapy, you cannot regain most, if not all, of your mobility.

"Now listen to me carefully," he went on. "I've seen patients with even more severe trauma walk again. But this requires a lot of physical therapy. Miss Bennington here comes highly recommended as a therapist." He glanced over at her. "And since your uncle is having your accommodations set up with the equipment necessary for your recovery," he glanced over at Uncle Brandon again, "I feel confident that if you follow her advice, I see no reason why you can't go home soon."

Getting out of here sounds great, I thought, *but what about my parents?*

"You'll need to take it slow and easy," he cautioned. "Many patients try and rush their recovery, and end up hindering their progress. We don't want that happening to you, now do we? So, slow and easy, all right? Your body needs time to heal itself. A positive attitude and patience are essential parts of your recovery."

I sighed heavily; it looked as if I had a very long road ahead of me. "Patience," I repeated, in a deep, raspy voice I no longer recognized. I reached up to my neck. "My throat..."

"Oh, that's to be expected. Your throat was badly bruised by some sort of cable that got tangled around your and your mother's—" He stopped suddenly and glanced over at Uncle Brandon.

"What? What about...my mother?" I demanded, my throat hurting with each uttered word. "How bad is she?"

"Faith, you really shouldn't talk," my uncle reminded me, as he reached for my left hand. "Should she, Doctor?"

I looked over at Sara and pleaded with my eyes for her to answer me. "I...I'm afraid she insists on knowing," she conveyed.

The doctor merely lowered his eyes and glanced over at my uncle. I quickly swung my gaze in his direction. I found him glaring at Sara as if he wanted to do her bodily harm. Then his expression deliberately softened when he noticed I was watching him.

"Leave us," he said, as if dismissing two servants, his gaze never straying from mine.

Once they had left, he came around to the right side of the bed, where the guardrail was already down. He eased down on the edge of the bed, then reached over and took my right hand in his much larger ones. Gently he lifted my hand to his lips and kissed my fingers. I knew from the way he was acting that something was desperately wrong with one or maybe even both of my parents. *It must be terrible,* I thought, noticing his reluctance to reestablish eye contact.

"Faith, as your uncle, this duty falls to me, and I'm not good at these things." His eyes clouded over as tears welled up around the lower lids. "Your father...my brother...he...he did not survive the crash."

I felt instantly numb from head to toe. A whirlwind of emo-

tions began swirling around inside my brain, seemingly paralyzing
the parts of my body that hadn't previously been affected.

"Your mother..." He paused, tears flowing from his eyes. It
seemed this was the hardest part for him. "She...she passed
away...day before yesterday." He quickly got up and removed a
handkerchief from his jacket pocket. Dabbing at his eyes, he
moved toward the window.

My heart began to pound a cadence like the drumbeat of a
death march. Something inside my head soon joined it, keeping
perfect time with the rhythm. Tears welled up in my eyes; a large
lump formed in my throat. I was sure my heart was going to burst
wide open at any moment. Instead, I found my anger boiling over
as I came to grips with the fact that he had misled me to believe
they were still alive and "in good hands."

"Why didn't you tell me!" I screamed, as loudly as I possibly
could, though my throat burned like I had swallowed something
hot.

He spun around on his heel, his eyes growing large. "Faith, I
didn't—"

"You could have *told* me!" I rebuked, my throat aflame. "You
lied to me! You let me think they were only injured!"

Sara burst into the room at that moment and saw me raising
my head. "Faith, you shouldn't—"

"Get out!" I exclaimed, though it came out as more of a
growl.

"Miss Bennington, I think you should leave. This is
between—"

"Not her, *you*!" I growled, gesturing toward the door. "Get
out! Get out of here *now*!" I shrieked, shaking my fist at him.

"Faith, please!" Sara admonished, as she slowly approached
the bed.

"Ju...just get him *ou-u-ut*!" I screamed, my hand falling back
on the bed, whereupon I broke into uncontrollable sobs.

Sara quickly placed her hand behind my head, catching it
before it hit the pillow. "I...I think you should leave, Mr. Neilson,"
she said softly, slowly lowering my head onto the pillow.

"But will she be all right? I—"

"She'll be fine," she assured him.

"*Ge-et...ou-ut!*" I growled through my sobs. "*Li-ar!*"

"Faith, I only—"

"Mr. Neilson," Dr. Rosemund's calm voice interjected,
"please come out into the hall, if you would. Give her a little
time? She's had quite a shock."

"I'm so sorry, Faith," Sara said, caressing the side of my face.

Without thinking, I reached out and pulled her to me. I was aching to be held by someone, anyone but my uncle.

"So very sorry," she breathed into my ear.

"Oh God, why didn't I die, too?" I wailed. "I want to die, too!"

"I can't let that happen, sweetheart," she said, softly. "You're here for a reason."

I knew Sara had uttered the words, but what I heard was my mother's sweet voice. I wailed in agony at the pain that was wrenching my heart into a million tiny pieces. The hurt was so great that I prayed for death to claim me right then and there. A few moments later, to my utter relief, blissful darkness came and liberated me from the relentless torture of my broken heart.

Chapter
3

I drifted back into the land of the living to find a very bright light in my eyes. I lifted my right hand to shield them.

"Thank God," Sara breathed.

"Faith, can you hear me?" Dr. Rosemund asked.

"Ye-yes," I managed to say, although my throat felt like I'd just set fire to it again.

The bright light went away abruptly, and although my eyes were quite heavy, almost like the first day all over again, I opened them a little wider.

"You gave us quite a scare, young lady," he said, peering down at me. "How do you feel?"

Movement behind him caught my attention and Uncle Brandon's face appeared over his shoulder. "I have a headache," I replied, glaring at my deceitful uncle, whose face abruptly disappeared from view as if it had been an illusion.

"Well, I believe we can fix that," Dr. Rosemund declared. "I'll prescribe a mild analgesic. Miss Bennington, if you'll hand me that chart. You're not allergic to any medications, are you?"

"Not...that I know of," I responded.

"Good," he acknowledged, as Sara handed the clipboard across the bed. "You're going to have to stop scaring us like this, young lady. I realize you had quite a shock today, but please, let's try and stay calm, shall we?" He looked down at the chart.

I shifted my gaze to my uncle, who had reappeared at the foot of the bed. I glared at him, the anger I felt over him misleading me bubbling up inside and threatening to erupt.

"And don't take all this out on your uncle," Dr. Rosemund continued, obviously noticing my expression and where it was aimed. "I told him it would be best not to upset you too soon. I was afraid you'd become overwrought and perhaps lapse back into a coma. He only did as I instructed. So, if you must blame or be angry with someone, let it be me."

My angry stare shifted to him.

"And me," Sara said, accepting the chart from the doctor.

The brief bits of conversation I'd overheard between her and my uncle did not fit with her statement. She'd been against him not telling me, so why was she taking up for him now? I'd thought she was someone I could trust; I was beginning to wonder if I'd been wrong. *Or was I mistaken about what they'd been talking about?*

"A nurse should be in shortly to give you something for your headache, and I'll check on you in the morning," Dr. Rosemund said, moving toward the door, my uncle falling in step behind him, his shoulders a bit slumped.

"Don't be too angry with him," Sara suggested, glancing down at the chart in her hand. "He was trying to protect you. We all were. We all knew it was wrong to let you believe..." She paused, still holding the clipboard in her hand and looking down, though her eyes did not seem to be focusing on the words. "Well, it just seemed the right thing to do at the time. We were all so happy to see that you'd finally come around; I guess we were afraid of losing you to that blissful darkness again."

Considering her use of the words "blissful darkness," I thought, *"So she really does know something about this."*

"Seems that may have been made a costly mistake, however," she continued, replacing the chart in the holder at the foot of the bed. "We may very well have lost your trust." She finally looked up at me, as if waiting for a response.

I merely looked away. The things that other people did for you on the pretext that they were doing it for your own good sometimes seemed worse than what they were protecting you from, because seldom did those things seem in to be in your best interest. Not to you, at least.

"He's hurting, too, you know." She had walked over to the window, her back to me. "Don't forget, he lost a brother."

At the mention of my father, tears welled up in my eyes.

"Do you know he spent every day at your mother's side?" she went on. "He did. When he wasn't checking on you, that is. He seemed to take it very hard when...she passed on. Or so I was told. And that happened not long before you came to. I think that when he told you she was here, he truly wanted to believe that himself."

"I saw...the way you...looked at him," I admitted, sounding

like Froggy from the old *Our Gang* kids' show. "I...should have known."

She sighed heavily. "I'm not very good at keeping secrets."

"You aren't...very good at...lying, either."

"And you shouldn't be talking," she admonished, turning and starting toward me. "I only wanted you to consider his reasons for what he did. He does seem to care for you, quite a lot, actually. And, from what I understand, he's your only family now."

I bit my lip and turned away, wishing none of this had ever happened. I wished my father had never even received that offer to make a movie out of his book and we'd never boarded that plane. The tears flowed like water, streaming over my cheeks. I felt the bed give when she sat down. "Why?" I murmured.

"What, sweetheart?" she asked, touching my arm.

"Why?" I repeated, and turned to face her. "Why did they have to die?"

"Oh, sweetie." She reached over and touched my cheek, wiping the tears away with her thumb.

I grabbed her hand, holding on to it for dear life, as sobs wracked my body. "Please...hold me?" I pleaded.

"Oh, of course," she replied, and gently eased her arms around me while slowly raising me up, her hand on the back of my neck, supporting my head.

It hurt like holy hell, but I managed to get my left arm around her shoulder, and held on as tightly as I could.

"Just let it all out," she whispered softly.

I did indeed release all the pent up emotions in a torrent of tears filled with anguish and relief.

When the residual spasms from all my crying claimed control of my body, I laid my head down on her shoulder. I was completely exhausted and yet felt better, in a sense. Calm and peaceful inside, I could almost let myself imagine that she was my mother, and none of this had happened. I could almost picture being back in our little house in Tennessee, my mother holding me while I cried over some petty little thing that had happened to me at school. I closed my eyes and tried to will myself back in time.

I felt my uncle's presence in the room, even before I heard the noise by the door. I raised my head in time to see the door closing behind his retreating form. A small part of me wanted to call him back and apologize, but I was too exhausted to go through another scene. Instead, I laid my head back on Sara's shoulder, enjoying the comfort of arms around me, the headache I had awakened with no longer in evidence.

"How is she?" a voice whispered.

"Fine, I believe," Sara answered.

"I...I just wanted to...check on her," the voice continued, a bit louder. I recognized it as my uncle's and didn't bother opening my eyes. "I'll come back later. That is...if she'll see me."

"Give her time," Sara said softly. "All of this is quite overwhelming for her right now. I know a little about what she's going through and... Well, just give her time."

I wondered if she had also lost a member of her family in her car accident, and was anxious to ask. Yet, I was *not* anxious to face Uncle Brandon at the moment. I still harbored ill feelings toward him. I knew I should be mad at Dr. Rosemund and Sara, but I wasn't. Neither of them had actually lied to me; they had merely sidestepped my questions. In the conversation I had overheard between my uncle and Sara, although I couldn't be sure of exactly what they were talking about, I did clearly remember him saying that he knew what was best for me and "it"—whatever he'd been talking about—was his decision to make. I heard the door slowly close and Sara's rubber-soled shoes squeak on the floor as she walked toward the window.

"He truly cares for you, you know," she announced. "He's probably doing the best he knows how."

My eyes flew open and I looked in her direction, wondering how she knew I was awake. She was staring at me, arms crossed.

"How'd you know?"

"I've watched over you for almost two weeks now," she answered. "I could tell by the change in your breathing."

I turned away and stared at the door. "He lied," I said simply, sounding much worse than Froggy today.

She sighed heavily. "Sometimes people lie for a good reason. Or at least...what they think is a good reason."

"L-like y-you." I paused and cleared my throat. I sounded awful, like a stereo speaker with a loose connection. "I...I heard you...ar-arguing w-with him, out there."

"You need to rest your throat," she admonished, turning back toward the window.

I watched her for several moments, assuming she'd make excuses for her own lie concerning how she had thought it was best not to tell me the truth, but she made no effort to do so. I respected her for her silence. It was much easier to deal with than a lot of justifications.

Besides, I was having a hard enough time just dealing with myself. *Why hadn't I forced the issue? I could've demanded to know. Why didn't I?* Could it be that somewhere deep inside I knew, and didn't press the issue because...I didn't really want to hear it said aloud? *To hear it from someone else's lips would have made it all too real, wouldn't it?* And I hadn't wanted it to be real! Didn't want it to be true. *It's not true! I don't want to even think about it anymore!*

My stomach grumbled, offering me the perfect distraction. "I...I'm hun...gry," I announced.

She quickly turned around and looked over at me, her eyes darting back and forth as if searching mine for the answer to some question she had yet to pose.

The corners of my lips quivered. I wanted to say all was forgiven, but couldn't bring myself to broach the subject again. She must have understood, for she smiled and started for the door saying, "Well, I'll just see if I can't do something about that."

"The fortuneteller stared into her eyes. 'You will soon take a journey,'" Sara read aloud, using an exaggerated German accent for the fortuneteller. "'And you will find love along the way. But...you will find danger, as well.' Marianne pulled her hand away quickly. She did not like the ominous tone of the woman's voice. And she did not care for all this hocus-pocus nonsense. 'Wait,' the fortuneteller called, as she started for the door. 'There is more I must tell you.' 'I think I've heard enough,' Marianne replied, as she opened the door. 'You should beware of the handsome one, who will lead you astray,' called the fortuneteller. Marianne bolted out the door, leaving it ajar. She did not care to hear any more of—" Sara glanced up and paused as the door to the room slowly opened, though not all the way.

We both waited in silence for someone to appear, but the door closed again. She looked over at me.

I sighed heavily, for I had a feeling it was Uncle Brandon. "Tell him...I'll see him," I offered.

Sara got up abruptly and headed off to find him.

A few minutes later, the door opened again and my uncle quietly eased into the room, his shoulders slumped and his expression remorseful. He turned and closed the door behind him, then ran his fingers through his thinning hair, just like my father used to do.

Pushing the lump in my throat aside, I finally managed to say, "I'm...sorry."

"So am I, Faith. Oh, so am I." He rushed over to the side of the bed and took my small hand in his larger one. "I only meant to...to do what's best for you. That's all I ever want to do—what's best for you." He brought my hand up to meet his lips and placed a kiss on the back of it.

Softly, he continued, "I'll take care of you, Princess, always. All you need to do is ask and, if it's within my power, I'll move heaven and earth if need be to get it for you." He sounded so much like my father that I couldn't resist reaching up and touching his cheek. He caught my hand in his, as if desperate for my touch to linger, pressing my hand to his cheek and then kissing the palm. "I'm so sorry, Princess," he apologized, staring down at me, his eyes misting.

How could I not feel for this man, who did indeed seem to care for me even though he didn't know me? Perhaps if my father had been in a similar circumstance, he might have done the same thing. Had I been too quick to judge, too quick to lash out at someone on whom I could vent my frustration and anger over a situation that I had no control of? It wasn't his fault that the duty of wielding the pin that burst the bubble of my illusion fell to him. He was merely the closest one within range when the fallout came raining down. Of course, that didn't excuse his lie. But, as Sara had pointed out, he was doing the best he could. I could not say for sure what I would have done in his stead.

"So am I," I finally replied, tears welling up in my eyes.

"Oh, Princess, I'll take care of you, I promise." He reached up and wiped a tear from my cheek, then slowly leaned over and placed a lingering kiss where the tear had been. "It will be all right, you'll see. I'd give you the world if I could."

I grabbed hold of him as the tears began to flow in earnest. The one thing I wanted most in all the world was something his money couldn't buy. Money could not persuade the angels to give back the two souls now in their midst.

He kissed me on the cheek again and nuzzled against my neck. I felt the scratchiness of the soft stubble on his face, and was enveloped by the male scent and expensive cologne permeating his clothes. I could not say why, but it was a most disturbing combination, which made me want to pull away from him. The best I could do, however, was loose my hold on him.

He eased back and placed a kiss on the bridge of my nose. "I'm so glad you forgive me. I was afraid you'd hate me for the rest of my life."

"I don't hate you," I responded, although I wanted him to back off even further. Somewhere deep inside I felt a niggling sense of fear, as if the arms on either side of me were some sort of trap.

He must have sensed my discomfort, because he finally did pull back. "I...I guess I should let you rest now," he said, caressing the side of my cheek. "I'll see you tomorrow."

I nodded ever so slightly and offered a smile, although my heart wasn't in it. Not yet.

"Everything will be fine, I promise." He patted my arm. "I'll make sure of it." And with that, he turned and left.

Afterward, I cried in silence for all the happy times my parents and I had shared, times there would be no more of. This reminded me of a line from a very short song my mother had loved: "Preserve your memories...they're all that's left you."

The tear faucet was on high again when Sara returned; there was no hiding it. I assumed she might admonish me for getting myself all worked up, but instead she walked over and put her book down on the nightstand by my bed.

"I...I realize it's easier said than done, but you will get through this," she said softly as she gazed down at me. "That is, if I have anything to do with it, you will." She reached over and touched my cheek. "I won't lie to you and tell you I know how you feel, because I can't fathom a hurt so grave. I can only offer to comfort you."

"Please," I whispered.

With that, she sat down on the side of the bed, and then reached around me like she had the night before. This time there was no need to pull me to her, for the bed had already been raised. She rested her head beside mine, as my uncle had. It was different with her, though, because I didn't feel the least bit fearful. My tears continued to fall as she hummed an old tune my mother had often sung to comfort me. I knew it was silly, but I felt as if my mother and father were close by, watching, and perhaps even participating by using this stranger's body to comfort me. I pulled her close, as if she were indeed my mother and father both rolled into one. And I sensed in that moment that my parents would never be very far away.

We were soon roused by a knock at the door. "I believe that's dinner," she said, removing her arms from around me. "Feel up to it?"

I made a face and rolled my eyes skyward.

She snickered. "You mean you don't want your first real meal?"

My eyebrows shot up. I now remembered the doctor saying I could have "soft" food for dinner. "Yes, I...want it," I replied, my voice still very deep and raspy.

"Come in," she called, putting her finger to my lips, as she got up. "Rest that throat, hmm? Remember our deal?"

I made a fist once and then turned my attention to the short, elderly African-American woman placing the tray on the serving table by the door. "I didn't know you was here, Miss Sara," the woman said with a smile. "If I'd known that, I'da already been in to sees you."

"How've you been, Delilah?" Sara asked as the woman wheeled the table over to the bed.

"Oh, cain't complain," she replied, and flashed me an expansive grin. "How's 'bout you?"

"Pretty good."

Delilah then removed the top from the tray. "First meal, huh?" she asked, watching me look things over. The offering consisted of red Jell-O, mashed potatoes, and something hidden by another aluminum cover. "Hospital food can be pretty good, when you ain't et in a while," she remarked.

Sara chuckled and so did Delilah, as her eyes surveyed all my bandages. "Well, this he'ya food may not be the bes' in town, but...you's sho' got 'bout the bes' nurse I knows of," Delilah continued. "Yes'um, you's in good hands wit' Miss Sara here."

I grinned and looked over at Sara, wanting to hear more.

"Um-hmm...this he'ya woman got Mrs. Simmons back on her feet after she done gone and broke her hip, last year. Mrs. Simmons, she's old...must be over eighty and orn-ne-ry as the day is long. Mean old woman," she explained, as she removed the aluminum cover, revealing a bowl of chicken soup. "That old woman, she wouldn't let nobodys touch her, nor do nuttin' for her, neither. But her son, he hired Miss Sara he'ya, and in two weeks she had that ol' lady scootin' 'round 'cher on that there walker. Um-hmm, you's got yo'self a fine nurse. You just do what she says now and you'll get better. I guarantees that. Um-hmm."

Sara blushed.

"Well, you's enjoys yo meal, and I'll be back to get da tray da'rec'ly," Delilah added as she headed for the door. "Good to sees you agin, Miss Sara."

"Good to see you, Delilah."

With Sara's help, I nearly cleared the tray. It felt good to have solid food again. And even though it hurt to swallow, I ate everything except the biscuit, which was so hard it could have broken a window. I wondered who had decided this constituted "soft" food.

After she cleared away the tray and table, Sara picked up where she'd left off in the book. I lay there listening to her comforting voice, my eyes growing heavier and heavier with each passing moment. I fought to stave off the inevitable, until the need for sleep finally overwhelmed me.

Bright and early the next morning, Sara woke me for breakfast. She raised me up even straighter in the bed, and I suffered no ill effects. I fed myself this time, while listening to her and Delilah converse about a patient she had once cared for.

Uncle Brandon came in right after she removed the table, and for the first time, I took a good look at him. Although he reminded me of my father in physical appearance, he seemed much more sure of himself; his attire was a testament to that. His three-piece navy blue suit fit him perfectly, as if tailored for his body; the collar of his white shirt was stiff and smooth, as if he had just taken it out of the bag; a navy and white striped tie was knotted just so, and held in place by a gold tie clip bearing a dark blue *N*, for Neilson. His hair was combed back from his face, dark sideburns neatly trimmed, face smoothly shaven. He reeked of an expensive-smelling cologne that they sold in the finer stores.

The overall effect stated that he was rich and important. I assumed few who met him would have disputed that claim. He had an air of distinction about him that spoke for itself. I could see why my father hadn't wanted to run the company. Like me, he would have gone stark raving mad in all those fancy duds. He was a T-shirt and jeans man, especially around the house, and most other times, as well. Like me, he preferred comfort to style.

"Good morning," Uncle Brandon said in a cheerful voice. "Ah, so we're eating this morning, are we? Feeling better, I assume?" he queried, nearing the right side of the bed. He didn't wait for a reply before continuing. "Who knows, you might be out of here a lot sooner than they think, hmm?" I merely smiled. He reached over and took my hand in his. "You've got your mother's eyes, for certain, but you've definitely inherited your father's tenacity." He patted my hand and winked. "Oh yes, I wanted to discuss something with you. Your future."

Future? I thought. *What's he talking about?*

"After you leave the hospital, you'll come to live at Shady Grove, of course," he continued. "I'm having a bed like this one placed in your room, so you can be comfortable. But, at your rate of recovery, I'm sure you won't need it long. And I've had a chair...a lift chair installed on the staircase."

A lift chair? I hadn't given any thought to the fact that I'd be in a wheelchair for a while. As a matter of fact, I hadn't given much thought to anything besides my immediate circumstances and the death of my parents.

"And we'll get you anything else you might need for a full and speedy recovery," he added.

I offered up a quick smile so as not to hurt his feelings, since he seemed so happy about all the plans he'd made for me, yet I felt like crying. Up until then, I had mainly been concerned about my parents, and getting better in order to see them. But that illusion was now gone. What if walking again was another illusion with which they were humoring me? *Why should I need an expensive lift chair if I'll be walking soon? Are they misleading me again? Dangling a carrot in front of my face just to keep my spirits up?*

I stared straight ahead as I envisioned myself in a wheelchair, receiving the news that I'd never walk again. For the first time, I felt the full weight of my situation. Reality came crashing down around me like a tidal wave. My emotions were tossed to and fro. I tried to hold back the tears, but it was no use. Emotionally, I was like an old rotten hosepipe; it didn't take much stress for me to spring a leak.

"Oh, Princess, what did I say?" he asked, concern and guilt mingled in his tone. "I didn't mean to upset you. I'm sorry, Princess, I'm so, so sorry." He brought my hand up to his face and placed a kiss on my fingers.

"It's...it's not your fault," I finally managed to say.

"Then what—"

"Mr. Neilson," Sara interjected from her place by the window, "after a shock like the one Faith's had, many times a patient is highly emotional. Their emotions are like a raw nerve. Even the slightest thing...or perhaps even nothing at all, will cause an emotional response. Sometimes it's anger, sometimes it's tears."

"I'm truly sorry, Princess. I'd rather walk through fire than hurt you again in any way." The tears welling up in his eyes seemed sincere. He kissed my hand again, and then placed it against his cheek.

There was a long silence, in which a tear trickled down his cheek and onto my hand. "Perhaps we should leave this for another day," he suggested, placing my hand back on the bed. "I'll let you get some rest now." He walked toward the door, his shoulders slumped as if he were in pain himself. "I'll be back this afternoon," he added, opening the door. He glanced back at me briefly, then was gone.

I felt guilty for crying and making him feel bad, but there was nothing I could do about it. The tears continued to trickle even after he left. One after another, they traced a path down my cheeks.

Sara finally came over and sat down in her chair beside the bed. "Did you ever notice that crying and laughing are similar emotions?" she queried.

I made a fist twice.

"Think about it," she continued, while retrieving her book, "When you laugh real hard, you usually get tears in your eyes, don't you?" I made a fist once. "They both make your stomach hurt, too, don't they?" She didn't wait for my response. "They're very similar in the way your body reacts, and yet they're at opposite ends of the emotional spectrum. But each has its own cleansing effect on the mind and body. Strange, isn't it?"

"Um...yes," I replied, as my analytical mind latched onto the stimulus she was providing. "Fear and...anger are...alike, too," I offered, after thinking about it for a moment.

"Fear and anger?" she questioned, one eyebrow arched skyward.

"Fight or...flight," I answered simply.

"Uh, yeah, I suppose they are," she agreed, looking quite satisfied, as if she'd succeeded in something she'd set out to do.

Realizing the tear faucet had somehow been turned off, I wiped at the remaining wetness on my face. "Thank you," I said, letting her know I understood what she'd done and that I appreciated it.

"Remember this moment," she said, with a wink as she opened the book. "I think it might come in handy. Especially during the next few weeks."

Chapter
4

She was right. My emotions were like raw nerves, and the slightest thing did indeed set them off. So, until their protective shell was repaired, I tried to bear in mind the advice she had given me. It didn't work, however. Over the course of the next several days, every time I turned around, I was crying. Not sobbing, per se, but merely weeping constantly, like one of those newfangled soaker hoses. What time I wasn't lamenting, I was sleeping. Even the simplest things wore me out, like changing gowns or being repositioned to prevent bedsores. But the most tiring time of all since my tests had been completed came two days later, when Sara got me up so they could change my sheets. This was my introduction to the wheelchair.

When she first wheeled it in, I cringed at the thought of being in it. As a kid, I would've jumped at the opportunity and thought it exciting, because back then I could have easily gotten up and walked away when it no longer intrigued me. Now, to be in it was to acknowledge the fact that I was crippled.

Sara must have sensed my reluctance. "Think of her as a friend, hmm? Because ole Nellie here," she patted the back of the chair, "she's gonna take you out of here."

Since she put it that way, how could I refuse? I didn't like feeling so helpless and dependent on everyone, and knew the chair could offer some semblance of independence.

I had assumed Sara would need an orderly's help to get me into the chair, but she didn't.

"This is the way you'll eventually move yourself, once we've built up your upper body strength," she explained. I watched curiously as she lowered the bed to chair height, let down the guardrail, and placed a smooth, slick board in the space between the wheelchair and me. "But until you're strong enough, I'll do it for you." She proceeded to show me how to properly position myself on the board, and then transferred me into the wheelchair.

I was quite surprised by her strength. Although slightly built, hardly over five-foot-six and 130 pounds, she handled me as if I were as light as a feather.

"They teach you how to do this so neither of us gets hurt," she said in response to the questions in my eyes.

She wheeled me over to the window, where my first glimpse of the city of Atlanta was not tremendously exciting. It was raining—a wind-driven rain from the looks of it, with a gray haze hanging over the tops of the tall buildings, which was about all I could see from my vantage point. March appeared to be going out like a lion.

My next great adventure came several days later, when Sara got me up for a bath. "I think you'll enjoy this," she commented, wheeling me out the door and down the hall. "This is no ordinary bath you'll be taking today. This'll be part of your therapy." I liked the way she always explained anything new to me. It was as if she eased me into it, just like she'd eased me into the chair.

When we reached two large silver doors, she pushed me onto the mat of an automatic opener and both doors swung wide. The room reeked of disinfectant. I grimaced at the smell, while looking around. A huge silver tub—more like a vat from a horror movie—loomed over in the left corner. A seated contraption hung suspended from a steel arm and extended out over the middle of the tub. After a quick survey, I reasoned that this was for lifting patients like me in and out of the vat-like tub, and grimaced at the thought of being strapped in it—stark naked at that—while the machine lowered me into the water.

I was quite relieved when Sara corrected my assumption, saying, "We'll be using this one over here." She pushed me to the right side of the room. "Your uncle's had one of these installed in your bathroom, so we'll go ahead and get used to it. I think you'll enjoy the jets." She stopped beside a white tub, which looked ordinary enough at first glance except for the four small silver holes running down the length of its interior and the grip bars on the sides, as well as the wall.

She turned the taps and water gushed out the four holes and began to fill the tub. After testing the temperature with her fingers, she turned the hot water up a tad and then began rolling up the sleeves of her white uniform. I soon found out why she always wore long sleeves. On the inside of her left arm—the one she had injured in the car accident—there were several long, straight scars that ran from wrist to elbow. Noticing my gaze, she offered no comment, and I asked no questions.

When she came over and removed my gown, I felt embarrassed. Of course, I'd been naked in front of her before, but not like this. Outside the familiarity of my room, I felt very exposed and wanted to cover myself.

"Eventually, you'll be able to get in and out by yourself," she explained, and then showed me how I could accomplish that. It took a bit of maneuvering, but she was soon lowering me into the tub of hot water. I grimaced as my stomach began to sting when the hot water reached above the demarcation line of my paralysis. It was odd, knowing the rest of my body should be feeling the same thing but wasn't.

"I'm sorry, but it does need to be rather warm. It's for your back and legs, to get the blood flowing and aid in your recovery. If it's too awfully hot, though, I'll cool it down for you."

"Uh, no," I replied, my voice still a bit deep and raspy, yet sounding much stronger and not so much like a distorted speaker. "It's fine."

She positioned me against the back of the tub, the water feeling good on my upper back. Once it stopped stinging, that is.

"Comfortable?" she asked, gazing down at me.

"Um-hmm."

"Your voice is getting better, hmm?"

"Yeah, but it isn't the same. It's deeper than it used to be and...still scratchy sounding."

"It'll more than likely return to normal. Just give it time." Her eyes drifted over my exposed body. "We'll need to keep those muscles in shape with therapy. You'll find it grueling work, but it'll pay off in the end. For now, though, we'll just keep them massaged, so they'll stay as...shapely as they are," she added, her eyes having traveled up my body to meet my gaze. She smiled. "You've got good muscle tone," she commented, her eyes embarking upon the return journey.

I felt a fluttering in my stomach as she reached out and touched my leg. Although aware of no physical sensations on my skin, in my mind I felt the way I thought I should if a man had touched me. Then again, every time any man or boy had touched me in the past, I'd felt dirty and repulsed because I knew what they wanted. She, on the other hand, wanted nothing from me, and surely had not meant this as a sensual touch. It was this fact that left me even more bewildered at my own reaction.

"You just relax and I'll be back in a second; there's something I need to get," she said, as she arose and turned the water off.

After she left, I felt the true helplessness of my situation. *If someone comes in, I'll just die!* I thought, seeing how far out of

reach my gown was, draped on the back of the wheelchair. When
the door did open a few minutes later, I cringed at the thought of
some man walking in on me. My hands automatically went to
cover my breasts, which left another area exposed. Upon seeing
her face, I breathed a sigh of relief.

"What's wrong?" she asked, seeming quite concerned as she
approached at a brisk pace. "You look scared."

"I was afraid someone else would walk in on me," I replied,
noticing she was holding something down by her side.

"I flipped the sign outside to read 'occupied.' No need to
worry; no one will come in," she assured me. "So far, we've
bathed you with hospital soap, but I thought you might prefer
something more...well, something that smells a little better." She
then opened her hand, revealing a pink bar of soap. "Think you
can manage on your own if I help you sit up?"

"Yes, I believe so."

She helped me into a sitting position and then handed me the
soap and a washcloth. I began bathing myself, careful to avoid the
bandages on my left arm, while she occupied herself by looking
everywhere but in my direction. I thought the soap was a very
thoughtful gesture. It smelled much better, being one of the per-
fumed brands enriched with bath oil. As I rubbed it over my legs, I
wondered how long it would be before I could feel this. When finished, I felt a lot better, and didn't smell like a hospital, either.

"Through?" she asked, as I laid the washcloth down. I nodded. "Okay, then I'll just wash your back, and we'll get you back
to your room."

She spent much more time on my back than she had when giving me pan baths. I could only assume she was trying to wash a
good bit of the hospital smell off, since she knew all about that.

"All right, we're through. Just let me get your towel." She
retrieved the towel from where she'd previously laid it on the back
of the wheelchair, and draped it around her neck.

Once she had me sitting on the side of the tub, she quickly
dried off my back, swung my legs over the side and turned me
around, then started on the front. I wanted to say that I could do
it, just as I had given myself a bath, but she was so much faster, I
let it go.

"I bet you have more boyfriends than you can count on both
hands," she commented, rubbing the towel lightly over my breasts.

"Uh, no...not really," I replied hesitantly, wondering why she
would broach this subject, especially now.

"Modest, are we?" she queried with a sly grin, then continued
over the rest of my body at a rapid pace, never lingering anywhere

else for very long. "All right, now let's get your clean gown on."
She put it on me and then tied it in back. "Now, back in the
chair."

I'll let you rest now," she said after getting me back into bed.
"The doctor should be here...in about two hours." She glanced
down at her watch and then pulled the cover up on me. "I imagine
you're pretty tired, but don't worry—you'll soon have your
strength back. At any rate, I need to run an errand. Remember, if
you need anything, just press this button." She indicated the red
button hanging from the guardrail she was raising. "I should be
back before the doctor gets here." And with that, she left.

This must be why she was so quiet before, I reasoned. *She had
something she needed to do*. With my own mind more at ease and
my body quite relaxed, I was asleep in no time.

I awoke to voices in the room. Dr. Rosemund was talking to
Sara. They were huddled around some type of cart, with their
backs to me.

"I'll need you to assist me," I heard him say. "If the wounds
on her arms have healed sufficiently, we'll apply a smaller bandage. If not, we'll..." His voice dropped so low, I had to strain to
hear what he was saying. "...condition of the head wound will
determine whether she leaves Friday, or maybe even before. As
you know, Mr. Neilson is pushing to have her discharged sooner
than I'd like, but since you'll be there... You will be starting physical therapy this afternoon, won't you?"

"Yes, I'm sure she'll be strong enough for a light session. She
had her first bath today, you know. Held up very well. She definitely has good muscle tone."

"That's always a good sign. Okay, let's wake her up and..."
He paused as he turned around and saw I was watching. "Oops...
Well, no need to wake her. So, how's my favorite patient?" he
asked with a smile, moving toward me.

"Fine."

"Good, good. Miss Bennington tells me you had your first
real bath today. Any pain, discomfort, dizziness?"

"No."

"Great. Now then, the next order of business is to change
your bandages. I've asked Miss Bennington to assist me," he
explained, as she rolled the cart—containing an assortment of
scissors, gauze and tape—up to the bed. "Let's raise you up, and
we'll start to work, okay?"

I merely nodded, wondering what the wounds looked like,
especially the one on my head. When I had inquired about this
previously, Sara had reported that she didn't know, since she'd

been hired after I was taken out of ICU. She also said she'd been
told I had several lacerations, but she was unaware of their severity.

As the doctor went to work removing the bandage on my forearm, I watched intently. A few seconds later, a thin cut running up
the outside of my arm was revealed. "Looks real good," he said
with a smile.

When the bandage on my upper arm was removed, it exposed
a longer laceration snaking its way up my arm and tapering off at
both ends—elbow and shoulder. It looked like I had railroad
tracks running up my arm. I assumed these two should not be so
hard to fix, but was reminded of Sara's scar, and speculated
whether there was something different about the skin on her arm
that made it a poorer candidate for plastic surgery.

"This is doing very well," he commented. "I think we can use
a smaller bandage here." He went to work doing just that.

By the time he got around to my head, I was a bundle of
nerves from imagining what would be revealed. Perhaps it wasn't
as bad as the bulk of the bandage implied. Perhaps the injuries
weren't any worse than the ones on my arm, and they'd simply
gone wild with gauze and tape.

When he finally started snipping the bandage, I once again
wondered if I had any hair left. I knew there was a short, spiky
growth on the right side where the bandage didn't cover, but
wasn't even sure whether or not hair would grow beneath a bandage. *Could this retard its growth?* I considered. I also speculated
on how big the wounds were, exactly how many there were, and
whether they'd leave awful scars like the ones on Sara's arm.

As the doctor slowly unwrapped the bandage, Sara watched
closely and I, in turn, watched her, to see what type of reaction
she had to my unveiling. I would use this to gauge how bad it was.
She must have felt my gaze on her, because she glanced down at
me and smiled. *Must not be that bad*, I thought.

"You're healing nicely. Very nice, indeed," the doctor commented, moving closer to examine something up there.

"Can I see?" I inquired.

"All right," he consented. "Miss Bennington, if you'd get her
a mirror, please. Before you do so, however, I want you to listen to
me carefully, Faith, okay?" He paused, gray eyes peering over his
bifocals. "Now, you have to remember that your injuries are still
in the process of healing, and actually aren't bad at all. The body
has enormous recuperative powers; and with time and a bit of
plastic surgery, I'm sure you won't even be able to tell they were
there. Believe me when I say you are healing very well, and what

you will see now is in no way a representation of the permanent state of things. So, let's try and stay calm, okay?"

As Sara handed me a small compact, I was no longer sure I wanted to see what had been uncovered. I looked at Sara, watching her face for any hint of what she thought of my injuries. I read nothing in her eyes or facial expressions. *That has to be a good sign,* I thought and opened the compact.

"Oh, my God!" I gasped.

"Remember, it's only temporary," Sara reminded me, as I surveyed the damage.

Seemingly in shock, my eyes traced the path of a long, jagged cut that started above my right eyebrow and ran horizontally across my forehead, curving upwards at a slight angle as it inched its way toward what should have been my hair line, but was only a very fine, light brown down. From this point, near the left side of my head, the wound took an abrupt 90-degree turn and continued across the top, where it tapered off.

Shifting the mirror to the left, where my ear had been covered, to my utter dismay, I found yet another laceration. This one was even more pronounced than the one across my forehead. It started near my temple, missed my ear by centimeters, and continued to grow progressively larger, slicing a straight path toward the back of my head.

Feeling my heart sink down to my feet, I stared into the mirror, unable to take my eyes off of what to me was a grotesque sight.

"Faith...Faith, look at me...look at me, Faith," Sara said in a stern voice as she reached over and turned my face toward her. She had already sat down on the left side of the bed. "Mine was far worse than yours, believe me. Now, tell me, can you see it?"

I looked at her, quickly searching her face for any hint of a scar, then turned back to the mirror. *She's lying to me,* I thought, staring at my hideous reflection.

Dr. Rosemund reached over to take the mirror from me, but I wouldn't let go. "Faith, we need to put on another bandage," he said calmly.

"Do it, then!" I growled.

He hesitated a moment, glancing up at Sara, then went to work while I watched. I felt numb all over. Still I stared into the mirror, so angry at the injustice of it all that I couldn't say a word, much less move a muscle. First, I'd been told I'd lost the use of my legs, although perhaps not permanently, or so they hoped. Then I'd learned I had lost my parents. And now...now I had been stripped of my dignity. All of my silky brown locks were gone; my

face and head were marred for life! Of course, it wasn't like I
hadn't already pondered these possibilities in my mind, but just
thinking about it was worlds apart from actually seeing it up close.

Soon my head was covered with another, somewhat smaller
bandage. "You're healing very well," Dr. Rosemund maintained.
"At this rate, I see no reason why you can't be out of here by
Thursday of this week."

"Did you hear that, Faith?" Sara queried. "Thursday. Isn't
that good news?"

Tears welled up in my eyes. Sure, I'd be out of here, but in
another strange place, to face...what? A new set of obstacles? That
long road of recovery that I'd previously envisioned stretched out
before me had suddenly grown much longer. I felt like someone
had removed a pair of binoculars from my eyes. What had once
seemed within my grasp now appeared to be miles away. Long,
rough, slow, agonizing miles for someone in a wheelchair. For
someone... *Crippled!* The word resounded in my head. My mind
began to taunt me with a childlike chant. *"Faith is a cripple... Got
a scar and not a dimple."*

How long will I be this way? I wondered. *How long before my
hair grows back?* Or before I could have plastic surgery? Who
would look at me now, the way I was? Or more to the point, *how*
would they look at me? With pity? Revulsion? Or would they
merely turn away?

"I'll check on you later, Faith," Dr. Rosemund said, as he
exited the room.

I didn't even acknowledge his departure, but continued to
stare into the mirror at my reflection: eyes that had once been a
soft blue with green highlights now seemed to be a piercing, cold
steel gray, filled with anger. The scar across my forehead only
completed the picture of a very ugly young woman. I didn't like
what I saw at all. I never wanted to look at myself again. I felt like
I had been slapped hard across the face by the unseen, uncaring,
and immensely cold hand of fate. And I wanted revenge! I wanted
to lash out at something, anything. I felt the rage boiling up
within me, and knew trying to stop it was useless. I grasped the
compact in my right hand.

"Faith, no, don't—" Sara reached for it.

Too late. The compact went sailing across the room, hit the
wall, and broke in half, the mirror shattering into a half-dozen tinkling pieces. *Shattered, like my whole world,* I thought, as I
watched the other half of the compact—containing the makeup—
skid across the floor.

"Faith, sweetheart," Sara began, as she touched my arm.

"Go away!" I growled, sounding like a dog that been cornered and was warning away a pursuer. I gnashed my teeth, knowing my voice would probably never be the same, either. *Nothing would!* "Just...leave...me...alone," I snarled, enunciating each word.

She didn't take her hand away. "Don't do this to yourself," she said, tightening her grip. "I know what you're feeling, I—"

"You know nothing!" I spat, trying to wrench my left arm from her grasp. I didn't want to be held or patronized anymore. "You know nothing at all about how I feel! Now, get away from me!" I pushed against her with my right arm, and she grabbed hold of it. I was able to get my left one free, however, and before even thinking about what I was doing, took an openhanded swing at her.

She blocked it and seized that one, too. "Stop, damn it!" she cried out.

I wiggled to free my arms, but she was too strong. She overpowered me and pinned my arms to the bed over my head. She was only inches from my face, her eyes wide and wild looking.

"Enough, goddammit!" she declared. "You can't get rid of me that easily. And yes, I do know what you're going through. Look at me. Damn it, I said look at me!" she demanded. Surprised at her ferocity, I complied. "You see this face? Well, sweetheart, five years ago, you wouldn't have recognized it. I sure as hell didn't! My face was a goddamned disaster area, just one huge mass of cuts and gashes."

I found it difficult to believe her face had ever looked as bad as mine.

"Oh yeah," she continued. "I wore a bandage all over, not just part of my head, like you. No, mine was all over my face, as well. I had two holes for my eyes, one for my broken nose, and one for my mouth—which was wired shut, by the way! And you think you've got it bad! Huh? You don't know what bad is!"

I turned my face away; her anger was too much for me to bear. I stared at her arm; the button on her cuff having slipped free, the sleeve was open, revealing her scars—which she obviously noticed.

"Oh, you think I'm lying about my face, do you? Why, because I have these on my arms? Well, let me tell you something, sweetheart, these weren't caused by the accident. No, I did this! Yeah, that's right, me," she added, answering the unvoiced question in my eyes. "I didn't want to live anymore! Now look at me and tell me again how much I don't know!" She let go of one of my wrists and then gathered them both up in one hand. "Look at me, damn it, and tell me I don't understand," she demanded, as she captured my face in her left hand and forced me to look at her. "I know a lot more than you think I do!"

The sight of her rage had cooled mine considerably. I had never had anyone talk to me quite this way, nor get this mad at me, that I could remember. She had sure taken the wind out of my sails. As I stared into her eyes, I realized she had left me with something else: a very strange feeling in the pit of my stomach. Before this, I had thought of her like my mother, but now...now she had shown me quite another side of her personality. She reminded me more of myself. The mother image I had held of her flew right out the window the moment she pinned me to the bed; my mother would never have done that. She would have left me alone. She would never have fought with me. I had a newfound respect for Sara. Uncle Brandon had been beaten by my rage, but not Sara; no, not Sara.

I studied the face that had once been so scarred, searching for any telltale signs. At this distance I could see faint lines here and there, but they were so light as to be barely discernable. There were no true remnants of the disaster area she had described. As a matter of fact, her face was beautiful. Her vibrant blue, slightly slanted eyes, finely arched eyebrows, upturned nose, and even the faint light brown moustache across her shapely upper lip were a very appealing combination. I found myself unable to take my eyes off those lips. Butterflies began to flutter around in my stomach, and I felt light-headed.

Slowly, she let go of my face and then my wrists. When she started to back away, I could not resist reaching up and touching her face. I knew there were still scars; they just weren't visible on the surface. When my hand touched her skin, the butterflies swarmed about erratically. Although I didn't understand why I was reacting this way, I knew I *liked* the feeling. My eyes traveled upwards to meet her gaze.

"Think we should ask your uncle to bring along two pairs of boxing gloves, the next time he comes?" she queried, a smirk forming at the corners of her mouth.

I found myself moving my hand slightly and running my thumb over her lower lip, tracing its succulent red path from one corner of her mouth to the other. She cleared her throat, I flinched, and she backed away just as the door to my room opened.

My uncle walked into the room, looking quite dapper in his dark brown suit, tan vest, and neatly pressed white shirt. "How's my Princess today?" he asked, sounding more cheerful than ever.

I looked over at Sara, who was getting up from the bed.

"Uh...better...now," I replied, as Sara's shoe crunched a shard of the mirror on the floor.

"What happened over there?" he questioned, spying pieces of the mirror lying all over the floor next to the table.

"I...I dropped my compact," Sara responded. "I'll just...go get something to clean it up."

"How come you weren't already cleaning it up?" he inquired curiously.

"Because...because I...I asked her to adjust my pillow before she left," I spoke up.

"Hmph. Well, I met Dr. Rosemund downstairs in the hallway. He said you'd be able to go home Thursday. I assume you were delighted to hear that?"

"Um... Yes, yes of course," I replied, watching Sara disappear around the door. "I...uh...I can't wait to see Shady Grove," I added, trying to sound happy, since I didn't want to hurt his feelings. I also didn't want him asking questions I didn't want to answer at the moment. I was having a hard enough time concentrating on what he was saying as it was, with my mind still on previous events. *Why in this world did I reach up and touch her lip?* I thought.

"You'll love it. I know you will. Your mother did, but...I suppose she told you about it."

"Uh...no," I replied. I saw his smile fade instantly. "I mean...no, I...I'd rather hear about it...from your point of view."

His expression changed abruptly, his brown eyes lighting up as he began telling me all about Shady Grove. I knew he loved horses and horseback riding, for he went on and on about the thoroughbreds he raised and the large expanse of land on which he rode them. I speculated as to whether I would ever be able to ride again.

I listened as intently as I could while he described his home in great detail, characterizing it more like Tara than even my mother had. I found myself profoundly wishing that my parents were here, and we could all be going there together. But, alas, that was not to be. Nothing could change what was. I knew they wouldn't want me to dwell in the past, so I allowed myself to be carried along by his excitement and enthusiasm. It seemed inevitable that this would be my future, for a while at least.

While listening to him expound further on the advantages of living at Shady Grove, I watched Sara clean up the broken shards from the mirror. I hadn't even stopped to consider that it was her compact. *Perhaps if I had known that, I wouldn't have broken it*, I thought. *Then again, none of the subsequent events would have taken place and*— I suddenly realized this was one of those times when, if I had to do it all over again, I wouldn't change a thing.

Before Brandon left, he placed a kiss on my cheek as always, promising to see me tomorrow. *Just two more days and I'll be out of here.* The thought excited me, and yet the future was frightening. How long would my recovery take? I looked over at Sara, who had been very quiet since cleaning up my mess. She was still sitting on the heating unit, staring out at the city beyond.

"Sara, how long will it take before...I can walk again?"

"That depends on a lot of different factors," she replied, her eyes never leaving the window. "Foremost is your body's ability to heal itself. Some heal faster than others, and that depends a great deal on your state of mind."

"What do you mean?"

"Whether or not you want to get better, and just how hard you're willing to work for it," she replied, still staring out the window.

I could tell there was something weighing heavily on her mind by the way she crossed and uncrossed her arms, then rubbed her hands up and down them as if she were cold.

"I'm...sorry about your compact," I offered.

"Don't worry about it." She shrugged. "I never used it anyway."

My mind replayed the scene right before Brandon came in. I remembered how she had backed away from me, and how I had felt at that moment. Why had I reached up and touched her lip? I still didn't know. But I did know I wanted to be close to her again. I wanted to feel her arms around me, the warmth of her embrace. *I wish you would turn around and look at me*, I thought.

"Sara," I paused, hoping she'd turn around.

"Hmm?" She didn't move a muscle.

"Is there something wrong?"

"No, just thinking about getting some fresh air, is all. Dinner'll be served soon, so I won't be long." She got up and walked over to the door, where she paused for a moment. "We...we'll start your therapy after dinner, so get some rest," she added, without even a glance in my direction.

Now I knew there was definitely something wrong. I wondered if it might be because it had stirred up some painful memories when she'd told me about her face. I assumed she probably just needed to be alone for a while. And who wouldn't, in her position, since she was on duty twenty-four hours a day? I had never really given this much thought before. I'd merely taken for granted that she would be here whenever I needed her. I realized

I'd been acting very selfishly, thinking only of myself when there were other people around me who had their own problems.

I must have dozed off, for when I opened my eyes again, a young Hispanic man was bringing a food tray into the room. "Sorry to wake you," he apologized, as he set the tray down on the table. "But your nurse, she did not answer when I knocked."

"That's all right. She would have woken me up anyway," I replied.

He pulled the table over to the bed and positioned it in front of me. I noticed he kept looking at my head out of the corner of his eyes.

"Where's Delilah today?" I asked.

"This is her day off," he answered, uncovering the tray. He gave me one last quick glance. "Everyt'ing all right?"

"Yes, thank you."

After he left, I raised the head of the bed to a more comfortable position. I was removing the cover from the plate when Sara walked in.

She looked over at me, seemingly quite surprised by what she saw. "Well, looks as if you can get along just fine without me," she observed, walking back over to the window.

I could tell by her demeanor that her time away had not helped. I tried to think of something witty to say, but all I came up with was, "It's because of you that I can do without you, for a little while, at least."

She smiled and then moved over to her chair by the bed. *Funny*, I thought, *how I consider this "her" chair.* "Have you eaten?" I asked.

"Yes. That's why I was late getting back."

I wanted to say something to try and cheer her up, but couldn't think of a thing, so I ate in silence. To my surprise, I found that I truly missed her being involved in everything I did. I wanted to be independent, yet adored the attention she lavished on me. *Perhaps that's it*, I thought. Maybe she realized I was depending on her too much, and this was just her way of loosening the apron strings, so to speak.

After my meal, I pushed the table as far away from me as I could possibly get it, so that she would see I was trying to be more independent. She didn't seem to notice, however; she merely sat there reading her book. I eased the head of the bed down and lay back, listening to the sounds of the hospital, all the while aching for her to say something...anything. She merely kept reading.

Finally, the young man came back for the tray. She still made no attempt to get up or even acknowledge his presence with more than a glance over her book. I thanked him.

About thirty minutes later, she got up, went into the bathroom, and emerged with something in a squeeze bottle. "Think
you're up to your therapy now?" she asked, without even looking
over at me.

"I guess so," I replied, not really sure what to expect, since
she hadn't explained anything about it. Yet, in a way, I was eager
for anything, as long as she would talk to me.

She placed the bottle on the table and then changed the sign
on the door to read "Do Not Disturb." She slowly closed the door,
as if she were contemplating something. She definitely had that
"lost in space" look, as my mother had always called it when I was
so deeply involved in my own thoughts that I blocked out everything else.

Pushing the table over to the right side of the bed, she finally
looked over at me. "We'll start with your legs," she said decisively.
"I'll rub them with the oil to stimulate the circulation of blood.
Then," she paused, lowering the bed, "then I'll turn you over, and
do the same to your back."

She pulled down the covers, exposing my seemingly lifeless
legs, and then sat down on the bed. Retrieving the oil, she placed a
small amount in the palms of her hands and rubbed them together
to warm it. A bit hesitantly, she began rubbing my legs. I could
feel nothing, yet closed my eyes, trying to imagine it, since it
looked like it should feel pretty good. My attempts at imagining
were to no avail, unfortunately, so I settled for watching.

"Was this part of your training?" I asked, desiring to break
the silence between us.

"Um-hmm," she answered, and then got up and went over to
the other side of the bed.

After massaging my left leg, she picked it up, bent it at the
knee, pushed it toward me, and then pulled it straight out. She
repeated the three movements—bend, push, pull—for at least two
minutes, without ever looking up. I was starting to feel like I was
just a job to her. When finished, she moved over and did the same
to the other leg.

"Okay," she said finally, "let's turn you over."

Crossing one of my legs over the other, she turned my torso.
Slowly, one body part at a time, she rolled me over. Although I
kept staring at her throughout, she never would meet my gaze.

Clearing her throat, she started rubbing oil on my back. Every
once in a while, I could feel what she was doing when her hands
moved above the paralyzed zone, then they would disappear into
the abyss again.

"All right, let's get you—"

"Um...would you...do the rest of my back?" I interrupted. "I'd like to know what it feels like."

"Pardon me?"

"I mean, I watched you do my legs and couldn't feel anything. I'd just like to know what it feels like."

"Very well," she agreed with a sigh.

Rubbing gently at first, her hands slid smoothly over my upper back. Now I knew what my legs had been privy to. Increasing the pressure, she moved up to my shoulders. I had been unaware of how sore they actually were. It felt as if she were kneading my flesh, but it didn't hurt. On the contrary, it felt good; and I told her so.

"Your shoulder muscles are tight," she said in response. "You're storing tension here. Are you worried about something?"

Finally she was talking to me. "You," I answered honestly.

She abruptly stopped, then resumed without a word. When finished, she repeated the process of rolling me back over.

"I realize it's none of my business," I conceded, as she rolled me over the last leg of the way, "but what's with all this silence? It's about to drive me up the wall."

She glanced down at me, her eyes a dark, watery blue. Several seconds passed, then she sighed heavily and sat down on the edge of the bed. "I suppose we should discuss this. Of course, most of the time this doesn't come up until later on; but, since I've seen it before, I suppose I recognize the first signs." She sighed again, as if reluctant to continue. "Sometimes, especially when a patient feels alone, they become...too dependent on their therapist, nurse, or whoever is with them most of the time. Do you understand?"

"Well, I suppose. But, there are only so many things I can do for myself. And...I try to do them, don't I?"

She shook her head. "No, I'm not referring to a physical dependency. I'm talking about an emotional one."

I considered this for a moment. The only way I could see that I was emotionally dependent upon her was when she held me while I cried. And I had only asked for that once. "You mean, I shouldn't expect you to hold me when I cry?"

"That, too. I mean... Yes, that was my mistake. I caused you to become more dependent that way. And now I need to remedy it."

"Well, why didn't you just say so? Why all the silence?"

She stared at me for a long time, as if she were trying to say something with her eyes that she couldn't bring herself to say with her mouth. "It goes deeper than that, Faith. I think we both know that," she finally answered.

"Oh, you mean me thinking of you like my mother. Well, I don't anymore. Not after this afternoon."

Her eyes opened wider, as if I'd hit the proverbial nail on the head. I searched through my memories of that afternoon, trying to remember what I could have done to upset her. Of course, it came back clearly: running my thumb over her bottom lip. I wanted to offer an excuse and say, *I only wanted to see if you were wearing lipstick.* But that wasn't the truth, and besides, I didn't think it would fly. At least, it didn't with me, because I hadn't given any thought as to whether she was wearing lipstick or not until after my finger touched her lip. *What were you thinking?* I questioned myself. *Hell if I know,* I silently answered. *It...it just...happened is all! It was an impulse! Just...just a stupid mistake! I...I felt grateful to her and...I was just showing that...wasn't I? Of course, I was, what else could it be?*

Instead of making excuses, I ended up going on the offensive. "Oh, you mean it's all right for you to show affection toward me, but I shouldn't reciprocate. Is that what you're saying? The patient-therapist relationship only works one way, hmm?" The words were tumbling out. "I shouldn't feel gratitude toward you? Shouldn't feel...anything, even though you're about the only person in this world right now I feel I can trust?" My bottom lip trembled, betraying my emotions.

"Faith, I..." She paused and looked away, shaking her head. Her eyes rolled skyward before her gaze settled upon mine. "You're...very emotional right now." She paused, the corners of her mouth turning up as if she wanted to smile. "I'm not the only person you can trust, you know."

"I'm sorry I've grown so dependent on you," I offered, my lip still trembling slightly. "But as I think you can tell, I don't really know my uncle that well. Matter of fact, I'd never met him until...the day I met you. I mean, he seems nice, but in the back of my mind, I know there's a reason my mother and father didn't like to talk about him. And that...well, it makes me want to keep my distance. Plus, whether he was protecting me or not, he still lied. I could tell you would've told me the first day. You wanted to, didn't you?"

"Hmph, well...I guess I can't fool you."

"That's part of it, too. My mother was like that. I could read her emotions in her eyes, too. You're very open with your feelings. I can tell that my uncle would put up a façade, and probably does quite often. His cheerful ways had me fooled into thinking my parents were... Well, I don't mean to judge him, but something tells me there's a lot hidden beneath that cheerfulness."

Sara frowned, nodded, and looked away. "I wasn't aware you'd never met him. Perhaps it's a bit too early for this talk, hmm?" She looked down at me. "And I guess there's very little I can hide from you."

"Nor I from you," I added.

She smiled. "This is one time I'll probably regret it when my patient takes her first step."

"Why?"

"Because," she paused, glancing down at her hands, "you won't need me much longer after that. My job will be finished, for the most part."

"Hmm. Well, can't we still be friends?"

"I...I suppose. That is, if you still want to be friends at that time." She fidgeted with her hands. "By then, though, you may hate me."

"Hate you? Why would I hate you?"

"'Cause you'll get tired of me pushing you so hard. That is, unless you're one of those unique people I haven't yet had the pleasure of meeting."

"My mother once told me that between love and hate, there's a very thin line. She said that in order to hate someone with a passion, you must have once loved them, because hate is love turned inside out. Sort of like laughing and crying: even though they're opposites, they are related. And if love can turn to hate, then hate can turn back into love."

She reached over and touched my cheek. "I hope you're right. I truly do."

"Read to me?"

"Sure." She reached over and retrieved the book from the nightstand and opened it to the first bookmark.

"Think we'll finish it before I walk again?" I queried.

She looked over at me and smiled. "I don't know," she answered softly. "We'll see."

I knew things were back to normal. I could only hope that they would stay that way.

Soon my eyelids began to grow heavy. I tried hard to fight the sleep that seemed to be commandeering my body. The last thing I remember was feeling her close to me, the scent of her perfume wafting around me as she whispered, "I'd read to you forever, if I could." Then she kissed me lightly on the cheek.

Sometime during the night, I awoke with a start and sat up. I had felt that my mother and father were right there in the room with me. I glanced around in the darkness as their voices replayed in my head. "Beware...have no illusions," they had said.

I broke down in tears; it had felt so real. Sara must have heard me crying, for I was soon aware of the patter of bare feet on the floor.

The night-light above the bed came on. "What's wrong?" she asked, a look of grave concern on her face.

"My parents...they were here...I...heard them..."

"Oh sweetheart, it was just a dream," she soothed.

"No, this was no dream; they were here. I could hear them...I could feel them," I blubbered.

"C'mere," she said, letting down the guardrail, then leaning over and putting her arms around me. "It was just a dream."

"No, I heard them. They...they said...'Beware...have no illusions.'"

She held me away from her and stared deeply into my eyes. I thought I saw tears in her green eyes. *Green eyes? But her eyes are blue, aren't they? Yes, of course they are, a vibrant blue. Could it be the light?*

"Your eyes. They're...they're green," I blurted out.

"Um...yeah, they are. I wear colored contacts," she explained.

Was this what my mother and father meant by illusions? Were they referring to Sara, who presented the illusion of blue eyes? Blue eyes like my mother's. Could she have known about my mother? Were they warning me about Sara for some reason?

"What's the matter?" she queried with a puzzled look on her face.

"Nothing. I mean, you're probably right. I must have been dreaming." I wiped my eyes. "It...it just seemed so real, that's all." I lay back on the bed and looked away. *Was it just a dream?*

"Well, you get some rest now. Tomorrow will be another big day for you. Dr. Rosemund said we should get you out for some fresh air," she stated, pulling the covers up over me. "I think you'll like that."

I merely lay there staring into the darkness, wondering what new set of obstacles I would be faced with next. Was the only person I truly felt I could trust the very one my parents had been warning me about? After all, hadn't she said that I shouldn't be emotionally dependent on her? And yet she had just put her arms around me once again. She had contradicted herself.

I suddenly felt very lost and alone. Could I, or more to the point, should I still trust her? Was there not a soul in this world I could rely upon? Yearning for the warmth, comfort, and security of my parents, I silently cried myself to sleep.

Chapter
5

Sara had been right; the next day was busy. After breakfast came my bath: I was stronger, more relaxed, and actually enjoyed it. When she pushed me back to the room, I didn't feel as tired, either.

Closing the door, she flipped the sign to read "Do Not Disturb." I wondered what was going on, as I was under the impression that massage therapy was relegated to nights. Leaving me by the bed, she went over to the closet. *What's she up to?* I wondered, watching her pull out two gift-wrapped boxes: one large, the other quite small.

"I...uh...I got you something yesterday while I was out," she explained, walking over to me. "I knew you needed them. Men sometimes don't think of things like this. I hope you like them."

Sara handed me the boxes. I didn't know what to say. Yesterday I'd have been thrilled to know she thought enough of me to buy me something. But now, I was having disturbing thoughts, questioning her motives.

"Thank you," I managed to say, hesitantly opening the small box first. Inside was a bottle of perfume: *Wind Song*, the cologne my mother had worn. "How did you know my mother wore this?" I charged.

"I...I didn't," she stammered in reply, her eyebrows darting up as if she had no idea what I was talking about. "I...I just went to the counter and smelled the different ones and...I liked this one. I...I don't know why, though. I'm sorry if...if I offended or...hurt you in any way. That was not my intention, believe me," she apologized, her blue eyes turning cloudy. "I'm sorry, I should've asked. I'll take it back. I'll get whatever kind you like." She reached over and took the perfume from me. "But, please,

open the other one. I think you *will* like it. Or at least I hope so."
The corners of her mouth turned up in a rueful smile.

I stared at her for a moment, searching for some signs of
deception. Finding none, I complied with her request. Inside, I
found an off-white nightgown and matching robe.

"I thought you'd need those," she explained, her smile uncertain. "I know how uncomfortable the hospital's backless 'negli-
gees' can be."

I had to admit, it was a beautiful nightgown. I hardly ever
wore one, however, because I preferred a cotton nightshirt or just
a T-shirt, which I found much more comfortable. Yet, she had
been thoughtful, taking my discomfort into consideration. Thinking back to the day before, I knew how thrilled I would have been
to receive this, and now I was just staring at it. *Why? All because
of something that could've been just a dream, could've been nothing more than an overactive imagination run amok.*

"Is it the wrong color...or size? I can always exchange it if..."
She paused, disappointment over my lack of enthusiasm written
all over her face.

"It's beautiful," I said softly.

"Well, what's—"

"You told Uncle Brandon my emotions were like a raw nerve,
remember?" I interrupted. "I really do like it. Please, help me put
it on."

Her spirits seemed to lift as she helped me out of the hospital
garb and into the nightgown.

"Lovely," she commented, as she backed away. "You're...very
pretty, Faith."

I blushed, not knowing what to say, for I knew this wasn't the
truth. I hadn't been pretty even before the accident, much less
now.

"Oh, I almost forgot," she murmured, reaching into the box
again. "I saw this and I thought...well, I thought we might fancy
up your...headdress." She pulled out an ivory-colored silk scarf,
displaying it across one arm. "What do you think?" she asked
uncertainly.

"You mean put that over my bandage?"

"Uh, yeah. I've seen it done before. It'll look like a turban,
sort of." She paused. "Tell you what, I'll fix it and if you don't
like it, we'll take it off, okay?"

I sighed heavily at the thought of the bandage. *Could she
really make it look better?* I wondered. *It's worth a shot, right?*

Once I agreed, she wheeled me over to the full-length mirror
hanging on the inside of the closet door. "Take one quick look,"

she directed enthusiastically. "Then close your eyes and keep them closed 'til I tell you to open them."

Looking at my reflection, I didn't see the angry girl of yesterday, but still I was far from happy with what I did see. Closing my eyes as she had instructed, I felt her moving about me, wrapping the scarf around my head. She fussed over adjusting it here and there, then finally told me to open my eyes. I looked up slowly and discovered my ugly bandage cloaked in the lovely silk scarf. Over on the right hand side, she had attached a small brooch: a butterfly with two tiny topaz stones for eyes. I felt like crying. She had taken something unattractive and turned it into a more dignified and appealing sight.

I looked older now. Gone was the naïve child of yesteryear, the floppy nightshirts with cute sayings across the front, her last hold upon childhood; her innocent eyes revealing how very little she knew about pain and loss. Before me was a more mature young woman, whose eyes reflected the severity of the pain and loss she had suffered. And whose breasts, I had to admit, filled out the cups of the shapely, low-cut nightgown rather nicely.

"You look lovely," she said, placing her hands upon my shoulders.

I looked up at her likeness in the mirror, tears welling up in my eyes. "Thank you," I said, putting my right hand on hers.

"You're very welcome," she responded softly. "Now, you're all ready for your foray into the outside world. When would you like to go?"

I knew she was changing the subject so I wouldn't dwell on the tears.

"How about right now?" asked Uncle Brandon's loud, cheerful voice.

I quickly glanced up at his reflection. *How had he slipped in without either one of us noticing?* But, oh, how handsome he looked. *Just like Father,* I thought. Except for the attire that screamed *I'm rich.* And his demeanor, straight and proud, which pronounced in no uncertain terms *I'm in control here. There's nothing I can't handle.*

"Princess, how beautiful you look," he said, as Sara moved off to one side. "I just can't take my eyes off you. So much like your mother...so beautiful." He approached the back of my chair, never taking his eyes off my reflection. "Did you do this for her, Miss Bennington?" he queried, his eyes seemingly glued to my image.

"Yes," she responded, backing away.

"Wonderful. I'll have to reimburse you. Princess, I'm so sorry

I didn't think to buy you something like this. I guess with everything that has happened, I've just been so busy, I... But I'll make it
up to you, I promise. You know men—they appreciate beauty, but
seldom know how to perfect it. You are beautiful," he repeated,
his eyes lighting up like he had just been given the grandest gift in
the world. "You do feel up to taking a short stroll, don't you, Princess? I'd just love to show off my lovely niece. It is all right, isn't
it, Miss B.?"

Sara had retreated, like she usually did when my uncle came
around. I watched her reflection as she turned away. "That's up to
Faith," she replied, walking over to her chair beside the bed.

I detected a note of disappointment in her voice. I knew she
had planned this for my first outing. Now he had walked in and
taken over, as he always did. What was I to do? I needed to get to
know my uncle better, since I would be living in his home. And I
already knew Sara, or at least, I thought I did. I reasoned there
would be time for other outings. Perhaps even today, although I
knew it wouldn't be the same.

Sara helped me into my robe and flashed me a rueful smile
before we left. Uncle Brandon then wheeled me out into the hall
and began to babble like a Chatty Cathy doll.

"I can't get over how beautiful you are," he said, leaning over
me while pushing me through the hall. "And how much you look
like your mother."

Since he kept broaching the subject of my mother, I thought
I'd take the opportunity to inquire about the time she'd spent at
Shady Grove. "Thank you," I replied. "I always thought my
mother was very pretty, but I'm sure my opinion was biased."

"She was *beautiful*," he said wistfully.

"What was she like when she was my age, when she lived at
Shady Grove?"

"She was like a breath of fresh air," he answered on a sigh.
His pace slowed somewhat, and I glanced over my shoulder. He
was smiling and staring off into space with a glassy look in his
eyes, as if he were reliving a memory.

I wondered why the mention of my mother should evoke such
memories. Was it a very happy time back then? My mother didn't
seem to think so. "I assume you were close to my mother and
father when they lived at Shady Grove?" I prodded, wanting to
pry more information from him.

"We...yes," he replied, clearing his throat. "Yes, the four of us
were...close. We lived in the same house, you know. The house is
big, but not that big."

Four? Oh yes, his wife, Vivian. "I suppose my mother and

Aunt Vivian were close?"

"Um, actually, no. They were never close friends, in that sense. They were worlds apart. Your mother was charming, graceful, sophisticated, and beautiful. Vivian was...too envious to be good friends with her," he stated rather coldly. "But enough of that, let's talk about you. What are you studying in college?"

"Psychology."

"I assume that was your mother's idea?"

"No, it was mine."

He pushed me up to the electronic doors that led outside, and we proceeded out onto the terrace of the third floor. A white wrought-iron railing enclosed the wide patio, where neatly arranged tables and chairs awaited patients and their visitors. We had it all to ourselves, however. Pushing me over to the closest table, he then took a seat in the chair beside me. A rather lengthy silence ensued as I took in my surroundings.

It was a beautiful spring day, the sun reflecting brightly off a tall glass building across the street. Traffic noises from the streets below wafted up on the warm breeze, which tinkled the wind chimes hanging from the ledge above. Life was moving at a rapid pace in the bustling city of Atlanta. Sequestered behind the walls of the hospital, I hadn't given much thought to the outside world. Perhaps I hadn't been ready. After all, life was still going on out there, when it seemed mine had stopped on March 3, 1993—the day of the plane crash.

The roar of a jet engine filled the air. All of a sudden I felt panicky inside, and struggled to fight the rising fear.

"Is this your first visit to Atlanta?" he asked, his voice sounding distant to my ears for several seconds.

"Yes, except for using the airport to make a connecting flight," I answered, remembering how my mother had been concerned whether we'd make our flight to L.A.

"Can't tell much about it from up there, can you?"

"No. It's like...being in a cocoon."

"Well, as soon as you're strong enough, I'll take you on a tour, show you the sights around here. We can even visit my office. Would you like that?"

"I guess," I replied, watching as the plane that I had heard disappeared into the clouds.

"You know you have a stake in Neilson, don't you?"

I turned to face him. What kind of stake was he talking about? To my knowledge, Father had never had anything to do with the business.

"You have inherited half the business. Your father never bothered with his inheritance, but then he never forfeited it, either. He merely ignored it," he said matter-of-factly. "And now, it's yours."

This prospect had never dawned on me. I'd always thought Uncle Brandon had inherited everything, and that was the reason why my father didn't stay at Shady Grove or have any part in the business.

He must have read my thoughts, for he continued. "He could have used his inheritance at any time. I mean, sharing the profits. He could not sell it, of course, not unless both of us agreed to the sale. I suppose that was my father's way of making sure the business stayed in the family. But your father was heir to half of everything. When he came home with your mother, I arranged to have the whole east wing redecorated for them. But Jonathan never seemed to want to have anything to do with the business, and now, all that should have been his belongs to you."

I was quite overwhelmed by all this. I knew he was telling me I was a wealthy young woman. Yet, I would have gladly given it all up to have my parents alive and well again—or even just a few minutes with them in order to say goodbye.

"I'll teach you about the business, if you'd like. Then you can assist me. There are always business parties to arrange, and a hostess as beautiful as you, why, you'd be the center of attention."

Oh yeah, I'd be the center of attention, all right, I thought. *But it wouldn't be the kind of attention you're talking about. Everyone would be staring at my scars and thinking, "How ugly," not "How beautiful."* I'd never even thought of myself as beautiful before the accident. Did he think I was blind? Or just a bubble brain who'd believe his every word, no matter how ridiculous?

"Every man needs a beautiful woman to help him," he continued. "We could be quite a team, especially with Jason there when he's through with college. He's preparing himself to fill my shoes one day."

Finding out I had inherited a fortune was one thing, but he was making plans for *my* future. I wasn't up to a confrontation on that subject—or any other—at the moment, so I tried to change the subject. "What about Ashley?" I asked.

A hint of sadness crept into his voice. "Your mother didn't tell you?" I shook my head. "We...we lost Ashley five years ago. She was killed in an automobile accident." He paused briefly then continued, as if answering an all too familiar question. "The car crashed through the guardrail of a bridge and sank into the water. They searched for days, dragging the river, but..." He raised his hand to his forehead and shielded his eyes, to avoid exposing me to his tears, I assumed.

I felt so sorry for him. Mother had told me how he'd lost his wife, Vivian: she'd committed suicide—shooting herself in front of Ashley when my cousin was thirteen. After that, Ashley had spent time in a psychiatric hospital. Now it seemed that he had lost his daughter tragically, as well. I now understood why he had not mentioned her, and why he sang Jason's praises. His son was all he had left. Except for me. This made it a little easier to under-stand why he doted on me so. I knew, however, that I could never replace his daughter, if that's what he wanted. I could never be anyone's daughter but *my* father's; yet I would try, for his sake, to understand him better. Perhaps one day, I'd even grow to love him.

"I'm sorry, Uncle Brandon. I didn't know."

"It's all right," he responded, waving his hand as if shooing away the memories. "You needed to know. I would have told you eventually." He looked down at his watch. "Hmph... Look at the time. I should get you back. I wouldn't want to wear you out on your first outing. And *I* need to get back to my office."

No words passed between us on the way back to my room. Clicking noises made by Uncle Brandon's shoes and the squeak of the chair's wheels on the tile floor as he pushed me down the long hallway were the only sounds to break the silence.

When we entered the room, Sara was nowhere in evidence. Uncle Brandon was furious. "I pay her good money to be here. And now that you need her, where is she? Probably off flirting with some orderly or doctor, I suspect," he said, his voice growing hard and cold.

"I'm sure she'll be back soon."

He stormed over to the bed and was about to call for a nurse when Sara walked in. "Where have you been?" he demanded.

"I went out for a walk while the two of you were out," she answered calmly.

"You are paid to be *here* when I—when Faith needs you."

"Please, Uncle Brandon—" I started to intervene.

"I'm paid to be a full time nurse and therapist, not a—" Sara paused, stopping short of losing her temper.

"Uncle Brandon, I'm sure Sara needs to stretch her legs from time to time. And I imagine she needs time away from the hospi-tal, and from me. I'm not the angel you believe me to be, you know. Besides, I need to be independent sometimes," I stated ami-ably, trying my best to ease the tension.

"I *pay* her to be *here* twenty-four hours a day," he declared.

"She is. She's here whenever I need her. I mean, she's here now. If you had left, I would have been fine. I knew she'd be back soon. And if there was an emergency, I could very easily call another nurse. I do know how to do that, you know. I'm not a child," I declared, thinly disguised irritation in my voice. I was determined to stop his irrational attack on Sara.

"Of course you're not, Princess. I can see that," he conceded, his tone becoming more tranquil as he looked me up and down. "But, please, Princess, just call me Brandon. Uncle sounds so...formal."

"All right...Brandon. Thank you for taking me on our little outing. I enjoyed it."

"I'm glad, Princess. I enjoyed it, too," he said, as he leaned over and kissed my cheek. "How would you like it if I brought Jason to see you?"

"I'd like to meet him."

"All right, that's what I'll do. Dinner is at six, isn't it? Then we'll be here around seven. If that doesn't interfere with your schedule, Miss Bennington?"

"That will be fine," Sara responded.

"Take care now, Princess, and get some rest. We want you strong enough for the trip Thursday. I'll see you this evening."

After he left, Sara helped me remove my robe and get back into bed. I was totally exhausted, although I didn't want to let on.

"How was your first trip outside?" she finally inquired, pulling the sheet up on me.

"Nice. I mean, I needed to get to know Uncle—I mean Brandon, and I found out a few things I didn't know. I don't understand why my mother never told me about my cousin Ashley."

At the mention of Ashley's name, Sara quickly glanced over at me. "Perhaps she had her reasons," she offered, as she sat down in her chair.

"Do you know about Ashley?" I inquired.

"Only what I read in the papers," she said solemnly.

"And what was that?"

"Something about a car accident."

"Did you know her?"

The question seemed to catch her off guard. She glanced over at me, then down at the floor, her eyes darting back and forth as if she were searching for the right answer. "I...I don't know really. Things from before my accident are...pretty fuzzy."

"Do you remember your accident?" I asked, intrigued.

"No, my father told me..." She paused and glanced over at me. "You need your rest," she asserted, changing the subject. "You've had a very busy morning, and I can see in your eyes that you're tired."

"No fooling you, is there?" I muttered, watching her reach over and retrieve her book.

She shook her head and smiled, as she opened the book to the second bookmark.

"Sara, thank you for the presents. I'm...I'm sorry about the perfume."

"I should've asked first," she responded. "By the way, what kind do you wear? I'll swap it."

"The last one I wore...the only one I really like is *Estee*, but you don't have to swap it. Brandon can have someone pick some up for me."

She cut her eyes over at me. "I'll get it for you. I'm only sorry I didn't ask you first."

"It was a good choice and...if it didn't remind me of my mother... Well, it's the thought that counts, right?"

She gave no response, but merely looked down at her book and started reading. I dozed off soon thereafter, and spent the remainder of the afternoon, except for a brief period of time during lunch and dinner, napping. Obviously, I hadn't realized just how exhausted I was.

Brandon and Jason came at seven, just as my uncle had said they would. Jason was a carbon copy of his father, except his hair was darker, almost black, unlike his father's medium brown. He greeted me in a rather cool manner at first. He wouldn't look at me and seemed very nervous about the whole situation. I wondered if I was that repugnant to him.

Then the conversation turned to the fact that I would be recovering at Shady Grove, and Sara spoke up. "Yes, Faith'll need help from all of us," she maintained, agreeing with Brandon's comment about all the staff being at my beck and call. "And there'll be times when I'll need someone pretty strong to help me with certain things."

"As I said, Miss Bennington, I have a staff of servants," Brandon reminded sternly.

"Well, I might need someone else with...a little more time on their hands. Someone with lots of energy."

"Then I'll hire someone. What is it you foresee them doing?"

"It wouldn't be a full-time job. Just helping out here and there, most probably with her therapy in the pool, getting her out and about when I'm—"

"I could help," Jason offered, glancing over at his father for his approval.

"Why, yes. Yes, I believe you'd be perfect for the job," Sara agreed, looking over at him. "We should be ready for pool therapy during the time you're on summer vacation. How old are you?"

"Fifteen," he said proudly.

"Only fifteen? Why, I thought surely you were seventeen, at the least," she remarked. He straightened up in his seat. "Think you could take Faith outside for me sometimes?"

"Yeah, sure," he replied, then turned to me. "I'll show you around the stables and let you meet my horse, Shane."

"I'd like that," I acknowledged with a grin.

From then on, he seemed more comfortable, and even smiled at me a couple of times, as if the idea of spending time with me was not so repulsive. I knew what Sara had accomplished, but Brandon seemed unaware of her manipulation and quite put off by the whole situation. But how could he object when I knew he wanted his son to make friends with me? I was relieved to know that it wasn't my looks that repulsed Jason. He was reticent because I was a stranger, a stranger he saw as not normal, one who would be invading his home. Something he'd had no say-so about until Sara opened the door for him. She'd offered him a choice about whether or not to participate and interact with us. I didn't doubt for one minute that he had been warned not to pester me in any way, which most assuredly had put him on the defensive.

Sara's very good at what she does, I thought, glancing over at her. I wondered how long she had been working at her occupation. And that, in turn, made me realize that I didn't even know her age. I had just assumed she was in her late twenties. I decided I would ask her the first chance I got.

Before leaving, Brandon asked to speak to Sara out in the corridor. I was afraid he was going to upbraid her about Jason, but when she came back in, her mood hadn't changed. She immediately began preparing everything for my therapy.

Pulling up the nightgown, she started on my legs. "How long have you been doing this?" I asked casually.

"Oh, about two years."

"How old are you?" I probed bluntly.

She looked up and smiled. "How old do you think I am?"

"Twenty...six?" I'd intentionally underestimated a bit, so I wouldn't embarrass both of us if she were younger than I'd assumed.

"I wish. Thirty-two," she replied, as she pushed my leg forward and then pulled it back. "Let's see...you're eighteen, right?"

"Twenty-two in another four months," I corrected. She gave me a rather odd look. "What's wrong?"

"Nothing. I just thought... Well, I've thought of you as a

child. I'll have to reevaluate my thinking, hmm?" She moved around to the other side of the bed. "Twenty-two and no steady boyfriends, hmm?"

"No. It seems they all want only one thing."

"Yeah, I know what you mean."

"Is that why you're still *Miss* Bennington?"

"Suppose so," she responded, rubbing my left leg with oil, working her hands back and forth, over and over again.

When finished, she turned me over, then stopped abruptly and looked at my nightgown. "What's the matter?" I inquired.

"Well, either I'll have to roll your gown up to your neck, to keep from getting oil on it, or..."

"Or take it off completely," I finished for her.

"Yes. I'd hate to ruin it. Would you feel too exposed?"

"Why should I, after the baths and that backless negligee I've been wearing?"

She smirked and wiped her hands on a towel she'd brought with her. Raising me up, she helped me remove the nightgown, then placed it over the back of her chair. After turning me over, she went to work on my back, massaging all of it without me asking. For a woman, she seemed to have strong hands. Then again, I'd never had a man massage my shoulders, except maybe for my father, so I had nothing to compare it to. When she leaned over me to get to my right shoulder, I felt the pressure of her body against mine. A chill rose out of the numbing abyss of paralysis and raced up my spine.

"Cold?" she queried.

I assumed she had noticed the chill bumps on my back. "Uh, no, not really."

A little while later, she started turning me back over. On the last leg of the turn, which put me flat on my back, her gaze fell to my breasts. Curious as to what was so interesting, I glanced down at myself and was embarrassed to find my nipples erect.

"Guess we better get you dressed before you catch cold," she suggested, quickly turning to retrieve the towel and wiping her hands once again, then picking up my nightgown.

While she was putting the gown back on me, I felt myself falling backwards; without my legs to use as counterweight, I reached out for the first available purchase: her neck. Her arms went around me posthaste and stopped my descent before I hit the pillow. Her face was only inches from mine when she laid me back. We stared into each other's eyes. When I felt her warm breath against my face, my stomach began to churn. I knew I should let go of her neck, but couldn't think straight. Too many things were

going on inside me, things I didn't understand at all. Things so
very new and exciting, I couldn't just ignore them, either.

"I'm sorry. I should have supported your back," she apologized softly, starting to back away, the expression on her face one
of guilt.

All I could think about was how I had hurt her feelings earlier, and all because of a silly dream. I remembered how she'd
brought Jason around so that neither of us had to be uncomfortable in the other's presence. *If she was my mother or even a sister*,
I thought, *I'd give her a kiss on the cheek*. And even though she
was neither of those things, I still felt the urge to do so.

"Thank you," I said, touching her face with my right hand.

"For what?" she asked, perplexed.

"Oh, for everything. The nightgown...fixing the
scarf...Jason..." Her eyebrows arched skyward. "Yeah, I know
what you did, and I appreciate it."

"You're welcome, but it wasn't that big of a deal."

"It meant a lot to me."

"Well, I'm glad that—"

Without warning, I interrupted her by attempting to plant a
kiss on her cheek. She turned her head at the last moment, however, and I ended up kissing her full on the lips. Strange sensations
shot down my body, disappearing into the numbness of my nether
regions. I had *never* felt anything like that before, despite the fact
that I couldn't feel anything below the waist. Neither one of us
seemed to know what to do at that moment. She turned quite red
with embarrassment, as did I. At least, my face and ears were
blazing hot for some reason.

"I didn't mean... Your cheek... You turned and..." The words
sputtered out of my mouth, and once again I sounded like a bad
cell phone connection, through no fault of my voice this time,
however.

"You...should get some rest," she asserted, reaching up and
removing my left hand from around her neck. "You have a big day
ahead of you tomorrow, and an even bigger one the day after."

I watched her as she put away the oil and set up her cot. I
couldn't help thinking about what had happened and how I had
felt when our lips touched. I wondered if it was just the shock of it
all, or whether there was more to it. Unable to go to sleep, I
watched her prepare for bed. After she dimmed the lights—leaving
on the soft night-light above the bed—and went into the bathroom, I heard the water running. I wondered how long it would be
before I could bathe by myself. *Perhaps when I get to Shady
Grove?* What would it be like, living in a mansion? Was it as

lovely as Brandon described? What about being waited on by servants? What would they be like?

Thoughts of my own home then crossed my mind. What had been done about that? Surely everything was still as we'd left it. *I'll need my clothes and stereo. I'll ask Brandon about that tomorrow. I'm sure he'll find a way to get them for me.*

It wasn't long before the bathroom door opened and Sara stole into the room, the scent of her perfume preceding her. I inhaled deeply, unaware of why, exactly, other than that I liked the sweet smell. I watched as she eased around the bed and over to the cot. I kept my eyes cracked just a smidgen to avoid detection, knowing she'd think something was wrong if she found out I was awake. I tried to mimic myself sleeping, though I had no idea what I sounded like. A few seconds later, she neared the bed, and I figured she'd expose my ruse. Instead, however, she rearranged the cover and then reached up over my head. Curious as to what she was doing, I opened my eyes wider to investigate. Her body was very close to my face, the thin material of her nightgown exposing her breasts to full view.

All of a sudden I felt *very* strange inside. My heart seemed to skip a beat. I heard a click, the room was plunged into darkness, and she withdrew. The image, however, remained: firm, nicely shaped breasts. *What? Firm, nicely shaped breasts?* I blushed from embarrassment at my own thoughts. Why in the world was I thinking about her breasts?

Well, they were right in front of your face, after all! a little voice inside my head answered. *How could you not notice them?*

That was true enough. I closed my eyes, hoping to rid myself of the image, but it lingered, as if it were imprinted upon the backs of my eyelids. *What in the world is going on with you? You're looking at another woman's breasts and...touching her lip... What the hell is wrong with you?*

You've been in an accident, remember? That little voice spoke up again. *Your head was injured. You were in a coma. You're not yourself yet. Your back was injured and now you're paralyzed from the waist down, so what kind of damage might have been done to your brain?*

Oh, now there's a comforting thought! What damage might have been done inside my head that they couldn't see or find with all their fancy tests? As I pondered all the odd feelings I'd been bombarded with over the last few days, I remembered Sara's concern that I might be one of those patients who became too emotionally attached to their nurse, therapist, or whomever. I latched onto this thought like a drowning person thrown a life preserver. I reasoned these strange feelings *must be* what she was referring to—*had to be* what she was referring to—because what other explanation was there?

You just want to be comforted by someone you feel you can trust, that little voice inside reasoned. *That's all it is.*

The next day I was presented with the task of lifting my behind off the bed every hour or so and rolling my own self over on my sides every 2 to 3 hours in order to prevent bedsores—the breakdown in skin caused by lying in one position too long. Although this didn't sound like it should be taxing, I soon found out it most certainly was. I now knew what Sara meant by building my upper-body strength, because I was actually shocked at just how weak I was. My arms were so tired by the end of the day that Sara had to do the turning for me.

Chapter
6

The big day finally arrived, and Dr. Rosemund was in my room before breakfast. He said I was free to go, but he'd be checking on me from time to time and wanted to change my bandages in a week. A few minutes after he left, breakfast arrived, with Brandon carrying the tray. On it was a red rose in a small vase.

"Good morning, Princess," he boomed in his baritone voice, looking quite debonair in a light blue suit and white sweater vest.

I was expecting more casual apparel, since he'd already informed me he was taking the whole day off just so he could be with me. It was evident now that Brandon would always dress according to his perceived status, no matter what the occasion.

He set the tray down on the table and then pushed it over to me. "Are you excited, Princess? I know I am. I can't wait to get you home, where I can visit more often. Oh, yes, I have a surprise for you. Miss Bennington, please retrieve the package I left outside the door." He never even glanced Sara's way as he issued his order. "I wanted to surprise you with the rose and your present," he explained, "but I saw the woman with your tray and...well, I thought I'd bring it in with the rose, because I wanted to serve my princess on this very special day." He smiled broadly and raised my hand to his lips. "Ah, yes," he said, taking the package from Sara. "This is for you, Princess. For your trip home." I started unwrapping the package as he added, "This is just a sample of what the future holds for you now."

I opened the box to reveal a pretty blue dress trimmed in white lace. I removed it from the box, thinking it looked like something my mother would have picked out for me when I was younger. It was definitely out of style: puffy short sleeves, low-cut bodice. But I knew from the feel of the silky material that it was expensive. I glanced over at him, not knowing what to say. I'd never owned a dress so posh. As a matter of fact, I had very few dresses. My wardrobe consisted of jeans, sweatshirts, and T-shirts. And, of course, a few blouses and polyester pants for formal occasions.

"Blue to match those beautiful blue eyes," he said softly.

"Thank you, Brandon," I reached out to hug him. He kissed me on the cheek, lingering longer than he had previously.

When he stepped back, his eyes drifted from my bandaged head to the dress. "Well, I should go and let you eat now. I have an errand to run anyway. But I'll be back in time to wheel you out those front doors and whisk you home, don't you worry." He winked and left.

Sara took the dress and put it on a hanger in the closet. When she turned around, I detected the worried look on her face.

"What's the matter?"

"Oh...nothing...nothing. We've got a busy day ahead, and I was just thinking about what needs to be done," she replied, and then headed for the bathroom. I knew she was preparing my bath.

Back in my room again, Sara helped me into the blue dress. I felt the least I could do for Brandon was wear it, even though I longed for a pair of pants and a blouse. She wheeled me over to the mirror, and I was surprised at how well the dress fit me, wondering how he had known my size. The blue color complemented my eyes as well as the stones of the butterfly pin Sara had given me. Something I had forgotten all about until now.

"Sara?"

"Princess!" Brandon boomed from the doorway, all smiles. "My, how beautiful you look! I knew you'd bring that dress to life! And I have something else for you," he beamed, crossing the room swiftly and handing me two packages.

"Thank you, Brandon, but—"

"Ah-ah-ah, none of that. Just open them."

I opened the first one to reveal a pair of low-heeled blue pumps. He quickly took these and handed them off to Sara. The other parcel, to my surprise, contained a very shiny, silky blue scarf, which matched the dress perfectly.

"I bought you *two* of every color they had," he stated proudly. "Now you can accessorize your wardrobe with a scarf to match. Miss Bennington, help her get dressed."

Sara put the shoes on my feet, then removed the pin from my turban. I held out my hand for it and she gently laid it in my palm, looking at my reflection in the mirror. I smiled and turned my attention to the pin. The blue eyes of the butterfly sparkled in the sunlight pouring through the window. *Real topaz? I wondered. Surely not. Sara couldn't afford something that expensive, could she?* I rubbed my finger over the small eyes: very smooth. As I tilted the pin to one side, the light refracted off the body and created a tiny rainbow of colors within. The body wasn't glass as I'd assumed, but some type of crystal. I looked up at Sara just as Dr. Rosemund entered the room. He motioned for Brandon to accompany him outside.

Sara was still preoccupied with the turban. "I love the butterfly," I said softly. She looked up at my reflection, her expression unreadable.

"Butterflies are free," she whispered, finishing with the turban. "Always remember that."

I handed her the brooch, wondering exactly what she'd meant by that. Was this her way of suggesting I would walk again?

Brandon walked back in and strolled over to me. "My, you do look wonderful, but...what's this?" he asked, as if he hadn't noticed the butterfly before.

"Sara gave it to me," I explained proudly.

He immediately looked over at Sara, his eyes growing small and cold. "Everything ready, Miss Bennington?" he asked, using that tone of voice he seemingly reserved for her alone.

"Yes," she responded, placing her hands on the grips of my chair.

"I will guide my princess in her chariot," he asserted, and smiled down at me. "I can't wait to get you home. Just wait until you see Shady Grove. I know you'll fall in love with it."

He wheeled me out to the elevator, Sara following close behind with our bags. He was acting as if she didn't even exist. When he did speak to her, it was only to give an order. Wheeling me through the lobby, he talked incessantly, like an excited child. Outside, a long black limousine was parked at the entrance. The back door was opened by a tall, thin, gray-haired man with piercing dark eyes, attired in black suit and tie.

Brandon made the introductions. "Faith, this is Charles, our chauffeur."

"Nice to make your acquaintance, Miss Neilson," Charles said in an uninterested tone, bowing slightly. He abruptly straightened up and stared straight ahead, as if he wasn't supposed to make eye contact with me.

"Nice to meet you, too," I responded, taking in his stiff demeanor.

Before I knew what was happening, Brandon had scooped me up out of the chair. Judging by appearance alone, he didn't look strong, but he most certainly was, because he handled me as if I were light as a feather. Of course, I knew I had lost weight, more than ten pounds according to hospital scales, but still I felt he had to be in fairly good shape to lift me so easily.

While he effortlessly placed me in the back seat, his clean-shaven face rubbed against mine. Richness exuded from every pore and his cologne filled my nostrils; it was nearly overwhelming, and not especially pleasant. He crawled in beside me and shut the door behind himself, forcing Sara to go around.

My, oh my, look at all the gadgets, I thought, surveying my surroundings. A small television, VCR, stereo system complete with CD player, and a small bar—rather well stocked—were all built into the wood-trimmed console in front of us. Soft classical music issued from the speakers concealed around the large back seat. The distinct aroma of leather upholstery mixed with Brandon's rich scent and permeated the air once Sara was inside and the doors were closed.

"Home, Charles," Brandon directed, his authoritative tone reminding me of wealthy people in movies, although their driver was usually named James.

I glanced over at Sara to see if she was as impressed by all this as I was, but she was staring out the window, looking rather uncomfortable. I wondered what was wrong, but didn't inquire. I'd save that for later, when we were alone and settled in at Shady Grove.

Finally, I'll get to see this awesome place I've heard so much about, I thought, and then wondered what his home would look like if his car was this nice.

A phone rang and Brandon quickly picked it up, an annoyed look on his face. "Yes?" he answered brusquely. "Did I not leave explicit instructions that I was *not* to be disturbed unless it was an emergency? Then handle it. That's your job." He cradled the phone slowly, seemingly reining in his anger with deliberation. "It's so hard to find competent help these days," he grumbled. "I haven't had a decent assistant since Raymond died. Now there was a real businessman." His tone was rapidly returning to normal. "He ran the business until I graduated college. Brilliant man...knew how to handle himself amidst the competition. Taught me everything I know. Groomed me to take over the company, just as I'm doing with Jason."

He glanced over at me and smiled, but his expression sobered quickly. "Oh, I'll teach you about the business. Wouldn't want you worrying your pretty little head about how your interests are faring. That is...if you even care anything about that."

"I don't know a thing about the business world, but I suppose I could learn," I responded, thinking I'd find out why Father disliked it so.

"Don't worry, you'll only need to learn enough to keep track of your interests and carry on a conversation at dinner parties. And speaking of parties," he added excitedly, his eyes widening with anticipation at what he was about to reveal, "I can't wait to introduce you to all my friends and associates at the party I'm giving tonight, in your honor."

I was taken aback at the thought of even being at a party, much less one given for me, especially when I looked so horrible. "A party, for me?"

"Mr. Neilson, I'm afraid a party might be too tiring," Sara interjected.

"I've discussed this with your doctor, Princess, and *he* assures me it would be fine, as long as you don't tire yourself out," he said, directing his comments to me alone, as if Sara were not even in the car, much less voicing any objection. "We thought it might be just the ticket to add some gaiety to your first night home." He patted my knee. I glanced down at his hand and he promptly removed it, as if he suddenly remembered I couldn't feel this gesture.

I glanced over at Sara to see her reaction to Brandon's statements. She was merely staring out the window, thinly disguised anger apparent in the set of her jaw.

"Yes, I imagine everyone will be eager to meet you, Princess," he continued. "Some of them knew your mother and father when they lived here, so I imagine they'll be asking questions about them. But, I'll be right by your side to deflect any...unpleasantness. I'm sure you'll have a wonderful time. Your mother always did.

"Now there was a lovely hostess," he rambled. "I've never seen a woman who could handle adverse situations like your mother. She reminded me of a swan. Harsh words, insults...they'd just glide right off her, like water off a swan's back, never penetrating. Yes, a beautiful swan, that was Marion." He snickered, seemingly at some yet-to-be-voiced thought. "Or, as one of my more flamboyant and eccentric directors once put it, she had such style that if she landed in horse shi—manure, she'd still come up smelling like a rose." He laughed softly, apparently at the memory replaying in his mind.

I glanced over at Sara to see if she was hearing the same thing I was. This time she was staring at his hands, blue eyes cold and narrow, her expression troubled, with a little residual anger mixed in. *Did she hear what I heard?* I wondered. Could she feel the same vibrations I was receiving? Brandon had been in love with my mother! There was just no other explanation for these constantly flattering references and the look in his eyes when he spoke of her, as if he were talking about a saint. I wondered if my mother and father had been aware of this.

"You inherited your mother's fine features, Princess. I hope you inherited her grace and style, as well, because I'm sure it would prove to be an asset in the future."

I wanted so badly to ask him if he had been in love with my mother, but held my tongue, aware it could possibly backfire on me. Suspecting is one thing, but bringing it out in the open to be dealt with is quite another. I wanted to know, and yet I didn't. Not right now, at least; so I endeavored to put it out of my mind.

Being in the center seat, I alternated between looking out one side of the car and then the other as we sped through Atlanta via a six-lane expressway. I had always envied people who could weave in and out of traffic like Charles, who made it look so very easy when I would have been on pins and needles.

We spent the next twenty minutes or so in heavy traffic, then the exits began to get further and further apart. More undeveloped land appeared; pine forests sprang up here and there, sharing their domain with oak, poplar, sweet gum, and pecans, all of which were already decked out in their spring wardrobes.

It was apparent I had missed the official start of spring, when the trees were just budding out: redbuds decked in lavish purple, Bradford pears clothed in stark white. Missed the early spring flowers: yellow daffodils, purple and white crocuses, and an array of variously colored irises and hyacinths which grew in the flower garden my mother had so carefully tended.

"What's the date?" I asked aloud, of no one in particular.

"April 21st," they responded in unison. Each one glanced over at the other, and then quickly turned away.

I could tell that these two were going to be a barrel of laughs whenever they were together. A short while later, we exited Interstate 75. Several minutes after that, Sara squirmed in her seat and lightly touched my arm, which she'd been doing all during the trip when she wanted me to see something of interest. I followed her line of vision, and there in front of us—a little ways off to the left—was a large pair of wrought-iron gates attached to a set of mammoth stone pillars, each supporting upon its top a statue of a sitting lion. Beneath one of the lions, the name "Shady Grove" was proudly emblazoned upon a brass plaque. Ivy partially covered two massive stone walls that extended for several hundred feet in either direction, giving way to a tall chain-link fence. The latter had been taken over by the clinging greenery, though the ivy had not been allowed to run amok. I could feel Brandon watching me as I formed my first impressions of what would be my new home.

The car slowed and the gates slowly swung open. I began to wonder if I were entering a home or a fortress as we crept slowly underneath an arch of black wrought-iron scrollwork and I caught sight of an older man in uniform standing inside a small wooden cubicle. Once beyond the gates, I knew why the plantation had been so named: groves of pecan trees lined the blacktop driveway and beyond, as far as the eye could see. The intertwining branches formed an arched canopy over the winding lane, bringing to mind the stately grace of the Old South.

As the thin ribbon of asphalt wound its way up a small hill, pecan trees gave way to high, well-manicured hedges on either side—the historic South fading into the neat progressive lines of a more modern era. The driveway then snaked around the small hill, the row of hedges leading the eye straight up to an impressive white mansion that loomed up ahead. It was beautiful, motion picture beautiful. I felt as if I'd been driven onto the set of *Gone With the Wind*, or at least a restored version of that house, what with the large Corinthian columns lined up along the front entrance like stone sentinels.

The driveway curved around a small courtyard where a fountain spewed torrents of water into the air, forming a lovely cascading effect. Beautiful flowers—large irises, late-blooming daffodils, pansies, snapdragons and many others—were carefully arranged in complementary colors, outlining the courtyard and circling around the fountain.

"Well, what do you think?" Brandon finally asked, seeming eager for my reaction.

I took one more look at the vast house, with its separate wing on either side. "I didn't expect it to be so...so...huge," I replied, totally in awe of the majestic beauty that surrounded me. "But it's...it's beautiful, like something right out of a movie."

"I knew you'd like it," he said proudly. "I have a suite all prepared for you. It's in the east wing, there." He pointed up to the last window of the wing closest to us. "It was your mother and father's when they lived here."

Before the car came to a complete stop, a young African-American man came bustling out of an impressive set of doors that opened into the house. He quickly covered the distance to the car, and stood waiting to open the door for Brandon.

"Get the wheelchair from the trunk, Sammy," Brandon directed as he got out. He then reached in and gently lifted me out of the car. "Welcome home, Princess." He beamed as he held me in his arms and kissed my cheek. "Let's get you inside, shall we? Sammy, bring that chair."

He carried me up the wide stone steps and across the threshold, like a groom would his bride. I could only wonder if this would be the only time I'd be carried across one, for my chances of finding Mr. Right seemed to have been considerably diminished.

In front of me now, across a vast foyer, loomed a substantial staircase. It reminded me of the one Scarlett floated down so gracefully in *Gone With The Wind*. Shiny walnut banisters led the eye upward to the second floor, where they branched off in either direction, connecting the opposing wings. The tinkle of glass brought my attention back to the elaborate chandelier hanging above us.

"Would you like to see the first floor now, or would you rather rest?" Brandon asked.

"I'd like to see the rest of it," I replied excitedly, glancing over his shoulder to find Sara standing in the doorway. "I feel like I'm in a dream world, and I don't want to wake up just yet."

"Put the chair over here, Sammy," he directed with a chuckle. A moment later, he carefully set me down in it. "First, I'll show you the library. I assume you'll be spending a lot of time in there. You do like to read, don't you?" he inquired, pushing me into a long, dimly lit hallway off to the left of the foyer. Before I had time to answer, he called over his shoulder, "Oh, by the way, Miss B., make sure Faith's bed is made ready. I'm sure she'll be tired when we're finished."

Stopping at a set of double doors, he swung both open wide. Too impatient to wait for him to push me inside, I attempted to maneuver myself. "Ah-ah-ah, not in my presence," he admonished. "I'll handle that. You are my *Princess*, remember?"

He wheeled me into the room slowly, allowing me time to look around. Bookshelves lined each wall, except for the right one, which contained a large fireplace, and the front wall, where two double windows reached nearly from floor to ceiling. It was indeed a library, a rather dark, but reasonably cozy one, with wine-colored leather chairs and sofas strategically placed throughout, each with its own table and lamp. Even though the heavy burgundy draperies, white lace curtains and partially opened Venetian blinds gave the room a formal appearance, something about the diffused lighting, as well as the aroma of leather and old books, appealed to my senses.

I could certainly get lost in a book in here, I thought. If I could get in here, that is; the mammoth staircase in the foyer presented a substantial obstacle in my mind's eye.

A little while later, when Brandon showed me the kitchen, he walked over to what appeared to be a wide closet door and opened it. To my surprise, it wasn't a closet at all, but a stairway. And at the bottom: a lift chair. "I'll teach you how to use that another day," he stated, closing the door and crossing back to me.

One by one, he showed me every room in each wing, except for one. Each room had the same dark wood paneling extending halfway up the 10-foot-high walls, just like the front foyer and the halls. When we passed by the one room I hadn't yet entered, located at the far end of the west wing, he remarked that it was his office, and explained that he allowed no one inside except for the one particular maid who cleaned it once a week. He said that if I ever needed him, I should buzz him on the intercom system, which linked all the phones in the house and would provide me with my own private access to him. Finally, he reiterated that I should never go into his office, for he was a stickler for his privacy. I didn't find that so very odd, since Mother never liked for me to bother Father when he was working. I figured that particular restriction would not cause me any hardship, especially as my uncle wasn't exactly my favorite person to be around, at least not yet.

He pushed me back to the front foyer and up to the staircase. "As I said, I will teach you about the lift chair another day, because today you are my princess and you deserve to be carried up the stairs." Suiting his actions to his words, that is exactly what he did. On the second floor landing, another wheelchair awaited me, and he eased me into it. "This one is electric. Just press this lever forward..." The chair jerked forward. "Back...left...right. Go ahead, try it."

I pressed the lever forward, and off I went down the long, dimly lit hallway. At the far end was a large window, partially covered by heavy draperies. The shapely figure of a woman stepped into the muted light. At first, I thought I was imagining things; the sun filtering through the lace panels gave her a surreal appearance. I could make out blonde hair, a dark blouse, and pants. Then she turned slightly and sunlight highlighted the side of her face. It was Sara. I hadn't recognized her without her stark white uniform. As we drew closer, she turned around and smiled, but Brandon did not even acknowledge her presence.

"Here is your suite, Princess," he announced, proceeding into the room ahead of me through a doorway off to the right.

I slowly maneuvered the chair through the doorway, the controls reminding me of a joystick on an arcade game. When I looked up, I couldn't believe my eyes. The room before me was decorated in blues and purples, my favorite colors. Everything—from the off-white wallpaper with its combination of tiny purple and blue flowers, to the dark blue of the curtains with their white lace sheers beneath, even down to the thick carpet with light blue and dark intermingling to give it a dappled appearance—could not have been more in tune with my own taste if I'd picked them out myself.

Inside the room were two chairs and a sofa, all of which had upholstery matching the wallpaper, making one of the chairs—positioned against the left wall near a window—seem to be a part of the wall itself. The remaining chair and sofa formed an "L" shape separated by a lamp and light oak end table. Artfully arranged on a matching coffee table in front of the sofa sat a collection of classic books by varying authors, the precision fanning of their titles suggesting more show than substance.

My attention was then drawn to an antique roll-top desk and floor lamp, strategically placed at the corner of the wall containing the door through which I'd entered. The top was closed, so I could only imagine the various cubbyholes, small drawers, and other assorted nooks and crannies that might well lie secreted inside. Since I'd always wanted one of these—although I never knew what I would use all those nooks and crannies for—I was positive, judging from the well-worn condition of its exterior, that I'd have fun investigating this one. There was no telling what miniscule hints of someone else's existence might be concealed within. However, that bit of curiosity would have to wait for another day.

Having realized at a glance that the wall to my right contained little of note besides a few pastoral prints and a small closet door near the far corner, I found it obvious that a necessary piece of furniture was absent. As Sara walked up beside me, I quietly asked, "Where's the bed?"

She smiled and gestured in the direction of my uncle, who was standing in front of a set of double doors I'd failed to notice. With a knowing smile, he dramatically turned and pushed both doors open wide. As if complying with his theatrics, light flooded across the threshold and into the room.

Ah yes, I thought, remembering he had used the word "suite," which I had not taken literally to mean more than one room, but merely as a fancy word for one's private quarters. Although I'd heard of old mansions like this having sitting rooms separate from the bedrooms, and even seen them on television, I had not expected this turn of events and was quite curious to see the rest.

Pressing the lever on the chair, I moved across the sitting room—albeit at a more leisurely pace than I would have preferred—and continued past Brandon, who remained by the door.

Feeling an immediate familiarity with the antique-white furnishings and their shiny brass ornamentations—not unlike the bedroom suite belonging to my parents—I allowed my eyes to drift around the room in an orderly, clockwise fashion. Knowing this would be my world for however many months it took for me to recover, I wanted to become acquainted with it right away.

Except for the antique-white wainscoting running halfway up the 10-foot-high walls, it was decorated in the same vein as the sitting room. The same curtains adorned a long window to my left, where two matching chairs sat facing each other, a white table— about the size of a card table—between them. My fondness for puzzles and any type of board or card game instantly leapt to mind. I assumed I would be spending a lot of time at that table, in the chair I currently occupied, trying to fill the unstructured hours within my day. As luck, or fate, would have it, the sunlight streaming through the window dimmed considerably at that precise moment, causing the Venetian blinds to cast a series of horizontal lines across that very area.

Moving right along and skimming past the tall off-white chest of drawers occupying the far corner—which held little allure—and onto the matching nightstand, complete with shiny brass swing-arm lamp, its blue shade perfectly positioned for reading in bed, my gaze was drawn to the rather low canopy bed itself. The blue canopy fabric, trimmed in off-white, harmonized nicely with the wallpaper as well as the matching spread. What had truly captured my attention, however, was the way the uppermost portion of the spread had been invitingly turned back on one side, revealing smooth white sheets that seemed to beckon to me from across the room. Lest I give in to the fatigue slowly settling into my bones, I forced my gaze to remain on course.

Near the long window next to the bed—perched like some overly large Barbie accessory—sat a lighted vanity, its sectional mirror angling out from opposite sides. Considering my present circumstances, I gave this only a passing glance, for it was far too obvious how little use I'd have for that particular piece of furniture. My gaze shifted to the matching armoire nearby, which held little fascination for me, then over to the far wall and what appeared to be the folding doors of a rather large closet.

Wow, lot of room for clothes...which I don't *possess,* I
thought.

"All the furniture belonged to your mother and father," Brandon informed me. "Of course, I had to have the bed lowered for
wheelchair accessibility."

I merely nodded in acknowledgment. *Well, that explains a
great deal,* I thought: *the sense of familiarity, my favorite colors,
Barbie's vanity.* All of which I was certain my mother would have
loved and had more than likely picked out. I wondered why they
hadn't taken the furniture with them, but I hesitated to inquire.
Matter of fact, I knew if I was going to maintain my composure, I
needed to avoid thinking about any of these things belonging to
my parents. Just considering that my mother had sat at that very
vanity brushing her lovely blonde hair, my father watching her, as
he so often did.

In an effort to distract myself from these thoughts, I absently
pressed the joystick. Instead of moving into the room, however,
the chair spun abruptly to the left. *Oh great,* I thought, taking my
hand off the lever. *Leave it to me to take the scenic tour.* Trying to
maintain my cool exterior, I found myself feigning interest in what
was essentially a bare wall, except for an adjustable table like
those in the hospital, and a small painting of a horse standing on a
hill against the backdrop of a stormy sky. *Well...now, that's appropriate,* I conceded, drawing a parallel between the stormy sky in
the painting and the turbulent emotions brewing in my own backdrop.

Needing a distraction more than ever, I pressed the joystick to
the left once again, and held it there until I was headed in the
direction I'd intended before my impromptu detour. In the process, I caught a glimpse of Sara standing across from Brandon in
the doorway. Although one eyebrow arched as if she were
impressed with my manipulation of the chair, a slight smirk,
which she attempted to hide, let me know my pretense hadn't
fooled her one bit. I could feel my cheeks color even as I eased
toward my previous destination: the closet on the far wall.

Upon closer consideration, I realized the large closet was
obviously an addition to the room, since a smaller door at the far
right end of this wall was set back much further. I couldn't help
but wonder where the small door led. *Does it lead to an adjoining
room?* I mused. *If so, whose? Will Sara be staying next door? If
anyone is next door, I certainly hope it is Sara.*

While fiddling with the joystick, trying to get the hang of
maneuvering the chair to avoid running into anything, my attention was briefly captured by yet another piece of furniture. A

matching dresser and hutch mirror, its knickknack shelves adorned with small figurines, occupied the wall on the far side of the sitting room doors where I'd entered. I perused the little girls and boys in their different poses and colorful outfits, pondering their origins. Had these belonged to my parents as well? Surely not. For if so, why hadn't they taken these with them? I could understand leaving the furniture behind, but such small items as these?

Despite my better judgment, I was just about to risk voicing this question when Brandon breezed by me. Obviously aware of my destination, he strode over to the folding doors of the closet and opened them with a flourish.

Assuming it would be empty, ready for me to fill with my own belongings or possibly already containing them since I'd made this request of Brandon, I was shocked to find *neither* of these to be the case. Not by a long shot. I could only gawk at the long row of clothing, none of which appeared to be mine. There were dresses of every conceivable color, most being the same basic out-of-style design as the one I was wearing; an array of skirts and silk blouses carefully displayed on sachet scented hangers; and on a long, two-tiered shoe rack below, matching low-heeled pumps in nearly every color of the rainbow.

I looked up at Brandon, who was grinning from ear to ear, seemingly very pleased with himself, and turned away. Although I appreciated the sentiment behind the purchasing of these expensive clothes, I didn't like the implications. It was as if he were dictating my wardrobe. And as I surveyed his taste, I grimaced at the thought of having to comply with his wishes. I wanted my own clothes, but how was I to tell him this again without hurting his feelings?

As my eyes strayed down the long row of dresses and shoes, I noticed something dark and decidedly longer at the far end. I inched the chair forward down the length of the closet until I found what I was looking for. Beyond the dresses were several pairs of jeans suspended from a multi-tiered pants rack. A number of polo shirts, a few sweatshirts, several pairs of cotton twill pants and matching blouses adorned regular run-of-the-mill hangers. Beneath these sat two pairs of Reebok tennis shoes: one white, one black. My face lit up instantly, for my first impression was that he'd honored my request after all. But it soon became apparent that these clothes and shoes were new. My joyous expression faded, but I was at least glad he'd provided some things I liked.

"What do you think, Princess?" he finally asked, walking over to me.

"I appreciate all this," I replied, reaching out and touching a pair of the jeans in order to see what brand they were.

"Where did these come from?" he asked, sounding a bit perplexed. "Miss Bennington," he snarled, spinning around toward her, "did I not ask you to pick out a few pants and blouses for casual wear?"

"I did," she responded evenly, crossing her arms.

"Dungarees, men's golf shirts and...and these handyman's pullovers... This is what you call casual?" he grumbled.

"Of course," she affirmed serenely. "That's the style these days."

He sighed heavily. "Skirts and blouses...perhaps even pants are casual wear. But these are dung-a-rees," he maintained. "Only poor white trash and niggers wear these."

"I wear them," I declared, "and I don't consider myself either of the two." He glanced down at me and I stared back boldly.

I resented his reference to "niggers." It was a derogatory term I felt should not be used to refer to any ethnic group. In accordance with Mr. Webster's definition of the word, I had met "niggers" in the Caucasian race.

"You should try a pair of jeans sometime," I added. "See how comfortable they are." His expression changed instantly, as if I'd hit him below the belt. I flashed him a quick smile and turned away, reading the tag on the jeans. *Perfect*, I thought. *The jeans that fit.*

I glanced back at Sara, whose face bore a concerned expression, and smiled warmly. "Thank you, Sara. Now I know why we played twenty questions yesterday," I said, referring to her inquiries about my choice of clothes and brand name preference, as well as her disappearance right after lunch while I was resting.

She returned the smile as I steered around Brandon and over toward the small door set back against the wall. "What's in here?" I asked. "Another room?"

"It's your private bath," Brandon answered, his voice returning to the cheerful tone he'd been using before. "Let me show you."

He swiftly came around me and opened the door. Directly across from this door was another one, leading into what I assumed was a bedroom like mine. Perhaps even the one Sara would occupy. I carefully maneuvered into the bathroom to find the usual accouterments, with the addition of grab bars and the like for the disabled. The tub, however, appeared to be newer than the other facilities. A window on the far end was draped in cottage-style curtains through which light filtered into the room.

"I even had a bathtub installed like the one you used in the hospital," he said proudly.

I smiled my appreciation, although I noticed the bathtub was not equipped with a shower, which was something I had enjoyed at home. I reasoned it would be a while before I could stand up by myself and take a shower anyway, so it really didn't matter right now.

I turned away and fiddled with the steering lever, trying to turn around. "Please, Princess, allow me," he said gallantly, putting his hand over mine.

"Thanks, but I need to learn to do this myself."

"Oh, of course," he conceded, withdrawing his hand. His cheerful demeanor fell away as he walked by me.

When I finally got turned around, he was standing at the door running his fingers through his hair, disappointment written all over his face. I had a feeling my homecoming was not turning out exactly the way he'd planned.

"Is this Sara's room?" I asked, motioning to the other door leading out of the bathroom.

"No, she'll be staying across the hall," he answered decisively.

"Oh, I just assumed because it was so close that—"

"She will be close enough across the hall, I should think," he interrupted. "I've had a nice room prepared for her." He glanced down at me as I passed by him and flashed me a smile that seemed as phony as a three-dollar bill. "That room is in need of repair," he went on to explain. "It's not easy keeping up twenty rooms, you know. Especially those up here, with the plaster walls."

"Oh, I can understand that," I acknowledged, remembering the faint aroma of fresh paint when first we'd entered the bedroom. "This bedroom is larger than the sitting room, isn't it?" I queried, changing the subject somewhat.

"Yes," he affirmed. "Yes, it is. There were originally three suites on this end of the wing. I had them renovated for your mother and father when they came home to live," he explained, seeming to warm to this subject. "We took out one bedroom here to make the bathroom and closet. And, of course, to add more space to this bedroom."

That explains the window in the bathroom, I thought.

"For the most part, the other rooms were left intact, only adding doors to join them together. I tried to maintain the integrity of the house and still give your mother and father their own private living quarters. The sitting room on the far end was used as a living room, for receiving guests; the other was a study for your father. The room next door was used as a den, I believe they called it. And this, of course, was...their bedroom." A touch of sadness entered his voice. "Your sitting room was designated...a nursery." He cleared his throat. "Perhaps when you're up on your feet again, I'll have the other rooms redecorated for you." The change in subject seemed to brighten his spirits somewhat. "Well, I should go now and let you get some sleep. You'll need to be well rested for your coming-out party tonight." His tone was almost cheerful again, as if just thinking about this event delighted him. "Let's get you into bed and get you some food first, though."

Coming-out party? I wondered, rolling over to the bed. What was he talking about? Wasn't that for young girls who were just starting to date? *I hate to be the one to burst your bubble, Uncle,* I thought, *but I've already come out. And done a few other things you wouldn't care to know about, and would more than likely disapprove of.*

"This isn't a hospital bed, is it?" I inquired, as he picked me up and laid me down on the double bed.

"It's adjustable," he replied, indicating the remote control contained in a holder mounted on the right bedpost. "The hospital beds looked too small and cramped and wouldn't fit the bed frame, I'm afraid. I thought this would be far more comfortable for you. And not be a constant reminder of...your condition."

"Oh, I appreciate that," I said, in total agreement with his choice.

"I'm sure that later, when you need to sit up, Miss Bennington can show you how to adjust it to suit you. For now, get some rest, Princess. Lunch will be served soon, but right afterward, you get some sleep. I'd hate to find my guest of honor was too tired to attend her own party." He kissed me on the cheek and turned to leave. Glancing in Sara's direction, he paused. "Nurses dress casually these days, do they?" he inquired, looking her up and down.

I knew he was referring to her black blouse, jeans, and tennis shoes. The change in her attire had taken me by surprise, as well. But it was a nice surprise.

"I thought Faith would feel more at home if she wasn't constantly faced with a nurse's uniform. Sort of like the bed," she answered unemotionally.

He sighed heavily and started toward the door.

"Brandon," I called, and he quickly turned around. "Thank you for everything, especially this room. I know you went to a lot of trouble and expense to have all this done for me, and I want you to know I do appreciate it."

"You're welcome, Princess," he responded with a winning

smile. "If there's anything else I can do for you, just let me know."

"I hope you're using my inheritance to do all this," I added, thinking of the expense.

"Don't worry your pretty little head about it, Princess. I'll take care of all that."

After he left, I requested that Sara help me change into something more comfortable.

She agreed, walked over to the chest of drawers on the other side of the bed, and produced a pair of neatly folded long-sleeved purple pajamas. "I know it's not a nightshirt, but I didn't think that would be appropriate with...*him* popping in and you getting in and out of bed. But anyway..." She paused and unfolded the pajamas. "Now, madam, these are 50 percent cotton, 50 polyester and," she held up the top and bottom separately, "as you can see, they are plain. No frilly decorations to scratch you." I knew she was referring to a previous conversation concerning our choice of nighttime apparel.

"All right!" I proclaimed joyfully. "I don't have to ask who chose those, now do I?"

She cleared her throat. "He picked out some frilly nightgowns and robes. They're over there in the armoire."

I grimaced. "Guess I'll need to wear them sometime so I won't hurt his feelings, hmm?"

She shrugged. "Which would you rather have today?"

I glanced down at the dress I was wearing, which was binding beneath my arms, the new bra making me itch. "I wore *his* dress, so now I want *my* pajamas," I declared.

She grinned and proceeded over to the bed, where she helped me changed into my soft new pj's.

"Thanks for the jeans, shirts, and Reeboks," I said, as she pulled the cover up over my legs. "And, oh yeah, the other pants and sweatshirts and pajamas and... Well, just thanks for everything."

"You're welcome." She chuckled softly and turned to leave.

"And, Sara," I added, causing her to pause and turn around. "I do like you better in jeans. The nurse's uniform would've been a constant reminder. This way, you look more like...just a friend."

"I want to be your friend," she said softly, easing down on the side of the bed. "And as your friend *and* your nurse, I must ask you, please don't overdo it tonight. Let me know when you start to feel the least bit tired, okay? I mean, I know you feel strong and I know your uncle said the doctor thinks it'll be all right, but you

haven't fully recovered by any means. And in a situation like a
party, where you're excited and having fun meeting different people, you tend to overlook your body's warning signals. So please,
try and take it easy, hmm?

"This won't always be the case, I promise," she continued, as
if reading my mind. "I won't always be hanging over your shoulder, so to speak, and nagging you. But for tonight, I think I
should. Bran—your uncle means well, I'm sure, but I don't think
he realizes your limitations at present. Every time he's ever seen
you, you were full of energy after resting a considerable length of
time. So please, let me know if you get tired. I'd much rather have
you or *him* a bit disappointed over leaving a party than retard
your progress unknowingly. Do you understand what I'm saying?"

"Yeah, no dancing on the tables for me tonight," I quipped.

"Exactly," she agreed with a smirk.

I lightly touched her hand. "I'm glad Brandon chose you for
my nurse."

"So am I," she responded. "Now, get some rest. If you need
me, I'll be in your sitting room. I'll leave the door ajar." She got
up and started toward the door.

I watched her walk across the room, her snug-fitting jeans
hugging the contours of her shapely hips and making a very light
swishing noise as her inner thighs rubbed together. "Sara..."

"Hmm?" She stopped at the double doors and turned around.

I wanted to ask: *Do you really believe I'll walk again?* But
instead, I stared at the nearly bare wall by the doors, which I
immediately realized would be the perfect place for my stereo system and television. "Umm... Do you think Brandon could have my
stereo and television brought here?"

"I don't see why not."

"And some of my old clothes? I mean, I like the ones you
picked out, they're great, but..."

"You have the others all broken in, right?" she acknowledged,
hugging the right door against her body. "And let me guess, you've
got a favorite pair of jeans you're thinking about, and they're
frayed here and there, but fit you like a glove, right?"

"You've got a pair of those, too?"

She chuckled and nodded. "Got a hole right here in the knee.
Most comfortable pair of jeans I own." I laughed along with her.
"I'll ask about it," she offered.

"Uh...on second thought, you'd better not." I suddenly
remembered she and my uncle were not on such great terms with
one another. "Maybe I should do it myself."

"You're probably right. He doesn't seem to like me very

much, does he? Oh well, that doesn't matter. I'm not here for him; I'm here for you. And if you like me...well, that's all that counts. Now get some rest. And that's an order," she declared, her voice very deep and decisive on the latter sentence as she moved through the doorway.

I couldn't help but laugh, because I knew she'd been mimicking him and the way he gave orders. "I do like you, Sara, a lot," I called after her.

There was no response, except the slight squeaking of the old hinges as she pulled the doors together behind her.

After she left, my thoughts turned to my parents. It wasn't that I hadn't thought about them before, I just hadn't let myself dwell on it. Now, however, the tears started to flow; I missed them something awful. Alone in a comfortable bed, dressed in comfortable clothes for the first time since the accident, I once again cried myself to sleep.

Chapter
7

The afternoon passed quickly because I slept most of the time. After dinner, Sara and I picked out a long-sleeved black dress—one of the few that were rather plain—that would hide the bandages on my left arm as well as the scratches and bruises on my right. It also covered my legs, which I knew people would be staring at, wondering about my paralysis.

Sara spent considerable time arranging the black silk scarf for my turban, trying to make sure the bandage was completely concealed. She also suggested we use makeup on my hands to disguise the bruises. It didn't completely cover them all on my left hand, but did a fair job of camouflage. She also used a little on my face, around my eyes, to conceal the lingering bruised circles from my head injury. When allowed to see the result of her labors in the vanity mirror, I could hardly believe my eyes. I truly did favor my mother, much more so now than ever before. Was it only the dark brown hair that had made me believe otherwise?

"Now, the finishing touch." She handed me a bottle of perfume.

"*Chanel No. 5*?" I queried, looking up at her.

She merely nodded and shrugged.

I smelled of it. It wasn't bad. I wouldn't want to wear it all the time, but since this was supposed to be a special occasion, I decided I'd try something new.

"Did you buy this?" I inquired, dabbing it on my neck.

"No, it was here on the vanity, along with all this makeup."

Surely Brandon hadn't done this, had he? He'd picked out a few frilly nightgowns, but what would he know about makeup? What did he know about clothes, for that matter? And yet he'd certainly supplied me with a wardrobe filled with what he liked, hadn't he?

"You're very pretty, Faith," Sara commented, looking at my reflection.

"Thank you." I felt my face flush. "Why aren't you getting dressed?" I inquired, noticing her nurse's uniform. "Aren't you coming to the party?"

"Oh yes, but Brandon wants me to wear my uniform and...act like a nurse." Two fingers of each hand formed quotation marks in the air. "Which means I stay in the background. So, you're on your own for a while. Remember what I said now..."

"Don't get too tired," we said simultaneously.

"You're incorrigible," she muttered, squeezing the muscles of my shoulders. "Brandon will be here soon, so I'll..." She made walking motions with her fingers in the direction of the door. "Have a wonderful time."

When Brandon knocked and entered my sitting room, I was waiting for him. He stopped in his tracks; his mouth dropped open. "You are *absolutely* beautiful," he declared, his eyes lighting up. "Your mother would be sooo proud." He finally moved toward me, holding out his right hand. "Might I have the honor of escorting you to the ball, my beautiful princess?" he inquired gallantly, as he took my hand and placed a kiss on the back.

"Why, thank you, kind sir," I responded, playing along. He extended his arm and I put my left hand on it while moving the chair's control with my right.

"Your guests await you," he announced as we neared the door.

All of a sudden it hit me that I wouldn't know anyone there except him, Jason, and Sara. This disturbed me. I didn't feel ready to face all those strange people, alone; I wanted Sara beside me. She had been my emotional rock for nearly four weeks now. I marveled at the brief amount of time it takes to become very attached to someone, especially when you're in desperate need of something to cling to. I now knew just how truly dependent upon her I was. I glanced over at her door, then down at my hands, which were lying still in my lap.

Brandon had preceded me through the door, but now turned around. "What's the matter, Princess?"

"I...I'm a little nervous. All those new people, and... Look at me, I'm—"

"You're beautiful," he interjected, kneeling down in front of me. "Simply beautiful. And you wouldn't want to disappoint all the people who came to meet you, now would you?"

I sighed heavily and glanced back at Sara's door one last time.

"No, I wouldn't want to do that," I agreed halfheartedly.

"I'll be right here beside you the whole time, Princess," he promised, as he got to his feet.

Would he? I wondered, as we started down the long hall. Despite my fears, I was about to find out.

He carried me down the stairs and placed me in the manual wheelchair. As he wheeled me into the enormous living room on the east wing, every head turned our way and conversations abruptly came to a halt. I felt like someone had turned a spotlight in our direction; there had to be at least forty pairs of eyes trained on us.

"May I have your attention, please," Brandon requested, though no one had to be silenced or prodded. "I'd like you to meet my niece, Miss Marion Faith Neilson." Heads began bowing amongst the crowd of assembled guests as they turned their attention to me. A waiter then walked up beside Brandon with a glass of champagne. "She will be living at Shady Grove now, and I'd appreciate it if you'd make her feel welcome. Faith," he paused, turning toward me and holding up his glass, "from all of us...a hearty welcome and sincerest wishes for a speedy recovery." Everyone clapped.

I felt like a bee trapped inside a jar, with curious and strange eyes staring at me from the outside.

Jason was the first to come over to me. "Welcome to Shady Grove, Faith," he said with a smile. "I...I hope we'll soon be friends." He then glanced up at his father, who nodded. This made me wonder if Jason was being truthful or just playing a part like an actor in a movie.

Needless to say, that was my last contact with a familiar face—besides Brandon's—for a while. My uncle wheeled me into the crowd of people and started introducing me to everyone. I heard so many names, I couldn't recall any of them clearly a second after he uttered them. Each one who had known my mother commented on the remarkable resemblance; I began to wonder if I should have shaved my head and donned a turban years ago.

Not a one had anything negative or unpleasant to say. Yet, after Brandon finished with the introductions and became involved in a business discussion, not one soul seemed interested in me any longer. I listened as my uncle and his friends discussed mutual funds, CDs and, of course, the stock market. Needless to say, I found this boring, since I had little to no knowledge about such matters, and I started looking around for Sara.

I hadn't caught even a glimpse of her all evening and was beginning to wonder if she had come down when I overheard two women behind me talking about my turban. They evidently thought I was deaf as well as paralyzed. One said that she "wouldn't be caught dead wearing something that hideous" on her head. I found out then and there that I was no swan, like my mother, nor was I even close to being a duck; these remarks did not glide off my back, they penetrated and stung. I wheeled myself away as fast I could to get out of earshot, all the while feeling the scars on my left arm complaining clearly that this sudden, vigorous activity was not to their liking. Finally I thought I'd found a safe place, only to overhear:

"Pitiful, isn't she?"

"Yes, poor thing."

"I don't know, but I heard she was paralyzed for life."

"No, Bill said Brandon told him it was temporary."

"Well, you know how Brandon is... Don't you remember how long it took him to accept that Ashley was dead? He had them drag the river three different times."

"And you think he's just being optimistic?"

"Let's just say, Brandon didn't get where he is by being ruthlessly honest." This was followed by a giggle from both voices.

That did it. That was the last straw. I was getting out of there if it killed me! I headed toward the door to the foyer, my arms screaming in agony, when my chair suddenly came to a halt. "Going somewhere?" asked a familiar voice from behind me.

"Yes! Out of here," I whimpered.

"Whoa," Sara said, placing one hand on my shoulder and leaning down. "Hold those tears. These kinds of people can be very cruel, but let's not give them the satisfaction of seeing you cry, hmm? Think now, what would your mother do?"

"I don't care," I grumbled, struggling to hold back the tears. "Wait a minute, how did you know what happened?"

"I've been...close by; I've heard things. I know how they can be. And you're not the first one in a condition like this to face such a crowd. My clients are people who can afford to have a private duty nurse/therapist, remember? I've seen it happen before. *These* people will never change."

"Then what do I care what they think?"

"Because this is your world now. Brandon has tossed you out here in this pool of sharks—against my better judgment, I might add—and now you have to swim or be eaten. So, which will it be, hmm?"

"Damn," I cursed softly, wiping my eyes.

"Believe me, if I thought I could get away with it, I'd slug the old biddy," she admitted, squeezing my shoulder. "But, I can't, so...let's turn you around and stroll over there." She motioned to a table set up in the corner where an elderly lady was serving drinks. "Tears go down easier with a little pop."

Leave it to Sara, I thought, *to pull me out of a bad situation and make me laugh.* I glanced up at her. "Slug the old biddy?" I asked with a snicker.

"Yep, right between her beady little eyes."

I laughed heartily. I wanted to show them their cruel remarks hadn't touched me. *At least, not as long as Sara's around*, I thought.

She pushed me over to the refreshment table, where champagne and wine were being served. "'ello, Miss Faith," said the short, elderly lady with a decidedly unrefined British accent. I noticed right away that she dropped a lot of her consonants as if swallowing them. "I'm Celia, your maid."

"Nice to meet you, Celia," I responded, hoping this would indeed prove true.

"Nice to meet you, too, mum. What can I get for ya?"

"A pop will be fine, thank you. Better make that two," I corrected, glancing over at Sara.

"Yes, mum, right away. Good to see sum'un who doesn't take ta the drink, these days," she commented, rummaging under the table. "Sorry I wuz to hear about your accident, mum. All of us here would like ta wish you the speediest of recoveries."

"Thank you, Celia."

"Yes, mum." She handed me the two sodas.

"Have you met my nurse, Miss Benn..." I paused as Sara looked down at me, giving me the eye. "I mean, Sara?" I finished.

"Yes, mum, we've already met. Enjoy your stroll 'round the estate, mum?" she inquired of Sara.

"Yes, thank you, I did," Sara replied. "Now we'll just have to get Faith here well enough to do the same."

"Yes, mum. That would be very good. Very good indeed."

Sara wheeled me away from the table and out of hearing range of everyone else as best she could. Several people glanced at us, and I just knew they were talking about me. Some were the faces of people I vaguely remembered being nice to me only a few moments before.

"You'll get used to it, sweetheart," she said as I handed her the glass of soda.

"I feel like a gunfighter in this movie I saw once," I expressed, surveying my surroundings.

"Hmm? How's that?"

"He said he always sat with his chair against the wall to avoid being shot in the back."

She laughed and squeezed my shoulder. "That's a pretty good analogy. Not bad advice, either, in this sort of crowd."

"Faith...Faith?" It was Brandon again. "I've been looking all over for you. You shouldn't be way over here. You should be the center of attention."

I wanted so badly to say, *Oh, but I am...I'm the bulls-eye on a target, and your classy friends are damn good shots!* But instead I merely complained of being tired, so he wouldn't push me out there again.

"All right, Princess, I'll carry you upstairs, then."

"No...no, please, stay with your friends. Sara can manage, can't you?"

"Of course," she responded, but her eyes said she wanted desperately to make another comment. What it could have been, I didn't know.

"Stay with your guests and have a good time," I insisted. "Make my apologies for me, I'm sure they'll understand." *And then they can talk about me all they want,* I felt like adding, but held my tongue.

He agreed, albeit reluctantly, and as soon as we finished our drinks, Sara and I were on our way to the kitchen and the lift chair.

"I know this isn't the best time to learn to use this thing," she admitted, "but I'm not strong enough to carry you up those stairs. Believe me, if I could, I would." She paused, looking things over. "Okay, now listen to me and this'll be a cinch."

"Uh-huh," I commented, my tone suggesting I didn't believe her.

"Oh you," she teased, bending down to free my lifeless feet. When she did, I couldn't help but notice the dark roots where her hair parted. I wondered why I'd never noticed this before. "Come on, now," she said, coaxing me to help move myself into the chair.

Together, we tackled the lift chair, and within twenty minutes I was safely in my room, lying on the bed while Sara massaged my back and legs. I had bitten my lip several times, holding back the tears that threatened to fall when I thought about the disastrous party, but when Sara was helping me put my pajamas on and mentioned walking again, the dam finally burst.

She held me in her arms. "You're just not ready to face that kind of world yet. But one day, you will be."

When she started to leave, though I knew it was silly, I felt very alone, like a child without its usual night-light. For several weeks she had been only a few feet away, but now she'd be across the hall. Not so far for someone who could walk, not so far for someone who could crawl, even; but to me, unable to do either, it seemed like miles.

"Sara, please don't go," I requested. "Please...stay here tonight?"

"I can't, Faith. There's no cot."

"This bed is large enough for two. Please? At least until I fall asleep. Just this once..." I pleaded, sounding more like a whiny child than I had in many years.

"All right, just until you fall asleep. First, though, let me change my clothes. Besides, I'm sure your uncle will be up to tuck you in and give his *princess* a kiss, hmm? And how would it look if you and I... Well, I'll be back *after* he leaves."

Sara was right, Brandon did come up a little while later to kiss me goodnight. I had the sinking feeling this was going to turn into a nightly ritual. He lingered longer than usual against my cheek. I could smell the alcohol on his breath as he mentioned my perfume and his eyes turned glassy. He appeared lost in some memory, but I wasn't sure of whom. I just didn't like the way he was looking down at me.

"Where did you get these?" he asked, his forefinger motioning to the pajama top.

"Sara." He groaned. "I asked for them," I lied.

He glanced from me to the pajama top. "Your mother let you wear these?"

"I'm twenty-one years old, Brandon, I'm not a child. My mother had no say-so over what I wore anymore, and she wouldn't have objected anyway. She'd want me to be comfortable, so I can rest."

"Well, yes...of course," he acknowledged, clearing his throat and backing away. "I...I have...guests to entertain. I'll see you in the morning, Princess."

After he left, Sara came back, closing the sitting room door and the two double doors behind her. Hesitantly, she lay down on the bed beside me.

"I...I feel so alone, Sara. If it wasn't for you..."

"Shh...it'll be all right. Time heals, sweetheart. And soon you'll be running circles around me."

"I...I heard one woman saying I was paralyzed for life. Is that true?" I asked, finally voicing the question I had been avoiding for quite a while.

"I'm hurt, Faith," she said, sitting up and looking down at me. "Really hurt. Do you truly believe I'd lie to you about that?" She stared at me, her contact lenses not in evidence.

"No. I just... Well, it scared me is all."

"I'm not lying to you, Faith, and neither is Brandon. Not about this, at any rate. I heard the doctor say he felt the paralysis would be temporary. Why would he lie to me? Why would I lie to you, for that matter? What purpose would it serve?" I shrugged. "That wouldn't be in your best interest," she asserted, still staring into my eyes.

"Why do you wear blue contact lenses?" I asked, curious as to the answer and also desiring to change the subject, for I wanted to accept her word on the issue of the paralysis.

"You don't miss a thing, do you?"

"I try not to."

She sighed heavily and lay back on the bed. "Blue eyes look better with blonde hair, or so I'm told."

"But you're not a natural blonde," I stated.

"Oh, you're terrible...just terrible," she teased. "So what else have you observed about me, hmm?"

"Oh, that you have pretty *green* eyes. And they're far more interesting than the blue ones you pretend to have. I think you're sad inside for some reason. And...you and Brandon have a mutual dislike for one another."

"My, my," she said, rolling over on her side to face me and propping her chin up on her hand. "I'll have to be careful, or you'll find out all my secrets."

"I intend to," I responded teasingly, though I was also being truthful.

We both smiled and gazed into each other's eyes. I felt those strange feelings again, along with the desire to be close to her. I wanted to be as close as we had when I'd accidentally kissed her on the lips. Just the memory of that brief moment made my heart beat faster. My eyes fell to her lips, and I found myself wanting to kiss her again. Reacting on impulse, I reached over and touched her face.

"You're becoming too dependent on me," she said, reaching up and removing my hand. "I can't... You...you need your rest. Please don't..." she objected, as I touched her arm when she started getting up. "I know it's my fault and...I know—"

"What I feel...is this dependency?" I interrupted, curious as to why I felt so strongly about her.

"Yes," she replied, rolling away. "If you had someone else...someone you could trust and felt close to...you might not feel this way. Just remember, it will pass in time."

Will it, Sara? I wanted to ask. *Will it go away like my paralysis? Leave along with it, perhaps? When I take my first step, will I walk away from you? Or will you walk away from me?*

The days passed, turning into weeks, and I grew stronger. My feelings for her, however, did not pass; they seemed to become even more pronounced, building in strength like the muscles in my arms and upper body. Sara had me lifting hand weights—two-pound dumbbells to start—and doing every conceivable exercise she could think of, or so it seemed. And every day she backed away a little further, making me do more for myself. I missed her catering to me; I missed her touching me as she moved me about, because after two weeks' time I was doing a lot of things all by myself.

I began to move from the bed to the chair and from the chair into the tub and back again, all under my own power. She was always there, of course, watching every move; but she would not intervene unless I truly needed help. I did feel more independent, and yet I longed for her to be by my side. It seemed the more she backed away, the stronger my feelings became, instead of diminishing, as I assumed they were supposed to. I didn't dare let her know this, because I feared she'd back away altogether and leave me with no emotional crutch whatsoever.

I took solace in the physical therapy, and especially the massage therapy, because these soon became the only times she touched me. I wasn't starved for that type of affection, however, because Brandon touched me a lot. And he did indeed spend more time with me than he had before. He was pleasant company, for the most part; although while he was there, Sara would leave, which I didn't find pleasant at all. Sometimes, I'd catch a glimpse of her out the window, walking around the grounds, looking quite as unhappy as I felt. Or so it seemed. Then again, maybe that was just wishful thinking on my part.

They all tried to get me outside for short trips, but I didn't want to leave the security of my rooms very often. Here, I was Faith the brave, in control of her small environment, where she could move about as she pleased. Out there, I was Faith the cripple, no longer in control of this outside world that presented so many obstacles. I seldom even went downstairs, though I had mastered the lift chair and could get around fairly easily. It was always so tiring, and for what? To get a book Celia could very easily bring up with my meal? It just wasn't worth it to me.

A week after I got to Shady Grove, Dr. Rosemund came out to remove the stitches in my arm. Two weeks later, he removed the ones on my face, checked on my progress, and applied a new bandage. After gauging the strength and lack of sensation in my legs, he didn't seem pleased with the results. He spoke to Sara outside the door in hushed tones. Whatever he said seemed to worry her, and she was lost in thought for the rest of the afternoon.

After dinner one evening, Brandon relieved her, saying he had a surprise for me. But, before I received it, I'd have to agree to a short trip outside. I knew I needed to get out, so I finally relented. He took me out by the pool and to the tennis courts. I assumed this was a way of making me want to walk. But to me, walking meant facing the outside world again—and losing Sara. Neither was an appealing thought.

When we returned to my room, I was shocked to find a massive white entertainment center on the wall in front of my bed. A very expensive stereo system lined one side, a 27-inch television and expensive VCR covered the other one. Brandon promised I would have cable hook-up before the end of the week; but he never mentioned my clothes from home or my own stereo system, which I'd asked for twice now.

Jason was home on summer break, and it was he who handed me the remote control. "This operates everything," he explained. "It's a universal remote."

I was at a loss for words. I hugged his neck, and then hugged and kissed Brandon for getting me something I desperately wanted, even if it wasn't my own.

Jason taught me all about the remote and how everything worked. Brandon made a selection from the classical music he had purchased for me, and a Bach concerto filled the room. This brought Sara to the sitting-room door. It was obvious she hadn't been in on this. She did, however, smile and wink at me before disappearing again.

When I inquired about her later, as Brandon and Jason were leaving, my uncle informed me he'd given her the night off. He went on to impart that this would soon become a routine thing, since I no longer needed her around twenty-four hours a day. Then he said he'd be back to tuck me in. *What about my therapy?* I wondered, but didn't ask. I assumed she must have felt I needed a night off as well.

After changing my clothes, I maneuvered myself into the bed. Looking over at the chair by the window where she usually sat, reading or just staring outside, a lonely, forlorn feeling flowed over me. One day, she wouldn't be here at all. I wouldn't need her anymore, and she would leave to help some other patient like myself. The thought depressed me terribly.

Brandon finally came up and tucked me in, making me a bit uncomfortable with the way he kept looking at my breasts. I wondered if he could see through the nightgown I had on, which he had selected. He asked why I no longer wore the perfume he liked so well, meaning the *Chanel No. 5*. And I replied that I didn't feel pretty right now.

"Perhaps if you put it on, you will feel prettier," he offered, walking over to the vanity and retrieving the bottle, which he brought to me. "Please, it's such a lovely fragrance."

I dabbed some on and handed it back; he inhaled deeply and then set it on the nightstand. "Your mother used to wear this, you know," he remarked, his eyes taking on that glassy appearance.

"You were in love with my mother, weren't you?" I blurted, the words falling from my lips before I had the chance to stop them.

He merely stood there for a long time with his eyes lowered. I assumed he was carefully considering his answer. "Living here, in the same house, we...became close. Your father...was away a good deal, trying to promote his first novel, so your mother and I did spend a good deal of time together. I had a...deep, abiding respect for her. She was a strong woman, despite her overt compassion for the hardships of others. I came to admire that about her. I suppose you could say I loved her, in my own way, yes."

"Did you have an affair with her?" I asked pointedly, noticing the cloudy look in his eyes when he spoke of loving her.

"What?" he asked, as if he hadn't heard me.

"I said, did you have an affair with her?"

He turned away abruptly, as if I'd slapped him in the face. "No!" he answered vehemently. "Your mother was far too loyal to your father to ever... No, we did not have an affair!" He rapidly moved toward the window, shoving his hands deep into his pockets, rattling the change in his right one. "It's getting late. You need your rest. I'll check on you tomorrow." He walked over to the door and then turned to me as he opened it. "Your mother was a wonderful woman, Faith. She never betrayed your father. One day, you might understand about lonely people: sometimes they live in the past, when the future holds little enticement for them." He walked out then, leaving the door slightly ajar.

I couldn't help but wonder what it had been like for him to love my mother, knowing she would never return that love. Is that why Mother and Father left? Did Mother know and tell Father, so he would move her away from here in order to avoid torturing Brandon? Is that what it had all been about?

I laid my head back and sighed heavily. The perfume on the nightstand caught my attention. Why was it here on the vanity? Had Brandon put it there for me to find? If so, why? Seems he would only be opening up old wounds, time and time again. Then again, perhaps as he'd said, he lived in the past because he felt the future held nothing for him. Now *that* I could relate to. My future seemed a constant uphill road, a slow climb for me. And once over the top, I would eventually lose someone who had become my best friend. The thought saddened me immensely. Hadn't I lost enough people in my life?

I did know something about loneliness, because I had felt it creeping up on me little by little each day that Sara grew more distant. As I lay there, I started to wonder what she was doing right now. Was she visiting her family? She rarely spoke about them. She'd only answer questions, never offering any details; and to be honest, I hadn't asked that many questions. I knew she had a father and a younger brother, and that she lived near Atlanta. Where her mother was or what had happened to her, I didn't know. I never pressed the matter too far, because Sara would get very uneasy and sad when I asked too many questions. I hated to see her that way. She'd retreat inside herself and close off all the doors behind her. Of course, then she would usually leave, only to come back later—her old, cheerful self. But losing her for even that brief period of time was not worth the acquired knowledge to me.

As soon as I turned off the lamp by my bed, I heard a noise out in the hallway. It sounded as if someone was dragging their feet and moving awkwardly. The footsteps stopped outside my sitting-room door. Muffled by the carpet, they continued to my bedroom door, where they paused. The door slowly squeaked open and my heart started beating very fast. *Who could this be? Brandon? Why's he here again? Why's he dragging his feet?*

The footsteps continued over to Sara's chair by the window. The light from outside struck the side of a face, the blinds casting horizontal shadows across the features. It was Sara. She sat down in her chair rather hard. I could make out her silky white blouse as it moved up and down to the rhythm of her heavy breathing.

What's she doing here in the dark? I wondered. *Why's she walking so funny and breathing so heavily?* The faint smell of alcohol drifted over to me. Could she be drunk? *Sara? Why?*

Her breathing returned to normal after several moments, and she straightened up. The light struck her face when she looked over at me.

"Did you have fun?" I inquired.

She flinched at the sound of my voice. "Je-sus H. Christ! I...I didn't know you were still awake."

"Obviously."

"I just wanted to...to check on you before I turned in."

"Turned into what?" I quipped, reaching over and switching on the lamp.

"Good God!" she hissed, shielding her eyes. "Cut that damn thing off!"

I was quite surprised by her appearance. Her hair was not in its usual coif, but long and flowing, falling around her shoulders. She looked quite nice, yet a bit worse for wear. Her white silky blouse was wrinkled, with smudges around the collar and shoulder; her jeans bore a few creases high up on the legs that I knew could only have been made by them being off her body for some length of time; one leg of her jeans wasn't even tucked into the calf-high black leather boots she was wearing. All together, except for her hair, her appearance was rather masculine. And the strangest part was, I liked it.

The silence in the room was deafening as she finally removed her hands from her eyes and looked over at me. Her expression was one of guilt, pure and simple.

"Did you have fun on your night off?" I asked again.

"Uh...not really," she responded, looking away.

"It would appear you did," I remarked, staring at her blouse. "Was he good looking?"

"Who?" she asked, sounding perplexed.

"Whoever wrinkled your clothes. Or should I say, whoever removed them?"

"Oh...you! Damn it, you don't miss a thing, do you?" she muttered, standing up.

"I try not to," I replied, watching as she stumbled forward several steps. I thought she had regained her balance, but then she hit my wheelchair with the toe of her boot. Stumbling forward, then sideways, she fell headlong onto the bed and across my lap. "Drunk, too, I see," I remarked, as she slowly sat up and looked over at me.

"You don't have to be so...so damn high and mighty," she declared, attempting to get up. As she did, she must have pressed against my leg somehow, and I yelped in pain. "I'm sorry, I didn't—"

"I felt that!" I gasped in utter shock. "I...I thought I felt it when you fell on me, but wasn't sure... I mean...but I definitely felt that!"

"Really?" she questioned, straightening up. "You actually felt pain?"

"Yes, I did." Tears leapt into my eyes.

"Let's see," she said, fumbling with the covers and finally

pulling them back. She pressed against my right leg. Nothing. Then did the same to my left one.

"I feel that!"

"Close your eyes," she instructed.

"I didn't imagine—"

"Close your eyes, damn it," she demanded.

I did as ordered. I felt nothing for a while, then...slight pressure on my left leg. "I can feel that on my left thigh! I can really feel it!" I proclaimed, opening my eyes.

"Yes, I believe you did," she agreed, sitting down on the bed beside me. "Dr. Rosemund said you should have regained some feeling by now. And I thought I was failing you when he told me you should be making better progress." Tears welled up in her eyes as she looked down at me.

"But you haven't. I did feel that! I swear!" I grabbed her around the neck, throwing caution to the wind.

She held me tight as tears of joy ran down both our cheeks. I hadn't realized that such a small thing could feel so wonderful. I *would* get better! I *would* walk again! I *would...lose Sara!*

I pressed her closer to me. I didn't want to lose her! I needed her. I had no family except for Brandon and Jason; I had no friends either. I needed her desperately! I pressed my lips to her neck, expressing the affection I felt for her. Her perfume tantalized my senses, making me aware of how very close our bodies were. I could feel the softness of her silky blouse above the low-cut bodice of my nightgown, her body against mine.

"Please...don't leave me...Sara," I pleaded, my voice breaking with emotion.

"I'll have to one day," she responded. "Remember, butterflies are free? And you're the most beautiful butterfly I've ever seen. One...I cannot keep." She tugged at my arm, urging me to let go of her neck.

As she pulled away slowly, her face came so close to mine that I felt an irresistible urge to kiss her, despite her alcohol breath. Which is exactly what I did, scaring my own self. My heart skipped a beat when my lips touched hers, and fluttered wildly, as if it had wings. For a few fleeting moments, she allowed the contact, almost as if she enjoyed it. I felt her lips part slightly, and her tongue flick across my own. *Oh God, that felt good!*

Abruptly she pulled away, got up, and left the room without a word, seemingly a more sober person than when she'd entered. I merely sat there and watched her leave, feeling quite numb all over. I had deliberately kissed another woman! And I had enjoyed it! *Oh God, what is wrong with me? Why do I feel this way?*

Before, I had blamed my feelings on dependency, just as she had said; but could I blame *this* on dependency? Could I blame this on the excitement or sadness of the moment? Or would I have to accept the responsibility? Had I become attracted to another woman?

But that was preposterous! Wasn't it? Yet I had kissed her, wanted to be close to her. So close, in fact, that I could feel her body next to mine. Didn't I watch her when she walked across a room, taking note of her shapely hips as they swayed back and forth? Didn't I purposefully look and admire her cleavage when she bent over in a low-cut blouse? *Yes,* I had to admit: I had done all of these things and more. And thinking back, hadn't I always felt fond of female teachers, especially the coaches? Yes, I had. But it only felt natural to do so. I'd never thought of it in *these* terms before, however. The concept of having unnatural tendencies scared me.

I lay awake for a long time, turning things over in my mind. There had to be another reason, because I was not ready to confront the possibility that I might be...*homosexual.* Even the word itself sounded horrible! They were immoral, evil people, weren't they? At least that's what they taught in the Baptist church we'd attended. God had destroyed Sodom and Gomorrah because of this type of immoral behavior; Lot's wife had been turned into a pillar of salt just for looking back. The few entries in psychological texts—I hadn't gotten far enough in my schooling to learn much on the subject—still weren't sure whether homosexuality was a choice or a product of some biological component. Either way, however, most religions deemed it an unnatural behavior. And I had been told there were still laws against such deviant relationships.

What must Sara think of me? I wondered. *Oh God, I'd die if she thought of me as evil! And what if she turns her back on me?*

I made up my mind then and there, that no matter what I felt, and no matter how hard it might be to resist, I would never, *ever* let those feelings show again.

Chapter
8

The next morning, to my amazement, Sara was back to her old chipper self and seemed to have suffered no ill effects from the previous night, except for a headache. She did change my schedule, though. We had our therapy session after lunch instead of before bed. I could still feel pressure on my left leg, which she said was a good sign. The only thing truly different was *my* attitude. I tried hard to fight the feelings I had once enjoyed. For instance, when she put her hands on me, I tried to tell myself, *It does not feel good, it feels awful.* In reality, I enjoyed it immensely. My body seemed bound and determined to disagree with my mind.

That afternoon I overheard a heated discussion between Sara and Brandon concerning my electric wheelchair. It wasn't the first time she'd broached this subject, yet she now had Dr. Rosemund's clout to back her up. My electric wheelchair was moved downstairs, and the manual one installed in my room in its place. I wasn't exactly thrilled with this new arrangement, because it meant more work for me, but that was the general idea. I needed more strength in my arms, and moving around in the chair would help, or at least that's what I overheard Sara tell Brandon.

Days dragged by as I fought my feelings for her. I tried to direct more of my affection toward Brandon—Jason having left for summer camp almost as soon as he got home. My uncle seemed to relish the attention, so I assumed I was doing the right thing. He threw several dinner parties, which I grudgingly attended, staying just long enough for the meal, then retiring to my room. Business conversations were just not my cup of tea.

During this time, I grew stronger and stronger, moving in and out and around in my chair with great ease, even venturing outside on the patio, usually with Sara following close behind. When we'd pass the indoor pool, she'd bring up the subject of starting therapy in the pool, which would be good for my legs and back. She was just waiting for Dr. Rosemund to give his okay for the head wound to be immersed.

She had already started working on the mobility of my legs, but I didn't seem to have any controlled movement yet. My left leg spasmed occasionally and my right regained feeling, but I couldn't move either one. I could tell this was disappointing to Sara, but there was nothing I could do about it. Most of the body parts above my legs had regained feeling, slowly but surely, and were in working order, for which I was very grateful. The "junk bag," as I called it, had not exactly been my best friend and I was glad to be rid of it, despite its essential function in elimination.

Even though my recovery was moving along, albeit at a much slower pace than anyone had expected, I became depressed over my inability to "cure" my attraction for Sara. I took a decided downhill glide into the abyss of my own dark, tortured soul. Needless to say, I wasn't happy with what I found there. Depression is like quicksand: the more you try to fight it, the lower you sink. And the more I fought my attraction for Sara, the more depressed I became. There seemed no way out of the endless cycle or the bottomless pit of despair.

A month or so before, I had been happy just to be able to get out of bed on my own; now this was a normal occurrence. I mechanically got out of bed, bathed, dressed and, when we weren't engaged in some type of therapy, watched TV or listened to music for the better part of every day. I had no desire to do anything else. Not even talk to Sara. She tried hard to get me outside, but I just didn't have the energy to do anything beyond my daily routine. She worked with me, trying to help me stand up by myself, but my legs would buckle, she'd inevitably catch me, and those *bad* feelings would surface again. That's when I'd plunge even deeper into the abyss of my despair.

Brandon called Dr. Rosemund, but there was nothing he could do. He, in turn, referred me to a psychiatrist, who came out and asked me question upon question, to which I offered curt replies. I overheard this analyst say that he'd concluded I was giving up on walking. He wasn't far off base, either, because I had given up on walking—and on life. I felt I was the worst sort of human being there was: a *homosexual.* The thought left a nasty taste in my mouth, one I refused to make worse by verbally sharing my "unnatural" feelings. I wanted no one to know about this, especially not my uncle. Of course, I had no idea how he might react. But images of being committed to an insane asylum tormented my waking and sleeping thoughts, which in turn helped keep my big mouth shut on the issue.

The psychiatrist prescribed an anti-depressant. It gave me severe headaches, and after only three pills—three days spent in bed, my head throbbing and my stomach nauseous—I refused to take any more, and no one forced the issue.

Dr. Rosemund finally approved pool therapy, suggesting it would be good for my back and legs and apparently hopeful it might help with the depression. Brandon was so optimistic, he purchased six bathing suits for me. And Jason—back home from a month away at summer camp—volunteered to help Sara haul me in and out of the pool.

The first day, I struggled into my swimsuit by myself, not wanting Sara touching me any more than she had to. She came into my room wearing a short robe and I immediately noticed her legs, which made me feel awfully dirty. I wished the chlorinated water in the pool would cleanse away my impure thoughts, but I knew better than that.

At the pool, Sara disrobed, and I tried hard not to look, but she was soon in front of me: black bathing suit cut low in the front, backless to her rump, and arched high over her shapely thighs. She and Jason picked me up and carried me into the water. I wanted him to stay, but he left me in her arms and went back inside the house. She carried me over to the side of the pool, where I eagerly grabbed hold of the drainage trough.

"Relax, Faith," she soothed. "You told me you could swim and weren't afraid of the water, so what's wrong?" I offered no reply. "Don't you trust me?"

"Yes."

"Well, just relax. We'll start off by massaging your legs." She turned me around to face her and took hold of both legs, stretching them out in front of me. "Perhaps we'll get some response today. Wouldn't it be great to make some progress?"

"Yeah."

"You sound sooo enthusiastic," she remarked, rubbing my legs while I gripped the trough with both hands.

I struggled to think of something, anything other than what she was doing. It didn't work, however; all I could think about was *her*. Unlike a few weeks back when I couldn't feel her touching me, I now felt nearly every nuance. And needless to say, it was far better than any fantasy I had ever conjured up about it.

When finished massaging, she held on to my left foot and tried to get me to move it by concentrating. Time after time I tried, but nothing happened.

"Faith...I just don't understand it," she said, anger tingeing her voice. "You should be taking your first steps by now. All the feeling has returned and... I...I just don't understand it."

I gazed up at the clear glass ceiling of the indoor pool, watching a small white cloud pass overhead. *What do you want from me?* I felt like asking. *I can only do as much as I can do.* Instead I said, "Maybe I'm paralyzed for life." I watched a bird land on the ceiling. *Wonder what it would feel like to fly.*

A few fruitless moments later, Sara walked over to the steps of the pool and got out. I thought she was going to get Jason and end the session, but instead I heard the door leading from the house to the pool area slam shut and the lock click into place. I then saw her walk over and lock the outside door. From there, she went over to the chair where her robe lay and let her hair down. I watched as the silky, bleached-blonde mass fell loosely around her shoulders. She did something else I couldn't see because her back was to me, and I chastised myself once again for even watching her. And especially for wondering how the fine downy hair running up her backbone might feel against my fingertips.

"Now, let's try this again," she said sternly, approaching me.

I could tell she'd taken out her contact lenses because her green eyes bored into mine. I looked away, wondering why she had made such a change in her appearance, and why she'd felt it necessary to lock the doors. *What possible good will this do?* But I didn't ask.

"Faith, concentrate," she directed, holding my left leg in her hand again. Nothing happened. "You're not concentrating, you're not even trying," she admonished, her tone revealing her frustration. "I don't know why I waste my time, because you...you obviously aren't even interested in trying."

I merely stared at the ceiling.

"Faith, look at me." I felt her coming closer, sliding up the side of my leg. "I said, look at me," she reiterated, touching the side of my face. I turned away. "Oh, I see...the little princess wants to remain in her castle today, does she? Poor Faith," she chided. "Poor, poor, crippled Faith. Shall I feel sorry for her?" Her tone was mocking.

She was starting to make me mad. I pulled myself down the side of the pool, trying to avoid a confrontation.

"Going somewhere?" She stepped in front of me and grabbed hold of the trough with her left hand, blocking my passage with her arm. I turned back toward the other side, and she did the same with the other arm. I was trapped. "Trying to avoid me, aren't you? Well, I won't let you. You can't get rid of me, because *I* won't give up on you, even though you have obviously given up on yourself. So, it seems like we're stuck with each other, hmm?"

I offered no response. I merely pushed against her arm, trying to get away.

"Oh no, you aren't going anywhere. You're going to explain to me why you've given up." I still offered no reply. "What is it, you too comfortable, hmm?" I pushed against her other arm. "That's it, isn't it? The pretty, little princess in her ivory tower; everyone waiting on her hand and foot, catering to her every whim... You're spoiled, you know that?"

"Stop it," I grumbled, holding back my anger, my tone quite low.

"Oh my, she said two words to me." Her tone was high-pitched and mocking. "I've been richly blessed. The fair princess, she speaks. And when she speaks, everyone obeys, right?" Her tone had changed, revealing her irritation. "Well, I'm sorry, but I don't cater to spoiled little rich girls."

"Shut up!" I growled.

"Why? Does the truth hurt? And the truth is, Faith doesn't want to walk, does she? Well, does she?"

I offered no response.

"Of course not, she's too damn comfortable in her ivory tower, isn't she? Isn't that the reason? Oh yes, she has everything she needs: a television, stereo system, and cable...with every premium movie channel they have, so she can watch those monthly showings over and over and over. Do you realize that's all you do?" she accused. "Watch TV and play that incessant classical music of Brandon's, while you waste away up there feeling sorry for yourself? But what I really want to know, Faith is why. I don't understand; explain it to me! Why would a beautiful twenty-one-year-old woman, with her whole future ahead of her, want to lock herself away in her room? I need to know why." She paused, allowing me time to answer, which I didn't. "You want everyone to feel sorry for you, is that it? *Don't upset her, you know she's a fragile child*," she said, mimicking words I'd heard Brandon use many times in the past few weeks.

"I'm not a child!" I exclaimed, prying at the fingers of her right hand so she would loose her grip.

"Oh no? Well you could've fooled me! You're acting like a child right now. A spoiled...rotten...child!" she declared, drawing out the last three words, making them sound vulgar.

Before I realized what I was doing, I turned halfway around, drew back, and slapped her across the face. She responded by grabbing both my arms near the elbows so I couldn't strike another blow.

"I told you before, you won't get rid of me this way! Now, we're going to get to the bottom of this thing if it takes all day. And now that I have your complete and undivided attention, tell me why you're not even trying to walk."

I struggled to break free of her hold, but she pressed me back against the side of the pool. "Goddammit, Faith, answer me! Why don't you want to walk?"

"Y-you!" I screeched.

She looked at me quizzically, as if this wasn't what she'd expected me to say. "What the hell do *I* have to do with it?"

"You'll leave me!"

She loosened her grip somewhat, but continued to stare at me. "Are you trying to tell me you don't want to even *attempt* to walk, because if you do, I'll leave?"

"Yeah," I admitted, tears welling up in my eyes.

"Faith, sweetheart, we've got a long road ahead of us. I'm not going anywhere just yet."

"You will, you said so," I reminded.

"Well, I'll be leaving sooner than you think, if you don't at least start trying to make some progress. Oh yes," she continued, reading my horrified expression. "Your uncle's already talking about letting me go. He seems quite content with your progress so far. He's giving up, just like you. I have another week. After that..."

The thought of losing her sooner than I had expected turned on the old tear faucet. I felt as if my heart were about to burst.

"Oh God, what've I done?" she muttered, throwing her arms around me. "I've made you so dependent on me. I'm sorry, Faith. I...I thought I was doing the right thing, trying to be a friend and not just a nurse. I thought—"

"It's not you, it's me!" I blubbered. "It's all my fault. You...couldn't have made me...love you."

I felt her flinch. "Yes, yes I did. I...I wanted you to," she admitted, easing back to face me. "I...I wanted you to love me, because I'm...I'm just so selfish."

"No, Sara, it's not you, it's me," I attempted to explain. "I'm...I'm a terrible person...a horrible, evil person!" I hung my head in shame.

She pulled me close, my cheek landing on her shoulder. "How can you say that?" she half-whispered.

"Because...I want you...all to myself!" I confessed.

"I think...we're both guilty of the same thing," she admitted softly.

There was a long silence. Slowly she eased back again to face me. She was so close that I felt an overwhelming desire to kiss her once again. I stared deeply into her beautiful green eyes, wondering what she would do if I did. Would she pull away forever? Afraid of taking the risk, I hesitantly reached up and touched her face instead.

"I tried to...to make you see," she said, her eyes tracking slowly back and forth, as if searching mine for understanding. "Perhaps I shouldn't have backed away, but...things were..." Her voice trailed off as her eyes swept from my mouth to my eyes and back again.

And then it happened. The impulse was overpowering. My control vanished. I didn't even stop to think about it until my lips touched hers ever so briefly. I drew back, astonished by my own actions and extremely fearful of what her reaction would be. My heart fluttered inside my chest, racing wildly as she gazed deeply into my eyes. I watched her expression change from anguish to something softer, more alluring. And then she leaned over and kissed me back. Not lightly, as I had her, but a full-blown kiss, with all the trimmings.

I'd never felt such sensations before, never even knew I could. They flowed over me like waves of delicious warmth. No male— boy or man—had ever caused me to feel this way.

I pulled her closer, feeling the dampness of her skin against my own. Sweet sensations crept down my spine; my heart was beating like a drum in my ears, drowning out everything except the soft sounds of our sighs as the kiss grew more passionate. A veritable Fourth of July fireworks display was going off in the pit of my stomach, sending out sparks that filtered down to my lower abdomen. Longings I had never before experienced swept through my body like a roaring fire intent on consuming me.

Without warning, she broke away from our passionate embrace and took a step back. Her eyes fell to my breasts, and then beyond. Tingling sensations raced up my spine.

Her previous expression changed quite quickly, and a smile began forming at the corners of her mouth. "Don't look now, sweetheart," she announced, her eyes slowly traveling back up my body until they locked with mine, "but you're standing on your own two feet."

My eyes widened in disbelief as I became conscious that she was no longer holding on to me. My gaze slowly drifted down to my legs. Indeed, I was standing on my own two feet, with no support whatsoever. I could even feel the concrete bottom against my toes. I quickly glanced back up at her, wondering how this had happened.

"Wonderful!" she beamed, taking a step forward to the place she'd occupied only moments before. "It's one small step in the right direction, sweetheart!"

I squealed with delight. At that moment, I couldn't remember ever being so happy. I felt like *two* enormous weights had simultaneously been lifted off my shoulders. Which I was happier about—standing on my own or being kissed in return—I didn't stop to contemplate. I reached out and pulled her close. "Oh, Sara, I—"

"What's all this about?" boomed Brandon's baritone, laced with undeniable suspicion.

I turned in his direction while still holding on to her shoulder with one arm. I wondered how long he'd been standing there and how much he'd seen. "I...I can stand by myself!" I cried out in sheer delight, just in case he hadn't been privy to previous events.

He gazed down at me, his expression cool. "That's...very good, Princess. Is that what all the commotion was about? The servants came and told me you two were screaming at each other." He eyed Sara skeptically. "What was all *that* about? And why was the door locked?"

"I felt it best if we weren't disturbed," Sara responded. "I...I was trying a tack that was a bit different."

"Different?" he asked, raising one eyebrow.

"Yes, she wasn't responding to anything, especially kindness. So, I...I thought if I got her mad enough, maybe I'd at least get *some* reaction."

"And it worked," I intoned, still hanging on to her.

"What did you say to create such a commotion is what I want to know?" he pressed, the agitation in his tone increasing.

"She called me a spoiled rotten child," I answered, still looking at her. "And...I slapped her. For which I'm truly sorry."

"At least it worked...in the end," she added, gazing into my eyes.

For a moment, I was lost in those green depths. My world consisted of the two of us and what we had shared. I forgot about Brandon standing there.

"I'm not sure I approve of your methods," he said, breaking the spell between us. "But I suppose the end justifies the means in this instance."

When we both looked up at him, he was still eyeing us suspiciously. I wondered just how much he had seen or overheard. Surely, if he had seen everything, he'd say something about it.

"Sampson," he called toward the house, "tell Jason to come down here. He's probably in his room."

In his room? I had completely forgotten that his room over-looked the pool. *Did he see us?* I wondered. I looked up to ascertain whether I could make out his window. Indeed I could, but didn't see him.

"Can you stand for *me*, Princess?" Brandon asked, his voice calmer and sweeter in tone. "Or do I need to make you angry, too?"

"No, I...I think..." I paused, removing my arm from around Sara's shoulder, "I think I can do it again." She took my hands to steady me, then slowly let go and backed away a few steps.

"See," I said, turning my upper body toward him.

The momentum of the turn must have been too much for my legs, for I lost my balance and began falling back toward the side of the pool. Sara grabbed both my arms and pulled me in against her body. My head came to rest on her chest. I could hear her heart beating rapidly and feel the dampness of her skin against my cheek. Those strange feelings returned again, but instead of fighting them, I now allowed myself to enjoy them. Sara had proven, with that one kiss, that I was not alone in how I felt. That in itself was quite a relief!

"I'm afraid you're not quite ready for spins and turns yet," she said teasingly, then reached down and swept both my legs up into her left arm. "But we'll keep working on it, every day, hmm?"

"Yes, every day," I responded, wrapping my left arm around her neck and pulling myself up into a more comfortable position.

"Must the doors remain locked each time?" Brandon inquired in a cold voice. "What if something should happen? The servants couldn't even—"

"That was only for today, Mr. Neilson," Sara interjected, cutting him off. "I thought it best that no one come running to her defense. There'll be times when she'll get pretty angry with me. She'll probably rant and rave and," she paused, looking down at me as she carried me through the water to the steps, "those are the times I'd prefer no interference."

"Interference?" he questioned. "I don't understand why you feel you must be so hard on her that any of us would feel the *need* to interfere. You know she's a fragile child."

Sara and I looked at each other and fought back the laughter I knew was just under the surface. I remembered how she had mocked those very words only a short while ago.

"Your technique may have worked today, but you may also have done more harm than good," he added.

"I believe she's stronger than you give her credit for. She's pretty headstrong and quite...stubborn," she maintained, though in a teasing tone.

"All right. You can both stop talking about me as if I'm not even here," I declared. "I'm not a fragile child, Brandon. To you I am, because I'm your niece. And I'm sure my father would treat me the same way. But Sara's right, I am headstrong and...I am stubborn," I added with a smile.

"Hey, what happened to you?" Jason inquired of me as he walked up beside his father. My, how they did look alike, except Jason wore a smile instead of Brandon's hard, cold stare. "When I left here a while ago, you'd hardly say a word. Now you're smiling. What gives?"

"Seems Miss Bennington is a...miracle worker," Brandon replied, a hint of envy in his voice.

"Looks that way," Jason agreed, moving down the steps to help Sara carry me to my chair. "It's good to see you smiling again."

"It feels good," I said cheerfully, relieved that he obviously hadn't seen any of what had gone on between Sara and me. "Perhaps this afternoon, we could finish that puzzle we were working on?"

"Really?" he asked, excitement coloring his voice. He helped Sara position me in my chair. "I've wanted to come see you more often, but you were..."

"Always so tired and rude?" I finished for him.

He nodded ever so slightly. "Would you tell me the story about the old hermit?" he asked, his voice soft and low. I assumed he didn't want his father to overhear.

"Sure." I remembered the first time I had told him about the hermit and the legend surrounding Windell's Point; how he had seemingly hung on every word I uttered. "If you'll tell me a few things as well."

He cut his eyes over at me and then quickly looked away. I knew he didn't like to talk about his family, but I did. The history of our family went back a long ways, and I wanted to learn more about it. I also wanted to know more about Ashley. Her body not being found was a juicy mystery I'd been dying to sink my speculating teeth into. Yet whenever I had asked about this, he'd always say, "I was away at school all the time."

"Miss Bennington, why don't you let Jason escort Faith to her room. I'd like to talk to you," Brandon said sternly.

My heart sank. Why did he want to talk with her? Had we not explained everything to his satisfaction? *Evidently not. How much did he see?* I wondered. *Is he going to fire her?* If so, what could I do to prevent it? Sweet Jesus, I felt helpless!

"I'll see you later," she said softly. "Try to get some rest before lunch." She must have noticed the worried look on my face, because she added, "I'll be up soon, I promise."

Jason walked beside me as I steered my chair back inside. He asked me what had happened to change my attitude, and I told him the same selective truth Sara had told Brandon. Unlike his father, Jason merely nodded and accepted it. When we reached my room, he left so that I could change, saying he'd see me after lunch.

I went into the bathroom and struggled to remove the wet bathing suit. It had been simple to get into, but it was hell removing it; it was sticking to my body like peanut butter on loaf bread. And I'm sure it didn't help any that my mind was elsewhere.

Finally I was able to get out of the garment and dry myself off. Needless to say, I had to dry the chair, too, because the seat was wet from my soaked bathing suit. I slipped into one of the nightgowns Brandon had picked out, just in case he came up anytime soon, hoping it might lighten his mood to see me wearing one of his choices. Then I wheeled back into the bedroom and maneuvered into bed, all the while thinking about Sara and what Brandon was saying to her.

I watched the digital clock on the VCR count off the minutes. Ten went by. Fifteen... twenty...I was getting worried now. *Twenty-one...Was that footsteps? Twenty-four...twenty-five... What could they be talking about so long? Twenty-nine...Thirty! He saw us and he fired her, I just know it! Thirty-two...God in heaven, what will I do now? I can't lose Sara, I just can't! I'd die! I'd just...Was that footsteps? Yes, thank God, here she comes!*

"What happened?" I questioned as she strolled into the room, all smiles, wearing her jeans and a black tank top.

Putting her finger to her lips, she shut the door behind her and then came over and sat down on the side of the bed. "He was angry about me making you mad, but he couldn't argue with the results," she answered softly. "But, he...um...he's uncomfortable with...the way you 'hang all over me,' as he put it."

"Did he see—"

She shook her head. "I don't think so. Surely he would have fired me for that, hmm? Results be damned. No, I...I think he's a bit envious, to be honest. He was probably ready to get rid of me, and this kind of screwed up his plans."

"Thank God for that!" I declared with relief, wrapping my arms around her neck. "I'm sure glad you did what you did."

"So am I."

"Oh, Sara, you don't know how long I've wanted to be close

to you like this." Tears were threatening, clouding my eyes.

"Me, too," she admitted. "But you've got to be careful about your displays of affection," she cautioned, pulling back to face me.

"You mean I shouldn't do this?" I leaned over and kissed her lightly on the lips.

"*Especially* that," she replied, all the while reaching up and touching my face. "I don't know if...if this is right for you. Perhaps I'm being selfish and you're just so emotionally dependent that—"

I interrupted her with another kiss. I didn't want to talk about anything negative. I only wanted to be with her, feel her close to me—especially her soft, full lips. I wanted to experience those wonderful sensations again and again and again.

After a moment or two, she pulled away. "Sweetheart, listen, we *have* to be careful. Anyone could walk in at any time. And I'd hate to see the fireworks if it was Brandon."

"But I want to be close to you. I want to—"

She put her finger to my lips. "I know. So do I. But there's a time and place for everything. And right now is not the time for this. Lunch'll be served soon, and I have a feeling Brandon'll be here shortly." She gazed into my eyes and started to reach out, then seemed to think better of it. "God, if I ever did anything to hurt you, I'd..." She shook her head. "I'm not sure about this, you know? But I know I...I care for you deeply, and I have for some time now. That still doesn't give me the right to...take advantage of you. I shouldn't—"

"I'm not a child, Sara," I reminded, ignoring for the moment her comment about taking advantage of me. "I know what I feel, I just had no idea you felt the same way. I was afraid you'd find me disgusting for having such thoughts, especially after you backed away before."

"I did that because," she paused, looking down at our hands, which were clasped together, "what happened in the pool today would've happened much sooner if I hadn't. And," she paused again and looked up at me, "are you sure it's not just a flight of fancy? I mean, you shouldn't get too involved if—"

"I've felt this way for quite a while. I've been fighting these feelings for well over two months now, maybe even longer. They're not going to go away. I already found that out myself...the hard way." I sighed heavily, rubbing my thumb over hers and squeezing her fingers. "I thought I was pure evil for having these thoughts about you. But they felt so good, you know? They were just...always there, whenever you were around. And...even when you weren't. When you kissed me today, it... God, Sara, it just felt sooo right!" I paused, gazing into her eyes and loving what I saw there. "I've had quite a few boyfriends...men...whatever." I glanced down at our hands, feeling a bit embarrassed. "They kissed me and...other things. Well, only one went...past the demarcation line, so to speak. We didn't—" I glanced up at her, and she nodded in understanding.

"But, anyway, I...I felt kind of...I don't know...numb about the whole thing, you know? I didn't *feel* anything when they kissed me. I mean, I didn't feel what I thought I should, or maybe more to the point, what I wanted to. So how could I let them do more? But when you kissed me...Whew! I felt things I'd never felt in my entire life. Things I thought I should've felt with them. And...oh God, Sara, don't tell me this is wrong! Please don't." Tears were welling up in my eyes once again.

"Shh," she admonished, reaching up and stroking the side of my face. "I don't think it's wrong, Faith, I just...I don't want to take advantage of you. You're so young and—"

"How can you take advantage of me when I kissed you first?" I interjected.

"Well, I'm older and...and I've been with...other women."

"Oh." This was something I hadn't given much thought to, since I'd been the aggressor. At least until today, that is.

"Then there's your situation," she continued. "You're so vulnerable right now and so—"

"Don't you dare say fragile," I admonished, glancing up at her. "To quote you, 'She's stronger than you give her credit for.'"

"You're incorrigible," she said with a smile.

There was a noise from my sitting room, and we both glanced toward the closed double doors. Sara quickly got up just as Brandon opened the doors without a word of warning or even a knock. This hadn't really bothered me before, but it did now. And it was something I could put a stop to. The hard part was, how to do it without making him suspicious or hurting his feelings?

"Hello, Princess." He smiled broadly, then gave Sara a quick once-over as she headed for her chair. "Since you made such marvelous progress this morning, Miss Bennington, perhaps you'd like the rest of the day off? That is, if you're through with your...therapy? I'll take over now. I'd like to spend some time with my niece." His gaze swung over to me. "You'd like that, wouldn't you, Princess?"

"Um...yeah, sure," I replied halfheartedly. I didn't want Sara to leave. I wanted to spend the day with her.

I glanced over at her as he turned toward the door, waiting for

Celia to bring in the tray. Good old Celia was spry for her age, but after climbing all those stairs with a tray of food in her hands, she moved rather slowly by the time she got to my room, bless her heart. Sometimes she even rested in my sitting room before going down again. This was one time I was thankful for her slowness.

Sara smiled and winked. I knew she was telling me this was just the first of many times when our secret relationship would have to wait. "I think I'll go into the city. Is there anything you need, Faith?" she inquired, obviously using this as a cover for our attention to one another, in case he turned around and took notice.

I glanced over at Brandon to be sure he wasn't looking. He still had his back to me, his hand on his hip, watching Celia. "You," I mouthed silently. She smirked and arched her eyebrows playfully. "I...I think perhaps some perfume," I finally said aloud, trying to prolong her stay. "Would you check for me? It's on the vanity."

She strolled over there and saw that the bottle of *Chanel No. 5* was only half empty and the big bottle of *Estee* contained a little less than that. I used it sparingly, what could I say? She turned and gave me a questioning look.

"On second thought, I'd like to try something different this time. Something..." I glanced over at Brandon, who was taking the tray from Celia to place on the table. "Oh, pick something out for me, would you?"

"A saleslady in one of the stores in the mall sprayed some *Liz Claiborne* on me the other day as a promotional gimmick. Have you ever tried that?"

"No. But if you think it's nice, perhaps I should."

"What's wrong with the perfume on your vanity?" Brandon asked, a hurt look on his face as he pushed the table toward me. "Your mother wore that, you know. She loved it. It has a wonderful scent," he said, his eyes shifting to that glassy look. He glanced down at me and must have noticed my expression. I was getting very tired of him wanting me to do, say, and wear things like my mother. It was as if he were trying to make me over to be her or something. "Oh well, I guess it's as they say, a woman's prerogative to change her mind. Or in this case...her perfume." He offered up a fake smile. "I'll reimburse you, Miss Bennington, unless you need the money beforehand."

"No, I think I can handle it," she responded, starting for the door.

I wanted so badly to say *Don't go!* but instead called out, "See you later." She responded with a wave over her shoulder.

"I...heard about...the breakthrough, mum," Celia said breath-lessly as Sara passed by her.

Sara smiled. "She did all the work. I just did all the yelling."

Celia chuckled. "Yes, mum, ya did do... sum of that, ya did. And Miss Faith...she did her share, too," she added with a sly smile.

I couldn't help but smirk, wondering how much she had over-heard. Or just how many of the servants had been within hearing distance.

"Yes, I...believe I did," I admitted, as Brandon moved the table over in front of me.

"Ya know, mum...sumtime a person needs...a good shout now an' again. 'Tis 'bout as good as...a first-rate bawlin', it is." She glanced up at Brandon and then lowered her eyes. "Will ya be needing anything else, mum?"

I looked around at the tray and thought about how slowly she had moved into the room and how she still sounded a bit out of breath. "I'm not sure. Perhaps you should stick around, I might want some more of these mashed potatoes or these biscuits."

Brandon quickly turned and looked down at me. "Have a healthy appetite today, do we?" he inquired. "You usually don't eat enough to keep a bird alive."

"Yelling takes a lot out of you," I answered teasingly.

Celia chuckled. "Ya sound sooo much better, mum. Why, you're even smiling. That's a sight for sore eyes, that is, mum. A sight for sore eyes, indeed," she repeated, glancing over at Bran-don. "I know you must be very happy 'bout that, sir."

"Yes, I am," he responded, his tone a bit cool, however. "Thank you, Celia. If she needs anything else, I'll let you know."

"Very good, sir," she said, and turned to go into the sitting room. "Oh, by the by, mum, shall I tell Cook ta make sum'thin' special for your dinner?"

This was a question she'd asked me every day since I'd arrived, and I had never made a request. "Spaghetti," I replied, remembering the chef was Italian. He was one of several servants I had only a brief acquaintance with, unlike Sammy and Celia, the latter of whom I saw on a daily basis.

"Spaghetti, yes, mum. Sight for sore eyes, that's just what it is," she repeated, disappearing into the sitting room.

When I looked up from removing the silverware rolled up in my napkin, Brandon was staring at me. His gaze softened when I smiled. "She's right, you know. This is a sight for sore eyes. But...tell me the truth, Princess, wasn't Miss Bennington..." He paused and my heart skipped a beat. *He saw us!* "...a bit rough on you today?"

I breathed a sigh of relief, which I made out was a deep breath before an explanation. "No, not really. I...I guess that's what I needed." I placed my napkin across my lap. "But I don't want to dwell on whether she should've or could've done things differently. It worked, and that's all that matters. I mean, I have been—excuse my language—a real pain in the ass. Even to myself. And as a neighbor of ours once said, and I quote, 'Sometimes you have to hit a jackass with a two-by-four just to get his attention.' I guess whatever works, hmm?"

He merely stared down at me as I shoveled peas into my mouth. I was quite hungry, which surprised even me.

"Your father allowed a neighbor to talk to you in such a manner?" he questioned.

"Oh no, he wasn't talking *to* me. He was talking to Father about his son-in-law. I wasn't supposed to be listening. Or at least, they didn't know I was."

There was a brief silence, then he asked, "Your father was happy without...all this?"

I could only assume he meant Shady Grove, the business, the money, and all that those things entailed. "He seemed to be."

"Would you..." He paused and walked over to the window. Taking a quick look at the chair Sara always occupied, he moved around the table and sat down in it. Resting his elbows on the arms, he steepled his fingers beneath his chin. "Would you tell me about your life, Faith? I've...I've never asked before, I know, but..."

"What do you want to know?"

He spent most of the afternoon with me, except for a couple of hours when he stepped out, allowing Jason to visit as I had promised. Brandon mainly wanted to know about my mother, which I'd assumed was his reason for asking in the first place. He rarely wanted to talk about my father. I knew there had been a grave deficiency in their relationship or a serious rift somewhere down the line, because they each seemed to have wanted to forget the other had ever existed. I began to see why the Christmas cards and birthday cards were short-lived subjects in our house. My father must have known about Brandon's feelings for my mother. Was this what had caused him to leave everything behind, and cut his brother out of his life?

Jason was a breath of fresh air compared to Brandon. We went into the sitting room, where the puzzle we had worked on over spring break was still lying on the coffee table, waiting for its disassembled pieces to be put back together again. Jason immediately asked about the hermit and the legend of Windell's Point. As I related the story, which had been told to me by the neighbor with a jackass for a son-in-law, Jason listened with wide-eyed interest.

"The legend went like this: Back during the Civil War, actually near the final days, there was a group of soldiers transporting a gold shipment which had been commandeered from the Union troops. As the story went, these soldiers had decided that if the South would ever rise again, they would need more than big dreams to get it off the ground this time around. So these soldiers carried the gold deep into the mountains of Tennessee where, it was rumored, they buried it on or near Windell's Point. All of them were subsequently killed, so no one came back to claim it. At least, as rumor would have it, no one ever had.

"It was said an old hermit, who lived up in the mountains, found the gold back in the early 20s. Of course, gold is no good to anybody unless you spend it. So the old hermit took some into town, where the shopkeeper became suspicious about him coming into so much money. Didn't take long before a group of men followed the old hermit home one day, to see just where he was getting all this money. Well, the men never found the stashed loot, but the old hermit turned up dead and missing one eye. The legend went on to say that the old hermit's ghost roams the point at night, looking for his missing eye."

Jason seemed intrigued by the story and had a fine time speculating about where they'd hidden the gold. Or at least, where he'd have hidden it if *he* had been *them*. Then he switched tacks to the old hermit and suggested that the old man had moved the gold, because that's what he'd do. And he'd hide it good, too.

I allowed him to rattle on and on, then finally asked him to fulfill his end of the bargain. I wanted to hear about Ashley. His mother's suicide in front of Ashley and his sister's subsequent stay in a psychiatric hospital intrigued me. This time, he told me what he knew.

"Father said my mother committed suicide while Ashley watched, but...I heard the servants say...Ashley had blood on her hands." He whispered the last few words, as if someone might be listening. *Ah,* I thought, *he doesn't want Brandon to hear him telling me this.* "And they said my father claimed Ashley had killed her," he added, still whispering.

I gasped inwardly at the thought of a teenage girl killing her own mother. That just couldn't be. "Oh, they were probably just saying that. Someone probably made it up," I offered.

He shook his head. "I don't think so," he disagreed quietly.

"Celia was the one telling it, and I've never known her to lie. I heard her say that Father only told everyone Mother committed suicide in order to protect Ashley. He didn't want her to go to jail, so he made them all promise not to reveal the truth to the police."

"Oh, that can't be true," I said, dismissing it. "Someone would have told. That many people can't keep a secret like that."

"Would you have wanted to send Ashley to prison?" he queried, glancing toward the door.

He had me there. *What would I have done?*

"Celia also said Ashley tried to kill Father and.. that's why she was put in a hospital. She said that Ashley was like a crazed animal, blood dripping from her hands...clawing at my father." He shuddered.

"You're making this up, Jason. Just to have a story to tell me, right?"

He slowly shook his head. "Ask Celia yourself, if you don't believe me."

"How old were you at the time?"

"I was just a baby. I don't remember any of that stuff."

"Was Ashley crazy when she came home from the hospital?"

He thought for a minute. "I was little then, but I don't think so. Still, she did act funny sometimes, especially around Father. I remember when she used to come in my room and play with me; she was lots of fun. Somehow she always talked me into doing things that I didn't really wanna do." He paused, as he looked up from the puzzle. "Oh, not bad things. Usually it was just something I was afraid of, like...like the time I fell off my horse. I never wanted to see another horse again after breaking my arm, but Ashley talked me into getting back on him while she held him." He paused again and smiled. "I love horses now. I can see why she did it. She knew I was just afraid. She was the one who talked Father into letting me have Shane for my own. He was going to sell him, 'cause he was a bit wild, but Ashley broke him of his bad habits and now...he's mine."

"How did she act funny around your father?" I probed.

"She always left when Father came around, except..." He stared off into space for a moment, as if collecting his thoughts, "...except when I was in trouble. She'd back away from Father, but she'd never leave me alone with him when he was mad. She'd stand up for me, sometimes. Like with Shane. She proved Father wrong."

"You spent a lot of time with her," I said, though it was more of a question than a statement.

"Yeah, in the summer. During the school year I only came

home at Christmas. Father thinks it's best I stay at school on other holidays," he explained with a rueful expression. "Except this year, he let me come home on spring break and for the funer—I mean, to meet you."

I ignored his reference to my parents' funeral. "It must be very lonely for you. Don't the other boys go home?"

"Most of them. Ashley used to come up on holidays, before..." He didn't finish.

I knew he was referring to the accident. "Where did she go to school?" I asked, trying to change the subject after noticing the overt sadness in his eyes.

"She stayed here. Father hired tutors for her since she had missed so much school, being in the hospital for three years."

Three years? If she were in her right mind, that must have seemed like an eternity. I started to wonder if the version of the story he'd overheard was indeed true. Three years was a long time to recover from just seeing something horrible, wasn't it?

"She did go to school at some point, didn't she?" I queried, wondering what she did after graduating, so to speak.

"Yeah, she went to college here. I mean, in Athens. She wanted to be a doctor."

"A doctor? What kind?"

"A psychiatrist, like you. Father told her they'd never let her be one, though, because of her history. Whatever that means." I could tell he was relating things he had overheard. "But Ashley wanted to prove him wrong," he added, a hint of sadness entering his voice again. "I wish she'd never gone to college."

"Why?"

"Because, Father said...it killed her," he mumbled, staring down at the puzzle that now seemed far more interesting. He scratched his forehead and wrinkled up his nose. I knew I had pried long enough.

After Jason left, I crawled into bed feeling very tired. I slept until dinner. Celia brought my requested spaghetti, which was delicious, and I started asking her some general questions about Ashley. But somehow I ended up far afield, because Celia seemed uncomfortable with the subject.

"Did you know my mother when she lived here?" I asked at one point, thinking to get back to Ashley in a roundabout way.

"Yes, mum, very nice lady. Pretty too, just like you, mum. Wuz very sorry ta see your parents leave, I wuz. Never got to say goodbye."

"Why not?" I asked, onto the scent of other game now.

"Left rather sudden, mum. Miss Marion even left 'er toiletries, right there on the vanity."

"You mean the perfume and makeup over there was my mother's?"

"Yes, mum," she replied, in a tone of voice suggesting she was trying to convince me of something I didn't believe. "Ya see, Mr. Neilson, he wouldn't allow anyone in here, least not 'til you come. Then he redecorated. But still...he wouldn't let anyone touch them things there. Now I think he wants you ta have 'em, mum."

I nodded. The conversation was turning my way, and I didn't like that. I was no mystery. "Did you know Mrs. Neilson? Vivian, I mean?"

"A'course, mum. She wuz a nice lady, she wuz. Not like your muther, but nice. God rest her soul."

"Perhaps one day we'll sit down and have a talk about my mother and...and some of the relatives I'll never get to know."

"Yes, mum," she agreed, albeit a bit hesitantly.

After dinner, Brandon came up and spent the remainder of the evening with me. He reminisced about his days at boarding school and college, recounting pranks he and his cohorts had played on their teachers. I gained a new perspective of him that evening. From the things he told me and the manner in which he related them, I assumed he could be very vindictive and devious. I knew he was jealous of Sara; I had seen it in his eyes on more than one occasion. But there was nothing I could do about it. I couldn't bring myself to be any closer to him than I already was. There was just something about the way he kissed my cheek that left me feeling cold and uneasy. What should have been a quick peck had gradually become a long, lingering kiss. I was quite relieved when he finally left.

Afterward, all I could think about was Sara. Not to suggest I hadn't thought about her all day. I had. But I knew there was no sense dwelling on the fact that I wanted to be with her, because I couldn't. Now, however, I felt I could. I glanced over at the clock on the VCR. It read 10:05. I was usually asleep by now, and she knew it. I started to wonder if she was having second thoughts about what had happened between us.

A few moments after that, I heard a noise outside the door. It slowly opened, and Brandon walked in with a glass of white liquid in his hand.

"Princess, I noticed that your light was still on. I thought you might like a glass of milk before retiring," he explained, closing the door behind him.

His attire was not the usual. He was wearing a robe over a

pair of pajamas. *So, he doesn't sleep in those three-piece suits,* I thought. *Wait...how'd he see the light in my bedroom from the other end of the hall?*

"You had a very exciting day," he continued as he neared the bed. "I thought you might need a little something to help you sleep. I know I do when I've had an unusually active day."

"Thank you," I said when he handed me the glass.

"Well, goodnight, Princess." He leaned over and placed a lingering kiss on my cheek. "I'll see you tomorrow. Sweet dreams."

After he left this time, I couldn't help but wonder why he was being so unusually attentive. Perhaps he was just happy that I'd come out of my depression and made a breakthrough in my therapy. Or maybe he was envious of my attention to Sara and the fact that he knew she would get to see and be a part of all my "firsts," so to speak. Whatever the reason, the milk was a nice gesture.

I downed half the glass while watching the minutes tick away on the clock. *Where could she be? Has she gone out again? Who had she been with that night she came in with her clothes all wrinkled? What other woman had been...* I shook my head. I didn't even want to think about her being with anyone else in a social way, much less that way. Yet the thought did cross my mind that she would be much more experienced in these matters. This sent a tingle up my spine.

Would our relationship progress that far? I wondered. I hadn't really given it much thought. I'd been concentrating only on what I wanted at the moment: just kissing and holding. I realized I was like a teenager again, only thinking of the simple and perfunctory steps, not the whole picture. *Probably because the whole picture is too uncertain,* I thought. *I'd be totally lost. I wouldn't know what to do.* Then again, I assumed I wouldn't be the first person to want something and not know what to do with it when they got it. According to Sara, there were others like myself—she being one—and then there were "the other women." I knew Sara wasn't a bad person, so I wasn't either, right? It wasn't as if I'd chosen to be attracted to her, I just was.

I must have dozed off, for when I opened my eyes she was sitting on the side of the bed, gazing down at me. I tried to raise up, but my head felt heavy, as if I'd been awakened from a deep sleep. I struggled to keep my eyes open. "Wh-where..." I paused and cleared my throat, rubbing sleep out of my right eye. "Where have you been?"

"I've been here since before dinner," she replied, taking my hand in hers.

"Wh...why didn't you come see me?"

"I did. I came in here right after I returned, but you were asleep and I didn't want to disturb you. I knew you needed to rest."

"But...after dinner you..."

"Brandon was here, sweetheart. And I thought perhaps it was best that...we take some time to think things over. Especially you. You had an emotionally draining day today. You need to think this over before you rush into anything."

"I don't need to think," I countered, batting my eyes and fighting back the need for sleep, which was threatening to overpower me.

"Well, you need to rest. I can tell you're very tired."

"Sara, please, don't go," I gripped her hand as best I could. "Stay with me."

"Maybe some other time. You're in no shape for company at the moment."

"Please, don't go. I...I don't know why...I'm so sleepy...I guess it was the milk."

"What milk?" she asked sharply.

"Brandon was...nice enough to...bring me some."

She got up abruptly and I tried to follow her with my eyes, but they were just too heavy. The last thing I heard was the sound of tinkling glass. It reminded me of the day I broke her mirror.

Chapter 9

The next morning I felt groggy until Sara brought me a cup of coffee after breakfast. I usually drank only orange juice, but since she'd gone to all the trouble, I figured the least I could do was drink it. Needless to say, it helped. I assume the caffeine jolted my tired system back to life again. The next thing I wanted was *her*. Of course, she sweetly reminded me that there was a time and a place for everything, and this wasn't the time for the lip-lock I wanted to put on her.

After breakfast, I got dressed for our morning therapy in the pool. Although tired, I was determined to make some small progress. After Jason performed his transport duty and left us alone, Sara began massaging my legs, and for the first time in quite a while, I allowed myself to enjoy it to the fullest. I didn't close my eyes to do so, either, because I could hardly take them off her. Observing the way her arm muscles contracted and the way her breasts jiggled slightly as she massaged me, I also found myself wondering what she looked like underneath her bathing suit. I had seen female bodies in the buff before, but never really felt anything other than slightly embarrassed to look directly at them. But now things were different. Or was it just Sara?

I could tell she was shapely, all the smooth curves in all the right places. I especially liked the arc of her shapely behind, which protruded beneath the backless bathing suit and swayed from side to side when she walked. I wondered what it would be like to have her next to me, my hands wandering over her posterior.

This brought to mind my last boyfriend in college, Howard Banks, and how badly he'd wanted to have sex with me. I can't say he wanted to make love, because Howard was all hands. There was only one thing on his mind: SEX. I remembered we were at a party one particular night, and I'd had a bit too much beer. Howard had been after me for a long time to at least let him feel me up, as he called it. Of course, I was curious about sex myself, and allowed him to coax me into an unoccupied bedroom, where he laid me down on the bed *tout de suite*. In only a few moments, Howard had my blouse unbuttoned, my bra pushed up across my upper chest, and my pants unzipped.

I was allowing all of this, even though I didn't feel anything more than curiosity. I'd listened to the other girls talking about how it felt when their boyfriends kissed and fondled them, remarking about the deep, overwhelming urges that prompted them to go even further. Some even went into great detail about the sexual act itself, which was interesting, to say the least. Yet when I was lying there with Howard atop me, my right hand on his behind and his mouth on my left breast while the fingers of his right hand fumbled around between my legs, I knew this wasn't right. I didn't want his hand there, much less anything else. So I made him stop for a moment, and then seized the opportunity to get up and leave. I knew I didn't want my first time to be that way, even if I remained the last virgin on campus, as my friends called me.

As Sara's hands worked their way up my left leg and I felt her warm thigh against my skin, my thoughts wandered to just how it would feel to be with her the way I'd been with Howard. Would it feel different? Better, perhaps? It definitely seemed like it might, since just the thought of having her on top of me made me tingle all over and sent delicious, tantalizing sensations down to my lower abdomen. *Are these the urges the other girls had talked about?* I wondered.

"Are you cold?" Sara asked, snapping me out of my daydream.

"Uh...no...why?" I responded, looking up at her.

Her eyes fell to my chest, and a rather sly smile formed on her lips while one eyebrow arched skyward. I followed her gaze. My nipples were erect, pressing against the material of the white bathing suit. I instantly felt embarrassed, yet just as swiftly realized that for her to notice, she must have been looking at my body while I was daydreaming about hers. Unlike when guys looked at me, which made me uncomfortable, this gave me a warm feeling inside. *Seems I'm not alone with my steamy thoughts. Does she find me as attractive as I find her?* I tingled all over again at the thought of being with her. I wondered if I should tell her what I was thinking. Would it be too bold? Was it too soon? Would she tell me this wasn't the time for such thoughts?

Damn the torpedoes, I thought, *I have to say something or I'll bust a gut.* "You have a...beautiful body," I remarked hesitantly.

She looked up at me and smiled. "Thank you. So do you," she responded, running her hand slowly up the inside of my thigh.

I hadn't expected this; it caught me completely off guard. Strange, delicious sensations flowed down to one particular area of my body, setting my toes to tingling. She glanced away, then slowly moved over between my legs and started working on the opposite one, as if unaware of what she had instigated. Making her way slowly up the inside of my leg, she watched me intently, the slight smile on her face leading me rethink my previous assumption. She knew exactly what she was doing. *And she does it well*, I thought, as those same sensations crept down my body and came to rest in that certain area once again.

Looking around the pool area carefully, she even glanced up at the windows overlooking it before her eyes came to rest on mine. She never broke eye contact with me again as she moved her left hand up my leg, keeping it on top and in plain sight, massaging as usual, while her right hand eased around underneath and inched its way up my inner thigh. I nearly lost my grip on the pool edge when her fingers came close to that oh-so-special and now very sensitive region. Things were definitely coming alive down there, like never before. Was the temporary paralysis responsible for this, or was it just Sara? At any rate, there was hardly any doubt in my mind now that *anything* involving her would feel different. *Enormously* different, in a very pleasing way.

When she saw my wide-eyed reaction, she eased her hand back and then continued to massage my leg in the usual fashion, all the while staring deeply into my eyes.

"You...um...you have a stimulating touch," I finally managed to say.

"Thank you. You're quite stimulating yourself," she replied, arching one eyebrow. "Just watching you... Umph! But enough of this; we have work to do." She patted my leg and moved down to my foot, where she started my exercises.

I sighed heavily. My body was all worked up, seemingly expecting something that hadn't happened. My stomach felt tight with anticipation. Never had I felt this way before, and I didn't want it to end.

"See if you can press your foot against my hand," she directed, moving on with her task.

How can she just turn it off like that? I wondered. Then again, she was the one doing the touching, *not* the one being touched.

"Concentrate, sweetheart, you can do it." I tried to set my mind on moving my foot, but nothing happened. "Let's pretend that...my hand is something you really want, okay?" she suggested, moving her hand an inch or so away. "The only way you can get it is to move your foot."

Even though I tried, I couldn't visualize anything I wanted that would involve using my foot to get. "I guess I'm not good at pretending. I'm sorry."

She stood there for a moment, and I was afraid she'd attempt making me angry again, but instead, she positioned her body in front of me. "Touch me," she said softly, a smile forming near the corners of her mouth.

I was a little confused as to what she meant until I noticed that her right breast was directly in front of my left foot.

"Don't you want to touch me?" she asked, arching one light brown eyebrow.

I wanted to say, *Of course I do, but I hadn't planned on touching you with my foot!* Instead, I merely concentrated on doing what she asked.

"Well, if you don't want—"

"I'm trying, okay?" I was desperate for my foot to move, but it just lay there like a knot on a log.

"Close your eyes," she suggested. "Relax. Think back to a few moments ago. I had my hand on your leg...just like now." She ran her hand over the calf of my left leg. "Only difference is, now you can touch me, if you'll just move your foot." There was a long pause as I envisioned the previous scene again, putting her within reach. "Think of it as your hand. This is your hand," she added, slowly inching her finger down the side of my foot. "Now reach out and touch me. You're so close, so very... That's it... That's my girl...little bit more...Yes!" she exclaimed at the same time that I felt the warmth of her body against the bottom of my foot.

Oh, how I wish this was my hand, I thought, opening my eyes to see that my foot was indeed resting against her breast. She quickly let go of my leg and maneuvered her way between them. Hugging me tightly, she declared, "You did it, sweetheart. I knew you could!"

Exhilaration flowed through me, listening to the happiness in her voice. She was more excited than I was!

When she pulled back, I noticed a single tear careening down her cheek. "Can you still stand?" she asked.

"I...I don't know."

Quickly sweeping up my legs in her arms, she carried me out into the middle of the pool, which I assumed she did to prevent me from hurting myself if I lost my balance again. Standing me up, though still holding my hands, she backed away. After a moment or two, she let go altogether. I could still stand on my own.

She smiled and reached out, taking my hands in hers. "Walk to me, Faith," she urged.

My eyebrows shot up. I was barely standing and only just moving my foot, and now she wanted me to perform a miracle and *walk?*

"You can do it, I know it. Just move each foot slowly," she urged. Nothing moved. I was a statue. "Come to me, sweetheart. Don't think about it, just look at me. Keep your eyes on mine. I want you here...with me, Faith. I...I want you in my arms," she added softly.

Oh, how I wanted to be able to walk into her arms at that moment, but it seemed impossible.

"Please, I need you, sweetheart," she prodded. My left leg flinched and jerked, then slowly moved forward. "No, no, don't look down," she admonished. "Look at me. That's right. I need you, Faith. I missed you so much yesterday. I wanted to hold you in my arms last night, and..." She paused and bit her lower lip. "Come to me now."

My left leg jerked, and my foot moved swiftly. It scraped across the bottom of the pool, peeling the hide off my big toe, which in turn caused me to lose my fragile balance. I plunged headlong into her waiting arms.

"I didn't mean you had to do it quite so quickly," she chuckled. "But I'll take it any way I can get it," she added, hugging me tightly. "You did it, you really did it! You've taken your first step!"

Tears trickled from my eyes. I wasn't sure whether I was laughing or crying. I only knew that this meant one day I would walk again. I could only hope that when that day came, I would still be able to walk into her waiting arms.

I wanted so badly to kiss her and revel in the joy of the moment, but suddenly a series of loud noises rang out within the enclosed space. We both looked up to find Brandon staring down at us, clapping enthusiastically. I could feel Sara tense up as she loosened her hold on me. *How long has he been there, and how much did he overhear?* I wondered. *And what might he do about it?* My big toe started to throb and sting, as if my body were suggesting there was more pain on the way.

"Wonderful, Princess...just wonderful! Soon you'll be walking the grounds with me," he proclaimed cheerfully as he sat down and began removing his shoes. *What's he doing?* "We'll have to

celebrate this momentous occasion," he continued, rising up out
of the chair in his stocking feet. He quickly removed his jacket and
tossed it over the back of a chair, then proceeded down the steps
into the water, fully clothed. "I know! We'll have a party! Yes! We
haven't had a big party since your arrival. Splendid idea, don't you
think?" He waded through the water toward us, his white shirt
gradually darkening as it absorbed water.

"I...I don't know. I... Why would those people care that I
took my first step?" I questioned, remembering the last party and
those dinner parties I'd hated.

"They'd rejoice at my happiness, of course," he responded,
his tone suggesting I had asked a silly question. "I'll have to call
Lynn and tell her to get on this right away."

I knew that once he'd called his secretary, there would be no
forestalling him. "But..." I paused, as he reached out and swept
my legs up, removing me from Sara's embrace. "But it's such short
notice," I protested, feeling as if he had just stripped me of my
happiness.

"Yes, it is Sunday. You may have a point there," he agreed,
turning and carrying me away from her.

I felt so helpless; all I could do was glance over his shoulder
in order to make eye contact with Sara. She, however, was glaring
at his back, frowning profusely, her hands clenched by her sides.

"Perhaps next weekend, then. Yes, that will give everyone
plenty of time to prepare," he continued, moving up the steps.
"You're so much like your mother, Princess...so levelheaded. I
guess I got a little carried away." He glanced toward the patio
doors, and then seemed to think better of that idea. "Friday... Yes,
that would be much better." He turned and eased me down into
one of the patio chairs.

"I...I won't feel comfortable around all those people, Brandon. I still have to wear this turban and—"

"Oh, that's no problem," he said, handing me my towel. "I
already have a solution for that. It was going to be a surprise,
but..." His gaze fell to my breasts as I began drying off. "Well, it
still can be. Just don't worry your pretty little head about anything, Princess. I'll take care of everything. You'll have anything
and everything you need to be the belle of the ball." He bowed
enthusiastically, then quickly turned and left, water streaming
behind him from his soaked clothing.

I turned toward Sara, who was just coming out of the pool. I
could see the disappointment written all over her face. "I'm sorry
he—"

She held up her hand and shook her head. "One of *those*

times," she said, walking over to get her own towel off the back of my chair.

"Sara, I..." I wanted to say something about the events in the pool, how I hadn't liked him taking me away and how I wanted to thank her, but I knew the mood was broken. And there'd be no retrieving it. This made me angry. "Wonder what the hell that was all about?" I questioned aloud.

"Jealousy, I suspect," Sara answered. "He's envious of... You're bleeding!" she announced, rushing over to me and squatting down by my foot. "How did this happen? Did Brandon—"

"No." I shook my head when she glanced up at me. "I did it trying to get to you."

Her eyes darted back and forth searching mine, while her expression changed from worry and anger to the soft one I had come to know and love. She started leaning toward me, then seemed to have second thoughts as she glanced toward the house. I knew she was thinking he might appear again at any moment. "We...um...I'll need to take care of that. We can't have you bleeding all over everything." She took the end of her towel and wrapped it around my toe. "Damn," she hissed softly.

I wanted to reach out and at least touch her in some small way, tell her that I was disappointed, too. But I didn't want to tempt fate. "I don't want this party," I voiced instead, changing the subject.

"You're the only one who can stop it." She glanced up at me. "And I don't envy you that task, 'cause he's all puffed up with pride right now, as if *he* made it happen." She sighed heavily. "To tell him you don't want this party would be like sticking a pin in a balloon."

She was speaking of him as if she knew him well, which puzzled me. *Perhaps she's just a good judge of character,* I reasoned. Either way, this was not my main concern at the moment. Finagling my way out of this party was. I sighed at the thought of having to endure another party—and at the loss of the moment he had ruined, which I'd wanted to savor. How many more times would he do this? Was there more to his coming into the pool after me than just his enthusiasm over me walking? Sara had suggested jealousy. Why should he be jealous of Sara?

Back in my room once again, I was struggling to remove the wet bathing suit when I realized I hadn't brought any dry clothes into the bathroom with me. Rather than have to pull the straps on the bathing suit up and right back down again, I left them hanging off my arms and wheeled over to the chest of drawers to get a T-shirt and a pair of shorts.

I just loved the new shorts and T-shirts Sara had picked up for me on one of her many outings. One hundred percent cotton, and more comfortable than anything I'd ever worn. She said that a friend had recommended them to her, and once she'd tried them, she fell in love with the way they fit. She just knew I'd like them, as well, and sure enough, once she put them on me, I didn't want to wear anything else.

I pulled out a neatly ironed and folded purple-and-white striped T-shirt and solid purple shorts, laying them on top of the chest, then moved aside and was reaching into a lower drawer for a pair of clean underwear when I heard the door open.

"Oh great," I said, not even looking up. "Would you help me? This damn thing is sticking to me like glu—" My voice caught in my throat when I looked up to find Brandon staring at my chest. My hand latched onto several pair of underwear and quickly pressed them to my exposed breasts.

"You are beautiful...just like your mother," he said in a dreamy voice, as his eyes lifted to meet mine.

"What the— Don't you ever knock?" I stammered, anger apparent in my tone.

"I...I'm sorry, Princess. I..." He paused as I raised one eyebrow and cut my eyes toward the door. I didn't want to have to tell him to get out, for I was afraid I'd really lose my cool. "Yes, well..." he said, then slowly turned around and left.

I breathed a shuddering sigh of relief and just sat in my chair with my underwear pressed tight against my chest. I couldn't bring myself to move. I felt exposed, helpless, and numb with embarrassment and shock.

Sara showed up a few moments later, rapping lightly on the door as she peeked around it. She glanced around, looking for me; her smile faded instantly when her eyes met mine. "What's wrong?" she asked, her expression signifying her confusion. "Are you doing this...because of me?"

I shook my head and bit my lower lip.

She closed the door behind her. "Then what's wrong? Why are you holding yourself like that, with your underwear... Why was the door open?" She asked the questions so fast I didn't have a chance to answer. "Wasn't Brandon just... What did... What the hell happened in here?" she finished, rushing over to me.

"He...he walked in on me. I thought it was you and—"

"Is that all?" she inquired, her face an angry visage.

"He...he said—"

"What? What did he say?" she prompted.

"He said I was beautiful..."

"Yes, and..." She was prodding for more.

"He said, 'You're beautiful...like your—'"

"Mother," she finished for me, placing her hand on my arm.

"He was her lover, wasn't he?" I asked, considering the implications. "My mother was...unfaithful to my father...with his own brother!"

"You don't know that, sweetheart. Listen, he could have walked in on her, just like he did you. You know he never knocks, he just barges in wherever he pleases." She tried removing the underwear from my tightly clenched hands. "Sweetheart, come on now, we need to get you out of this wet bathing suit," she insisted, placing her hands over mine. "And I don't think you'll need but one pair of these, hmm?" she quipped, making an attempt at levity.

"How could she do that to my father?" I asked aloud, still thinking about how this tarnished my mother's image.

"Faith, listen to me." She turned my face toward her. "You can't blame your mother for something that might or might not have happened. Don't destroy her memory just because of something Brandon said. If, and I do mean *if,* he ever saw her naked, she might have been as innocent as you are now. Sweetheart, don't do this to yourself. Your mother left here, right? She left with your father, didn't she? Now why would she do that if she were having an affair with Brandon?"

"He had a wife."

"All right, let's stop this right now. There's no sense looking for old skeletons in the closets when there more than likely aren't any. I'm pretty sure Brandon loved your mother, but I doubt she loved him. Don't you think she'd have to have been a fool not to see through him? And your mother was no fool, was she?"

"No, she wasn't. She...loved my father, or...seemed to."

"Stop second-guessing what you know to be the truth, then. Your mother was still in love with your father; you told me so, remember? And you know it's true, right?" I nodded. "Well then, let's forget about it, okay? I don't like seeing you so upset; it just tears me up inside."

I hadn't really thought about how my state of mind might affect her. She was more than likely right; he probably had barged in on Mother when she'd lived here, and she'd mistaken him for Father, as I'd mistaken him for Sara.

Out of the blue netherworld of my thoughts, the question of what my mother would think of my relationship with Sara jumped up and slapped me in the face. Would she think it vile and disgusting? I pondered the question as Sara helped me out of my bathing suit, and concluded that I had no idea what my mother would think. I could only hope she would have been accepting of my feelings for Sara. Once we'd had a long chat, that is. I had no idea how my father might feel, either. And I truly wasn't in the mood to ponder either question for very long.

Once I was dressed, Sara helped me into bed. "Feeling better?" she asked, taking my hand in hers.

"Yes," I replied. "I shouldn't have questioned my mother's integrity."

"Nor yours," she added.

How could she have known what I was thinking? I wondered.

"Your eyes give you away," she explained, as if replying to a question I had asked. "You do need to take your time, though, and be absolutely sure. I won't pressure you in any way. Be sure that it's me you want and not just...someone close, in bodily form. Otherwise, we both could get hurt. Believe me, I know. Don't make the mistake of letting sex play the most important role in your thinking. It's only one part of the big whole. And if sex is all you want, it's all you'll get. But not from me."   .

I stared at her, not really sure what message she was trying to convey.

"Don't get me wrong, now; I'm not saying sex is bad," she went on. "Far from it. I think it's the ultimate way of sharing yourself with someone else, when you love them. But without true love, it's just...empty. Passion is fleeting, and lust...well, it can be used in cruel ways. Love...real love, that's what lasts."

"Have you been with...many women?" I couldn't help but ask.

"Yes," she answered honestly. "There for a while, I was pretty wild. That's why I'm telling you this. I don't want to see you go down the same road I did. People can be very cruel, even those who say they love you," she added ruefully.

I reached up and touched her face, wondering how anyone could be cruel to someone like her. "I won't be cruel, Sara," I said softly.

"No, I don't believe you would. And I don't want to see anyone hurt you, either." She turned away and looked toward the door. "I'd rather die first."

We both fell silent. I didn't know what to say, and she seemed to be retreating inside herself again. I wondered if she was trying to tell me something with her last comment. Was I in some danger of being hurt? If so, from where? By whom?

I suddenly remembered the dream I'd had months ago. "Beware of illusions," my parents had said. That was the same night I had noticed Sara's blue contact lenses. I looked into her eyes now, wondering again if *she* was the illusion. Would she have second thoughts about us and leave me here alone and broken-hearted? Who was the other woman she had been with that night? Was there someone else she wasn't telling me about?

All of sudden, hit by the realization that her eyes were neither green nor blue at the moment, I blurted out, "They're brown!"

"What?"

"Your eyes, they're brown."

"Oh, yeah, well they change like that sometimes. That's another reason I wear contacts. Some people find it...rather spooky, how they change like a chameleon."

Was she the illusion my dream warned me about, this woman with the chameleon eyes? After all, she was a very secretive person, revealing very little about herself. Whenever I asked, she'd always say, "The past is fuzzy. I don't remember a lot before the accident." Yet she seemed to carry around a lot of deep-seated sadness and anger. Then again, perhaps that sprang from the fact there were things she didn't remember. I knew I would be lost without my past, like a ship without a sail cut adrift on a stormy sea.

I glanced back up at her, feeling sorry for doubting her. She had been nothing but kind to me—always there, always helpful, and always loving. How could I even question her intentions? As she gazed into my eyes, I watched hers slowly turn back to green again. It was fascinating to watch the change in her expression correlate with the change in her eyes. Those warm green eyes that were so inviting, tempting, and filled with mystery tugged at my heartstrings.

"Is this the right time?" I asked, so softly I barely heard the words myself.

She smiled and leaned forward, her face hovering very close to mine. "Sometimes I think you read my mind," she whispered. Her gaze shifted to my lips. "If I didn't know better, I'd swear you were teasing me, just to see if I can resist you."

"Can you?"

Her gazed shifted back to my eyes again. "My body says no, I can't, but my mind must say yes. Otherwise, I'll... Don't look at me like that," she murmured, referring to my dissatisfied expression. "I told you to take your time. I know I lost my head today in the pool. But you're so enchanting...there's so much innocence in those baby blues...such impatience, too... asking for things you know nothing about."

"I haven't asked."

"You don't have to. It's all right there in your eyes. I know what you want, and when the time is right, you won't have to ask." She quickly pecked me on the cheek. "Get some rest, I'll be back soon." She hesitated a moment before she got up, looking down at my right arm where I was reaching out to her. "Did I do this?" she asked, quickly turning my arm slightly.

I peered down to see what she was talking about. "You mean that?" I asked, pointing to the light brown, oval-shaped mark on the underside of my right arm.

She nodded, guilt written all over her face. I shook my head and explained that it was a birthmark. She commented on how it looked just like a light bruise made by someone's finger. I then told her, as well as showed her, how it always remained about the size of my own index finger.

"How come you never noticed it before?" I inquired.

She shrugged. "Maybe the same reason you never noticed my eyes changing color?" She had me there. I reached out for her. "Ah-ah-ah," she cautioned, and moved away quickly. "Like I said, get some rest."

After lunch she came back with a small bag in one hand and a questioning look on her face. Pressing her behind against the doors, she shut them slowly. "I've got something I want you to listen to. I don't know whether you like rock, but—"

"I do," I said, readily. "As long as it's not hard rock."

"Well, this isn't, believe me. You know," she paused, removing a compact disc case from the bag, "I've been waiting for you to ask me for some more...up-to-date music. But you never did, so I assumed you didn't like it."

"I do. I just...didn't want to bother you, back then."

"Oh." She turned on the stereo and put the disc in the CD player. "Well, I've got a lot of tapes and CDs at home. I could get them sometime, if you'd like. Or I could buy you some. I mean, whatever kind of music you like, I'd gladly—"

"Love songs," I interrupted.

"Excuse me?"

"Love songs, that's my kind of music."

She turned around and smiled. "Well, good. Listen to this song, track number..." she looked down at the case, "...number nine. I'll be back later, and you can tell me what you think." Smiling once again, she walked out.

"Good, Miss Bennington, glad I caught you," Brandon said from the sitting room. "You can have the rest of the day off. I'd like to spend more time with my niece."

I couldn't hear Sara's reply, if she even gave one, but my heart

sank at the thought that Brandon had once again ruined something else for me. *Doesn't he ever have work to do at home on the
weekends?* I wondered.

He politely knocked on the door and waited for me to answer.
I turned the stereo off via the remote and then invited him in. He
walked through the door as cheerful as ever, acting as if nothing
had happened. Through the open door behind him, I saw Sara in
the hall, watching. I felt better knowing she wasn't eager to run
off.

"Well, Princess, how would you like to go on a tour of the
stables? Jason is eager for you to meet Shane," he said as he
walked over to me.

I had never been to the stables because it was too far from the
house and down a very rocky gravel road. Wheelchairs were not
made for such obstacles, so I had always shied away from going.
"I suppose. I'd like to see Shane, but you might end up having to
carry me if the chair won't go over the gravel."

He smiled. "That would be fine by me. I'd gladly carry you
anywhere, Princess, you know that." He placed his hand on the
back of my chair.

"Jason said Shane was once pretty wild, but Ashley broke
him. Did she really do that?" I asked, changing the subject as I
maneuvered myself over to the side of the bed.

He gave me a hard look. "Um...well, yes...um... You get yourself together or...whatever it is you females do, and Jason and I
will meet you downstairs."

*Not even an escort down the stairs? Boy, Ashley's name sure
got rid of him fast. I'll have to remember that.*

Right after he left, Sara returned. "What's up?" she inquired.

"Going to the stables to see Jason's horse."

"Oh, he's a beaut. You'll like him."

"You know him?"

"Well, I take walks around the place sometimes when you're
asleep, or when Brandon takes over. At night, though, I'm never
far away," she added, as if this were something I should know.
"Need some help with those jeans?"

"Yeah, all I can get."

She helped me to my feet and then held onto me from behind
as I pulled the jeans up. "Is Brandon coming up to get you?" she
queried.

I could feel her warm breath on my neck; it made me feel all
tingly inside. "No, he said he'd meet me downstairs. Why?"

She shook her head and shrugged. "Got 'em on yet?" she
asked near my ear. Those delicious sensations flowed over and

through me once again. "This is the first time you've been on your
feet outside the pool. How does it feel?" she queried.

"Very good," I replied, enjoying it immensely. "Who's teasing
who now?"

"Payback's hell, isn't it?" she questioned, slipping her arms
around my waist. "You got those jeans on yet?"

"You're not helping any."

"I wasn't trying to be helpful," she admitted, and lightly
kissed me on the neck.

Basic instinct must have taken over, because my response to
this stimulus was to move my head to one side and offer her my
neck for more stimulation. She teased my neck with her soft lips
several more times while her hands roamed over my T-shirt-clad
stomach, then started moving toward my breasts.

"Damn," she swore softly, stilling her hands and pressing her
lips to my neck. Sighing heavily, she withdrew and held me out
away from her body. "I always lose control, don't I?"

"One day, Sara, it won't be so easy for you to get away from
me," I said teasingly, glancing around at her.

"Ah...now that'll be the day."

"And you won't have to walk the grounds alone, either."

"I look forward to that," she acknowledged, easing me down
into my chair.

"I love you, Sara." The words tumbled out of my mouth with
ease.

"I love you, too," she responded without hesitation, and
placed a kiss on top of my turban.

We both heard Brandon's voice in the hallway, so she quickly
bent down and helped me put my feet in the footrests. I touched
her hair; it was soft, but dry—from the hair color she used, I
assumed. "What color was your hair?" I queried.

"Dark brown, why?"

"I just wondered what you looked like—you know—natural.
How come your eyebrows aren't dark, then?"

"I had them done too. Dark brown eyebrows looked rather
peculiar with blonde hair. Gave away my secret too easily," she
replied with a sly grin.

"Princess, there you are. I was afraid you had fallen
or...something. What's taking you so long?" he inquired, glancing
down at Sara as if he knew what the problem was. "I didn't know
you needed help with that. I thought you did those things yourself
now."

"I had to get Sara to help me into these jeans after I struggled
for so long with them," I lied. "She was just nice enough to do the

rest while she was here so I wouldn't keep you waiting."

He grunted. "Are you ready now?" His tone bordered on impatience. I nodded and eased the chair forward.

"Have a good time," Sara said.

"She will," Brandon answered before I even had a chance to. "And we'll take real good care of her. You really shouldn't worry about her so much, Miss B. Soon she'll be walking and will no longer be *your* responsibility."

I didn't like the way he stressed "your." I could tell Sara didn't either. It made me sound like a piece of merchandise to be handed over to someone else at some point in the future. He was also reminding her that her services would no longer be needed at that time, which was something I didn't *even* want to think about.

Brandon had a surprise for me before we even reached the stables: a recently blacktopped path that ran parallel to the gravel drive. Sometimes he could definitely amaze me.

I enjoyed the stables; the horses were gorgeous. I knew why Jason had picked Shane the moment I saw him. Dark brown with a beige mane, he stood out from the others, whose manes were either of the same color as their body or black. I couldn't help but be reminded of Sara and her bleached blonde hair against the dark brown roots.

Jason fed his horse and asked if I'd like to do the same. So I did. Shane bent down to receive the morsels in my hand, his light brown eyes with their dark brown specks perusing me carefully. I found it hard to believe he had once been wild, what with his kind eyes and gentle manner.

Love, I thought. *Love can do this.* Jason's love for the horse and Ashley's love for Jason had turned this wild animal into a gentle and loving friend.

"One day, maybe you'll be able to ride him with me," Jason offered. "He's not wild anymore."

"I wouldn't bet money on that," Brandon remarked. "He's still got that wild streak like his mother. She *never* lost it."

"His mother?" I queried.

"Oh yes, wildest horse I've ever seen. One of my hands acquired that horse for me. Bad choice. Never could ride her."

"Ashley could," Jason interjected.

"Had to fire that man after he'd worked for us many years," Brandon continued, ignoring Jason's comment. "He turned out to be no better than his choice in horses. People are a lot like horses, you know. Some are proud, dignified, and respect discipline. Others are wild from the day they are born, and you can't teach them a thing."

I knew he was most assuredly making reference to some particular person. And I had a feeling it was Ashley.

"Well, let's finish this part of the tour, shall we, Jason? I'd
like to show Mari—Princess, here, some other places she hasn't
seen yet."

He'd made a slip and almost called me my mother's name.
Why did she still hold such a special place in his heart? I wondered. Twenty-two years later, and him a handsome, wealthy man:
couldn't he find someone else to give his heart to? I assumed from
what I had seen at the first party—women flitting around him like
moths to a flame—that he could have just about any one of them.
But perhaps that was a problem in itself. For often it is that which
we cannot have that we desire most.

After the stables, Jason left us, and Brandon pushed me back
toward the house at a leisurely pace. He talked constantly about
the businesses he and I owned. The holdings of Neilson Enterprises were so diversified it was too hard for me to keep track of
them. Plus, my mind was preoccupied at the moment with something far more interesting: *Sara.*

Finally we made it back to the house. The flowers lining the
pathway behind the mansion were beautiful. Brandon noticed the
attention I paid them and picked some for me. I thought this a
noble gesture. Taking me beyond the hedges and around the
indoor pool, he pushed me toward a white gazebo with pink, blue,
and lavender flowers planted around it in a perfect circle. I did so
love these colors, and remarked about them as he steered me up
the ramp he'd had installed when I first began venturing out. The
same one I hadn't used very much.

"Your mother loved this place," he remarked as he sat down
on one of the benches in front of me. "She called it her thinking
place."

"Why didn't you ever marry again?" I inquired, changing the
subject. We'd already had this conversation about my mother the
first time he'd brought me here.

"Oh..." He sighed heavily. "Vivian's death was hard on me.
Taking her life like that... Then there was Ashley to deal with. I
couldn't very well ask a woman to come in and take over a house
when I had a daughter with such erratic behavior."

"You mean she wasn't all right after thr—being in the hospital?" I corrected myself, because I knew he hadn't revealed how
long she'd stayed in the hospital; Jason had told me that part.

He glanced up briefly, then his gaze dropped back down to his
hands, which were intertwined in front of him. "I'm afraid not.
Oh, she was fine with animals—horses, dogs, cats—but not with

people. I suppose she felt she couldn't trust anyone, not after what her mother did."

"What about now? I mean, you're alone, except for Jason."

"Oh, I don't know. Too old, too set in my ways, perhaps." He sighed. "And of course, you're here now, so I don't—"

"But I won't be staying indefinitely," I interjected.

"Why not?" he asked tersely, his expression shifting abruptly from sadness to concern.

"I have a home. When I can walk again, and I'm sure that will be soon, I intend to go back and..." I paused, realizing I hadn't given this much thought lately. Now that Sara was in the picture, what was I going to do?

"And?" he prodded.

"I suppose I haven't given much thought to what I would do after I got there. I've been so busy just...taking one day at a time."

"Stay here, Princess. There's no need for you to go back. I'll give you anything and everything you need," he said, a pleading tone to his voice, as he stared at me.

"I need to go back. Even if only to settle things and...say goodbye to..." I paused once again, a lump swelling in my throat this time.

Until now I hadn't wanted to think about my parents' gravesites. When I had first inquired about this, in the hospital, Brandon had assured me there was no need to worry, everything had been taken care of. *Concentrate only on getting better.* I didn't even know anything about the funeral or where they were actually buried. Had they purchased a cemetery plot? I didn't know, and until now, hadn't wanted to think about it. It was easier for me to think of them the way they had been—the way they were in my memories—rather than where their bodies might lie. I suppose I felt that as long as I didn't see a headstone, I could keep them alive. Now it seemed it was time to think about the inevitable: saying goodbye.

A tear formed in the corner of my left eye. "I have to go back and say goodbye," I finished.

"No, you don't, Princess," he said, softly. "They're...not in Jackson Falls."

"Not... Where, then?" I stammered.

"They're here."

"In Atlanta?"

"No, Princess," he answered hesitantly. "They're *here*...at Shady Grove."

My mouth fell open. "You mean to tell me my parents are buried somewhere on this estate, and you haven't told me?" I accused.

"This is the first time you've asked. I...I didn't think you wanted to know. You never asked before."

"Yes, I did. I asked about the funeral and everything. You said it had all been taken care of."

"It was," he said evenly, turning away from my wrath. "If you had asked where, I would have told you. But you didn't."

I sighed heavily. "You're...you're right, I'm...I'm sorry. I should've asked. I...I suppose I really didn't want to know. Seeing head...Well, it would seem so final. Maybe it's better that I didn't know. But I do want to..." I paused. "I'll want to...go there, soon."

"Yes, of course, but not today, hmm?" he suggested, touching my hand as if pleading with me.

"No, not today," I agreed. "Maybe tomorrow. Where is this place?"

"Out there." He pointed toward an open field. "Close to those pecan trees you can barely see from here. All the Neilsons are buried there." I merely nodded in understanding. "So you see, Princess, you have no reason to go back," he added, trying to sound cheerful again.

"Yes, I do. There's the house and—"

"I can take care of that for you, I know of a real estate—"

"No." I shook my head. "It's more than just selling the house. Sooner or later, I'll have to take care of my own affairs. And I'll take care of this one...when I can walk again."

To hear myself say the last few words felt strange. Everyone around me had uttered them at one time or another, but not me. I was too scared I never would walk again and all those big dreams would come back to haunt me. Now, however, I was reaching for the future in order to say goodbye to the past. *How ironic!*

I hadn't realized how much I had changed over the past few weeks spent in my melancholy state. There were only a few tears now, when before I would've cried buckets at the drop of a hat. At the moment, I felt numb. Little did I know this was merely the calm before the storm.

Chapter
10

I ate a light dinner that night; I didn't feel very hungry. Brandon stayed with me most of the evening. He was quiet and subdued, which was unusual, because he normally talked incessantly about the business. I was relieved at the change and found him pleasant company, considering that I was stuck with him. Unlike the previous night, when I saw his mischievous side, tonight I was treated to quite the opposite. Kind and gentle in his tone and manner, he did nothing to make me uncomfortable.

His about-face made me wonder about us all. I, too, had different sides to my personality, which was something I'd become more aware of since being around him. I wasn't exactly the same to every person I met. We all seem to react to the stimulus around us, more often than not. And he must have been reacting to our trip to the gazebo. I knew it had reminded him of my mother, for he brought her up several times on the way back. I was also aware how my questions might have inadvertently reminded him of how alone he was.

Watching him stare out the window many times over the course of the evening, I felt sorry for him. *What's he looking for?* I wondered. Or was he even looking out there? Perhaps he was looking inside himself—the private thoughts of a lonely man, who had everything except the woman he wanted most. *To love someone for so long without ever having them must be pure torture,* I decided.

After he left, my thoughts turned to my own private world. I flipped on the stereo and started the CD player. The intro to track nine was beautiful: the sound of tinkling chimes and an organ. Then the young woman began to sing about a love that was new. She was telling her lover she wanted to take things slow, asking that her lover wait a while before they went too far. She promised she'd be worth the wait.

Listening to the song, I could see why Sara had chosen it. Several times, I felt as if she were in the room, saying these things to me. I understood what she had been trying to say that afternoon. What she could not get across easily in her own words, the song lyrics did.

As I thought back over the past few months, I could more clearly see the emotional roller-coaster ride I had not been aware I was on. My initial thinking of her like a mother figure had abruptly given way to the recognition of those feelings for what they actually were. This realization had then prompted me to fight those unnatural tendencies for all I was worth, up until yesterday, when I'd released them, setting them free to be expressed. I could now see how, over the past few days, I had allowed these previously pent up and suppressed emotions to sway my better judgment. Now I understood why so many young girls became pregnant. Sexual desire is a driving force that requires temperance, which takes time to learn. This was something I hadn't given much thought to before, since I'd never really had such overt sexual feelings. Was that perhaps one reason why they were so intense now? Or was it just because the guys had been pushy, and Sara was being anything but? Was I chasing her because I felt she was pulling away from me? Isn't that what I needed to control, the instinct to chase that which kept trying to elude my grasp? My, oh my, how things had changed in a few short months.

I had to struggle to get my jeans off, but finally managed. I changed into my pajamas and got into bed, waiting for Sara to come and say goodnight. I didn't think Brandon would be back; he'd already chastely kissed my cheek and expressed his nightly sentiment.

A few moments later, the door slowly opened and Sara walked in wearing a thin blue nightgown. I wondered why she wasn't wearing her robe as usual, but didn't inquire. I liked the view too well to want to spoil it. She backed up against the doors, shutting them. "Did you like the song?" she asked, moving toward me.

"Yes. And I understand. I'm sorry that I've been so—"

She stopped me by putting her finger to her own lips. "Don't apologize. There's nothing to be sorry for. I only wanted you to understand why it would be better to wait, not make you feel guilty. So, no more I'm sorrys, hmm? Now, how was your day?" she inquired, sitting down on the bed.

It amazed me sometimes how quickly she could change the

subject.

"Fine. I...I'll be visiting my parents'...graves tomorrow."

She looked surprised, and a bit concerned. "How will you get there? Isn't that a long trip?"

I explained about the cemetery beyond the west wing. I still felt numb talking about it, as if I had no feelings.

"Are you sure you're ready for this?" she questioned, still sounding apprehensive.

"I...I don't know. I don't feel...anything; I'm just numb. I feel as though I should be sad; tears should be flowing, but... I mean, I'll be saying goodbye tomorrow, and..."

"Not necessarily," she said softly, fiddling with my fingers.

"What do you mean?"

"Well, you have no memories of them here. What I mean is, sometimes it takes a long time for a person to let go of loved ones, especially in your case. Normally, you would confront your memories day after day and thereby come to terms with their deaths gradually, but you've been taken out of that familiar environment. Back there in...Jackson Heights, is it?" I shook my head, but didn't offer to correct her. "Well, you know what I mean. Back there is where you'll most likely say goodbye. Because in your mind, they're still there, aren't they?"

I nodded. "Yes, that's...that's how I remember them."

"Don't feel guilty about feeling numb. People handle grief in different ways. And they say there are stages you go through. Being numb is one of them."

Looking into her eyes, I felt that she was right. This was more than likely a stage I was going through. And perhaps inside I knew I would not be saying goodbye tomorrow; for to me they weren't here, they were still in Jackson Falls.

"How'd you get to be so smart?" I asked, taking her hands in mine.

"Didn't you know, it comes naturally," she teased, obviously trying to lighten the mood.

"I missed you today."

"As I did you. I brought back some tapes and CDs. You'll be dancing before long, and I knew you'd need some music to boogie down to."

"Will you dance with me?" I queried.

She smiled. "Every chance I get. I'll make sure I fill my name in on every line of your dance card."

"What dance card?" I questioned, thinking this sounded like something out of the Stone Age.

"Oh, I'm sure as old-fashioned as Brandon is, he'll give one of those gala affairs commemorating the Old South, somewhere around Labor Day; and by that time, you'll be on your feet and the men will be lining up to dance with the pretty Southern belle."

"What put you in such a good mood?" I asked, deliberately changing the subject.

"Oh, I don't know. Could be because you took your first step. Or...because Brandon goes back to work tomorrow, and I can have you all to myself." Her voice dropped an octave or so on the last phrase while she leaned in closer, her eyes glowing with happiness.

She looked so utterly beautiful that I wanted to kiss her. Instead, she lightly pecked me on the lips and then pulled back. Her eyes darted from my lips to my eyes and back again. "Before I came in here, I told myself I wouldn't do this, and yet I find it very hard to resist you," she admitted, her tone deep and sultry, her face moving closer until her lips met mine.

One kiss led to another and another, growing in intensity with each parting and reuniting of our lips, until I felt my pajama top being lifted. I gasped as her hand surrounded my left breast. The suddenness of this action sent a million sensations rushing downward, where they hit bottom and exploded outward like fireworks.

"Damn!" she cursed softly, "I've got to get out of here." Pulling away, she got up and left me lying there, breathing heavily and longing for her return.

I hadn't meant to scare her off. Not in the least. I'd wanted her to continue. I would've given her complete control over my body without a moment's hesitation. And that was one thing I'd never done before. I'd always been in control, at least in this area; there had been no melting beneath a male's touch. Yet, I had definitely felt as if I were soft butter and she, a warm knife...and I wanted to experience that again. I tingled from head to toe, desiring more. Much more! I wanted to get up and follow her; breeze into her room and crawl into bed with her; give up my long-held virginity; experience the wonders of my sexual awakening; touch, kiss, caress, fondle...whatever seemed right at the moment.

Inhaling a shuddering breath, I then let it out ever so slowly, resigning myself to merely remembering what had happened tonight. After all, she was the one who wanted to take it slow, so she was the one in control. All I could do was follow her lead. Well, most of the time, that is. It wasn't as if I didn't have a *few* ideas of my own.

We spent all the next day together. I took another step forward, slower but a tad more confidently. She informed me that the next stage would be daily trips to the hospital in order to use their therapy equipment, because I needed to work on exercising my lower body and learn to walk all over again using parallel bars for support. The idea of getting out and about with Sara was intriguing. We could *truly* be alone then, and I definitely liked the sound of that. I also liked the idea of what would come after I was able to move better: a walker. This represented freedom from the chair, and also meant Sara wouldn't be able to walk away from me as easily.

The previous night's incident was never mentioned by either of us. I think somehow we both knew that soon enough, perhaps sooner than she expected, we'd be together. We played a few of the tapes and CDs she had brought from her house, and during the love songs we stared at each other from across the room. If anyone else had been in attendance, it would've been quite obvious how we felt. But no one could know; it had to be our secret.

Dinner came far too quickly, and Brandon came up as usual. He said he had informed the servants we'd have a small memorial service for my parents that very evening. In a way, I appreciated the gesture, but I didn't want a big production. The formal funeral had been months ago, and I would've preferred having only Sara and myself in attendance on this occasion. But he insisted, and with Brandon, there was no arguing, most of the time. He liked making a production out of the simplest, most personal things.

Sara helped me into a plain black dress, but no words passed between us until Brandon arrived. Then all was quiet again as we made our way to the gravesite. We took the limousine, of course, moving slowly down the narrow dirt track. It was quite a good ways across the field, much farther than I had assumed. It turned out to be a fitting place for a cemetery. The black wrought-iron fence surrounding the site and its matching archway over the entrance—emblazoned with the name NEILSON—blended in well with the pecans and oaks, whose branches overhung the oldest of the headstones. One of these dated back to 1829, when Jackson David Neilson had passed away. I assumed he was the one who had built the house.

The wrought-iron fence had been freshly painted, or so it seemed, and as Brandon opened the gate, it squealed a minor protest. I glanced up at the archway and wondered how many who *weren't* born Neilsons were buried here. He wheeled me over to the left side of the graveyard. I perused the headstones we passed; some were green and weathered with age, exuding a sense of history.

Brandon stopped abruptly, bringing my attention back to

what lay before me. Staring me in the face were two new head-stones: "Jonathan David Neilson, Beloved Father and Husband; Marion Renee White Neilson, Beloved Mother." There it was, carved in stone. There was no denying the fact now. They weren't still happily going about their lives back in Jackson Falls, as I often wanted to believe. It had just been easier on me to think that one day they might walk through the door, and everything would be all right again. But here it was before me in big bold letters, clearly stating, "*They're not coming back!*"

I started to tremble, and Sara placed her hand on my shoulder. I could hear a voice that sounded like Brandon's, but I didn't understand the words, nor did I care to. Gripping the arms of the chair, I stared at the headstones, shutting out everything except the memories that flooded my mind. Freeze-frame moments flashed by in rapid succession: happy times we'd shared...laughter ringing in my ears...my mother tucking me in at night...my father in his study, pecking away at his typewriter...the day he got the letter proposing the movie deal...leaving for Hollywood...

Hands were touching my arms on either side as blurred images moved past. Whispered words mingled with the stiflingly hot breeze, sighing in and out around me. I offered no response. I was as still as a statue, completely numb from head to toe, my eyes as dry as any desert.

"Perhaps we should leave now, Princess," I heard Brandon say as he kissed my cheek.

"No," I finally managed to utter. "I...want to be alone."

He seemed to accept this and started away. "Miss Bennington," he called, as if prompting her to leave as well.

"Stay," I requested tersely.

She squeezed my shoulder, as if to say she wasn't going anywhere. "I'm sure she'll be all right, Mr. Neilson. Give her some time. I'll push her back to the house when she's ready," she offered.

"I'll wait," he countered.

"No, Brandon, I'm sure you have more important things to do," I said, without even considering his feelings.

The silence that ensued once he left was deafening. "I...I can't cry!" I finally voiced, growling the words like a mad dog. I could feel the rage building up inside me. I knew this should be sorrow, but what could I do about it? *What's wrong with me?*

Sara bent down beside me. "Don't punish yourself. Remember what I told you?"

"Punish myself!" I exclaimed in disbelief. "They're the ones who've been punished! And for what? What did they ever do to deserve this?" I shrieked.

"Why do you think death is a punishment?" she inquired calmly.

"Because their lives were cut short!"

"I don't know, but I've heard it said, 'Only the good die young.'"

"Bullshit!" I shouted.

"Then tell me how *you* feel, Faith."

"Feel?" I growled, gritting my teeth. "I feel cheated, that's how I feel! I feel angry! I feel so much ang...ger! It just doesn't make sense! Why were they taken, and not me? Hmm? Why my little brother, and not me? Can anyone answer me that?"

"I don't believe so. Least of all me."

"I just want to know why? Why them? Why now? Why the hell did we ever get on that plane?" I screamed, not caring who heard or how it might sound.

All at once, the dam burst. The Sahara of my eyes finally gave up the water just beneath the surface, and tears poured down my cheeks like rain. My heart felt like it would burst wide open at any moment. "Oh, God, why?" I blubbered.

Sara held my hand while I wailed in agony from the pain I felt inside. My stomach literally ached as some force within pushed to relieve all the emotional pressure that had been building up for the past few months. My body I likened to a pressure cooker; my mouth, the steam escape valve, venting all those pent-up emotions; my eyes, the lid, bubbling over with excess liquid.

It took over half an hour before the tears subsided, but afterward I felt somewhat peaceful. Just like a summer thunderstorm brought the rains that cleansed the earth, the storm inside me had been a cleansing experience too. As Sara slowly pushed me toward the house, I requested she take me around to the gazebo.

We sat in silence side by side—Sara on the floor by my chair—until the sun descended behind the trees, its bright red glow highlighting the underbelly of the clouds to the west in an array of increasingly lighter shades of pink. The crickets began chirping, the cicadas commenced their eerie trill, and the tree frogs soon joined the late evening chorus that would carry on throughout the night. The cooing of a mourning dove somewhere close by filled the air with a lonesome sound. A few minutes later, the call of a chuck-will's-widow drifted up to us from the direction of the stables.

"Shane is a beautiful horse," I commented, finally breaking the silence. "I know why Jason picked him."

"Why?"

"He's different. That lovely beige mane of his, and those eyes... It's hard to believe he was ever as wild as they say."

"Don't we all have a wild streak?"

"What do you mean?"

"A rebellious side that...wants to do something even though you know it's probably the wrong thing to do."

"Hmph. Yeah, I know about that side. It's hard to control sometimes."

"You can say that again," she remarked, holding out a piece of pine straw, the three separate strands braided together.

"It's hard to control sometimes," I repeated obediently, admiring her handiwork.

She glanced up at me and we both grinned; it seemed to ease the tension between us considerably. Even though the references had been vague in those previous few lines, we both knew we were indirectly discussing our relationship.

"Hey, look," she announced, pointing to the east. I followed her gaze and saw a bright orange moon barely peeking its head above the tree line. "Isn't that beautiful?"

"Um-hmm, very," I agreed.

A hush fell over us once again while we reverently admired one of Mother Nature's most mysterious wonders: the moon. It seemed to be an enormous fireball in the sky, but I knew it had no light of its own. It was merely a reflection of its daytime counterpart and benefactor, the sun. All the folklore that had grown up around this changeable nocturnal reflection of the sun was amazing to me. Some people even feared it when it was full, but not me; just like the ocean's tide, I could feel her working her magic on me.

How many lovers have been seduced by this illusion and its magical pull? I wondered. A full moon was considered romantic, but did anyone ever stop to wonder why? Was it because of her gravitational pull on the earth, more so than her light? If she could move an ocean, what force must she exert on us as individuals, without our being aware of it?

A cool breeze floated up the little rise where we sat and I looked over at Sara, wondering what she was thinking. The breeze tossed short strands of her hair, which had slipped out of her coif, to and fro. They danced around her forehead and flitted about her ear. I speculated once again what she had looked like with her natural coloring. Her olive complexion against the blonde hair gave the appearance of someone who spent a good deal of time in the sun. And of course, our time in the pool had only darkened her skin to a richer hue. I tried to imagine what she would look like •

with dark brown hair.

This reminded me of my own hair. Day by day, it was slowly growing out, but I still had only enough to make me look like a boy with a crew cut. The scar stood out against the light brown stubble, winding its way across my forehead to my right eyebrow. Of course, the turban I always wore now—in place of the bandage, which had been removed the last time Dr. Rosemund came out— still covered this up. But I still couldn't imagine how Sara could think I was beautiful. The phrase "love is blind" seemed to be whispered in my ear by the incoming breeze.

"Princess, what are you...two doing out here?" Brandon asked as he quickly ascended the steps of the gazebo. From his tone of voice and the expression on his face, I knew he'd first assumed I was alone. I realized that from the path, Sara would have been out of sight sitting on the floor beside me. "Shouldn't she be inside, Miss Bennington?"

"Just a little while longer. I want to stay until the moon climbs above the tree tops," I requested, giving him what he apparently expected from me: my best whiny brat impression.

"Moon?" he muttered, as if not understanding why I would want to see this.

"Yes, over there." I pointed toward it.

He sat down on the bench behind us with a heavy sigh. Sara seemed quite uneasy about his presence and got up a few seconds later, walking over to the rail at the entrance. *Why does Brandon make her so uncomfortable?* I wondered. Was it just because of their mutual dislike? I had thought Sara stronger in character than that. Or was it that she felt our closeness in his presence might reveal our true relationship?

"I suppose I should have known I would find you out here," Brandon commented in a soft voice. "So much like your mother, you are."

I gritted my teeth, for I wanted to scream, *I am not my mother, can't you see that?* Yet again I held my tongue.

"Oh yes, I nearly forgot," he added, "I've arranged for a hair-dresser to come out tomorrow."

"A hairdresser?" I repeated. "Brandon, I hardly think I need—"

"Ah-ah-ah, let me finish, Princess. I know it was supposed to be a surprise, and I was planning to be here, but things came up down at the office and I have to take care of them. I just wanted to let you know he would be bringing several wigs for your approval."

"Wigs?"

"Yes, of course, for the party this weekend. You remember you remarked about your turban? Well, here's your solution."

That damn party again! Without coming right out and telling him I despised his friends, I had been unable to persuade him not to give the party. I'd relented, reasoning that he didn't ask a whole lot of me usually, and just because he'd interrupted my new love life on a few occasions was no reason to deprive him of his happiness. I'd just slip away early. Now, however, he wanted me to do something else for him. I'd never worn a wig before. As a matter of fact, I'd never even seen one up close—at least, not that I was aware of. The thought of donning one had never even crossed my mind. Now that it had, I couldn't help but wonder what I'd look like? *An old lady,* was my first reaction.

"I don't know what your hair was like before," he continued, "but I assume it was as beautiful as your mother's. So I picked out several that reminded me of her—subject to your approval, of course," he added hastily.

Of course is right, I thought. *If I do wear a wig, which I doubt, I'm certainly not wearing anything I don't approve of.* As a matter of fact, the whole idea would take some getting used to. I looked over at Sara, who was merely staring off into the distance while she twirled a piece of pine straw between her fingers. *Perhaps if she likes it, it might be all right.*

After I changed for bed, Brandon came up to say goodnight and brought another glass of milk. I wasn't thirsty and knew how it had affected me the last time I was tired, but drank a few sips to let him know I appreciated the gesture. His goodnight kiss lingered longer than usual, as he rubbed his face against mine. "Get well soon, Princess," he whispered.

A few minutes after he left, I took another sip of the milk. It didn't taste like ours at home, but of course, no two dairies are the same. As I lay there waiting for Sara, I could feel sleep silently creeping up on me.

Finally, she appeared in the doorway, wearing her robe. "I think I'd better say goodnight from here," she suggested, holding on to the side of the open door and twisting the knob nervously.

"Is that what you really want?"

"No," she replied, still twisting the knob back and forth, her eyes scanning the room like a fly searching for a place to land. "But I think it would be better if..." She paused, her gaze coming to rest on the nightstand. "Who brought the milk?" she questioned, frowning.

"Brandon. Why?"

She shrugged. "I...I don't know." She rested her forehead

against the door. "There's just something about...a glass of milk. Every time I see it, I want to get rid of it. But I can't say why," she added, shaking her head. "There's so much I've lost."

"What do you mean, lost?"

She sighed heavily and glanced up at the ceiling. "I've been meaning to tell you this for a while now, but...I just... Well, it never seemed the right time or..." She paused, looked down at her feet, and tapped her forehead against the edge of the door.

She had me worried. "What is it, Sara?"

She sighed again, her forehead merely resting against the door's edge now. "Remember I told you that I didn't recognize my own face when I woke up in the hospital?"

"Yes."

"Well, that wasn't just because it was such a mess, which it was." She looked over at me and lifted her head from the door. "It really was; much worse than yours, by a long shot. But, that's not the real reason I didn't recognize it. You see, Faith, I had amnesia."

That explained a lot. "Amnesia? You mean you couldn't remem—?"

"Still can't," she interrupted, fidgeting with the doorknob. "And that's why I keep saying that everything before the accident is fuzzy. Truth is, I don't remember."

"You mean you don't remember anything about your past?" I asked, aghast.

"Not really. There've been a few flashes...a few things that...I don't know...feel familiar or something, but nothing I can *clearly* say is a memory."

"What flashes? What things feel familiar?" I was intrigued.

"Oh it's just little things, like...the milk and...this house, for instance. I feel like I...either visited here before or maybe lived in one similar, or something."

"Maybe you knew Ashley," I interjected, trying to make some sense of her familiarity. "Maybe you attended one of Brandon's parties?"

Her eyes took on a faraway look, as if she was trying to remember something. "I doubt it, but...I couldn't say one way or the other. And that's the worst part: I just don't know." She was fiddling with the latch now.

"What about your father, can't he tell you anything?"

"He said I lived with my mother until the accident."

"You mean she was..."

She nodded before I could finish the sentence. "He said she...died instantly. But I have no memory of her. Unlike you, I couldn't even mourn her properly. She was a stranger to me. I...I don't even know where she's buried."

Although I felt sorry for her, I was fascinated with the amnesia and wanted to keep her talking, so I said, "It must be hard on you. Not knowing, I mean."

"Sometimes, like now, when I remember little flashes of things..." She paused as she crossed the room to the vanity. "I often wonder what she looked like. My father said I look like her, except for my hair and eyes. That's another reason why I changed them. I guess I thought if I looked more like her, it might trigger some memory, but I suppose my face changed a great deal after the accident."

"Didn't your father have a picture of her?"

"Just a small faded snapshot. You can't tell much about her."

"What about pictures from your home? Surely—"

"The house burned down while I was in the hospital. Vandals broke in and..." She shook her head sadly. "All the memories I might've recalled through familiarity, they all...went up in smoke, I guess you could say." She seemed to be trying to dismiss her sadness with humor.

"Can't he tell you anything about her? I mean, surely there are relatives or—"

"My parents were never married," she interrupted, sighing heavily. "She left home because she was pregnant. Didn't keep in touch, though he claimed he'd tried to find her." She frowned at her reflection and then looked away. "She had no relatives, no husband."

"Where was the accident?"

"Outside of Atlanta."

"You mean you were living around here, close to him, and he didn't know?"

"No, he lived in south Georgia, down near Columbus."

"I thought you said you lived here in Atlanta?"

"I do. I have an apartment in Smyrna. And no, I didn't go to live with him," she added, as if anticipating my next question. "I spent a long time in the hospital. Then he rented me an apartment so I could be close to the doctors, plastic surgeons, and everything. After that, I started school here and..." She drew a deep breath. "You have to remember, I...I didn't know him very well."

"How often do you see him and your little brother?" I inquired.

She ran her index finger over the vanity top as she stared into the mirror, frowning at her reflection. "I...I don't have a brother, Faith. I...I don't even have a father now. He died not long before this job came up."

She had lied to me.

"I know there's no excuse for lying," she went on. "It...it was just easier somehow than telling the truth. Especially when I'm not sure what the truth is...for me." Her frown deepened.

"What do you mean?" I asked, crossing my arms over my stomach. I realized as soon as I did this that it was a defensive posture, designed to ward off any blows to my solar plexus where she had already, figuratively, hit me only moments before.

"There's...there's just a lot of things he told me that, well, they don't add up."

"Are you saying you think he lied to you about something?"

She quickly turned away from the vanity, then walked over to her chair and plopped down. "Perhaps. I'll let you be the judge of that," she finally responded, glancing over at me. "Sara Bennington, this is your life," she quipped. "Or at least, according to my father."

She then related her history as it had been told to her. Her mother had run off to Atlanta because she hadn't wanted to marry her father. The duplicate birth certificate Sara had obtained after all her identification went up in flames with the car listed her as being born in Atlanta on December 14, 1960, to Amy Jackson. The father was listed as Leon Bennington. According to her biological father, Leon Bennington was nowhere to be found at the time of the accident, and he had no idea who Leon was or if he even existed at all, since her mother had never changed her maiden name.

Her father knew nothing about her previous life, other than the fact that she had lived in a rundown house on the south side of Atlanta. Her mother had no living relatives, and no friends that he could find. As she had mentioned before, vandals had broken into the house they had shared and somehow set fire to it. Sara had never seen it, because by the time she was up and around again, the lot had been cleared and another foundation had been laid on the site.

It was obvious Sara was disturbed over the fact that she hadn't known her father, even before the accident, and then suddenly he walked into her life and took over. Obviously suspicious, when she'd asked how he'd found out about the accident, he explained that he'd read an article in the paper about her mother dying in the crash. But he could produce no proof that he was indeed her father, other than the picture of her mother and a small black-and-white snapshot of a little girl on horseback, which he said had been sent to him many years before with no return address after he'd snooped around looking for her. He reasoned that Amy had wanted to appease him with these small tokens. But the snapshot was so faded and worn, Sara had no way of knowing whether this was indeed her childhood image or that of some other little girl.

I sighed heavily when she finished. "Lots of unanswered questions, hmm?"

"A lot," she agreed. "And I know this gave me no right to lie to you, but I didn't want you feeling sorry for me. And I didn't want that analytical mind of yours going to work on my Swiss cheese of a life history. I wanted you to concentrate on yourself."

"Well, at least you've finally told me. But would you have, if I hadn't pried?"

"Eventually, I suppose. I mean, how do you just come out and tell someone something this...odd? What if what I'm telling you now isn't the truth? I have no way of knowing if I'm lying to you right now or not."

"You're telling me the truth as you know it, right?"

She nodded. "But do you see why I didn't tell you before?"

I frowned. "Why the little brother, though?"

She shrugged. "I don't know." She was staring out the window. "I guess maybe I've always wanted one. But see, I don't even know if that's true. I have no way of finding out what I was like before the accident or...or even if it was my fault," she added, as she quickly got up out of the chair. "I'm sorry, I think this conversation has degenerated into something I don't like. And I'm sure you'd rather not have a liar for a...friend." She started for the door.

"Sara." She stopped, her hand already on the knob, but didn't make any move to turn around. "You've helped me put my past behind me, helped me get through...so many things." I paused and nibbled on my bottom lip. "Maybe it's time for me to return the favor. We...we can both put the past behind us and...walk into the future together." Tears welled up in my eyes, and I tried to will them back. Through my watery vision, I saw her hand slip from the doorknob; her shoulders start to shake. I knew she was crying, too. "Are you coming over here, or are you gonna make me get up out of this bed and come to you?" I asked.

She turned around slowly, looked at me through tear-filled eyes, then covered the distance between us in only a few strides.

"What did you do after you got better?" I inquired once we had both stopped crying.

"I enrolled in college," she responded on a sigh, as she leaned her head back against the pillow propped beneath it. "Like you, I wanted to be a psychologist, but...I couldn't hack it." She reached down and fiddled with the sheet between us. "I mean, I didn't even know who *I* was, how could I help anyone else find themselves? Anyway, my therapist talked me into trying this. And five years later, here I am. Don't get me wrong; I love the job. It's very rewarding to help people. Especially someone like you," she added, looking over at me.

She was so close, lying only a few inches away, and yet I knew nothing would happen between us. "Where did all the women come in?" I queried, feeling a smile forming at the corners of my mouth.

"Ah... I wondered when you'd get around to that one. Well," she paused and turned her fidgeting fingers to the belt of her robe, "I...umm...I had a crush on my therapist to begin with." She cut her eyes over at me. I grinned. "But she was straight as an arrow. Then I met this girl in college, and we had a thing for a couple of months. My first, I suppose. And then, let's see...there was a...succession of them—women I met at bars or through mutual friends."

"You mean none of the relationships lasted?"

"No, not more than a couple of months; some, not that long. I...I just couldn't commit to anyone for very long, or else they didn't want to stick around."

This frightened me a bit, because I wondered if I was letting myself in for heartbreak. I hadn't given much thought to the future of the relationship. I'd been too busy reveling in my newfound feelings to think past losing my virginity.

"That's why I want you to think about this carefully, before we go too far," she continued, turning over on her side to face me. "I feel more for you than I have for anyone, but who knows what will happen later on." Her eyes darted back and forth, searching mine.

"What's that saying? 'Tis better to have loved and lost, than never to have loved at all," I remarked softly.

"You're incorrigible, you know that?" she teased, reaching over and touching my hand. "No matter how I try to keep my distance, you still end up luring me in."

"Could be because I want you here," I responded, searching her eyes now.

"Such innocence." Her hand moved up to my face. "It scares me to think I might unwittingly hurt you."

"If I do get hurt, it'll be my own fault, right?" I heard myself say. "I started this, after all."

"Well, I'd better go," she asserted, withdrawing her hand. "It's getting late and—"

"Stay with me a while longer, please." I reached out for her hand, but ended up grabbing one side of the belt to her robe.

"No, that wouldn't be a good ide— Hey, let go of that."

"Stay," I pleaded, tugging on the cord.

I hadn't meant to untie it, hadn't even thought about this happening when I tugged on the belt, but her robe suddenly gaped open. Underneath, she wore nothing but a pair of blue panties. A lump formed in my throat as I gazed upon her naked torso.

She slowly pulled the end of the belt from my hand. "You didn't expect this, did you?"

I slowly shook my head, unable to take my eyes off her breasts. She started to pull her robe back together, but I reached out again, this time catching hold of her hand. "Please, don't." She gazed down at me, her expression saying that she wasn't sure about allowing this intimate perusal of her body. "You've seen mine," I reminded.

The sides of the robe slipped from her hands and fell back to their previous positions. She then laced her fingers in mine, seeming a bit embarrassed. My eyes memorized her body, taking in every curve, every line, and every freckle on her shapely form—at least, every one of these within my view. And what a view it was. Her breasts were firm and round, light brown aureoles just starting to tighten, the darker nipples becoming erect beneath my gaze. I tried to get my hand free, but she held on tightly and shook her head slowly. I wanted to touch her so badly I felt as if my fingertips were itching with desire, but I knew she was right. That would have to wait.

My gaze met hers again, searching for something, anything to change the subject, or else I felt I would go crazy with desire. "So, did your father have chameleon eyes?" I queried, shattering the moment to hell and back.

"Chameleon eyes?" she repeated with a chuckle, slowly letting go of my hand in order to put her robe back together. I recaptured one of her fingers, not wanting to lose this enticing and intriguing sight just yet. The back of my hand brushed against her stomach. "Umm..." She moaned and squeezed my finger, "I don't really know, actually," she continued, answering my question while at the same time letting go of my finger and pulling her robe back together. "I never noticed. I guess so, since I don't have my mother's eyes. Why?"

I cleared my throat and sought to discard my wanton thoughts so that I might proceed with the conversation I'd started. "Um, isn't there any way to find out more about her? I mean, surely *someone* knew her?" I was still staring at her robe, knowing now exactly what lay beneath it and just how very beautiful it was.

"My father said he couldn't find anyone."

This got my attention. *No one knew this woman? That didn't sound right.* "Well, did you see the article about the accident? Maybe that might tell you something."

"No, I never did. That's an idea. Leave it to a clever mind like yours to think of that," she replied, patting my hand, which was lying by her naked leg. "I suppose I didn't really want to know a lot at the time. Like you, I had enough to do just recovering. I guess I always hoped someone would recognize me."

"Do you want to find out now? Try to fill the holes in the Swiss cheese, so to speak?"

"Yes and no. I guess I'm afraid of what I might find. I mean, these flashes...they're not...Well, they make me feel...angry and scared. Like...like the milk, there," she said, eyeing the nearly full glass. "To you, it's just a glass of milk, but to me there's a...foreboding feeling associated with it. I...I'm afraid my life wasn't a happy one. I often wonder if it's best that I don't know. Maybe I can't remember because I don't want to."

"But won't you always feel empty inside? I know I would. Maybe that's why you can't make a commitment to anyone. You scare yourself away, because without your past, you don't truly know who you are."

Several moments passed as she considered this. "You'll make a fine psychologist one day, sweetheart. Mark my words, a fine one," she remarked, touching my face again.

"You would've, too. The way you manipulate people."

"Manipulate?" she repeated, removing her hand. "Who have I manipulated?"

"Let's see..." I pulled myself up straighter in the bed. "There's Jason, for one. Getting him to come around, and take part in helping me. Then there's me, of course. You manipulate me all the time."

"When?" she asked, with a sly grin.

"In the pool. And you know, you're pretty good at it, too." My eyes traveled downward, coming to rest at the top of her robe, which was still slightly open. "You accuse me of teasing you, when you do the same thing to me," I added, referring to the fact that she had been nearly naked underneath her robe. My eyes traveled back up to meet her gaze and gauge her reaction.

"You think you have me all figured out, don't you?"

"Not yet, but I'm working on it." I reached over and ran my fingertip along the collar of her robe.

"You're quite a challenge, you know that? You're truly testing my resistance, aren't you?"

"I wouldn't say testing." My finger proceeded down to where the two sides joined. I knew what lay underneath that robe, and was dying to get my hands on all of it.

"Oh, right. It's more like you're wearing down my resistance." She removed my hand and intertwined her fingers with mine. Gazing into my eyes, she rubbed her thumb back and forth over my fingers. Then slowly she leaned over and kissed me ever so lightly. "Good night, Faith." She quickly got up from the bed.

I wanted to reach out and pull her back, but she was too quick. I fell back against the pillows, frustrated and exhausted. I started to reach for the milk, then remembered her foreboding feeling about it and decided against it. I turned off the light instead and settled back.

Once again I had let my feelings lead me. And like the night before, I was left frustrated. I couldn't help but wonder what I would do if I ever pushed things too far, and she suddenly stopped playing this little cat and mouse game. I was being very aggressive and selfish in this situation, and I knew it. But it was so hard to resist once those feelings took over. I felt like I was rapidly turning into a Howard: all roamin' hands and rushin' fingers, with one thing on my mind. And I didn't know the first thing about what I was rushing into.

Chapter
11

After pool therapy the next day, we were both surprised to find several men in the room next to Sara's, moving out furniture and assembling the very equipment she'd previously mentioned as being the next stage in my therapy.

Sara walked into the room while I looked in from the door. "Where did this come from?" she inquired of a burly man tightening the bolts on an exercise machine.

"We're from Blanchard's—" The man started to name his company, but Sara interrupted.

"No, I mean, who ordered this?"

"A Mr. Neilson," he replied, glancing over at his companion. "Is there a problem?"

Sara hesitated, her gaze falling on the other young man, who was assembling a pair of parallel bars to a long flat mat of some sort. This reminded me of a large treadmill, although it appeared the mat was stationary. She eventually shook her head. "No, no problem," she answered, tight-lipped.

"Are you the therapist?" the young man inquired.

"Yes."

"All the paperwork is over there." He pointed with his screwdriver to a slim stack of papers on the floor by the door. "You'll need to sign the one on top saying you received this."

Sara merely nodded, walked over, and picked up the papers, along with a pen that had been left on top. She read the first page, frowned, then said, "Let me know when you're finished. I'll need to check things over. I'll be next door."

"What's wrong?" I queried, as we entered my sitting room.

She hesitated. "He had the equipment brought here," she responded, still tight-lipped. "I wanted to get you out, even if it was just going to the hospital and back, but I suppose this will be more convenient." She paused and sighed heavily. "Well, the important thing is we can start this stage of your therapy right away." She flashed a rueful smile.

I could tell she was disappointed; so was I. I'd been looking forward to those outings together. I hadn't, however, been looking forward to being around a lot of other people during my therapy. This turn of events was a mixed bag, and one relegated to the back burner after lunch, when the hairdresser showed up as Brandon had promised.

Pierre was a thin, short man, with conspicuous black, wavy hair and striking light brown eyes. His French accent was fake, an affectation presumably to impress his customers. He hadn't quite perfected it, for even I could detect the Southern drawl marring his performance. It was quite humorous, actually, and I found him thoroughly entertaining. As he touched my face, he made a comment in French. I had no idea what he'd said, but Sara looked over at me and translated. "He says you're very pretty." When I inquired as to how she knew French, she frowned in consideration, then shrugged her shoulders and got that faraway look in her eyes. *She's found another hole in the Swiss cheese,* I thought.

"Mademoiselle, your uncle has selected three choices for your approval," Pierre explained, opening three square silver boxes. "First, we will try zis one."

He pulled out a wavy blonde wig with hair the color of Sara's and placed it over my turban. It was awful. I looked like a blonde version of Betty Boop.

"Too full," he decided, promptly removing it. "Let's try zis one." He placed a wig with long, flowing blonde hair on my head. "No, no, no, zis does not fit your face."

I had to admit, I did look rather odd. The hair even looked silver against my skin, rather than blonde.

He discarded it as well. "Your uncle said zis one reminded him of your mother," he related, bringing out the final selection.

I immediately noticed that the nearly shoulder-length blonde hair had already been styled and set the way my mother wore it, the ends turned under like Streisand's. As Pierre placed it on my head and arranged the sides, I found myself gazing at a reasonable facsimile of my mother. I looked more like her now than ever before. Even if the nose was not the same and my lips were a bit fuller, I could still see her features in my face: rosy cheeks, bow-shaped lips, small chin, and the pale pigment of my skin. Or did I look so much like her only because I no longer had the lovely original to compare the reproduction to?

"Ah yes, mademoiselle, zis is your color. Yes, I could transform zis into a work of art," he proclaimed, fussing with the front edges to arrange it around my face.

"But the turban..." I pointed out the way the part displayed it.

"No need to worry, Pierre will take care of zat." He looked at my reflection in the mirror, then brushed the hair down in front and over to one side, covering most of the turban. "I could sweep it ovair to zee side like zis, give you a part here. Or... give you bangz. Yes, I believe bangz would be better. You like?" he queried, repositioning the hair in front.

"I...I don't know," I replied, seeing a face too much like my mother's staring back at me. Then again, I'd always wanted to look like her, and now was my chance.

"Can you take zis tur-bon off?" he asked.

I shook my head. "The scars are too bad."

"Might we have a look? Pierre can do won-derz with zee makeup, and your scar might be eazier to hide zan zis tur-bon."

I relented, and he unwound the turban to reveal my scarred head and face. I know he didn't mean for me to see it, but I noticed the expression on his face when he first saw the disfiguration. He looked up at my reflection in the mirror and flashed a fake smile, however. I sighed heavily while he repositioned the wig on my head, fussing around with the sides again, and pulling them forward into bangs.

"Yez, yez, I zink I could make zis work, with a little makeup here and...across here." He nodded and smiled at my reflection. "What do you zink?"

"Sara? How about it?" I queried, feeling I was not the best judge of this situation at the moment.

"Please, Mademoiselle Sara..." He moved aside and Sara's reflection appeared behind me.

She looked at me oddly for only a brief moment, and then the corners of her mouth turned up in a smile. She arched her eyebrows and slowly nodded.

"Yes, Pierre, I'll take it, but you must do something about the underside."

"Un-der-zide?" he asked, bewildered.

"This thing is making me itch under here."

"Oh, oh, Pierre can fix zat, oh yez. No pro-blem zer." He lifted my chin ever so slightly. "You have lovely features, mademoiselle. Zis will be a pleazure. Shall I inform your on-cle zat I will be returning Friday afternoon to perform your tranz-forma-zi-on?" he said, his tone implying he was teasing me.

"All right. Friday at..." I glanced up at Sara for help.

"Make it in the late afternoon, Pierre," she suggested. "I'm sure she'll be sleeping most of the day."

When Brandon came to my room later that evening, he was thrilled with my choice. He began chattering away about the upcoming party, informing me that since the Fourth of July fell on the same weekend, he'd decided to combine the two special occasions into one gala event. As Sara walked in with the dinner tray, trying to save poor Celia a few steps, Brandon promptly relieved her for the evening. Then he left to eat his own dinner.

Sara dropped in again on her way out. "Why don't you go to the library and look up that article on your accident?" I asked.

"All right. To satisfy your curiosity, I will. See you later."

Brandon and Jason visited with me until well after nine. I only half listened to their conversation, because my mind was on Sara. I hoped the article might tell her something that could be useful in tracing her past, and I was curious to know what she'd found out.

Around ten-thirty she came in, still dressed in her jeans and a white men's shirt—epaulets on the shoulders—open to the waist and worn over a black tank top. She flopped down in her chair as if she were worn out.

"Well, what did you find?" I asked, eager to end the suspense.

"A very small article," she replied. "Didn't tell me anything I didn't already know."

"I'm sorry."

She waved the gesture away. "It was worth a shot," she acknowledged, and started removing the pins from her hair.

"I suppose." I was disappointed.

"Hey, don't go feeling badly about it. Oh yes, I found an article about Ashley. I had a copy made for you. I thought you might be interested in it, since she was your cousin and all."

My curiosity was on the rebound. "What does it say?"

"I don't know. I didn't take time to read it." She shook her head and ran her fingers through her hair to straighten it.

She was so beautiful when she let her hair down that this distracted me for a moment. "Um, you didn't find anything at all on yourself?" I questioned further.

She shook her head as she stood up. "I guess the daughter's recovery is not newsworthy," she replied, reaching into her back pocket and withdrawing a folded sheet of paper. "Here's that copy of Ashley's. And mine is in there, too. I assumed you'd want to read both." She stared at the mimeograph paper as she walked over to hand them to me.

"Do you know how beautiful you are?" I asked, admiring the

way her hair fell around her face, framing it with the silky tresses. "Read," she said with a smile. "I need to go change."

After she left, I unfolded the warm sheets of paper, which contained slight indentions where they had been molded against the curve of her behind. The first sheet was the small article on Sara. ONE KILLED IN SEMI MISHAP, the headline read. The article went on to say that early Saturday morning, December 28, 1987, a tractor-trailer truck jackknifed on Highway 85 South, just north of Fayetteville. According to the driver of the semi, one Dick Broswell, an oncoming vehicle swerved to avoid a collision with him, and the driver lost control of the vehicle on the wet payment. The 1982 Sunbird plunged a hundred feet down an embankment and crashed into a tree. Mr. Broswell rushed down to the vehicle, which was catching on fire; the driver was lying on the hood. He reportedly carried her to safety only moments before the car exploded. The vehicle was later found to belong to Amy Jackson. Her daughter, Sara Bennington, was listed in critical condition.

I sighed heavily after reading it. Sara had been the driver of the car. I couldn't imagine how she must feel, wondering if she could've done anything differently. I knew this was a guilt she would carry around for the rest of her life.

I put this page aside and took a look at the other copied article. It was considerably longer, probably in proportion to the net worth of the victim. MILLIONAIRE'S DAUGHTER MISSING AFTER CAR ACCIDENT, it read in big bold print. The article detailed the distress of multimillionaire Brandon Jason Neilson and his request that the river be dragged in an attempt to find his missing daughter, Ashley Marie Neilson, 22, after her car plunged into the Chattahoochee River on the night of December 30, 1987. Evidence at the scene—skid marks and a deer with two broken hind legs—suggested that Ashley had unsuccessfully swerved to miss the deer and had lost control of the 1987 Camaro convertible on the slick pavement, tearing through the guardrail and landing fifty feet below in the rising waters of the Chattahoochee River. The man who came upon the accident and subsequently called the authorities had ventured down to the river, but had not gone in because of the swift current. Unable to guess whether or not Ashley had escaped, he was quoted as saying, "It was just too dark to see anything, with the rain and all. I figured the best thing I could do was find a phone and call the cops." Sergeant Collinsworth of the Atlanta police had issued a statement saying, "All the evidence seems to suggest she was thrown through the windshield of the vehicle, so we'll continue to search." The reporter made note of the torrential rains that had fallen over that weekend, which had raised the level of the river several inches, making the current very swift and substantially hindering the rescue efforts.

The story continued with the prospects of finding her alive; the first attempt to drag the river, which had proved futile; and the ongoing search that had been launched the next day and had so far come up empty. It included many details about her life, where she had gone to college, and what she was majoring in—psychology. Actually, it sounded more like a eulogy than a news article on a missing girl. It was obvious to me the reporter had already made up his mind she was dead. Brandon was the only one holding out any hope that she had survived.

I refolded the papers and laid them both on the side of the bed for Sara. The question of Ashley possibly being alive was a moot issue with me now. Obviously her body had been washed down the river by the rainstorm. I could see, though, why Brandon wouldn't give up so easily; there was always that lingering hope that maybe, just maybe, she'd somehow escaped. But that was only a tale for the movies or a good book. Things like that didn't happen in real life.

However, things like Sara's fate did. And now she was walking around without a past. I assumed the latter made her afraid to look too far into the future.

A few minutes later, Sara walked back in with her robe open, revealing a pair of black silky pajamas underneath. I wondered when she had acquired those, as I didn't remember seeing them before. "So, what did you find out, Miss Detective?" she asked, closing her robe and tying it together.

Is she teasing me? I wondered. "Umm...she drove a Camaro convertible," I replied. "Must have had good taste."

"Camaro? Hmm... Yeah, pretty good taste."

"That reminds me, what kind of ride do you make your escape from this place in?"

"A black Trans Am," she replied, arching her eyebrows. "Her name's Rosa Lee."

"Rosa Lee?" I queried with a snicker.

She smiled. "Hispanic girl I used to know. She was sleek, dark, and moved like greased lightning."

I turned away and crossed my arms over my stomach. She started to snicker now, as she sat down on the side of the bed. "What else did you find out?" she queried.

I didn't even offer a reply.

"Oh, come on, sweetheart," she said playfully, rubbing my arm. "I was only teasing."

I merely stared at the floor, not even offering to look her way.

"You flatter me," she admitted, though taking her hand away. "Truthfully, there was no Rosa Lee, okay?" She smirked. "I just added that part to see how you'd react."

"Did I perform well for your amusement?"

"Faith, come on, I was only teasing."

"I know, to see my reaction, right?" I faced her. "And I gave you one, didn't I? I'm jealous, okay? Next time we're out in the yard, take one of those yellow flowers and put it under my chin. It'll turn bright yellow, I guarantee it."

"I...kind of like that," she said softly, as she put her hand on my left leg and moved it up to where the covers ended. She looked up at me, then hooked her finger around the covers and pulled down, ever so slowly.

"Uh-uh," I objected, grabbing hold of it. "You can just keep your hands to yourself."

She grinned and took her hand away. "Feisty, aren't we?"

"Um-hmm. So, you going to take me for a ride in...Rosa Lee, sometime?"

"Sure, whenever you want. Although Brandon might not approve."

"Oh, I'm positive he wouldn't approve of me riding in a car named after one of your...lovers," I said haughtily, glancing away. "Come to think of it, I'm not sure I want to..."

My voice drifted off as she reached up and turned my face toward her, then laid one on me. And boy, did she ever! She pressed me back against the pillow; I wrapped my arms around her waist.

"There was...no Rosa...Lee," she stated through her kisses, while her right hand made its way up my left side. "And...I want to...take you...away with me."

"Do it," I said breathlessly, hoping she wouldn't stop.

"Oh, Jesus, Faith, how I want to." She broke away and stilled her hand, resting her forehead against mine. I could see the anguish on her face as she uttered, "But I can't. You know I can't."

I wanted to say, *Why can't you?* But I knew what she meant. I had to get better before we could make plans like that. This was just passion talking. And mine was screaming out, *Please, don't stop this time!* But I knew she'd already regained control of herself. "Then just take me for a ride, hmm?" I suggested instead.

"But Brandon..."

"It'll be our secret," I whispered.

"No, it won't; the servants will know."

"Well, it'll go down like this, see," I explained, doing my best Edward G. Robinson impression, which wasn't very good. "We'll sneak out by the back stairs, and if the guards see us, we'll make a run for it, see."

"What happens if they catch us?" she asked, playing along.

"We'll let 'em have it, rat-a-tat-tat," I responded, imitating a machine gun.

She backed away and started laughing. I glanced down, feeling a tad embarrassed, wondering if she thought I was an utter idiot. "You're something else, you know that?" she finally said, lifting my chin so that our eyes met.

"Yeah, but you're not sure what yet, right?"

"No, I'm sure you're funny, unpredictable, stub-born..." she replied, dragging out the last word, as she moved in closer, "...kind and...adorable as hell." She paused as her eyes darted down to my lips and back again. "You're also very beautiful and...desirable."

She leaned down and kissed me again. This time, I was determined that she wouldn't get away so soon; I wrapped my arms around her neck and held on tight. Her kisses grew even more passionate than before as she seemingly sought to devour my mouth. Her lips were soft, warm, and wet. I felt like I could never get enough of them, never get tired of feeling them against my own. I completely forgot about wanting to hold her there, and brought my hands around to her face when she came up for air. Brushing the hair back from her face, I let the silky strands slide through my fingers and followed them downward to the top of her robe, where I then proceeded to trace a path from the middle of her chest to her belt. She kissed me on the cheek and continued down the side of my face while my fingers untied her belt. Slowly, I worked my hands underneath the robe and around to her back, while she progressed down my neck. Needless to say, by this time, I was on fire.

"You're not going to give up, are you?" she asked breathlessly, as she straightened up to face me.

"No," I whispered, pulling her back down for another lip-lock.

Moving my hand around her side, I touched her breast through the silky material. A series of wild sensations soared through my body as she moaned. All I could think about was having her next to me—touching, caressing...and whatever came next.

"Stay with me, Sara," I pleaded between kisses. "I...don't care...if we do nothing more...than this. Please!"

She let out a soft whimper and plunged her tongue deeper inside my mouth, where I caressed it with my own. We moaned simultaneously. Her right hand once again made its way up my side, and this time reached its destination. When she placed her hand on my breast, I let out a loud sigh I felt everyone in the house could've heard.

She broke away and removed her hand slowly. "No, Faith, this isn't right. I can't... God, don't look at me like that."

"Stay with me," I pleaded.

Her eyes darted back and forth, searching mine. I knew she wanted the same thing I did, I could see it in her eyes. She slowly reached up to the bedpost and pressed the button lowering the head of the bed, and then turned off the light. I tingled with anticipation, which suddenly transformed into apprehension. *Oh, God, I thought, she's stopped playing cat and mouse. Now what am I going to do? I don't know the first thing to do beyond fondling her breasts. What will she expect of me? I've been so aggressive up 'til now, what if she's disappointed when I don't know what else to do?*

You'll muddle through, I told myself, feeling the bed give on my left side and the covers being pulled back. I didn't know what to do, because turning over to face her would have been awkward at best. Instead, when I felt her slide under the covers, I reached out for her hand. It wasn't her hand I found, however; I touched soft, naked flesh. *Oh, God, no clothes!* A lump formed in my throat. I swallowed hard and ran my hand over her silky smooth skin. Fireworks went off inside my mind and body. I wanted her to come closer, but remembered myself saying, "if we do nothing more than this." I was trapped in a web of my own making, unless she took things further.

A few moments later, she rolled over on her side and my hand fell to the mattress as she moved closer. I could feel her breath against the side of my face. I wanted desperately to roll over, but instead reached out again. This time I found her arm.

"Would it be better if I turned the light on?" she asked.

"Yes," I replied, and struggled to reach the lamp myself.

The dim rays illuminated the bed, and I could see her in what I thought would be all her glory. But she wasn't naked. She had removed her robe, but she still had on her pajamas. The naked skin I had touched was her leg, where the shorts had been pushed up when she got into bed.

"Not what you expected?" she queried, running her hand over my arm.

"No, I thought you were—"

"I know what you thought," she confirmed, her fingers leaving my arm to trace my lips. "But you didn't know what to do, did you?"

"Er.. huh-uh," I admitted, shaking my head slightly.

"You felt helpless, didn't you?"

"Umph. Well, I couldn't—"

She silenced me by putting her finger to my lips. "Now do you understand why I want to wait? I don't want you feeling helpless like that. And I don't want to feel like I'm taking advantage of you. No, now," she admonished, as I started to speak, "just listen for a moment. I want you; you know I do. But I want you to be able to move away or walk away if you want to, understand?"

"Yes, but that could take months."

"Not necessarily. But even if it does..." I turned away, feeling rejected because I was crippled. She gently brought my face back around toward her. "Even it if does, Faith, won't it be better? Listen to me. Some people date for years and never—"

"That was years ago," I snapped, immediately regretting voicing this argument.

"All right, tell me, how do you picture the first time we make love? I know you've thought about it. I certainly have. Or are you just after a quick roll on your bed, hmm?"

I glared at her for that last remark, but knew I deserved it. As a matter of fact, I'd reminded myself of a couple of my boyfriends when I threw the argument back that dating without sex was something people used to do years ago. I was reminding myself of my old boyfriends more and more here lately. But, my God, it was so hard not to want her close! I'd finally found what I'd been looking for all these years, and what I'd been avoiding, as well. I had finally found my wings, and now was eager for my first test flight.

"Well?" she prodded.

"I...I don't know what I imagined it being like. I..."

"Wouldn't you like to be able to roll over here right now? Touch me, kiss me...crawl on top of me?"

"Yes," I admitted, my stomach tensing up with anticipation, thinking how much I'd like to be doing that right this minute.

"If we wait, sweetheart, it can be beautiful. Remember the song...I promise, I'll be worth the wait," she whispered in my ear.

A tear formed in the corner of my eye and rolled down the side of my face.

"Bear with me, sweetheart. I know I've caused a lot of this, because I want you as much as you want me, if not more. But I promise, it'll be better this way."

"So what should I do, tie my hands and put glue on my lips before you come in here at night?" I asked sarcastically. I shook my head, knowing this was not how I meant it to sound. "I...I didn't mean that. It's just..."

"I know." She put her finger to my lips. "I know all too well. We just shouldn't go any further than this, hmm?" she added, running her finger around my lips. "I'm not a man who feels that he can't turn it off, but...I could very easily go too far, too soon, if you're persistent. As you can see, I'm not immune to your charms. Nor am I immune to losing my head, for that matter. And you're wearing my resistance down, that's for sure. More happened here tonight than I intended."

"Sara, I love you."

"I love you, too, Faith."

She stayed that night until I fell asleep, I suppose. The last thing I remember was the feel of her arm draped across my side.

The next few days went by pretty quickly, what with the new therapy added in. I was able to move my legs a little more using the parallel bars and maintain my balance standing in the pool. Walking—well, that was another matter; that would take time. Sara was her usual cheerful self, but I was a bit restrained, trying to control the urges inside myself. I'd had my wings clipped and was slowly adjusting to life without thoughts of flying, for the time being.

As Friday approached, I resigned myself to the reality that she'd made the right decision. At this point in my recovery, sex of any kind would have been a bit strained. I knew it would definitely be much better if I could move around easily. Her way was best for both of us. I had just been far too eager to jump headlong into this new and exciting experience.

Friday came, and Pierre offered to trim my own hair, free of charge, evening up both sides before applying the wig. I had to admit, he performed quite a transformation. When Sara saw the finished product, she thought it was nice, but voiced her own questions about my original hair color. When Brandon saw it, however, he nearly flipped. He went on and on and on about how he couldn't get over the resemblance. I was now a living doll. Not just a princess, but a living doll.

Yes, Chatty Cathy's string had definitely been given several good yanks that night, and many was the time I felt like pulling out his batteries—and would've, if he'd had any. This time he introduced me to everyone as his princess and a living doll, embarrassing me to no end. I noticed several people looking at us both quite strangely, although most seemed more accepting of me this time. I suppose I looked a bit more "normal" to them, even though I was still in a wheelchair. Several of them even came over and started a conversation with me.

When I had first considered wearing the wig—looking like my mother, the way I had always wanted—I'd never envisioned the way other people would see me. I'd always heard blondes had more fun, but I'd never heard a wig could get you many future offers from eligible men. But it did. Or else my uncle had set me up. I wasn't exactly sure which.

While I was slowly buzzing through the crowd in my electric chair—which I had insisted on, since I didn't want to be Brandon's "living doll," pushed around the room in her carriage the entire evening—I was accosted by a young associate of his, who stepped in front of me and boldly introduced himself. I wanted to tell the brash Mr. Graham that he took quite a risk doing this because I was a horrible driver, but instead I smiled and said it was nice to meet him. Needless to say, those four few words were just what he wanted to hear. And throughout the remainder of the evening, I couldn't shake him. For some unknown reason, the pleasant young man—in his late 20s, with dark brown, neatly trimmed hair and thin moustache to match—seemed intent on being with me. Of course, he wasn't really a nuisance; I just didn't want to mislead him in any way.

Toward the end of the evening, when I'd had a few glasses of champagne that he'd insisted on getting for me, he asked if I'd like to take a stroll with him. At first I made some comment about my driving and sweetly refused. But then I noticed Sara standing across the room by the buffet table, having an animated and seemingly enjoyable conversation with a rather attractive woman about her age. I was suddenly extremely jealous. Now I was the one with the chameleon eyes, because the green-eyed monster, jealousy, certainly had me by the throat. Sara turned and glanced over at me, holding two glasses of champagne in her hands, one of which she handed to the woman next to her. I promptly turned back to Mr. Graham and accepted his offer.

While we strolled around the pool at a leisurely pace, he talked mostly about himself, as all men tend to do. He told me his plan was to one day own a large corporation like Brandon's. He was a junior associate at present, but moving up rapidly. I knew he was trying to impress me, but I was only half listening. I couldn't keep my mind off Sara and that woman. Although I'd gotten jealous once before over the name of her car, which turned out to be her way of teasing me, this was real. That green-eyed monster was rapidly eating away at me.

Brandon had arranged a spectacular fireworks display, but I

didn't enjoy it nearly as much as I could have if Sara had been by my side instead of the brash Mr. Graham. From our separate positions on the patio, I glanced over at her on several occasions, envy crawling around inside my heart upon seeing the attractive woman standing next to her. And although Sara raised a glass of champagne in my direction on one these occasions, this did not allay my fears in the least.

Up in my room, with three more glasses of champagne under my belt, I lost my cool and blew up at her. I demanded to know who the woman was. I was sure I'd met her, but how was I supposed to remember all those names? Sara explained that she was someone she had met at another party thrown by a patient's family, and that the woman was interested in working with disabled people.

Continuing in the same vein and not straying from the asinine character I'd already been displaying that evening, I demanded to know who the other woman was—the one she had slept with quite a while back before we even started dating, or whatever it was we were doing. No sooner had she begun explaining than I cut her off and would not let her continue. I could tell from her unconcerned tone of voice that this person had been a one-night stand. And so I lit into her again.

"I thought you said if sex was all I wanted from you, I wouldn't get it. And yet isn't that what you did with that one?" I accused.

"That's different," she responded. "I was drunk, and she was coming on to me."

"Now you sound like a man. 'Well, who's going to refuse it when it's thrown in your face?'" I declared, mimicking a few guys I'd heard voice this excuse to their girlfriends. "Was she *that* irresistible, Sara? Just because she could move her damn legs?"

"Faith, you're drunk," she proclaimed, and then turned and exited the room posthaste.

She was right. I was drunk, I was way out of line, and I was *completely* out of control. The green-eyed monster had nearly strangled me with envy, and I'd tried to drown it with alcohol. The end result being one very jealous, cantankerous drunk—namely me. After taking my tight dress off and struggling out of the chair in a drunken stupor, I must have passed out on the bed, because the next thing I remember, Sara was putting a nightgown on me. Although I don't remember a lot about what happened during that time, I do remember touching her and pleading with her to make love to me.

Needless to say, the next morning I had one hell of a hangover and felt like a complete jackass. I vowed never to drink like that again, no matter whom I saw Sara talking to. When I apologized for my asinine behavior as soon as I laid eyes on her, she said that she forgave me.

This episode passed, as did many more disagreements and arguments; for it seemed the stronger I became, the more she pushed me; the harder she pushed, the more tension developed between us. Of course, the kissing and making up was well worth the arguing.

My birthday came around on the twelfth of July, as it did every year, and Brandon wanted to throw another gala ball, but I wanted no part of that. It was *my* birthday, and I thought I should be able to have the things I wanted. And all I wanted was a small party with a few friends. Needless to say, that evening my small party turned into another gala performance because he invited all his friends as a surprise. I was surprised all right, but not in a nice way. I grinned and bore it for as long as I could, then sought the privacy of my own rooms, where Sara had to calm me down because I was ranting and raving about him spoiling my party.

July stormed its way into August, and August burnt its way into September. By this time, I was on my feet and using a walker for support. No longer confined to the wheelchair, I trudged about the house and grounds, slowly but more independently. Every morning now, instead of the pool therapy, Sara and I took walks around the grounds. We weren't able to cover up little displays of affection as easily now, so they became infrequent at best when we were outside the privacy of my room.

Jason would be returning to school after Labor Day, and I already missed him, for he'd begun withdrawing, as if preparing himself for the inevitable. Brandon had grown more demanding of my time, seemingly in step with my progress and his slow, but deliberate ushering of Sara into the background, where he seemed to feel she belonged. Sara and I no longer spent any amount of time together in the evenings. She had me from eight a.m. to four p.m. only; he took up the remainder of my evenings, sometimes staying long past eleven, which I knew was his usual bedtime.

He also began growing more insistent that I wear the wig in his presence, even though my hair had grown out and Pierre had cut and styled it for me. It was short, but at least it was mine and not a scratchy old wig. Sara thought my hairstyle was cute, and I grew to like it as well. It was cool and easy to handle, but I didn't like the color. It was coming back a mousy, dull brown, which no one had a satisfactory explanation for. Soon I began ignoring Brandon's request for me to wear the wig, and he finally stopped asking.

My relationship with Sara was tranquil. I no longer pushed her for more than she was willing to give during those few stolen moments before bedtime, but we were still close. Sometimes too close for Brandon's tastes, I assumed, from the remarks he'd make now and then, though he never came out and said anything directly. He continued to bring me a glass of milk on occasion, to which Sara still had an aversion. I drank very little of it.

To occupy my free time, when Sara and I were not working and Brandon wasn't demanding my undivided attention, I tried to solve a few mysteries. Ashley's death was a moot issue, so I turned my attention to her mother's death. Why had Vivian committed suicide in front of her thirteen-year-old daughter, I wanted to know? I got nowhere with that one, either, because any of the staff who had known her would only clam up at the mention of her name. Brandon's orders, I assumed.

I then turned my attention to Sara's Swiss cheese of a past. But that was a wash, too, for I didn't have the resources that a private investigator would. Yet I knew there had to be a way to find out, and one day I intended to do just that.

Labor Day came, and just as Sara had predicted, Brandon threw a big party. It didn't have a Southern theme, however. As a matter of fact, there seemed to be no theme at all. It was just another one of his business parties, as far as I could tell. I quickly grew bored, retiring to my room for a few moments of peace, hoping that Sara would follow. But she seemed to think it best if she kept her distance. Instead, I saw her walking around the grounds by herself.

Seeing her down there, as well as my own reflection in the window pane, I seriously began to think about leaving sooner than I had intended. This house had become a prison for both of us. She was being pushed out the door, while I was being kept inside.

"Sara, I want to leave here," I stated bluntly when she sat down on the bed that night.

"What? Where will you go?"

"Well, I thought we could leave together, but...I guess I was wrong about that, huh?" I looked away, my feelings hurt that she hadn't jumped at my proposal, despite its ambiguity.

"You mean you'd really take a chance on me?" she asked softly.

I looked up, wondering how she could ask such a thing. "Of course."

"Have you really thought this over? You'd be alone in my apartment, because you know I'm never there."

"You mean if I was there, you still wouldn't come home?"

This time she looked away. "I...I've never made a commitment to anyone, Faith."

"Yes, you have. You make a commitment to your patients."

"That's different; that's a job."

"Oh, I see. So, all along, I've been just a job."

"You know better than that. But my job requires me to be away from home a lot. I mean, I'm living here, Faith. I have lived with each patient in their fancy houses."

"Does the job require this? Or is this your way of not having to return to an empty apartment?"

"Damn," she cursed, as she got to her feet. "Stop shining that goddamn analytical spotlight of yours on me."

"Truth hurt?" I asked softly.

"Damn it, Faith," she cursed and flopped down in her chair.

"Do you love me, Sara?"

She offered no reply, but merely stared out the window.

"Not enough to make a commitment and live with me, huh?"

"What would we live on? Love?" she asked, her tone bordering on sarcasm.

"Oh, money worries you, huh? What, you think I'm sponging off my rich uncle here? I've got news for you, sweet cheeks, I inherited half of Neilson enterprises the same day my whole world went straight to hell in a hand basket." I crossed my arms over my stomach and turned away.

"I...I wasn't aware..."

"Does money change everything, Sara? Think if I have money, I won't miss you if you..." I bit my lip and willed the tears back. "Just forget it. It was a stupid idea." I reached over, grabbed my walker, and got out of bed.

Ambling into the bathroom, I shut the door behind me and broke down in tears. It was obvious she hadn't come to terms with her past. Nothing had changed for her: I was still a job she could walk away from when things got rough. And I assumed she preferred it that way. Perhaps she was even considering walking away now. I was stronger, I was up on my feet, and I was, for the most part, independent of her, so now she could leave without a guilty conscience. But she was going to take my heart with her, ripping it right out of my chest when she passed through those front doors.

It took a while, but I finally got myself together again and opened the door to the bathroom. I half expected to find her still sitting in her chair, but she wasn't. I sighed heavily and started making my way over to the bed.

"Faith?" She put her hand on my shoulder, and I nearly stumbled all over myself trying to get away. She'd scared me half out of my wits. "I'm sorry, I didn't mean to frighten you, I thought you saw me," she apologized.

"Saw you? Where the hell *were* you?"

Pointing toward the bathroom door, she said, "You walked right past me."

I now saw a rectangular hole in the wall near the bathroom door that looked like a small door itself, except it was only the height of the wainscoting—a little over four feet—and there was no apparent handle. "What the hell is that?"

"I think it's some kind of secret passageway. C'mere and look." She gestured to it and even helped me turn around.

"How did you find this?" I queried, bending over and looking into the dark little opening.

"I was just standing here by the bathroom door and..." She paused as she looked up at me, then quickly looked down and cleared her throat.

"Go on," I prodded. I was too intrigued by her discovery to revisit our previous discussion.

"Well, like I said, I was just standing by the door, and I leaned up against this wall here..." She demonstrated how she had leaned up against it with her behind, one leg bent at the knee, the bottom of her foot resting on the wall. "And it sort of gave with my weight. So I went and got your nail file, and... Well, I made a mess of the paint in a few places, but..."

"Who gives a flying fig about the paint?" I murmured, taking a few more steps forward, then bending over the walker and peeking inside the darkness of the small space. I was a little afraid of going in; too many late-night horror movies, I suppose.

"Boo," she hissed next to my ear.

"Damn you, Sara! Did you go in here?"

"A little ways, not far," she replied, leaning over my shoulder to see around me. "Too dark, and I haven't got a flashlight, have you?"

"What do I look like, a Boy Scout?" I retorted.

"Not by a long shot," she quipped, right next to my ear. I looked over my shoulder at her; she merely smiled and arched her eyebrows. "I feel like this is one of those Abbott and Costello movies. Remember those?" she asked.

"Never liked 'em."

"Me neither, but I'm sure we look like them right now, me peeking over your shoulder like this."

"Think Abbott and Costello had a thing—?" I stopped short, remembering our previous discussion.

She gazed into my eyes. "I'm sorry, Faith. Please, give me
more time. I mean, I love you, but I'm so afraid of hurting you.
That's what I wanted to say to you. I was standing out here, debat-
ing whether to barge in or not. I didn't want to knock because I
was afraid you'd tell me to go away." She paused, giving me time
to digest this information. "I do love you, Faith," she whispered,
putting her arm around my waist. "So much," she added, and
placed a kiss on my neck.

"What is this?" I asked, clearing my throat and trying to
inject a bit of levity. "You get me in a small, dark, cramped place
and take advantage of me?"

"Sounds like a good idea to me," she teased, squeezing my
side.

"Oh, be serious," I remarked, looking back into the darkness.

"I am. We could use this as a hide-out," she suggested.

"Um-hmm. You're all talk, I know you. Know where we can
get our hands on a flashlight?" I asked, changing the subject. "I'd
like to check this out. I wish there was more light in the room,
but..."

"I know where I can find a candle," she offered.

"Oh great, and have it blow out on us while we're looking
around, hmm?"

"Knowing us, we'd be the ones to blow it out," she snickered.

"You *are* in an Abbott and Costello movie. Now cut it out;
I'm being serious here."

"Okay, seriously, Faith, what do you think we're going to find
in there, hmm?"

"I don't know. What are you suggesting?"

"That we wait until morning, round up a flashlight, and then
check it out. Makes no sense to do it now. Hell, with our luck,
we'd end up making enough noise to wake the whole house."

"Well, you're the one who opened it," I reminded, glancing
over my shoulder. "Don't blame me for getting my curiosity
stirred up."

"Ooh, you're a hellion when you're mad," she teased, breathing in my ear.

"And just who pulled your string, missy?"

"You did. You made me think I might lose you. I don't want
to lose you, Faith," she admitted, placing her face next to my ear.
"Please, give me time."

"Like you've given me time to heal?"

She merely cocked her head to one side. "Come on, we'll save
this for in the morning. Right now..."

I saw the look in her eyes as they darted back and forth,

searching mine. I knew she was asking me to forgive her and reassure her that things were all right between us. Just as she had done for me so many times when I had made a mess of things.

I nodded in agreement, and she helped me back up and turn around. "How are you going to get that thing shut?" I asked, watching her attempt to close the door and realizing she had nothing to hold on to once she could no longer get her fingers around the edge of the panel.

"Must be some way of doing this," she remarked, looking at the side of the door. "I mean, whoever built the damn thing surely made a way to shut it from this side. Don't you think?"

"What's that down there by the molding? No, there," I directed. "See that place near the very bottom of the door?"

She pulled the door open to reveal a small piece of what appeared to be leather, painted white and nailed to the inside of the panel. She maneuvered it out a little ways and then used it to pull the door closed.

"Look at that, the way it's painted and lays down behind the molding, you can't even see it," she said, astonishment in her voice. "Now we have our own secret door," she added in a ghoulish voice, arching her eyebrows up and down. She stood up and faced me. "Shame it doesn't run between my room and yours, hmm?"

"Maybe it does," I suggested.

She shrugged. "I doubt it. But we'll find out tomorrow." She looked back at the opening, the tiny nicks in the paint being the only visible indications of its presence. "Never was much good with a knife. Couldn't cut a straight line to save my life. Remember those damn little scissors they always gave you to cut with in grade school?"

"Sara—"

"Dull as shit, and then hurt your hand when you used 'em. And they wanted you to have fun. Give me finger paints any day. Remember how that stuff used to smell?"

"Sara—" I said again, louder.

"What, sweetheart?" She put her arm around my waist and started helping me toward the bed.

For a moment, I was afraid to mention it, but felt I had to. "Sara—"

"Yes, Faith?" She stopped and looked at me questioningly. "What? What is it?"

"You remembered," I said simply.

"Huh?" she inquired, obviously not comprehending.

"The holes in the Swiss cheese are filling in."

She stared at me for a moment, then looked down at the floor. Inhaling sharply, she mumbled, "I did remember, didn't I? Those little scissors...the finger paints..." She paused, looking awestruck. "I even remembered the smell."

"How about the Abbott and Costello movies?"

She stared at me as her mouth dropped open and tears welled up in her eyes.

"You didn't like 'em, but you remember 'em," I added, my eyes becoming misty, as well.

"God, I love you," she stated, and grabbed me around the neck, nearly knocking me off balance.

"Sara..."

"Hmm?"

"I think you should go to your room now," I whispered in her ear.

She blinked her eyes a couple of times and looked over her shoulder at me. "I love you." Words so soft and beautiful uttered in a sleepy voice, the expression in her drowsy green eyes affirming their sincerity. All of a sudden, she frowned. "What the hell?" She abruptly sat up in the bed and looked down at me. "What did... I didn't drink anything, did I? What did I do?" she questioned, seeming quite bewildered.

"You fell asleep, that's all. Believe me, when you do *that*, I'll make sure you remember it the next morning," I quipped.

"What time is it?" She ran her fingers through her hair.

"Four-thirty," I replied, having read the clock only moments before.

"Damn, the servants'll be getting up soon."

"What? How do you know what time the servants get up?"

"Huh?" She shook her head. "What the hell did I just say?" She rubbed her eyes.

"I think you're still half asleep. Go catch a few more hours, and then I want to find out more about our secret door."

"Huh? What secret..."

"Just go get some sleep," I suggested.

She got up slowly and glanced around the room as if she didn't recognize it, then made a beeline for the bathroom. I waited a good while for her to come out. Thinking she may have gone back to sleep on the john, I started to get up and go see about her.

Just then the bathroom door opened. "My head's a fucking mess," she muttered, half stumbling across the room. "Goodnight," she added, and walked out the door, leaving it ajar.

"I'll say," I agreed with her first assessment. Getting out of bed to shut the door, I couldn't help but wonder if the emotional upheaval of the night before had something to do with her regaining bits and pieces of her memory. "I hope it all comes back for you," I said quietly, closing the door. "And I hope there's nothing bad, like you think."

Chapter
12

"Where'd you get the flashlight?" I asked, as she aimed the dim beam of light into the small, dark entrance.

"I poked around downstairs. There's a lot of stuff in the basement," she replied, the beam of light coming to rest on a wall just a few feet away.

There were rows of shelves, starting about three feet off the floor and extending up over our heads. The highest shelf was about six feet up, and wider than the rest. Perched precariously near its edge was an old tin can: *Maxwell House—good to the last drop*. The rest of the shelves were bare, except for years of accumulated dust and cobwebs. She panned the light around the periphery of the small closet-like space and found two more sets of shelves—same height and width—running down the length of the side walls.

"What do you think? Should I?" she asked, motioning to the coffee tin.

I nodded, wondering what we might find. She bent down, went inside, and picked up the coffee tin, bringing down dust and cobwebs with it. "Here, hold the flashlight," she said, handing it back to me, then brushing a cobweb out of her face. She slowly looked inside the tin, as if afraid of what she might find. A smile twitched at the corners of her lips. "We found ourselves a bloomin' fortune," she announced, glancing around at me.

"What?" I asked, getting excited.

She reached in the tin can and brought out something in her hand. Slowly extending it in my direction, palm up, she opened her hand, revealing two Indian head pennies, an old Liberty half-dollar, three Mercury dimes, and a broken pendant with a red rosebud on it.

"Like I said, a *bloomin'* fortune," she reiterated with a big smile.

"Oh, you."

She giggled like a little girl while putting the coffee tin and pendant back.

"What are you going to do with the money?" I queried.

"Save it for our future."

"Oh, so you *do* think we have one?"

A smile graced her face once again as she exchanged the money for the flashlight. Illuminating the walls again and even looking behind the panel door, she asked, "What do you think, some type of closet?"

"I don't know. Closet doors usually open up to the outside, not the inside. Don't they?"

She nodded agreement. "I hadn't thought of that. So what was this, do you think?"

"Maybe some secret storage room?" I was still standing in the bedroom, itching to go inside. "I do know that whoever made it didn't want it seen from the outside."

"Yeah. And it hasn't been used in a while. I went through two, maybe three layers of paint to get— Hold the phone," she announced, running her finger down the side of one of the shelves.

"What is it?"

"There's a separation here and..." She paused, grunting as she pushed on the shelf. "C'mere and hold the light."

I pushed the small door open wider, its old hinges squealing a mild protest. Then I ducked down and maneuvered into the small space. It was a tight fit: the two of us, *and* my clunky walker.

She handed me the flashlight. "I felt this thing move a while ago. Let me try again." She pushed on the shelf with both hands. The coffee tin above her head rattled with the force of her shove, and the wall—from about head height down—opened like the other small door. We both glanced up at the tin can. *If she hadn't moved that,* I thought, *it might've hit her in the head.* "Shine the light in there," she said, sounding a bit excited herself now.

"Guess that shoots down our little mystery, hmm?" I said, peeking over her shoulder.

She took the flashlight from me. "Closet in the sitting room?" she queried, motioning up toward the steel rod overhead that ran the length of the space.

"That'd be my guess," I answered, noting the doorframe a few feet away, highlighted by the beam of light.

"Only one way to find out." She ducked down and moved over to the door. The hinges squeaked as she slowly opened it, and light edged into the closet from the window across the way. "What do you think...an adjoining closet?"

"I don't know," I murmured. My first thought was that it had been a hiding place for slaves. Yet that didn't make much sense. *Slaves hiding in the house? Don't think so.* My second thought was about Sherman's march to the sea. It was said that in the final days of the Civil War, after General Sherman fought his way into Georgia, Union troops pillaged, plundered, and even burned their way from Atlanta to the coast of Savannah. How this plantation had survived intact, I had no idea. It made sense to me that this may have been a hiding place for the plantation owner's valuables, and I suggested as much to Sara.

"Could be. It has two entrances, so somebody wanted to be sure they weren't trapped in here," she commented while searching the other walls of the sitting room closet for more niches or hidden doors. "Nothing there." She pulled the small door shut in the same way she'd closed the other one the night before, another piece of leather. The hinges protested again, and the tin can rattled. "Wanted to be sure these doors stayed hidden and could be closed from this side," she remarked.

I merely nodded in agreement.

She panned the light around the hidden closet some more. I now noted that the interior walls were paneled with unpainted, rough-hewn wood, unlike the sitting-room closet. My second impression still held water for me. It stood to reason this space would have been built on short notice if the owner had feared being ransacked and robbed by Union troops; ergo, the rough unpainted wood.

"You're probably right," she noted. "The sitting-room closet was probably downsized. It probably takes up enough room to fool the eye, so no one would even suspect this was here."

"Wonder why those shelves up there are wider?" I queried aloud.

"Your guess is as good as mine," she responded, reaching around me and pushing on the far left hand set of shelves. She sighed heavily when it didn't move. "Damn, I thought we'd found something. I was all ready to find more hidden doors, an old staircase, maybe even a tunnel out to the road for quick escapes." She glanced over at me, disappointment written all over her face. "Pretty silly, huh?"

"No. I had expectations, too, you know. I couldn't wait to get in here." I was more disappointed than I was letting on. I'd had high hopes of finding something old and valuable in this hidden space. As a child, I'd dreamed of being an archaeologist, or at least finding something important that had been hidden away for years and years. Guess that's why I liked the story of the old hermit and Windell's Point.

This thought reminded me of Jason, and then Brandon. I wondered if either one knew about this. "Wonder if this is what Brandon meant about maintaining the integrity of the house?" I voiced aloud.

"Oh, you mean the renovations? Hmph," she grunted. "Stands to reason he should know about it. But then again..."

"Then again, what?"

"Like I said before, I went through a few layers of paint—at least two, maybe more. So it's possible he doesn't know. He doesn't live on this end, after all." She glanced over at me and shrugged. "Speaking of paint, that reminds me, I need to go back to the basement and try and find this color, so I can touch up those nicks out there."

"Why bother?"

"Well, just in case he doesn't know, then we'll have ourselves a secret hideaway." She arched her eyebrows suggestively.

"It's hardly big enough for *that*," I countered.

She shrugged again. "Just a thought. Can't blame a girl for trying."

"I hear you, I just don't believe it. What's come over you?"

"I don't know, maybe it's the mystery...the intrigue... Or it could be having you trapped in such a small, dark space." The latter was said in a sinister voice as she wrapped one arm around my waist. "Didn't I tell you I was a vampire?" She leaned over swiftly and attacked my neck.

"Nooo. I believe you neglected to share that little bit of information. But," I turned my head to one side allowing her better access, and hissed like a vampire in the movies, "who's really trapped with whom, hmm, my dear?"

"I love you, Faith," she whispered in my ear. "Believe me, this is as hard on me as it is on you. Maybe more so." She nibbled on my neck as both arms wrapped around my waist, flashlight and all. "God, how I want you right this minute." Her right hand began moving toward my breast.

I didn't want her to stop, but I felt she should. She was only teasing both of us. "Ah-ah-ah," I said, grabbing her hand. "Remember, you don't want to take advantage of me."

She groaned. "Oh well, guess our little mystery and adventure is a wash, huh? Well, I should get out of here first so you can turn around easier."

"That might help."

Maneuvering the walker around was hard enough, but even more so in such a tight space. I finally managed it, however.

"Now to find that paint," she suggested, shutting the hidden door behind me.

"It's not that bad. Besides, what does it matter if he knows we found it?"

"How are you going to explain what I was doing by the bathroom door?"

"Hmph. Well, I'll...I'll say I hit it with my walker."

She glanced down at the molding. "Won't wash," she objected. "You'd hit the molding first." She flashed a half smirk as if to say, *You know I'm right.*

"So, what happens if you can't find the paint?" I didn't want her leaving right away. I had designs on finishing what she'd started in the hidden closet.

"Well, then I know a..." She bit her lip and didn't finish.

"Know a what?" I prodded.

"I know a woman who has her own painting company."

I sighed heavily. "One of your exes, I assume?"

"I don't have exes. They're just friends. It's not like I went around promising these women anything and then not delivering. What they may have assumed is something different."

"You mean as long as you didn't say 'I promise to love you and live with you,' you don't owe them anything, is that it?"

She frowned. "I seldom said I love you, come to think of it. That should've told them something, right?"

I sighed heavily once again and started toward the bed. "Whatever."

She followed behind me. "I'm a terrible person, hmm?"

"I didn't say that. But why didn't you ever stay with any of them?"

"I don't know. It just never felt right, somehow. Maybe I just wasn't right, up here." She tapped her head.

"You've been making excuses and running for too long, Sara." I sat down on the bed and made eye contact with her.

She glanced from me to the unmade bed. "Yeah, well, I'd better go look for that paint." She abruptly wheeled around and left the room.

Two disappointments in one day! I fell back crossways on the bed and made a sound with my lips like a tired horse.

For several weeks, right after her initial memory breakthrough and our shared disappointment about the hidden closet,

Sara became withdrawn and spent a lot of time in her room. She was slowly regaining tiny bits and pieces of her memory. I could tell it was frustrating for her. It was almost like being handed puzzle pieces, a few at a time, which you tried to fit together and make sense out of without knowing what the finished product should look like. And there was no box readily available where you could just reach in and draw out more pieces to consider, if these weren't to your liking.

Slowly, day by day, as the weather grew a little cooler, Sara started acting more like her old self. She stopped trying to force the memories, which seemed to have their own agenda about how and when to surface, as well as how much to reveal. The Swiss cheese was filling in, but it seemed to be a selective filling, which might well take years or possibly never be completely whole again.

September breezed into October, and the trees started putting on their autumn coats of many colors. From my window, I could see what I called a small patchwork quilt starting on the sloping hills surrounding the estate. Shady Grove was a beautiful place, but it was not a place where I had been happy for very long.

Halloween came, and Brandon threw an elaborate party. He even hired some carnival people to set up a haunted house out on the grounds. I dressed up as an elderly man. I figured that, aside from an elderly woman, this was the only thing that went with a walker. Since I didn't want to wear the wig, I merely donned a hat. Sara came up with a coat and a pair of women's pants that were too long in the inseam. I pulled the pants nearly up to my breasts and put on a thin belt, then blacked out a tooth for good measure.

Of course, as he escorted me down the stairway, Brandon frowned on my choice, but I wasn't about to wear the fairy princess outfit he'd chosen for me. My excuse to him was "I've never seen a crippled fairy." And I wasn't about to walk around with wings on my back that I couldn't use, at least not amongst his so-called friends. In my opinion, that would be asking for trouble. Someone would inevitably remark, "I thought fairies could fly," and I'd get pissed. And besides, at this of all parties, where everyone was free to dress any way they chose, I wanted to be me, not someone Brandon had managed to gussy up to look like my mother.

Entering the living room, where the buffet and drink tables had been set up, I looked around for Sara. She had refused to tell me what she would be wearing, which made me a little uneasy at first. But then again, I'd always enjoyed a good mystery.

Everyone was dressed a bit unusually at this little bash, or so I thought, taking in all the masks and expensive-looking costumes.

At first I didn't like the masks because I couldn't tell who was who. After roaming around a while, however, I started to enjoy guessing whose face was hidden under what mask. Cleopatra was Lynn Darbon, Brandon's secretary. The old hag was none other than Celia. Julius Caesar was Brandon's vice president, and Zorro was Kevin Graham, the man I had met at a previous party and couldn't seem to lose. I was relieved to see him accompanied by a Cinderella whom I didn't know. But that was nothing new; I actually knew the names of less than a third of the people milling around.

Finally giving up on finding Sara in the living room, I made my way out to the haunted house. Surely I would find her there.

As I maneuvered my way through the small hallways, dummies covered with fake blood popped out of walls and coffins; spiders, bats, and other assorted creepy crawlies scuttled, flew, or moved in some fashion in order to frighten the passerby. And despite telling myself I wouldn't do it again, I jumped and yipped every time. Nearing the end, I noticed a very real-looking dummy over in a dark corner, and was prepared for this one to jump out at me or do something equally as scary for the finale when the figure spoke. I nearly leapt out of my shoes right then and there.

"Meet me upstairs," a sultry voice whispered.

"Wh-What?" I asked, trying to calm my racing heart.

The figure stepped out of the darkness, and I was face to face with Elvira, Mistress of the Dark. It took me a few moments to recognize Sara underneath all the makeup and long dark hair. I glanced down at the costume and was not surprised to find she filled out the dress better than Elvira herself.

"Meet me upstairs," she said seductively, running one long, red fingernail over my lips. "And make sure you aren't followed."

"Why?" I called after her.

She didn't even glance back as she disappeared into the darkness of the haunted house. I wasn't sure what she was up to, but definitely wanted to find out. The plunging neckline on that dress was enough to make me want to take the stairs two at a time. Of course, that was out of the question, since I could barely manage one.

I strolled back to the buffet tables and got something to eat, mingled around, killed a little time, and hit the champagne table twice for good measure. I found Brandon a while later and thanked him for the wonderful party, kissing him on the cheek for emphasis, since I had enjoyed this one more than the others. I especially liked the fact that he hadn't seen fit to drag me around introducing me to everyone.

As he returned the kiss, narrowly missing my mouth, I could smell the liquor on his breath. I told him I was going to bed early, all this excitement having worn me out. He seemed to buy my story. Either that, or he was just too far gone to care. He said he'd give me my goodnight kiss right then. I made sure I turned my head so that his lingering, wet kiss landed on my cheek. "Love you, Princess," he whispered. I merely nodded.

I knew he loved to play host and sometimes drank too much, although I'd never seen him sloppy drunk. But I had seen him pretty happy, and I could tell by his bloodshot eyes, he was bordering on quite happy. It wouldn't take long before he'd be chatting up the single, intoxicated ladies.

I moved slowly through the crowd, making my way back to the kitchen. Usually the parties were contained in the living room and patio area, but tonight there were people everywhere. I passed one couple necking by the double-door refrigerator. It appeared neither one was in any condition to care who was watching. To me, it was like catching a glimpse of an X- or at least R-rated movie, because you could tell by the way they were going at each other, something was definitely going to happen. Scenes from the movie *Fatal Attraction* flashed through my mind as I saw his hand lift her skirt. *Garter belt, no less*, I thought, and kept moving.

Holding on to the walker, I sat down in the lift chair and ascended the stairway. *Nothing like riding backwards up a flight of narrow stairs while holding on to a bulky walker*, I thought. At the top, I heard noises from the east wing and looked down the long hallway. The only light I saw was coming from my sitting room. Sara had told me to meet her upstairs, so I proceeded down the hall, wondering what she was up to. I heard voices behind me and saw a couple entering one of the bedrooms on her side of the hall. I wondered if Brandon knew they were up here.

I went through the lighted sitting room, turned on the bedside lamp, and glanced around. The room was unoccupied. I felt disappointed for a moment, but then reasoned that she might not have anticipated me coming up this soon, so I went to the bathroom and removed my costume. Since I knew Brandon wasn't coming up, I donned only the top of my pj's. It was rare, having a chance to be reckless.

I had just climbed into bed when the light in my sitting room went off. I assumed it was Sara and she wanted to scare me, so I dimmed the lamp. "Princess," called Brandon. My heart sank. "Are you all right?"

"Yes, I'm fine, just a bit tired, as I told you."

"Well, I thought I'd say goodnight before you went to sleep," he said, as if he didn't remember doing so downstairs. Evidently, he was further gone than I'd presumed.

I noticed he carried a glass of milk in his hand. "Thank you," I said as he put it down on the nightstand. "Goodnight, Princess." He placed a long, lingering kiss on my cheek.

After he left, disappointment settled over me. I wondered if Sara had meant for me to meet her in her room. So, I got up, put on my shorts, and walked across the hall. She wasn't there, either. *She must have meant much later on,* I reasoned. Crossing the hall again, I glimpsed another couple disappearing into the darkness of one of the rooms; I was glad the walls were thick. I walked back into my bedroom and shut the double doors. I considered locking them because of the people coming upstairs, but still held out hope that Sara would soon be walking through them.

Turning around, I immediately noticed that the dim light, which should have been coming from my bedside lamp, was instead emanating from a large candle on the nightstand. Before I even had a chance to ponder this mystery, I heard a noise off to my right and my heart jumped up in my throat as a figure stepped out of the shadows of the bathroom. It was Sara.

"Holy-moly!" I gasped, noting the long, black, revealing negligee, which wasn't the costume she'd been wearing previously, although it appeared she had retained the wig since her hair was still dark. "You scared the shit out of me! Where have you been?"

"I've been waiting for you," she answered in a deep, sultry voice, as she moved toward me.

"Well, I've been right here, I just stepped out to—"

"Shh! No, please," she interjected, placing a finger against her own lips. "Don't say anything, Faith." My eyes had followed this movement and then slid over to her hair, the dark, silky mane highlighted by the candle's glow. *Great wig,* I thought absently, my gaze following those flowing tresses down to the plunging neckline of the negligee, which was cut into a V shape that ended just about her navel.

I swallowed audibly as she drew closer, the sheer fabric molded to her breasts. "There's something I want to say to you," she whispered, stopping in front of me. My gaze lifted to meet hers. Candlelight danced in those soft green depths. "Remember when I said someday we'd be together?" She reached up and took my face in her hands, leaning in closer still. "Well someday...is tonight," she breathed against my lips.

When our lips touched, a barely audible moan issued from my throat. A fire ignited in my loins as her wet tongue parted my lips and slid inside. My heart skipped a beat and my legs trembled while our tongues embarked upon that intriguing mating dance.

My heart was racing as she eased back from our passionate lip-lock. "Sure you're ready for this?" she inquired, her face hidden in shadow now. I could only imagine her eyes darting back and forth, searching mine as they often did.

"Y-Yes," I answered breathlessly.

She moved off to one side and I heard the door being locked behind me. Putting one arm around my waist, she took the walker from me with the other, setting it aside. "You won't be needing this anymore tonight."

My legs trembled as she led me to the bed. My heart was racing ninety miles an hour, my body tingling with anticipation. When she sat me down on the side of the bed, her gaze held mine for several heartbeats. Slowly, she reached out and touched my face. I kissed the palm of her hand. She smiled, and yet, I sensed a bit of hesitation on her part.

"What?" I ventured.

"I...I had this all planned in my mind, but..." She nibbled her lower lip.

When she offered nothing further, I finished for her, "But life isn't like the movies?"

"You got that right," she agreed, her thumb caressing my chin.

"Are you...having second thoughts?" I reached out for her other hand, our fingers interlacing without a moment's hesitation.

She shook her head. "No. I-I think I'm more nervous than you are." Her voice quavered. "I want this to be...memorable for you. I want everything...to be—"

"It doesn't have to be perfect," I interjected. "Let's just play it by ear, hmm? One kiss at a time."

This prompted a genuine smile. As she leaned over and our lips met once again, warmth surged through my being and my arms went around her neck. I lay back crossways on the bed, pulling her down with me.

"Oof!" she hissed against my cheek. I had felt her lose her balance and then catch herself with her elbows before her weight fell fully upon me. She quickly shifted her weight off to one side now. "Definitely not like the movies," she uttered, gazing down at me from her propped-up position.

"We don't know what happens between takes. We only see what they show us." My eyes drifted down to the negligee, where her left breast was barely concealed by the silky black material. I swallowed hard, feeling fireworks going off in my stomach. I wanted to see her body fully exposed to my view. I wanted to touch and explore.

Obviously noticing where my attention had strayed, she reached over and took my hand, placing it on her shoulder near the negligee's strap. No more prodding was necessary. My fingers inched beneath the thin material, my hand caressing her shoulder and arm while moving the strap out of the way.

I could feel her watching me as the negligee fell away, revealing her breast. My hand trembled as another fireball erupted in my lower abdomen. *Beautiful,* my mind declared, and my eyes were totally captivated by the sight of the light brown areole tightening and shrinking, while the budding nipple, a shade darker, gradually rose higher with each passing instant. The urge to touch this part of her anatomy, feel the changes as they happened, was overwhelming. I licked my lips involuntarily and met her gaze. Candlelight danced in those depths as she moved back just enough for my hand to slide off her arm and on to her breast.

A low moan escaped her lips, while a loud gasp exited mine. I closed my eyes as an intense explosion erupted in my groin area and sent sparks cascading in all directions. My hand did not leave her breast; however, it seemed to have a mind of its own now. I caressed the firm, round globe, my thumb rubbing back and forth across the burgeoning nipple. My analytical mind wanted to make sense of why this felt so good, but other forces overrode and silenced it.

The next thing I knew, she had one leg between mine, her hand on my thigh underneath the leg of my shorts. "We need to...scoot up...in the bed," she mumbled around the kisses she was showering upon my face and lips.

"Um-hmm," I agreed, but made no effort to do so. The hand in my shorts was inching beneath the backside of my underwear, the thigh between my legs pressing against the very center of my desire. I could hardly think, much less move.

"Get out...of these...clothes," she said, as if continuing her previous thought.

This somehow filtered through on a different level. *No clothes!* "You first," I said, and she moaned in response but didn't stop what she was doing: kissing my neck and caressing my backside.

"Sweet Jesus," she hissed, finally breaking contact. She sat up on the side of the bed, one breast exposed and the shoulder strap completely off her arm, dangling by her side. Her face bore a slight flush, her lips a rosy red hue; her hair framed all this in a dark oval. I thought she'd never looked more beautiful.

But I was wrong. For in the next few moments she was on her

feet, removing the other shoulder strap and allowing the negligee to slide off her body, forming a puddle at her feet. *Lovely* and *magnificent* were the words that came to mind as my eyes traversed the planes of her body. A trail of light brown fuzz down the center of her torso drew my eyes to the dark brown triangular patch of curls at the apex of her thighs.

In the next few minutes I realized just how right she had been about waiting until I could maneuver around on my own. Removing my clothes and properly positioning myself in the bed was not nearly as awkward or as hard as it could have been. I didn't feel helpless or vulnerable when she eased into bed beside me. As a matter of fact, while she hovered over me, her long hair falling around my face, I thought I had died and gone to heaven. And yet, in the next moment, I was once again proven wrong.

When her naked body touched mine—skin so warm, soft, and smooth—my breath left me completely. I was certain I was going to die right then and there. Moist lips caressed mine, an eager tongue probed the interior, and much-needed air was somehow drawn into my lungs. As with any fire, oxygen fed the flames of the inferno burning inside my loins. Every touch, every kiss, every sensation thereafter sent shockwaves throughout my system. The very center of my being was bombarded with one explosion after another as Sara slowly positioned herself between my thighs. We both moaned, though not quite in unison, hers sounding more like an echo of my own.

"Oh, God!" I breathed, my loins aflame and pulsing with lust.

"Sweet Jee-sus!" she hissed, pressing her lower body against mine.

My hands were soon in her hair, her lips sucking on my neck, our bodies moving in time to an intrinsic rhythm. In some distant part of my mind, it registered that the mass of hair in which my hands were intertwined was *not* a wig. I didn't dwell on it, however. Nor could I have, even if I'd wanted to, which I didn't. There were far more pressing issues at hand.

"I never dreamed...it would feel...this good," I murmured breathlessly.

"Oh yes, baby," she responded, her right hand trailing down my side, lips inching toward my mouth.

While she was kissing me, I felt her raise up slightly and slip her hand between our bodies. The first touch from her fingertips sent a shudder through me that rocked me all the way down to my toes. A small squeak emanating from my throat escaped our joined lips. A low moan was her response as fingertips inched further downward, stroking my desire.

I was now lost in an entirely new world composed solely of immensely pleasurable sensations. I could hear my moans and sighs as if they were coming from somewhere in the distance. It wasn't until a warm mouth closed around my left breast and a questing digit eased into my inner sanctuary that this world exploded and I was propelled into another one. I was floating, soaring, flying, and then blasting off into the outer reaches of some inner landscape, oblivious to everything else. I felt detached from my body for an all too brief and awe-inspiring moment. My body shuddered in response, gibberish streaming past my lips in a torrent. Colors resembling a fireworks display burst behind my closed lids. Tears stung my eyes as the scattered embers showered down around me like a fine mist of rain. "Uh-h-uh-uh-h," my mouth spewed forth over and over, as my lower body convulsed in spasms.

"Ahh, yes, baby," she softly whispered near my ear.

My body shuddered once more and then went limp as a dishrag. Tears sprang to my eyes in a surge of emotion that threatened to overwhelm me. I cried like a baby while she held me, raining kisses upon my face and neck.

"I'm...I'm s-s-sorry," I blubbered, once I regained some semblance of control.

"Shh...there's no need to be sorry, sweetheart," she soothed.

"But...I'm crying. I-I shouldn't cry...I should be...ha-happy."

She chuckled deep in her throat and nuzzled her face against mine. "Remember when we discussed how crying and laughing sometimes cause the same reactions—tears?"

"Umph" and a slight nod were the extent of my response.

She leaned up and looked down at me. "Well, this is one of those times when it's hard to tell the difference." A sweet smile graced her face as she reached down and wiped a tear from my cheek with her thumb.

"I-I love you, Sara," I blubbered.

"I love you too, Faith. So very much."

It took a while for the tears to subside and my emotions to return to normal, but once they did, I was ready, willing, and eager to at least attempt to bestow upon her the same pleasure she'd seen fit to provide in abundance for me. I felt awkward and clumsy at first, merely exploring the surface of her body. I found her nipples fascinating. The feel of those erect protrusions between my fingers was quite a stimulating experience. I had no idea how much more intoxicating these could be until I brazenly lowered my mouth onto one. She moaned in pleasure, her hand pressing against the back of my head, urging me onward. I sucked lightly on the engorged tissue, my tongue tantalized by a flavor I wouldn't soon forget. My taste buds seemed to erupt, sending lancing bolts of lightning down my torso, where they exploded inside my loins. She moaned louder and I sucked harder, and was rewarded once again with the unique taste sensations that had set the center of my desire pulsing.

"My...God!" I murmured, and went back for more.

She whimpered and shifted her left leg, which lay between mine, pushing it against my throbbing hub. My mind went blank as my body sought to satisfy its own urges by slowly rubbing against her leg. I was vaguely aware of her hand leading mine down to the dark brown thatch of curls at the juncture of her thighs. When my fingertips encountered the incredible warmth and moisture they found there, my own urges were suddenly shoved into the background. My hand once again had a mind of its own, my fingertips already inching their way into the silky, slick warmth.

"Oh yes," I mumbled against her breast. I couldn't ever remember these appendages encountering anything more inviting and exciting. "Show me how to please you," I whispered, my mouth leaving her breast for her lips.

She pressed my fingers against her, and then propelled them back and forth over the slick folds and protruding nub. She moaned in time with each slow stroke. In a burst of utter clarity, I now recalled what she had done to me. *I* took over from there, and moaned along with her when my middle finger slid effortlessly into her slick well of desire, the soft hot tissue initially yielding and encasing, then squeezing and relaxing in rhythm with each stroke.

"Uh-huh!" she breathed, her hand pressing against my back, her hips now arching and drawing me deeper. After a few moments, she urged, "M-More."

I wasn't sure exactly what she wanted, but pressed against her harder and raised up to gauge her reaction. Languid green eyes opened slowly and gazed up at me. "More of you...inside me," she murmured.

The mere words alone sent a shiver up my spine and heat rushing to my cheeks, and set off a series of volcanic eruptions in my loins. We moaned in unison as I sought to oblige her. She buried her face in the crook of my neck and her fingernails in the small of my back, her hips arching to meet each successive thrust.

"Oh yes, oh yes... Sweet Jesus, don't stop... Oh yeah, baby... Ung-h-h!" She shuddered several times. "Oh-oh-oh, ohhhh," she moaned, and her hips went still.

Her breathing was ragged, and I could feel her heart beating rapidly against my chest even as she showered my neck with light kisses. Progressing upward, she sucked on my earlobe and growled in my ear, while the inner walls of her desire contracted against my fingers. "Don't ever leave me," she whispered, wrapping both arms around me and then squeezing my buttocks.

"Never," I responded, feeling dampness against my cheek that had obviously come from her eyes.

Being with her that night was the most wonderful experience I'd ever had in my entire life. Our lovemaking far exceeded my expectations and fantasies. As we lay back, I expected this to be the end of our initial consummation, because in the movies the lovers usually smoked a cigarette afterward. Perhaps that's what they did in the movies, but resting was *not* what Sara had in mind. She didn't even let the flames of passion die down to embers before she was fanning them again, creating one hell of a raging inferno inside me.

"I could make love to you all night," she whispered.

"Please do," I responded, and meant it. I wanted to blend with her, become a part of her as we explored the realms of the most intimate of paths two people could traverse together.

It was also the shortest night of my entire life. Time slipped through our fingers like miniscule grains of sand on a windy day. There was no stopping it, no holding it back. *Time waits for no man...or woman.* The candle had burned out long before we drifted off to sleep in the wee hours of the morning.

When I awoke, I was curled up against her back, my arm around her waist, my body molded to hers as if we were two parts of a jigsaw puzzle that fit together perfectly. She was still asleep, and I felt as well as heard each soft sighing exhalation that passed her lips. Running my hand over her naked body, I took great pleasure in each and every curve within my reach. I tingled all over at the response from her smooth, firm breasts as I fondled each in turn.

Slowly working my way downward, I must have aroused her, for she moaned softly, then shifted her legs somewhat, allowing me entrance to the area I sought. I kissed and sucked on her shoulder, my fingers intent on exploring that most intimate and sensitive of regions. "Umm...Faith...oh...baby..."

"Yesss," I whispered, pressing my lower body against that lovely backside of hers.

She reached back and ran her hand over my thigh. "Ah, yes... Umm...are you sure you were a virgin?" she queried, her tone sonorous and smoldering.

"Um-hmm...why?"

"Umm...then you're a quick study."

"I had a good teacher."

"Ohhh?" She shifted her position and turned over on her back.

"Uh-huh. A very good one," I added.

She reached up and brushed a strand of curly brown hair out of my eyes as I repositioned myself beside her. Leaning over, I attacked her right breast. I had yet to cease what I'd started previously. "Oh, Faith..." she breathed, pressing against the back of my head.

All of a sudden, I felt her flinch. "Damn!" she hissed. "What time is it?" She raised up, taking me with her.

I glanced around at the clock on the VCR. "Ten after nine," I responded.

"Whew!" she sighed, sounding like air escaping from a tire. "Thank God. Brandon should be gone to work." She eased back onto the mattress, taking me with her once again. "Now where were we, hmm?"

I hated to tell her, but I didn't think Brandon would be going in to work today, because he probably had one hell of a hangover. Instead of worrying her needlessly, however—the door was locked, after all—I picked up where I'd left off.

"Awh...baby...oh yes... Awh, Faith...oh... yes... AWHH-HHH!" she exclaimed into the back of her arm, muffling the sound. Her body spasmed several times and then went limp. "Oh, Jee-sus," she breathed, taking her arm away from her face. "C'mere, you." I was just raising up in order to comply when there was a knock on the door. "Holy shit!" she cursed quietly, and started to get up.

I put my hand on her stomach. "Shh," I admonished. I didn't really care whether Brandon found out or not, because I was ready to leave this place. Him blowing his top would only hasten my departure. I hated to witness it, though. I couldn't imagine how hideous a scene it might be.

I waited for the next knock. It didn't sound like Brandon to me. "Y-yes," I called, trying to sound sleepy, which wasn't hard.

"Miss Faith," Celia called. "Breakfus', mum."

I felt the tension leave Sara's body as she breathed a very heavy sigh of relief.

"Umm, would you mind just leaving it on the table out there?

I...well, I locked my doors because of the party and I-I'm ashamed to admit it, but I have a bit of a hangover this morning and I'm afraid if I try—"

"Yes, mum," she called back, interrupting me. "I unnerstand."

"Thank you, Celia."

I heard her put the tray down. "Oh, by the by, mum, if you see Miss Sara, tell her I took her breakfus' back to the kitchen ta warm."

I ran my hand over Sara's stomach. "Yes, Celia, I'll tell her soon as I see her."

"Thank you, mum."

"Oh, Celia?"

"Yes, mum?"

"On second thought, would you mind taking mine back, also? I-I don't believe I feel up to getting out of bed right now." I was looking down at Sara and grinning slyly.

"Ya want I should come back at a certain time, mum?"

"Umm... I..." I cocked an eyebrow at Sara, wanting to tease her by asking, *How long do you think this'll take?* But instead I merely answered Celia, "No. Don't worry about it. I'll come down for breakfast, when I feel better."

"Very good, mum." I heard her footsteps receding.

"Are you feeling poorly?" Sara whispered, brushing my hair back.

I shook my head. "Fine as wine. And you?"

"Well, I was going to say that if you felt bad, I could try and make you feel better." She ran her index finger over my lips.

"On second thought, I feel *real* bad...just awful, in fact. I need a nurse right away. Think you could go find one for me?"

She grinned broadly and rolled me over on my back. "*I'd* better be the *only* nurse you let take care of you *this* way," she responded, and attacked my lips.

Chapter
13

After we both were sated for the time being, we went into the bathroom and took a shower. Not long after I'd arrived, Sara had purchased a hand-held showerhead that attached to the faucet so she could wash my hair without me bending way over; we had a fine time with it now, bathing and rinsing each other off.

"God, you're beautiful," I said, standing beside her as she dried herself.

"So are you." She turned her drying technique on me as I held on to the walker in front of me. "It's been quite a while since I've been able to do this. I missed it, a lot," she whispered in my ear while she pressed her lower body against my backside and cupped my breasts in her towel-draped hands.

"God, I never thought I'd ever feel this way," I admitted, taking one hand off the walker and reaching around behind me to caress her silky smooth buttocks. The towel dropped to the floor and she began manipulating my breasts, making me ache with desire. "My God, Sara, what have you done to me?"

"Made you my lover," she purred. "Just like I wanted you to be the first time I held you in my arms."

"Oh?" I glanced over my shoulder. "You do this with all your patients then, do you?"

"No, just the pretty ones." I popped her on the butt and was about to walk away, but she held on tight. "And you're the only pretty one I ever fell in love with," she added, placing a kiss on my neck.

"Keep that up, and we won't be going down for breakfast."

"Umm, going down is just what I had in mind," she responded in a sultry voice, then began devouring my neck while her hands sought other regions.

I knew what the term "going down" meant and was a bit apprehensive at the prospect, although quite aware at this point that I would hardly deny her anything she wanted.

We both heard the knock at my bedroom door. "Tell her you'll skip breakfast altogether," she whispered.

"I thought we took a bath so we'd be presentable when we went down to breakfast?"

"I changed my mind. I don't want food, I want *you*."

Another knock, a bit more insistent this time. "I've got to go out there and talk to her, or else she'll be worried."

Sara sighed heavily, then reached over and grabbed a robe hanging on the back of the door. Helping me into it, she suggested, "Get rid of her quickly." As I started walking away, she tapped me on the butt. "Hurry back. I'll be waiting for you."

I gave one last glance over my shoulder and sighed heavily. *Damn, she's beautiful! I love the color of her hair. I'm going to have to remember to mention that once I take care—*

Yet another knock broke into my woolgathering, and a voice called out my name. The voice did *not* belong to Celia, and I froze in my tracks.

"Sara," I whispered, "it's Brandon."

"Ah, Jesus H. Christ," she hissed. "What the hell do we do now?"

"Just stay in the bathroom," I advised. "I'll try and get rid of—"

He turned the doorknob. "Faith...Princess, are you all right in there?" he asked, his voice growing louder and his knock more insistent.

"Yes," I called. "I'm fine. I'm in the bathroom."

"What?"

"I said I'm in the bathroom. I'm fine," I shouted.

He tried the knob again. "Why is this door locked?"

"The party last night."

"What?"

He's hard of hearing, I thought. *Or else, suspicious.* "I'm fine, Brandon!" I yelled. "I'll be out in a little while."

He tried the knob again, seemingly for good measure, and then relented. "All right, I'll be waiting out here."

"Shit!" I exclaimed under my breath.

Sara walked up behind me. "Listen, you have to stall him in there, get him away from the door. I don't know how, but do it so I can slip out."

"How are you going to... Ah, the secret door." At the time, I hadn't been thinking about any situations like this arising. I was glad she had been.

"I'll go get dressed and... Where the hell is my gown?"

"Where you left it: on *my* side of the bed," I answered.

"Oh." She pushed by me and tiptoed over to get it.

She also picked up my pj's and brought them to me. I tossed them into the bathroom on the hamper and while she finished dressing, went over to the chest of drawers to get out a pair of loose-fitting pants and a matching T-shirt.

I was trying to think of a way to cover up the noise Sara was bound to make when she exited the sitting-room closet. "We should have oiled those hinges," I said. "Why didn't you think of that?"

"I did," she said, looking down at herself in her negligee. "But I'm afraid they'll still make noise."

"What? Did you plan for this?" I asked.

"It crossed my mind. Damn good thing it did, too."

"Princess, are you sure you're all right?"

I rolled my eyes at Sara. "Yes, I'm fine. I'll be out shortly. Let me get dressed!"

"Why is this door locked?" he asked again.

I sighed heavily. "Because I saw some of your guests up here on the east wing last night. I didn't want anyone stumbling into my room by mistake!"

"Oh," he said, as if this were a satisfactory explanation.

"Boy, he hates locked doors, doesn't he?" I whispered.

"A locked door keeps him from barging in wherever he damn well pleases," she hissed.

"Here, help me," I said, holding up my arms for her to grab hold of me so I could pull my pants on while standing up.

"Umm, those fit real nice," she said, running her hands over my lower abdomen. "But I'd better save this for another time, or else he'll be trying to knock the damn door down." She reached over and took the shirt from me and pulled it over my head. "No bra?" she queried.

"I haven't got time."

"Damn, I wish he'd go away," she said. While I put my arms through the holes, she reached around and cupped both breasts. "I shall return," she added, as if speaking to them.

"Why don't I just go down to breakfast instead of you taking the chance on sneaking out?" I queried.

"Well, whatever you think'll work. I just thought if he saw me in my room when you two were coming out of yours... Oh well, doesn't matter. Do it the way you feel best, I'll follow your lead. Just make enough noise with that damn thing that I know where the two of you are." She was referring to my noisy walker.

"I'm going down to breakfast, no matter what. I'm starving, aren't you?"

"I *won't* be joining you—I don't think it'd be wise—but I'll see you for our walk, hmm?" She placed a kiss on my neck. "I love you, Faith."

"I love you, too," I said as she tiptoed over to the secret door next to the bathroom. She had her hand on it when I called out, "I'm coming, Brandon. You know, I'm completely famished." I plopped the walker down on the floor hard, to cover up any noise she might make with the door. "How come you aren't at work? I thought this was Friday, not Saturday."

As I opened the door, he stepped in, his eyes immediately searching the room. They lingered on the rumpled bed as he said, "I...I didn't feel like going in this morning. Like you, I didn't feel very well." His eyes came back to rest on mine. "You say you're famished?"

"Well, when you purge your system like..."

"Oh, I see. Rough night? Your hair is wet," he noted.

I blushed for a moment. "See what happens when you rush a woman? Would you mind getting my brush for me? I think I'll skip blow-drying it today."

He walked over and retrieved my brush from the vanity. His eyes scanned the room once again. *What the hell is he looking for?* He had obviously talked to Celia. *Is he suspicious about Sara's absence?* That's when my gaze came to rest on the candle-holder: the candle Sara brought with her the night before, now a puddle of wax that had melted out onto the nightstand.

"Too much champagne, was it?" he asked, holding the brush out toward me.

I didn't offer a response, but promptly took the hairbrush, shoved the handle in the waistband of my pants, and proceeded out the door and into the sitting room. There was a mirror on the wall by the closet, and I moved over to it. "I...I guess I overdid it, hmm?" I asked, running the brush through my hair a couple of times and repositioning my bangs. I could feel Sara's presence in the closet, and thought I might even have heard a faint squeak. I cleared my throat to cover for it. I'd wanted to get him away from my room quickly, but things weren't working out that way.

I saw his reflection in the mirror as he scanned the bedroom one last time, then closed the door. "I'll have to have a talk with my guests next time. We can't have you feeling as if you have to lock your door at night."

Whew! Didn't see the candle! But wait, what did he say?

"And what's wrong with locking my door?" I inquired, tossing the brush over on the sofa. I was ready to go, and started making my way across the sitting room.

"Well, what if you fall or something and I...we can't get in to help you?"

I shrugged. "Well, I suppose if that happens, I'm sure my big strong uncle would knock down the door to come to my rescue." My tone was sarcastic, but I turned at the door and smiled sweetly, which seemed to confuse him. "A woman sometimes likes her privacy, Brandon. It was all right when I really needed help," I was through the door now, "needed someone around all the time. But now that I'm more independent, well, I don't like everyone just barging in on me. You understand, don't you?" I paused, watching as he considered that. "Well, of course you do," I added, answering my own question before he had a chance to. "You have your office downstairs."

He cut his eyes over at me, seeming a bit surprised. Then he frowned as we continued down the hall. "Yes, I...I understand, Faith," he said, letting out a heavy sigh. He knew I had him by the shorthairs on that one. *Otherwise he would've called me Princess.*

Frankly, I didn't understand what the big deal was anyway. I wouldn't care if Sara locked her door. And I doubt Sara would care if I did. She'd merely knock, and I'd let her in. Just as I would him, unless...I was otherwise engaged. I faltered a step as tingling sensations ran over my body from just the thought of exactly *how* I might be otherwise engaged.

"Princess?" he asked, placing a hand on my arm.

"Hmm?" I looked up at him.

"Didn't you hear me? I asked if you had seen Miss Bennington this morning."

I stopped as if truly concerned. "She's not in her room? Hmph." I shrugged and started walking again. "You gave her the night off last night, didn't you?"

He cut his eyes over at me, as if to say *of course, she has every night off.*

"Maybe she...got lucky."

"Princess!" he admonished. I shrugged and snickered. He made a huffing sound and changed the subject. "Will you be glad when you're walking on your own?" he inquired.

He might as well have asked, *Will you be glad when she's gone?* "Of course. I'll be glad to get rid of this thing," I said, glancing down at the walker.

"Time to start thinking about your future?" he asked as we neared the back stairs, although it sounded more like a statement of fact.

"Perhaps, but not this morning," I responded, wondering if Sara had made her getaway.

While I was eating at the servants' table in the kitchen—something Brandon didn't approve of, but I preferred because I didn't care to sit at that long dining table just to eat a small breakfast—Sara walked in the back door. It took me quite by surprise. *Now, how'd she get around to the back door? Must have sneaked out the front and gone around. Good thinking!*

Brandon looked her over from head to toe. Sara was wearing the Elvira costume from the night before. It was wrinkled in several places, and her hair was in disarray. "Good morning, or should I say...afternoon, Miss Bennington," Brandon said, glancing down at his watch.

"I...I'm sorry, Mr. Neilson, I...I think I had a bit too much fun at your...party, last night," she apologized, raising her hand to her head as if she had a hangover.

"Where have you been? I think it's time for your therapy session already and you're not even dressed for it," he said, his eyes surveying her cleavage.

Oh, how that burnt me up! Looking at me was one thing, but looking at her that way was quite another. Which is why I interjected, "I'm not exactly on my toes this morning, either, Brandon and, excuse me for saying so, but neither are you."

He straightened up and cleared his throat. "Yes, well, it was quite a party. But I must say, this should not happen again, Miss Bennington."

"Yes, sir," she agreed, hanging her head in shame.

I didn't like this at all. She was being too subservient to him, and it irked me. "I think I might be ready for our walk in a little while, if you're up to it, Sara. Or I can go alone today, if...."

"No, I'll..."

"I can do that, Princess," Brandon offered.

Oh shit. Why didn't I keep my big mouth shut?

"Oh no, Mr. Neilson," Sara began, "it's my job and, as you say, I should have been here on time. I'll just go clean up and take care of my duty. I've lost enough time already."

"Speaking of time..." He indicated with another glance at his watch.

"Oh yes, you should dock me for the..." She paused, looking down for her watch, which wasn't there. "However many hours I've lost," she recovered nicely.

"Oh, you can be sure of *that*." He looked her up and down with a rather odd expression on his face.

"Yes, sir," she said as she walked away.

"Is that a wig?" Brandon asked, of no one in particular.

I started to answer honestly, then thought better of it. I shrugged. "Must be. Looks like she's dressed as Elvira."

"Elvira?" he asked quizzically.

Boy, he's out of touch! "She was a late-night horror show hostess," I explained. "I'm sure you've seen her."

"No. I never watch anything but the news, I'm afraid."

Boring and depressing.

"And speaking of news, I suppose I had better check in with the office." He got up. "I'll see you later, Princess," he added, leaning over and giving me a kiss on the cheek for good measure.

I didn't know how Sara had managed it, but she'd obviously gone to great pains to pull the wool over Brandon's eyes. And I believed she had him pretty well convinced she hadn't even been in the house that morning.

In a way, I felt disappointed. In a dark little corner of my mind, I wanted him to find out. I wanted an excuse to leave, so we could be together anytime we wanted, but I knew this would only put undue pressure on Sara. It would be better if we both decided to leave together; however, if she didn't hurry things along, I just might move out without her. I was tired of him running my life, of having to answer to him all the time. Not that I wasn't grateful for what he had done, because I was; but I was tired of placating him and walking on eggshells around him.

Funny thing was, I wasn't sure why I was afraid of him getting mad. I'd never really seen him in a rage or anything that would account for my attitude, but I definitely had the feeling he could be a very undesirable adversary. Perhaps that was why my father never stayed in touch with him or wanted anything to do with the business. He might have known Brandon was not his ally, but his rival. And I had the feeling deep down inside that Brandon could be one vicious rival.

A few minutes later, Sara was back and dressed to kill, as they say, in a tight pair of jeans and a white shirt open to the waist, worn over a white tank top. I called Celia to bring her tray.

Sara tore into the food as if she were starving. "I thought you weren't hungry," I questioned.

"I'm ravenous," she responded. "And I'm not just referring to the food, either," she added, looking me up and down. "You do look good in that outfit. I don't usually like tan colors, but I bought it because you said you liked it. And I have to admit it looks really good on you."

"Thank you." I looked down at myself. I didn't see what she saw, but I was glad she did. When Celia came to clear the table, I noticed she kept glancing over at Sara with a rather odd expression on her face. "Is there something wrong, Celia?" I had to ask.

"Your hair, Miss Sara is...is that a wig, mum?"

Sara shook her head. "No, it's mine. I had it dyed back to the natural color rather than letting it grow out. Does it look that bad?"

"Oh no, mum, ya just...ya look...diff'rent with dark hair, is all. And, 'tis usually pulled up back here an'—"

Sara laughed at Celia's expressions, interrupting her. "I didn't feel much like fooling with it today."

"Yes, mum," Celia said, turning her head sideways. "I believe there's sumthin' else different, isn't there, mum? I mean, if ya don't mind my saying so?"

"No, I don't mind. What else?"

"You're smiling, mum. No sad eyes and...worried looks."

Sara chuckled again. "I suppose I am feeling rather good today," she agreed, looking over at me. "Thank you for noticing."

"Yes, mum." Celia then glanced over at me. "Parties can make a lass feel good, can't they, mum?"

"Sometimes," I agreed with a smile.

"Can I get you anything else, mum? More coffee or..."

I waved away her next offer. "We'll be going for our walk soon," I explained, not taking my eyes off Sara.

"Yes, mum. Very good then," she said, as she turned and started away. "Must be men," she mumbled, shaking her head.

Once she'd left the room, Sara and I both cracked up laughing. *If she only knew, it'd curl her panty hose!* I thought.

"We've got to get away from here, and soon," Sara whispered, once our laughter died away and we were left staring at one another. "God, I can't stand being this close to you and not being able to at least touch you."

"Who's pushing now?"

"I am," she replied. "I'd like to push you into old Rosa Lee out there and buzz you over to my place. Lay you back on my bed and... Umph...I've got to get out of here." She leapt to her feet and took a step backward.

"Where are you going?"

"I...left something in my room. I'll be back in a few moments to go on our walk."

"I like your hair," I acknowledged, as she took another step backward.

"I did it for you," she responded, glancing around us before her eyes came to rest on mine.

"Then I like it *a lot.*"

"I'm glad." She gazed into my eyes. "Umph! This is sheer torture. I'm in hell for sure," she ranted softly, backing out the door.

I felt the same way, but didn't say anything. I'd reined my feelings in for so long, it only came naturally to do so. Now, however, she was getting a taste of what I'd been through. I didn't enjoy her pain. Quite the contrary, I ached as well. But I did enjoy knowing she felt so strongly about me. *Perhaps the virgin wasn't such a disappointment after all.*

When she came down, she was carrying a light brown cane with an intricately carved head on the handle. "I picked it up in an antique shop months ago," she explained, handing it to me.

I glanced down at the end of the handle, which was carved into the head of a panther. *Interesting*, I thought, looking it over more closely.

"The last hurdle," she said softly. I looked up to find her nibbling on her lower lip, and I knew this meant tears weren't far from the surface. "Here, let's get rid of this bulky old thing," she added, moving the walker out of my way. "Try it, Faith."

I hesitantly put the cane down on the floor and gripped the handle. "The last hurdle, huh?" I questioned.

She nodded and nibbled her lower lip again.

I took a deep breath and struggled to my feet, both hands wrapped around the cane. When I went to move, I somehow got my feet tangled up between the table and chair and nearly fell over. She caught me, as always.

"Now, how many times have I told you, you're not ready for turns and dips yet?" she teased.

"Oh, you." I pulled away and regained my balance. "Well, move back. Let me see if I can learn to work this puppy."

"Puppy?" She backed up, giggling. "Where did you get all those cute sayings?"

"Oh, like a magnet picks up iron, I pick up these goofy sayings and..." I paused as I took my first steady step without the walker, "they pop out my mouth at the...damn-dest times," I finished, taking another hesitant but steady step.

"Well, looks like you've learned how to work that puppy, all right," she noted, and wiped a tear from her cheek.

We strolled around the grounds at a slightly slower pace so that I could get familiar with using the cane. I could tell I would soon be more mobile with it. I already felt much freer without the bulky walker. Yet when my left leg grew tired, as it often did, I found myself missing that steady old four-legged prop. Somehow sensing my discomfort, Sara genteelly offered me her arm for support. I graciously accepted, thankful for the comfort and reveling in the warmth and closeness of our bodies. When we resumed walking again, arm in arm, it felt so natural, I didn't even stop to think how it might appear to anyone else.

During our walk, she told me about her apartment in Smyrna, and how much she'd like to take me there. I relished the thought of being alone with her, without worrying about who could be watching or might walk in on us. We discussed possible scenarios for slipping off for a day. Shopping seemed the most viable excuse to offer anyone, even though I knew Brandon would want to go with me. He never liked Sara handling things that should be "family matters." Somehow I had to convince him that shopping was not a family matter, but "girl stuff." I'd also have to ask him for the money, since I didn't even have a driver's license anymore to prove my identity to the bank clerks. It irked me to have to go through him to get money from my own account, but as he had so eloquently pointed out long ago, I couldn't very well cash a check from my bed, and they wouldn't allow Sara to cash it for me; nor would he want her to. Which was why he had handled things since then.

As I looked up at her, thinking how I'd like to share my life with her, I decided it was about time I took control of things myself. First on the agenda would be a new driver's license, for which I might even be required to take a driving test in order to prove my ability post-accident. *This might have to wait a bit longer, after all.* It wouldn't be long before I'd need to take care of my parents' affairs: the house and their belongings. A few months ago, that day had seemed far away, but it would soon be a reality.

I didn't want to think about going into the house again, for I knew it would be filled with memories. Memories of happier days, which at times seemed to have happened so long ago and yet at others seemed like only yesterday. I dreaded the thought of going through my parents' belongings. What would I do with them? What does a person do when someone dies like that? Sara had been through the same thing, and not so long ago. She might know what to do.

"Sara, what happened to your father's belongings after..."

She glanced over at me. "Well, the house I still own." She looked away. "Lawyers advised me to keep it, along with the inheritance."

I was quite surprised. "Inheritance?"

"Um-hmm. He wasn't filthy rich like Brandon, but my father

owned several horse and cattle farms around Georgia, a large ken-
nel that raises greyhounds in Florida, and he had interests in several other areas. It all fell to me after he died, so I kept it. It
provides for the upkeep of the house, and the rest is deposited for
me. I just left everything the way he had it set up."

"You mean you own horse farms?" I asked, very surprised
that she'd never mentioned it.

"In name only, I guess you'd say. Other people handle that
stuff. I'd rather earn my own way. I mean, I never really knew
him. I'd...I'd feel...funny using his money. I even tried to refuse it,
but the lawyers said that since there were no other living relatives,
the state would get it; and his wish was for me to have it, so..."

"And *you* were the one worried about money?" I observed, a
touch of irritation in my tone.

"It's not so much the money, Faith. I just...I don't want to
hurt you. Money worries seemed... Well, they seemed a good
excuse at the time."

"And now?" I probed.

"What do you say we have lunch out on the patio?" she queried, changing the subject.

I knew she didn't want to discuss the subject anymore. "All
right, sounds like a fine idea to me. It's a beautiful day for it."

"Good, then I'll inform Celia of our plans."

She escorted me over to a patio table, then went inside to talk
to Celia. I sat there drinking in the fresh, cool autumn breeze.
Memories of the night before wafted over me with the warmth of a
lover's caress. The autumn leaves with their bright colors—yellow,
orange, red, and gold—danced in the gentle currents of air, their
leathery skins rubbing together and sounding like the rustling of a
thousand dancers' skirts, giving my eyes and ears a wonderful
treat.

"Very good, mum," Sara said, walking out onto the patio,
mocking Celia, though not in a derogatory fashion. "Don't you
just love that accent of hers?"

"You should've heard my mother—very refined British
accent. She could make ordinary words sound...beautiful."

Sara evidently noticed my mood slipping into sadness. "My,
don't you look wonderful today," she commented, sitting down
across from me.

"So do you," I acknowledged with a smile. Then I noticed
Celia approaching. "So, you own...two horse farms?" I queried,
saying the first thing that came to mind in order to change the sub-

ject.

"Three, actually. Randall Stables has horses and cattle, Marie's Pride has horses and greyhounds, and the Vivian Leigh, where he lived, is mostly cattle and only a few horses."

"Vivian Leigh?" I inquired.

"Um-hmm," she replied with a smile. "He must have had a thing for a movie star."

"Excuse me, mum," Celia said to Sara. "Cook would like ta know if you'd care for anything special?" Sara looked over at me.

"No, the usual soup and sandwich will do. Just ask him to include some ice cream," I requested.

"Yes, mum, very good." Celia glanced back at Sara. "'Scuse me, mum, but I couldn't help but overhear. Did ya say Randall Stables?" Sara nodded and looked up at her. "That wouldn't be Tom Randall, would it, mum?"

"Yes," Sara answered, glancing over at me. I shrugged.

"Now, that's a name I haven't heard in many years," Celia declared reflectively, as she looked off into the distance.

"Did you know him?" I inquired.

"Oh yes, mum, if he's the same one, mind you. Tall, dark an' handsome, as I remember him. Moved ta...Columbus, I believe it wuz. Has a stable down that way, don't he, mum?" Sara nodded. "Is he any relation to ya?"

"My father," Sara responded ruefully.

"Well, glory be. Tom Randall's daughter." Celia stared at Sara. "This is Thomas Clancy Randall, mum?"

"Yes. I believe his middle name was Clancy."

"Well, bless me muther. How is young Tom, if ya don't mind me asking?"

"He...passed away..."

"Oh no, I'm so sorry, mum. So very sorry, I am ta hear that. Tom wuz a fine man, he wuz. Yes, a fine man."

"How did you know him, Celia?" I queried, as Sara looked over at me. She knew my inquisitive mind was at work. And I felt we were hot on the trail of pieces of her past.

"Worked here, he did, mum. Stable hand. Worked his way ta being a trainer."

"He worked here?" Sara asked as her eyes grew wide. "When?"

"Oh, Tom's been gone 'bout...thirteen, fourteen years now, I'd say. Yes, that's right. He left right after Miss Vivian...took her life." The last three words were nearly a whisper.

Sara looked at me.

"How long did he work here, Celia?" I continued interrogating.

"Oh, wull, that would be hard ta say, mum. See, Tom, he grew up here. Matter-a-fact, he wuz born in the servants' quarters."

"Born here?" Sara asked incredulously.

"Yes, mum. His dear departed muther and father, they worked for the previous Mr. Neilson. Tom, he grew up rambling 'round here, following after his father, learning 'bout the horses and things. Grew into a fine man, he did. Always had a smile for ya and never an unkind word. Yes, that wuz me Tom. I wuz his godmuther, ya know." She glanced over at Sara, whose face was an unreadable mask. "Oh, I didn't mean ta go on so 'bout the dearly departed, mum. I'm sorry, truly I am."

"That's quite all right, Celia," Sara asserted, waving away the apology and flashing a wry smile. "Please, have a seat; tell me more."

Celia cleared her throat as if she were a bit uncomfortable. "Wull, I would, mum, but the cook, he'll be waiting for me."

"Perhaps you could join us for lunch, then," I suggested.

"Oh, wull, yes, mum. I'd be honored ta do so, I would."

After Celia walked away, Sara just sat there staring at me. I knew she was wondering why her father had lied to her, because if I remembered correctly she had said he was from Columbus.

"I assume he didn't tell you he was born—"

"No, he didn't," she interrupted tersely. "Wonder how much more he didn't tell me. Was my mother from around here?"

Hearing the anger in her voice, I shrugged. "Maybe Celia will know."

She stared at me a moment longer, as if she were looking through me. Then she quickly turned away and slumped down in her chair. I knew that her Swiss cheese of a past had just taken one hell of a blow from a cookie cutter. And Celia had been the one to unknowingly wield it.

"Just wait. Perhaps Celia will have some answers for you that'll make sense. I mean, maybe he moved away and came back or...maybe it's just a coincidence on the names and he's not—"

"Oh, get real, Faith!" she declared as she got up from her chair. "The woman was his godmother, for Christ's sake. She obviously kept tabs on him for a while. She knew about that stable and him moving to Columbus. And he *was* tall, dark...and handsome. He always had that goddamn smile plastered on his face. Bad part was, he wasn't anything like Brandon. You couldn't see through it, so the damn thing must have been genuine."

"Sara, please just calm down, there may be a logical explanation for all of it," I offered.

"Yeah, he fucking lied to me."

Celia joined us for lunch and Sara plied her with questions, explaining that she hadn't known her father because she'd lived with her mother, and that after her mother had died, she and her father had had only a brief few years together because he'd passed away in January of this year. Celia was very obliging and offered all the information she could. When Sara mentioned her mother, Amy Jackson, Celia shook her head and said she'd never heard of her, but that she might well have been one of Tom's girlfriends.

When Celia left with the trays, Sara got up and went over to the patio railing. After a long silence, she finally said, "I've got to go through my father's things. I didn't want to before. I felt he'd answered my questions the best he could, but now... You're right, you know, about this hanging over my head. With things the way they are up here," she motioned to her head, "I'll never be able to make a commitment to anyone. And...I want to do that with you, Faith. I really do," she added, as she turned around to face me.

I was touched by her desire to do this, but I could tell this revelation had turned our afternoon, which should have been peaceful and filled with loving glances, into one of unanswered questions and disappointment.

"I need to go to my apartment," she announced. "Come on, let's get you upstairs."

"Oh no," I protested. "You're not leaving me here to worry all day. I'm going with you."

"Brandon will probably have a fit if he—"

"Then let him. I'm going with you. I can walk now, I should be able to go anywhere I want. And if he doesn't like it... Well, he'll just have to get used to it."

"All right, all right. I'm not about to argue with you anymore. Just let me get my purse, and I'll be right back." She touched my arm on her way by.

What I felt should have been a long, lingering contact followed by tender glances, like a few hours earlier, was now only a quick pat on the arm between friends. I sighed heavily over yet another ruined moment. This time, it wasn't Brandon's fault. It wasn't anyone's, really.

And perhaps it's for the best, I thought. Finding out about her past was far more important than sitting here, yearning for each other. Besides, we'd be away from prying eyes. That part I liked. A lot!

Chapter
14

I was able to get in one last sip of my tea before Sara whisked me away to the garage. "Why are we in such a hurry?" I asked, moving along at a much faster pace than I was accustomed to.

"I want to get back before Brandon does," she answered, opening the passenger door of her shiny black Trans Am.

"Where did he go?" I inquired as she helped me inside.

"I don't know, but when I left word that we were going for a drive, Sammy said he was gone."

"I'm not afraid of him," I declared. "Why should you be?"

"He pays my salary, Faith."

"One you *don't* need," I reminded.

"Just get in," she muttered, starting around to the driver's side.

"I have money. We can move somewhere else, and I can pay your salary," I offered, as she got in and closed the door.

"Give me the cane, I'll get it out of your way." Putting my cane in the back, she propped it between the seats so it was within easy reach. "It's just better that we don't tempt fate right now, all right? All right?" she repeated.

"Okay," I agreed, looking over the infamous Rosa Lee, who was as clean as a whistle. "You always keep her this clean?"

"I've been expecting you for some time now." A sly grin graced her features as she put her hand on the headrest of my seat and backed out of the garage.

We seemed to fly down the winding road leading out of Shady Grove. Braking to almost a full stop but too impatient to wait for the gates to fully open, she steered around them at the first available opportunity, and then off we sped into the outside world. It had been quite a while since I'd seen anything except the grounds of Shady Grove. It felt good to be out from behind those gates; most of all, it felt good to be alone with Sara.

Gazing out at the surrounding scenery, I wished we were merely going for a lazy drive in the country. Why did Brandon have to rule my life?

I reached over and took her hand. "I'm sorry, I didn't mean to snap at you about getting away from here," I said softly. "I guess I just feel frustrated. He controls my life, and I don't like it, Sara."

"I know. I don't, either, but until you're on your feet properly and can take charge of your life, he'll stay in control. Gaining your freedom, well...it might not be as easy as you think."

"You talk about him as if you know him well."

"I...uh...sometimes I feel like I do," she confirmed with a decided frown. "I can...sense things. I don't know what to call it. But I just feel he's... Well, it's just not gonna be easy to gain your independence from him, that I can tell from the way he acts. He loves handling everything. Remember the exercise machine and parallel bars? I was all set to get you out of there, if only to the hospital and back, but he didn't...he didn't care for you leaving the house. I guess it could be that he didn't trust my driving..." She glanced over at me very briefly. I'm not sure what expression she saw on my face, but evidently she didn't like it because her tune changed somewhat. "Oh hell, maybe I'm making a mountain out of a molehill. All I know for sure is he's stubborn, very stubborn."

"Like someone else you know." I pointed to myself.

"Yes, indeed," she agreed, glancing over at me and squeezing my hand.

When we got to her apartment, she disappeared down a hall-way while I looked around. The place was plain and simple, but decidedly neat. Everything was arranged to be functional for one person. Missing were any family pictures, which added a homey touch to any house. The only decorations on the walls were the scenic paintings one could buy in any department store. There were no books lying open on the tables, no shoes on the floor, and no shirt or other apparel draped across the chairs, as would be the norm for an active home. Or at least, would be for mine. Taking a peek into the small kitchen, I saw no real evidence that anyone lived here, except for the one used coffee cup on the counter. It was obvious Sara paid rent, but that was about the extent of her involvement with the apartment.

My legs were getting tired, so I walked over and sat down on the sofa. A few moments later she came out, dragging a large box behind her.

"One of my father's associates sent this to me," she

explained, dragging the box into the middle of the room. "It's from his office. I haven't gone through it yet. I didn't think I needed to. I've been meaning to take it to the house in Columbus, but so far I just haven't gotten around to going down there since his death."

As she brought out a stack of papers, I eased down onto the floor beside her. She halved the stack with me and we went through them, finding nothing that pertained to Sara. We then proceeded to go through everything else in the carton, but still came up empty.

"Maybe his personal papers were at home," I suggested, handing back the last stack. I caught a quick glimpse of his birth date on a form he'd filled out some time ago. September 6, 1947.

"Yeah, I was afraid of that. Now I'll have to go to Columbus," she muttered with a frown. "Oh well, that can wait for another time."

"Good," I said softly, and scooted over a little closer. "We're quite alone here, no prying eyes... no one's gonna walk in."

"Uh-huh." She glanced at her watch.

"Forget Brandon, please, Sara. God, you made me wait so long, and now we're here, alone. No one knows where we are, and you're still thinking about him."

Her eyes darted back and forth, searching mine. "I hope you're right, Faith. I hope I don't ever cause any harm to come—"

I silenced her with a kiss. Our passions ignited faster than a match tossed into a pool of gasoline. Soon we were in her room, on her bed, making love with great abandon. I didn't know it could be any better than the night before, but it was. We even took another shower together, and despite my handicap, she turned this into a very erotic and sensual encounter. The feel of her warm, wet, slippery body against mine was one I wouldn't soon forget.

We ended up back on her bed—our bodies still damp, my hair quite wet. I could feel the moisture seeping into the comforter, even as I felt her warm, wet tongue leaving a trail down the front of my torso. Soon that warm, wet appendage flicked across my desire and set my loins ablaze. My hips arched involuntarily, begging for more of this tantalizing contact, and I was soon rewarded with my first encounter with a knowledgeable tongue and what it could accomplish. *Sheer unadulterated bliss!*

A bliss I longed to share through reciprocation. Although oral sex had always sounded like something I would never, *ever* want to do, I soon found myself going back on that erroneous conclusion. And *going down* on her.

With the first stroke, I was reminded of that tantalizing taste that had issued from her nipples. It only made sense that these two areas were connected in some fashion; I'd felt this connection for myself. My taste buds yearned for more of this tangy nectar.

She moaned with pleasure as I feasted upon her succulent, sensitive flesh, my tongue delving inside at intervals to capture the exquisite taste of her unique and intoxicating liquor. I held on to her bucking hips and rode the glorious, undulating waves of passion until she cried out. Her legs twitched, her whole body shuddered, and then she went limp. I stayed right where I was, unable—or perhaps more to the point, unwilling—to relinquish this intimate contact.

She shuddered once again from a long, languid stroke of my tongue. "Oh, God, Faith, please..." she pleaded, slowly moving away from my eager mouth.

But I'm not done with you yet, I wanted to say, but instead held my tongue, at least as far as vocalizing this thought. I could not, however, resist returning for more of the luscious sap still oozing from between her thighs.

"Oh holy hell!" she hissed when I plunged my questing muscle deep inside as if she were an ice cream cone, my tongue desiring to search out and savor every succulent drop of her creamy, molten essence. I wanted it all. I couldn't get enough.

Her fingers slipped into my hair, stroking and caressing while I gently lapped up the trickling juices. "Don't stop," she pleaded. "God, yes...like that. Oh yes, *just like that.* Oh, Faith...oh, baby...oh, G-g-go-od!" Her body shuddered once more, her legs trembling and closing tightly about my head. So tightly, in fact, I was unable to continue my ministrations. "Dear God, Faith...c'mere," she requested, her hand moving around to my chin and lifting it.

I kissed each inner thigh lightly in a parting gesture, quite aware of the moisture being transferred from my face, which was sticky with her juices. I wore this temporary mask of my ardor proudly while maneuvering up her body, all my senses seemingly heightened by this awareness. She placed a hand on each side of my face, her eyes growing wide as the amount of moisture registered with her senses. Sliding her hands over each cheek, she removed the residue, and then without warning, pulled me down and commenced devouring my lips.

"Can I go with you to Columbus?" I asked as we were getting dressed. At this point, I didn't want to let her out of my sight a moment longer than I absolutely had to. I felt I would follow her to the ends of the earth if she asked me to.

"Don't I wish," she responded, glancing over at me. "But

Brandon would surely become suspicious."

"So what? I can leave Shady Grove any time I want. I'm well enough now."

"Let's not rush things, hmm? You may be well enough for all intents and purposes, but leaving would...create a strain, right now. Just take it one step at a time," she replied as she tied her shoes.

"In other words, you aren't...you won't..." I paused, tears filling my eyes. Evidently she didn't share my enthusiasm over our time together. "It wasn't good enough, was it?" I blurted out.

"What wasn't?" She glanced over at me and, obviously reading my expression, added, "Oh, Faith! Sweetheart..." She moved closer to where I sat on the bed. "Good Lord, Faith, one has nothing to do with the other! Nothing at all! How can you think such a thing?" Her arm went around my shoulder. "I've tried to tell you, I don't want to hurt you. I... Sweetie, listen...let me get this...or at least *some* of this messy past of mine squared away here, okay? Otherwise, I might not be much good to...either of us. I mean, this is the first time since the accident that I've really considered delving into this. I guess I just kept assuming my memory would someday return, whole and intact, ya know."

"Like in the movies?" I suggested.

"Yeah, like the movies," she acknowledged with a heavy sigh. "And I can't say that this won't still happen, especially now that I'm looking into it. I've been warned that it could be a very frightening and painful..." She paused. "Well, very hard on anyone I might be involved with, that didn't know me before. Can you understand that?"

I nodded slowly. It was frightening now, merely thinking that if her memory returned she might well have a lover in her past and want to go running back to her. *Or him.* Which would be even harder to deal with, and I really didn't want to think about any of it right now. I needed to concentrate on myself, getting control of my life, which would allow Sara time to focus on herself and her past. "Do what you have to do," I said, drying my eyes. "And I'll do what I have to do."

"I don't like the sound of that, Faith. Sweetheart, Brandon isn't going to let you walk out of there that easily, I'm afraid."

"How can he damn well stop me?" I retorted.

Her eyes darted back and forth, searching mine again. "I don't know how, but...I just feel he'll try. He dotes on you, Faith. And just like you and I wouldn't want to give each other up, I don't think he'll give you up. He's made you his world for the last several months, and I doubt he'll give that world up so easily.

Especially if you just up and take off so quickly...*with me.*" One
dark eyebrow arched skyward.

I could hardly argue with her reasoning, even though she
made Brandon sound more like a lover than an uncle. "Well, he's
just gonna have to give me more freedom. I *cannot* continue to
live like this—in fear of what he thinks or what he..." I paused,
considering once again why I feared him. "Sara, why do you, me,
Jason, Celia...all the rest of us fear Brandon so? I've never seen
him angry but once, that day when you weren't around in the hospital. But he calmed down quickly enough."

She stared at me intently. "Honestly, Faith, I've seen a different side of him than you have." She looked away. "We've butted
heads on several occasions over what's best for you...your emotional well-being, your therapy. That's one reason I don't stick
around when he's there."

"I thought that was because you didn't like each other."

"That's part of it." She frowned. "But it goes deeper than
that, I think. Much deeper. The way he..." She shook her head.
"Well, he's just so damn pigheaded. Always insisting on having
his way. It's either his way or the..." She paused, and waved her
hand as if dismissing this thought. "Oh, never mind. You do what
you have to do. I only ask one thing: give me a few more days to
check into this past of mine. Celia is my only link to my father
right now. If you leave now, or your uncle fires me, I lose that link.
I know that sounds selfish but, Faith, in all these years, I haven't
really cared about my past, and now...because of you...because of
us...I want to know. I want to have this behind us *before* we start a
life together."

Start a life together? Then there was hope. I knew I needed to
carefully consider her request. She hadn't finished that sentence I
assumed would have gone, "It's either his way or the highway." I
wondered how many times he had threatened to fire her. And if he
ever did so, what might that mean to Sara's career, which she
seemed to love?

I reasoned that I'd lived with his firm hand on my life for several months now; what were a few more days? Especially since, if I
was brutally honest with myself, it wasn't so much Brandon I was
trying to escape as Sara I was trying to run to; desperately desiring to be alone with her, have her all to myself. Which is something that would not be easy at Shady Grove. I was allowing my
hormones to do my thinking again, and that could be disastrous in
the long run.

"All right, a few days then," I agreed, bending down and
tying my shoes. "How do you plan to go about finding out about

your father?" I inquired, changing the subject.

"His lawyer is on a retainer. I'm sure he can recommend a private detective. It's not just my father I want to know about, I want to know about my mother and the life I lost."

"I suppose that's a good idea. But can you afford a private detective?" I asked, remembering she didn't like the idea of using her father's money.

She considered this for several seconds before answering. "My father told the lies in the first place, it's only right his money should be used to find out the truth, don't you think?"

She immediately got up and retrieved her purse, then went to the phone and punched in the numbers from a business card. In a very professional voice I'd seldom heard her use, she got the ball rolling. Where it might end up, she had no idea; yet she seemed bound and determined to find out. And I could hardly blame her.

As I eavesdropped on her conversation, I thought back to the date I had seen on the form: 1947. I did the subtraction in my head. Her father would've been 45 when he died. And Sara was 32. It didn't take a genius to see that something was very amiss, unless he'd fathered her at the age of twelve or so. I suppose it wouldn't have been unheard of, but it was very unlikely. Then again, that could be the reason Amy Jackson had run off. But it didn't answer the nagging question of why Tom had lied about where he had lived.

When she got off the phone, I inquired about her knowledge of his age. "Did you know how old your father was when he...passed away?"

"No, why? What does that have to do with anything? Come on, we need to get back," she suggested, extending her hand for my support.

"According to the birth date on one of those forms, he was 45."

"So?"

"So, that would make him 13 when you were born."

She cut her eyes over at me, a familiar faraway look in their depths. "Damn, it just gets more complicated, doesn't it?" Her gaze shifted to the floor. "Seems the more I find out, the deeper the shit gets."

"Are you sorry I started this?"

"You? This all came about by accident, remember? Celia's the one who overturned my little apple cart, not you."

We rushed back to Shady Grove. When Sara drove up to the

front door, saving me quite a few steps, I noticed Celia outside
sweeping off the front steps. She looked our way, then the broom
slipped from her hands as her mouth fell wide open; she quickly
clamped her hand over it. I started to laugh at her odd behavior,
thinking she must be reacting to my being so bold as to go running
off without Brandon's approval, but then her reaction took an
ominous turn: she crossed herself in the Catholic manner, her face
turning as pale as a sheet. I glanced over at Sara, who had also
noticed her peculiar behavior.

"Celia?" I called, opening the door. "What's wrong? You look
like you've seen a ghost."

"Ye-Ye-Yes, mum," she stammered, continuing to stare at
Sara, who was coming around the back of the car to help me. "I...I
thought I had."

"What? Oh now, I know I don't look like my mother without
that wig."

"No, not you, mum. It's...Miss Sara."

Sara turned to look at her, even as she offered me her hand.
"What about me?"

"For a moment, mum, I..." Celia paused as she reached down
and picked up her broom. "I thought Miss Ashley had...cum back,
I did."

"Ashley?" I asked, quite puzzled.

"Do I look so bad that you thought I'd risen from the dead?"
Sara asked, obviously trying to lighten the mood.

"Oh no, mum, I mean, f-forgive me, mum," she stammered,
"But in those dark glasses, that car...your hair... It just...it
reminded me so much of Miss Ashley, God rest her soul." She
crossed herself again and closed her eyes.

Sara helped me to my feet and then took off the glasses, placing them on top of her head. She squinted in the bright afternoon
sunlight. Turning toward Celia, she asked, "Is this better?"

Celia merely stared at her and then glanced over at me.

"Sara doesn't look like Ashley, does she?" I queried.

"Yes, mum. I mean, no, mum. I...I suppose it's just the light.
'Scuse me, mum, but my eyesight isn't so good anymore, and...I
'spect my mind plays tricks on me from time to time," she mumbled, and she started into the house, leaving the steps half swept.

Sara looked at me questioningly. I shrugged. I didn't know
what to make of it. "Ashley must've had dark hair," I offered.
"Maybe even a *black* Camaro?"

Sara nodded in agreement, but glanced back at Celia's
retreating form, frowning.

I made my way through the front door, half expecting Brandon to be waiting for me— hand on his hip, demanding to know where I'd been. I had seen that pose many times when I'd wander about the grounds by myself and he'd come looking for me. To my surprise, and relief, he was nowhere in sight, or within hearing distance for that matter.

I slowly ascended the stairs, taking them one at a time, resting for a moment on each. The cane made walking up stairs *much* easier, yet I'd had quite a tiring day and my legs were complaining of fatigue. I took my mind off them by thinking about poor Celia and her reaction moments before. Surely Sara didn't look like Ashley, did she? I suddenly realized that I had no idea what Ashley had looked like. I'd only assumed she had features like Brandon and Jason. As a matter of fact, I didn't know what Vivian looked like, either. I decided this would be something to occupy my time while Sara went off to Columbus. I would ask Brandon for some old photo albums and get him to tell me more about our history. If I could, that is. Sometimes Brandon was more close-mouthed about the past than Sara was, and his silence was deliberate.

Before I got two-thirds of the way up the stairs, she joined me. Putting her arm around my waist, she whispered, "I wish I could just sweep you up in my arms and carry you, but, I'm afraid we might not make it halfway down the hall."

"You carried me in the pool," I reminded.

"That was different. Water creates buoyancy, makes you seem lighter. Besides, you've put on a couple of pounds since the days when I carried you around." I pinched her shoulder for that one. "Ouch! I didn't say that was bad. As a matter of fact, I think you've filled out rather nicely." She glanced down at my breasts.

"Oh, you, stop that. I have not filled out up there, and you know it. They just look bigger 'cause your hormones are going wild."

"You can say that again."

"They just look bigger..." I paused as she glanced over at me and we both started laughing.

Back in my room, she helped me into bed. Dinner would be served soon, and more than likely, Brandon would be coming in. I touched the side of her face as she leaned over me. I wondered what she had looked like before the plastic surgery. Not that it mattered. The thought just happened to cross my mind as I surveyed her lovely features. She'd mentioned that her father had told her she looked like her mother.

"Where's that picture of your mother?" I inquired as she sat down on the bed.

"In my room, why?"

"Can I see it?"

"Why?" she asked suspiciously. "Oh, don't tell me. The incident with Celia, right?"

"Well, I never saw the picture. I just wondered what you might have looked like before the surgery. Kinda get an idea of how my looks might change."

"Oh, come on, you won't be having major plastic surgery. They'll just redo this right here." Her finger traced the path of the scar that lay beneath my bangs. "And I don't think that'll change your beautiful features very much. It'll only keep you from being so self-conscious about it." She kissed me lightly on the lips, and then seemingly could not resist returning for more. I reached up and pressed the button on the remote, lowering the head of the bed and bringing her down on top of me. "Ah, God almighty, Faith! I've gotta get out of here." She pulled away. "You're a bad girl," she admonished, shaking her finger at me.

"Yeah, but you love it."

"Tease," she retorted, getting to her feet.

"Sara," I called as she started away, "the picture?"

"All right. To satisfy your curious mind, I'll get it. But like I said, you can't tell much about her. And you have to promise to be a good girl, or I won't come back."

"Cross my heart," I lied.

A few minutes later, she was back with a faded black-and-white snapshot. I immediately recognized one of the women in the photograph. "This is my mother," I announced, suddenly feeling very peculiar about this whole thing.

"Where?" she asked, leaning over to look at the picture.

"Right here." I pointed to the woman on the left. "This isn't your..."

"Oh no, no the other one," she assured me, as we both gave each other a puzzled look.

How coincidental that our mothers had known one another. But then again, this most assuredly meant that Sara's mother had been to Shady Grove and was more than likely friends, or at least acquaintances, with my mother back then. Yet Celia had said she didn't remember Tom courting anyone named Amy Jackson.

"Maybe if you showed Celia this picture, she might remember her. Who knows, maybe Celia didn't know they were lovers."

Sara raised her eyebrows. "According to that form you saw, my mother must have been much older than my father. What did she do, seduce a child?"

"Maybe I was wrong about the date or...maybe it was a misprint or..."

"He lied?" she finished for me. She sighed wearily. "I think he lied about a lot of things."

"Well, just show Celia the picture and see if she recognizes her."

"That doesn't mean that she's my mother, though. He may have lied about that as well." She nervously turned the photograph over in her hands. "Why don't you show it to her?"

"Why?"

"Your mother's in it. I mean, she might tell you more. If she recognizes her, that is."

I nodded. *Perhaps that would be better,* I thought. Then I could censor what I told Sara, in case it wasn't all good news. *Now who's thinking about lying to protect someone else?*

About half an hour later, Celia arrived with dinner. As she wheeled the tray over to me, I asked my question. "Celia, may I ask a favor of you?"

"A'course, mum. How can I help ya?"

"This picture," I said, holding it out toward her. "Do you know these women?" I didn't want to taint her observations by telling her one was my mother. I wanted to see how bad or good her eyesight was.

She took the picture and held it out at arm's length, then reached into her apron pocket and pulled out a pair of partial bifocals. Just as I suspected, her eyesight was failing.

"This one here is your muther, mum," she said without further hesitation, pointing to the photograph.

"Yes, I thought so. But, what about the other one?"

"Umm...face is a bit blurry," she observed. "But I'd have ta say this is more'n likely Miss Vivian."

"Vivian?" I asked, quite surprised.

"Yes, mum, 'pears to be." She studied the picture closer. "Oh yes, mum, that's Miss Vivian, all right. I 'member that outfit she's wearing. Your muther and Miss Vivian were fond of riding, they were. Seen 'em together quite often."

"You mean Vivian liked my mother?"

"Oh my yes, mum. Who wouldn't like your muther?"

"She wasn't envious or jealous?"

"Well now, who wouldn't be envious of your muther's beauty?" she replied, looking over her bifocals at me. "But Miss Vivian, she wuz a lady, she wuz. Never seemed ta let it show, leastwise not in my presence. Best I recall, your muther was Miss

Vivian's only friend. Besides young Tom, a'course."

"Tom? Tom Randall?"

"Oh yes, mum. He took care of Miss Vivian's horse, ya see, and you'd often see 'em talking from time ta time. I 'spect she felt by Tom like he wuz a bruther."

"A brother?"

"Yes, mum, they's 'bout the same age, ya see. Mr. Neilson, he...brought home a child bride," she said in a conspiratorial tone of voice, looking over her bifocals again. I could tell there was something she wasn't telling me. And from the way she quickly glanced back down at the picture, I knew she wouldn't be doing so, either.

"Are there any pictures of Vivian and Ashley here in the house?" I queried after a short silence, during which she handed the picture back.

"Umm... Yes, mum," she said, a bit hesitantly. "In...Miss Ashley's room."

"Ashley's room?"

"Yes, mum. Mr. Neilson, he's... Well, he closed off her room," she nearly whispered, glancing around behind her as if to make sure he wasn't close by. "I suppose that's cuz they never found her bod..." She paused, clearing her throat. "I think he still holds out hope she'll return."

"Where is her room?"

She looked at me rather strangely. "Why, next door, mum."

"Next door? I thought Brandon said that was part of my mother and father's old suite?"

"'Twas, but Miss Ashley requested those rooms after she came back from hospital. I suppose being in her old room may've been a bit too painful." She put her glasses back in her apron pocket.

"Thank you, Celia."

"Yes, mum," she said as she started away, then paused at the door. "May I say, mum, don't let Mr. Neilson see you." Her gaze went toward the bathroom door; the door to Ashley's room was on the other side. "He...he's rather particular 'bout anyone going in there."

Now *she* was alluding to being afraid of Brandon, so I decided this was the prime time to ask about it. "When Brandon gets mad, Celia, is he—"

She shook her head back and forth rather rapidly, cutting me off. "No one likes to see Mr. Neilson mad, mum. No one."

"How come?"

She was still shaking her head. "No, mum," she answered,

glancing down at the floor, head moving rapidly for a moment as if warding off some unsavory thought. "Is there anything else I can do for ya?" she asked, changing the subject.

I reasoned the type of behavior she was exhibiting came from years of practice—being a servant and knowing when to keep one's mouth shut. "No, thank you, Celia, you've been very helpful."

"Yes, mum."

After she left, I merely picked at my dinner, a thousand different questions floating through my mind. Tom and Vivian? Now why had Tom given Sara a picture of Vivian and told her it was her mother? Was he merely trying to give her some semblance of a family, since she had lost so much? Then why not give her the truth? Or was the truth too painful? And if so, too painful for whom—him or her?

Brandon came up after dinner, and I hid the picture underneath my mattress. I didn't want to explain where I'd acquired it. He stayed until well after ten, never even mentioning the fact that I'd been out of the house. Evidently, he had some close-mouthed servants. Or else they just didn't like talking to him. He kissed me goodnight, but I knew—as did Sara—that he'd be back with a glass of milk. He showed up, as presumed, and I took a few sips before he left—anything to get rid of him faster so I could talk to her.

When she came in, I imparted nearly everything Celia had told me. I thought she had a right to know all of it.

"Damn, this digging up my past is something else," she said, running her fingers through her hair. "The hole keeps getting deeper and deeper, but so far I haven't found out anything that makes sense. Other than the fact that he lied to me, big time."

"Want a diversion?" I queried.

"What?"

"Celia said that was Ashley's room over there." I gestured toward the bathroom and the room beyond. "Wanna go in and have a look around?"

"Why?"

"I don't know, get your mind off this for a while."

"*You* can take my mind off this, can't you? Besides," she began unbuttoning the front of my pajama top. "I'll be gone all day tomorrow, the next day, and maybe even Monday."

"What? You didn't say you'd be staying *that* long," I whined, stopping her on the second button.

"Well, I can't just rush down and right back. I need to take my time and look things over. Maybe I'll find something that'll clear all this up. Maybe he's not the same Tom Randall, I don't know."

I sighed heavily. "I'll miss you." I reached up and touched the side of her face.

Taking my hand in hers, she kissed the palm and then quickly got up. "Where're you going?" I demanded.

She didn't respond, but merely walked over to the stereo and turned it on. Picking up a cassette tape lying on top of the entertainment center, she put it into the tape deck, pressed rewind, and then went over to the door. I heard the lock click into place. On her way back, she pressed play on the tape deck. Soft, romantic music filled the room.

"You staying the night?" I asked as she started toward me, untying her robe.

Her head moved slowly back and forth in a negative manner. "Long enough, though." She sat down again and began kissing me.

I reached up and pressed the down button on the remote. The head of the bed descended slowly, and so did she, right into my arms. And this time, she didn't run away.

Chapter
15

"Faith?"

"Um-hmm?"

"I just wanted to say goodbye." She pecked me on the cheek.

"Never goodbye," I admonished. "See you later, maybe, but never goodbye." I pulled her close for a kiss. "Hurry back."

"I will." She eased away slowly. "You look so lovely lying there like that."

I glanced down to see what she was talking about. I was naked, lying with one leg bent at the knee, the other stretched straight out. I didn't see what the big deal was, but I was glad she liked it.

"Damn, I hate to leave," she said, her finger tracing a path from the middle of my chest downward.

"Then don't. Let the detective do all the work."

"That's tempting, but..."

"What do you think you'll find there, anyway?" I asked, rubbing sleep out of my eyes.

"That's just it, I don't know. Maybe something...maybe nothing. I can't just sit around here waiting. I have to *do* something. And besides, Brandon will want you all to himself most of the weekend, *as usual.*"

"We've got nights."

"Uh-huh, and then how do we explain why we aren't getting any sleep?" She ran her finger around my lips. "Look pretty suspicious if we're both tired all the time, wouldn't it?"

"I guess," I sighed heavily. "Frankly, though, I don't care who knows. But obviously you do, so you'd better get going, and pray that no one sees you leave."

"Why? I told Brandon I was going. I'm not keeping this trip a secret."

"No, but you might wanna keep that big red spot on your neck a secret, or someone might figure out where you got it."

"What? What did you do?"

"I got carried away." I pulled her down for another kiss. "Sue me," I mumbled against her lips.

"Jesus, Faith, look at that sucker," she said, staring at her reflection in the vanity mirror.

"Like I said, sue me."

"Did you have to put it so...high, in plain sight?"

"Well, at the time I was doing it, I didn't actually think about where I was or how it would look later. It just...kinda happened. I mean, it's your fault too, you know. If you hadn't done what you did, I wouldn't have done what I did."

Sara merely shook her head and grinned. "First time meeting these people in Columbus, and I have a great big hickey on my neck. Oh, I bet that goes over real well."

"Stay here, then."

"Oh-ho, no. And try to explain this sucker? No way, sister." She looked back at her reflection. "Wonder if it's too hot for a turtleneck."

"I'm sorry, Sara. I didn't mean to—"

"Oh, come off it. You know I'm not mad. Why should I be, hmm? It's only a reminder that I must have been pretty damn good last night, wouldn't you say?"

"I think I already did."

She chuckled. "Yes, I believe you did. In big, bold, red print, sweetheart."

The first day of her absence dragged by. I knew better than to expect to see her on Saturday but hoped she'd be back Sunday, even though she wasn't scheduled to return until late Monday. Meanwhile, on Saturday afternoon, while Brandon was out doing something, I took it upon myself to have a little adventure. My plans went awry, however, when I found the connecting door to Ashley's room locked. I went around to the entrance from the hall and found it locked, too. Back in my room, I sat down on the bed to ponder this initial setback.

Now, why would Celia tell me to be careful and not let Brandon see me if she knew both doors were locked? Maybe she thought I was going to pick the lock? But what do I know about picking locks? Nada, that's what! Oh, but wait... I might be able to find out where they keep the keys. Celia had said Brandon was particular about who went in there, just like he was particular about the one specific maid who cleaned up his office. And I had a sneaking suspicion who this person might be.

"Celia?" I began, when she placed my dinner tray on the table. "I have another favor to ask of you."

"Yes, mum," she said a bit hesitantly, as if she knew what was coming.

"You have 'em, don't you?"

"Have what, mum?"

Clamping my index finger and thumb together as if holding a key ring, and dangling it back and forth, I said, "Jingle, jingle, jingle."

She pushed the table over to me, a sly grin on her face. "Yes, mum," she murmured. Glancing toward the door, she hastily slipped one hand in her apron pocket, and then surreptitiously slid a key underneath the side of the plate. "I'll be back for your tray later, mum."

"Make it much later," I suggested with a smile. "And Celia, thanks."

"For what, mum?" she questioned with feigned innocence. "Just doing me job."

As soon as the door closed behind her, I pushed the table back, grabbed my cane, and got up. Within a few minutes, I was in Ashley's room.

Free of the dust and cobwebs one would expect to find after five years, the room looked like someone still occupied it, despite the musty odor that assailed my senses the moment I opened the door. There were toiletries, hairbrushes, a few bobby pins, and even an open jewelry box on the vanity, as if the occupant would be back at any moment. Across the room, a small closet door was standing open. Inside were many neatly arranged dresses, several pairs of jeans, a sweatshirt or two, and lots of blouses and skirts. I felt like I was intruding on a living person's private space. Brandon had seemingly kept everything the way Ashley had left it, but why? Did he really think there was any hope of her coming back? I shook my head to clear it. I needed to get down to the business at hand: finding a picture of my cousin.

I scanned the room, located what I was searching for on a dresser by the window, and made my way over there. The first picture was of Vivian. I could see the resemblance to the snapshot Sara possessed. Vivian had actually been rather pretty, her blonde hair pulled back in a French twist. This reminded me of the way

Sara wore hers. I wondered if Tom had told Sara that her mother wore her hair like this, since Vivian's hair was long and flowing in the picture he'd given her. I also wondered whether Tom had suffered from a crush on Vivian all those years ago. He'd obviously kept the photograph for some reason, and further, tried to palm Vivian off as Sara's mother. Did he wish she had been? After all, "Vivian Leigh" was the name of one of his properties.

I shrugged this thought away and admired the woman's features. She had finely arched, light brown eyebrows, a petite nose, full lips, and an oval-shaped face. I didn't see why she would have been jealous of my mother; she was pretty in her own right. *But seldom are we ever satisfied with ourselves*, I thought.

I then turned my attention to the picture on the other end of the dresser, which I assumed was Ashley in her late teens. The dark hair caught my attention first, then the face that was so much like her mother's. But instead of Vivian's sweet smile, Ashley had a hard look, as if she had not been a happy young woman. I glanced between the two pictures, back and forth, my mind seemingly searching for some connection that was just out of reach.

Moving closer to the picture of Ashley, I could now see why Celia had mistaken Sara for her, because there were definite similarities. I glanced back at the picture of Vivian with her blue eyes and then over to Ashley's green ones. *Green?* I questioned, leaning over closer. *Familiar green eyes!* I backed up rapidly, stumbled over my own feet, and sat down hard on the edge of the bed behind me. My hand went to my mouth, just as Celia's had that day on the porch. I didn't cross myself, however, for I hadn't seen a ghost: I'd seen the real thing. The eyes staring back at me from the photograph were Sara's.

But how could that be? It couldn't! And yet, the similarities were too striking to ignore. The resemblance was clear, in the set of Ashley's jaw and especially in the depths of those eyes. I had seen this overall expression on Sara's face many times. Usually when Brandon was around.

"Oh, my God," I said aloud, my mind struggling to make sense of the multitude of thoughts careening around in my brain. *But it can't be! It just can't be! Sara was in a car accident with her mother. The article was in the newspaper. We both read it!*

Just then the door to Ashley's room squeaked open, and my heart jumped up in my throat. *Brandon or Celia?* I was swiftly preparing myself for the proverbial shit to hit the fan when Sara peeked around the door. "I knew you couldn't resist coming in here," she said with a big grin on her face.

"Wh-What...are you doing back so soon?" I asked, knowing I

had a look of shock on my face and groping for some way to change it before she took notice.

"So soon?" she questioned, one eyebrow arching skyward, the grin slowly sliding off her face. "I couldn't wait to get back to you," she explained, walking toward me. "Aren't you glad to see me?"

"Uh, yes...yes, of course I am," I stammered, thinking how much I wanted to get her out of there, and fast. "Wh-what happened?" I started struggling to my feet.

"Oh, I decided to let the detective handle things, like you suggested. He'll probably have better luck than me. And besides, I've got something I couldn't wait to tell you." The smile was back. "There's no big rush," she added, when I nearly lost my balance.

"Well, Brandon might find us in here and he doesn't—"

"He's not home."

"How do you know that?"

"I saw Celia on the way in. She said to tell you she'd be up when he came home. Whatever that means."

"She...she gave me the key to this room. He doesn't like anyone coming in here. So let's go."

"Wait, don't I at least get a hug first?" she inquired, reaching out for me.

"Of course." I wrapped one arm around her neck. "I missed you terribly. Now let's go."

"Jesus, you're as jumpy as a cat on a hot tin roof," she noted when I pulled back. Her gaze shifted to our surroundings, and her expression changed dramatically.

"What's wrong?" I asked, my heart racing, wondering what she might be thinking.

"I...I don't know. I..." She glanced around at the walls. There were just a few pastoral scenes strategically placed here and there. "This was a young girl's room?" she queried, frowning.

"College age, I believe."

"Something's missing," she stated, her gaze sweeping the room again. "It doesn't feel right."

"What?" My heart skipped a beat. "What are you talking about?"

"No posters, no...individual touches." She shrugged. "So, Celia keeps things just like this, hmm?" She reached out and rubbed her finger over the bedpost, obviously checking for dust.

Afraid she was about to remember something that I didn't want to hear, I breathed a sigh of relief. And now that I looked around without an agenda, I realized she had a point about the room: it didn't feel like a place where a young girl had come of age. But I didn't have the luxury of delving into that bit of minutia right now.

"Come on, I'm getting hungry," I announced. "I left my dinner in my room. And I want to hear all about your trip."

"Okay, but hold on a minute. As long as I'm here..." She'd obviously noticed the dresser behind me, because she moved in that direction. "So, did Ashley look anything like me, or is Celia's eyesight..." She paused, her gaze landing on the picture of Vivian.

"Come on, Sara," I prodded, touching her arm.

She wouldn't budge. "Look at this, Faith. She...she could be...my mother."

"Oh no, there's not much resemblance," I lied. "Your father probably just had a crush on her or something and...and had a picture of her, so he gave it to you and—"

"Yes, there is," she interrupted, glancing up into the mirror, then back at the picture. "Look at the eyebrows, Faith. I don't tweeze 'em to make 'em arch like this, you know." She stared at the photo. "Her lips are a bit fuller, but that could be because of my surgery. Her nose is a little larger, but..." She paused, her eyes drifting to the other photograph on the dresser. She moved behind me and toward it so slowly, I felt like I was watching her on videotape, in slow motion. "Ho-o-ly shi-it!" she gasped, her lips starting to tremble. "Oh, God, Faith!"

I took hold of her arm. "Come on, let's get outta here. It's not what you think, it...it can't be."

"But you saw it, didn't you?" she asked, turning to face me. "That's me, Faith! And...and you know it, don't you?" Her eyes darted back and forth, seemingly beseeching mine.

"I know no such a thing. For all we know, the plastic surgery could have changed your features dramatically, and it's...it's just a coincidence you resemble her...a little."

"A little? Bullshit!" she exclaimed, wrenching away from me. "That's me. I know it. I can feel it," she tapped her chest, "in here. That means, I'm not...Sara Bennington." She paused, her mind obviously running wild. "I'm not Amy Jackson's daughter. Or even... Tom Randall's." She picked up the photograph. "I'm...Ashley Neilson. Jason is my brother, and Brandon...is my father." She spun around on her heel and faced me. "And that means you're my... Oh, God, Faith, what have I done?"

The look of horror on her face cut me to the core. The photograph slipped from her hands and crashed to the floor, the glass shattering. She glanced down at it, then up at me, her mouth agape. "I'm so sorry!" she shrieked, and bolted from the room.

I knew the implications of her statement; I'd already been considering that same thing only moments before. If it were true, we each had fallen in love with, and made love to, our own cousin. All these revelations were almost too much for me to bear; I knew they had to hit Sara even harder, because it was her life, her past, we might have unearthed here. It appeared the skeleton in the closet was one we hadn't even considered, one we perhaps didn't want to. At least, I didn't. Not even now.

I took off out the door as fast as my legs would carry me. I didn't want her to leave in her present state of mind. We met in the hall, and I noted her purse slung over her shoulder, keys in hand. "Where are you going?" I asked as she brushed past me.

She stopped abruptly, the look in her eyes disturbing, to say the least. It reminded me of a deer caught in a car's headlights. She offered no response, merely stared at me for several all too brief moments, her eyes changing color from green to light brown.

As abruptly as it had begun, the spell was broken, and she was walking away at a rapid pace. "Sara...Sara..." I called, my voice echoing down the long hallway after her.

She stopped momentarily at the staircase and glanced back. I didn't know what to say. No words would come out. Turning quickly, she disappeared down the stairs; and I had the sinking, all too real feeling in the pit of my stomach that she wouldn't be returning anytime soon.

Feeling like I was on automatic pilot, I wandered back into Ashley's room. Reaching down and picking up the broken picture frame, I saw Sara's eyes staring back at me. There was no mistaking this. The nose was a bit different, Sara's a bit smaller now. The lips were a fraction smaller, without so much of the previous pouty expression. The cheekbones were more pronounced, probably from losing the baby fat. But the eyes hadn't changed. They were the same sad green orbs I had come to love: windows into the soul of the person I had fallen in love with and made love to. The one person I had wanted to spend the rest of my life with.

I sat down on the floor and picked up all the broken pieces of glass, placing them back in the frame, bit by bit. In an apparent daze, I struggled to my feet and carried the wreckage over to a trashcan by the small desk. When I carefully turned the frame over, the shards of glass shifted, making a tinkling sound as they rubbed against one another. Larger pieces splintered into smaller shards when they toppled together into the empty trashcan. I couldn't help but wonder if I was listening to the sounds of broken dreams and shattered realities. If Sara truly was my cousin, what did that mean for us? I cringed at the thought of how horrified she had looked when she said, "Oh, God, Faith, what have I done?"

"Miss Faith?" Celia called from my room.

I walked out the door, the framed photograph still in my hand. "I'm sorry, Celia, but...I dropped this picture and... I'll try to get a frame to replace it."

Celia stared at the object. "It's all right, mum. I...I'll say I did it."

"No, Celia, I can't..."

"It would be better that way," she maintained as I handed her the key. "Want I should put it back for ya, mum?"

I hesitantly handed her the picture. "I'm truly sorry... I..."

"Think nuthin' of it, mum. It can be replaced."

"Thank you, Celia."

I insisted she take the tray with her when she left, though I hadn't touched my meal. I didn't feel like eating anymore. I merely crawled into bed and turned on the television to help silence the endless chatter in my head. Chatter that was trying to make sense of all the implications this newfound knowledge presented while at the same time desperately seeking to justify our relationship.

Oh, Sara, I thought.

No, no, she's Ashley now. Or rather, again.

NO! She can't be Ashley, I argued with myself. *She just...looks like her.*

But the photograph Tom had given Sara with Vivian and Mother in it...why would he do that unless...

He just happened to have a picture of Vivian, because he had a crush on her, that's all. Sara was in a car accident with her mother, Amy Jackson. We saw the article!

Ashley was also in a car accident; her body never found...

Oh, God, no, Sara can't be Ashley! It's impossible!

Is it?

Of course it is! Sara just happens to look like Ashley. A coincidence, that's all. Just a coincidence! Yes, there's no other rational explanation! And Sara will realize this when she's had time to sit down and think things over clearly. At least, I hope she will!

My God, what thoughts must be running through her mind? I couldn't imagine not knowing about my past, and then having something like this happen to confuse things further. *God, what a mess!* A mess *I* had created with my incessant curiosity.

Deeply worried about Sara, I went on and on in the same vein for the rest of the evening. Guilt became my constant companion, apprehension holding my hand in a death grip.

Brandon came up as usual, this time talking about some new

undertaking in which he was involved. My mind was elsewhere, naturally. By this time, denial had effortlessly edged into "what if it's true?" My mind was spinning its wheels, pondering the questions that perplexing conundrum would pose.

If Sara is Ashley, then why didn't Brandon recognize her? I wondered. *Or Jason, even?* But then, Sara's hair had been blonde, her eyes blue from the contact lenses she seldom removed until late in the evening. That is, until recently. Celia hadn't made mention of the resemblance until Sara had dyed her hair back to its natural color. And Brandon hadn't been around Sara much lately. Nor did they often make eye contact. Whenever dealing with each other in my presence, theirs was always a quick glance or nod. Most of the time, Brandon seemed to ignore her, as if she weren't even in the room.

Could this be why they didn't like being around each other? Did they have some type of effect on each other? Is that why Brandon didn't look at her? Had she reminded him of Ashley, thereby making it painful for him to be around her?

He finally noticed my inattentiveness, interrupting my thoughts when he inquired about the cause of my preoccupation. I lied, saying I was tired and not feeling well. Of course the latter, in itself, wasn't far from the truth, because I *was* sick. Heartsick.

I sat up in bed until the wee hours of the morning waiting for Sara. Even though my mind maintained that she would not return anytime soon, my heart still clung to the thin hope that she would.

The next morning, Celia woke me and inquired about Sara's whereabouts. I pretended I didn't know. I could only hope she would return soon. I desperately needed to talk to her; otherwise I felt I would surely lose her.

Afternoon came and went; still no Sara. As the hours slipped past, my heart sank lower and lower. I sat in her chair and gazed out the window overlooking the patio. I remembered all the times we had spent together, especially our first night in bed. Would everything be ruined now? If we really were cousins, then what we had shared was terribly wrong, wasn't it? Could love be wrong?

I sat right there until midnight, refusing my dinner and suffering through Brandon's chatter from across the small table between our chairs. I accepted the glass of milk, as usual. And this time, I drank it.

The next morning, my head felt heavy. I assumed it was from worrying so much and not eating. I asked about Sara, but Celia hadn't seen her either. After breakfast, Brandon was back. He informed me that he was taking the day off because he was concerned about me. He badgered me to let him escort me outside, and I finally agreed. I took his arm as we walked around, but all I could think about was the first time Sara and I had done this. I suppose, in my reverie, I acted as if I were feeling close to him, for he remarked about it as he put his arm around me. Comfort of any kind felt better than none at all, and at that moment, I readily accepted his.

When we finished our walk, we had lunch at the dining room table, which Brandon thought should be a treat for me. For his sake, I tried to show enthusiasm, but inside I was filled with grief. He escorted me to my room after lunch, and I ended up falling asleep in Sara's chair.

I awoke later and was headed for the bathroom when I caught a glimpse of taillights moving down the driveway. Although I only saw the rear bumper for a moment or two, I knew by the spacing of the lights that the car belonged to Sara. I hauled butt as fast as I could to the stairs and began descending them. It was my intention to commandeer Charles and have him drive me to her apartment, but Brandon met me at the bottom of the stairs.

"Good news, Princess," he said cheerfully, placing his arm around my waist. "You have been officially released from the doctor's care."

"Officially released?" I asked, puzzled.

"Yes. I spoke with Dr. Rosemund this afternoon, and he said that you're well enough to be released from constant medical supervision."

Yeah, well, great, I thought, knowing this meant that I could set a date with the plastic surgeon. But who cared about that at the moment? I sure didn't.

"Was Sara here?" I asked, ignoring his enthusiasm.

He looked puzzled now. "Yes, but... Didn't she come up and say goodbye to you?"

"Goodbye!" I nearly shrieked.

"Why, yes. I informed her of the doctor's decision, and she agreed that you no longer required her services. She went up the stairs and I assumed—"

"What?" I exclaimed.

"Why, Princess, what's the matter? Did Miss Bennington leave without a word of goodbye?" He didn't wait for me to answer, it must have been written all over my face. "She should be ashamed of herself! I will certainly report this—"

"No, don't...please. It's...no big deal," I countered, unable to stand the thought of causing Sara any trouble.

"But it's made you unhappy and that's a big deal to me. I have a good mind to get on the phone right this minute and—"

"No, please!" I pulled away from his embrace. "Please don't...don't do anything, she...she probably just... I was asleep. I fell asleep in the chair and...she probably didn't want to disturb me."

"But, Princess this has obviously upset you and—"

"Yes, at first. It was just the...shock; I'm fine now. Really, just fine." I forced myself to smile.

"Oh...well, that's a little better. A bit more like my Princess." He put his hand on my cheek. It took all the willpower I had to maintain that smile. "Now you can have the freedom you've been wanting," he continued. "No one watching your every move. And we can have this taken care of." He leaned over and placed a kiss on the top of my forehead, near the scar.

"Um, yes, that...that will be wonderful," I murmured, feeling a bit uncomfortable and taking a step back. "But perhaps we can talk about this another time? I-I'm feeling a bit tired now."

"Of course," he agreed. "I'll see you back to your room."

"Oh no...no, that won't be necessary. Really, I'm fine," I lied, unsure of how long I could continue with this particular charade. My legs felt weak as I started back up the stairs.

"Princess, what was it you came down for?" he queried. "I'll bring it up for you."

"Umm..." This stopped me in my tracks for a moment. "Ya know, I can't remember, what with all the...excitement." I shrugged. "Guess it wasn't very important, after all."

"You do look quite tired, Princess. Perhaps I should see you to—"

I snapped my fingers. "Oh, ya know, I just remembered. I was going to the library. Yes...I thought I'd do some reading, but now...I've changed my mind. I'm too tired." I rubbed one eye for emphasis.

"What book did you want? I could get it for you and bring it up with your milk. Then you can have it—"

"Oh no, I-I didn't have a particular one in mind," I interrupted him for the umpteenth time. "I'll find something tomorrow. Thank you anyway," I added for good measure, starting up the stairs again.

"You're welcome, Princess. I'll be up later with your milk."

I breathed a sigh of relief, hoping he wouldn't be up anytime soon, because with each step I took, I could feel my energy draining away. Not only were my legs a bit shaky, I felt weak inside, as well. This couldn't be happening. She couldn't do this to me! Could she?

I headed straight for her room. *She'll have to come back for her things*, I thought.

My heart sank all the way down to my toes as I entered her bedroom. She'd already removed her things. Tears welled up in my eyes as I slowly scanned the area, looking for something, anything that she might have to return for. But there was nothing.

Shuffling slowly back to my room, I felt as if I were dragging my heart along behind me. I lumbered over to the bed and plopped down. I could not believe she had left without even a word to me. Didn't she care about my feelings? Didn't what we had shared mean anything to her? *Obviously not,* I concluded, flopping over on my side. When my head hit the pillow, something crackled underneath. Pulling back the pillowcase, I found an envelope. My heart pounded as I tore into it. *Perhaps she wants me to go with her*, I thought. *Perhaps she'll be back to get me and then we'll...*

Dear Faith,

I love you with all my heart. And I'm very sorry, but I can't stay here any longer. I intended to come back and say goodbye, but I just can't bring myself to face you. Perhaps it's better this way, anyway. I'm sorry for what I led you into. Surely you must feel the utter shame of our relationship now. I won't subject you to that further. I wish you all the luck in the world. I know you'll do well. And despite the shame of what I've done, I wouldn't change any of the memories I carry with me. Not even one little bit. Please forgive me, Faith. I truly had no idea. Perhaps one day I'll read about my famous psychologist patient and smile. Maybe, by then, you'll be able to smile, too.

Sara

I knew she had written the letter hastily, for the handwriting was not her usual careful style. There was even a small round spot on the paper, which hadn't completely dried; the dark ink smeared on the word "further," presumably by a teardrop.

I burst into tears myself, clutching the letter to my chest. My heart was breaking into a million tiny pieces, each shard cutting away at my insides. I cried so hard, I didn't even notice Brandon was in the room until he spoke.

"Princess, why are you crying?" he asked, rushing over to me. "This should be a happy day. Now we can have that scar— What's this?" Before I had time to object, he pulled the letter from my hands. I started to voice a protest, but nothing came out. What did it matter, anyway? She was already gone; he could no longer fire her. And I really didn't care what happened anymore. My world was in utter shambles.

"Damn her!" he exclaimed, ripping the letter in half. "She-she seduced you, that...that perverted whore! I'll kill the bitch! I knew she was no damn good! But *you* liked her so much...and now I understand why! Oh, great God in heaven, tell me you didn't lay down with her!" he demanded. "You didn't, did you?"

"Ye-es," I blubbered, though not ashamed in the least.

"Goddammit!" he roared. "And I never suspected! But I should have. Oh yes, I should have. I saw her making you hang all over her and... Oh, Princess, it was my fault. Yes, all my fault for not making her leave sooner. I should have seen through her." His tone was softening. "Oh, you poor child...you poor, poor helpless child. Seduced by such a vile creature. But it's not your fault, Princess," he added as he knelt down beside me. "I know you're innocent."

"No, I'm...not," I corrected.

"Of course you are. You've never done this before, have you? Why, of course not; you're just a child. A sweet virgin," he said softly, touching my face. "Don't worry about this at all. No one ever need know; it will be our secret. You'll forget in time, forget she ever even existed."

"But...I love her," I wailed.

"Oh, great God in heaven!" he bellowed. "She has turned your head completely!" He stood up quickly and stormed over to the window. "Damn that pervert! I wish I'd known before..." His fist slammed down on the windowsill, rattling the pane. "I'll have her name smeared from here to...Timbuktu. She'll never work again in this town!"

"No, Brandon!" I shouted, sitting up. "She's not to blame, I am! Leave her alone, please!"

"Princess, she has...*defiled* you," he maintained, disgust in his tone. "Not only has she despoiled your body, she has turned your head and completely muddled your thinking."

"Leave her be!" I demanded.

He wheeled around and glared at me. All at once, I felt afraid. I'd never seen such a nasty, hateful expression on his face before. Out of habit, I instantly began searching for a way to appeal to his better judgment, because anger seemed to be getting me nowhere. "You said no one else need know," I began, dropping my head and looking ashamed. "If you do this, you'll surely...shame me. Please, Brandon," I pleaded. "Don't do this to me!"

"Princess, you know I wouldn't hurt you for the world, but

she must pay for this."

"At what price to me?" I prodded. "I think she's paying her own price now, a heavy one. Let her be, Brandon; please, just let her be. Promise me you will." I broke down in tears again.

He shoved his hands in his pockets as if he were stuffing his anger inside them, as well. Turning back to the window, he stared out into the darkness. "I...I suppose you're right," he said after several moments, his tone calmer. "No one need ever know. Time will heal all. I-I was going to throw a lavish party this weekend to celebrate...what I thought would be good news, but..." He paused for quite a long time. I was relieved that the angry storm had passed. "Perhaps it's still a good idea. We'll celebrate despite this. Yes, indeed we will. Perhaps that was my mistake, leaving you in the hands of a woman. Time with a man would do you good."

"Brandon, please, I don't—"

"All you need is male company. You'll soon forget all this disgusting nonsense with which she has filled your head," he said, as if he hadn't even heard my protest. "I'll arrange a date for you."

"No, Brandon, please I don't want to be—"

"I know what's best, Princess. You'll see that a man can offer you far more than she ever could." I started to voice a protest, but held my tongue because of the look on his face. "We'll speak of this no more," he declared, then quickly turned and left the room.

I fell back on the bed. I knew he was going to complicate the issue further, but I had no strength left with which to protest. I was mentally, physically, and emotionally drained. I curled up in a ball, feeling like a child: a helpless, angry, and most of all, broken-hearted little girl. Fate had played a cruel joke on both of us. It wasn't fair! Now I truly had lost everyone I dearly loved.

Feeling lost and alone, like a child without a home, I cried myself to sleep.

Chapter
16

Throughout the next week, I grew more and more depressed each day. I abandoned thoughts of running to her—trying to convince her it would be all right, whether we were cousins or not—for it seemed this parting was what she wanted. *Perhaps it even gave her the excuse she needed in order to walk away,* I reasoned.

Brandon tried to cheer me up, but it didn't work. I feigned a smile for him, yet inside I was crying deep, sad tears, which no one ever saw but me. Each night I drank the milk he brought and cried myself to sleep; each morning I felt dizzy and sleepy, which only led me deeper into the pit of despair.

At the end of the week, Brandon threw his proposed party. Young men I had never met before followed after me, each trying to outdo the other with common courtesies. They were supposed to make me feel like a princess, I'm sure, but I felt more like a bitch in heat, with all the studs in the neighborhood hot on her trail. These studs weren't merely responding to biological urges, however; they were onto the scent of money. I sensed this by the way they kept glancing over at Brandon, as if for his approval. I wondered how many greenbacks had been handed out to those willing to take on the challenge, and what the proffered payoff was for the one who caught me. Needless to say, I wasn't interested in any of them. All I wanted was Sara. I knew Brandon noticed my inattentiveness, because I saw him watching us while he downed one drink after another. Finally, when I'd had my fill of the drooling studs, I excused myself. I saw no sense in leading these young men on, only to please my uncle. I could not be something I wasn't, nor would I even try.

Upstairs in my room with a bottle of brandy pilfered from the kitchen, I locked the door and turned on the stereo to drown out the party below. I pressed play on the tape deck on my way by, while downing a big swallow of brandy straight from the bottle. The liquor nearly took my breath away as it burned its way down my throat. Blazing a trail down my esophagus, it slammed into the pit of my stomach and burst into flames, as if it had been concocted from the fires of hell itself.

I went over to her chair and flopped down, listening to the song that was playing. The female singer was crooning about being alone again...silence filling the empty room... I turned the bottle up again, tears stinging my eyes. The singer wanted to turn back the hands of time; they had kissed in a warm September rain, before her heart was filled with pain. She wanted to love that way again; she longed for wishes to come true. I turned the bottle up once more, my heart breaking, my eyes streaming tears, and my throat burning like I had swallowed embers of hellfire and brimstone. The song could not have been more appropriate. Funny thing was, I had never really cared much for it before, but now I grabbed the remote and rewound the tape.

"Play it again, Sam," I said aloud, then downed another big swallow. Gritting my teeth, I sucked in cool air. I was getting good at this. The next song began and I sang along. "Come back to me," I crooned, tears streaming down my cheeks. *And they said country was "crying in your beer" music,* I thought, and took another big gulp.

Next up was a song we had made love to. "Just great, just fuckin' great," I grumbled, then tilted the bottle up over and over as that beautiful memory played out in my head right along with the song. Remembering love this way was bittersweet, but it was all I had left. *Preserve your memories...they're all that's left you.*

Celia brought up my milk that night, which was quite a switch. And one I was thoroughly grateful for, because what she found was an intoxicated woman who needed to be put to bed. Noticing my red, swollen eyes, she questioned me about it, and I almost let everything tumble out. Yet even in my condition, I somehow managed to control my tongue and lay the blame on my monthly cycle. *At least this comes in handy every once in a while,* I mused, when she seemed to buy my excuse. In the next instant, however, she exposed my deception by adding that she missed Sara, as well.

"Whaddaya mean, as well?" I slurred, shocked at her inference.

"Very little slips by me, mum. Servants become invisible, but they're not deaf or blind," she replied, helping me up out of the chair.

"You're...very obser-vant, Ceel-ya," I slurred.

"Yes, mum," she agreed, catching hold of me as I stumbled. "I've seen ma share of...strange things. Not that you two are strange though, mum. Why, in my day, hardly anyone woulda given it a second thought, you two being so close. But today...Well, mum, the servants notice things."

"And what else...have you noticed?" I inquired as she sat me down on the side of the bed.

"Wull now, Miss Sara...she bears a striking resemblance to Miss Ashley. I 'spect ya noticed that too, after being in there." She gestured toward Ashley's room.

I cleared my throat and hiccupped. "Yes, I d-did." I nodded sadly.

"I 'spect she left on account of it?"

I merely nodded once again.

"I'm not condoning or condemning, mum, but if I wuz you, I'd have myself a look in the attic. Miss Ashley spent a good bit of time up there."

"Attic? W-What are you talkin' about?"

"This ol' house holds many secrets, like the castles of our kings and queens. Sum are best left alone, but uthers...could be helpful."

"Ex-actly what are you tryin' ta tell me?"

"Just have a look in the attic, mum," she replied, a bit of irritation in her tone now.

"I...m-miss her," I babbled, struggling to remove my clothes.

"I know, mum," she sympathized, helping me out of the dress. "You wuz very close." She went to get me some pajamas.

"Are we cousins, Ceel-ya?"

"Can't really say, mum. Tom wuz right fond of Miss Vivian, but...wull, I'd be afraid ta speculate."

"Would it be so bad if... I mean, we can't have kids or anything, so..."

"In the olden days, cousins wuz not too close for marriage," she offered.

"Why'd she have to leea-ve me, Ceel-ya?" I queried, as she sat back down beside me and I leaned my head on her shoulder.

"Oh, mum, maybe she'll have a change a'heart, soon," she soothed, patting my cheek with her hand. "Cum now, we need ta get ya dressed for bed."

The last thing I remember was Celia cutting off the light. "Goodnight, mum. She'll be back. Don' ya worry 'bout that."

The next morning, I had one hell of a hangover. Brandon came up after breakfast, but I think he was suffering from the same malady. He reluctantly left the room and eventually the house, when still feigning a headache, I didn't join him later.

Remembering bits and pieces of the conversation with Celia the night before, I wondered what could possibly be in the attic. *Secrets? What kind of secrets?* Needless to say, the intrigue pulled me from my bed. Despite the headache that lingered just behind my eyes, I got up and went looking for the attic.

Searching the east wing, I found nothing that even resembled stairs behind any of the unlocked doors, so I proceeded to the west wing. The last door on the left was my only hope, although it looked much like all the rest. Placing my hand on the knob, I expected to find one of two things: locked like the others I'd tried, or another unused bedroom. When I opened it, however, I immediately knew I'd hit pay dirt. A miasma of tepid air, like a warm breath, assailed my senses with the smell of cardboard, dust, and things long unused.

In front of me lay a steep stairway. Upon first glance, I thought it too steep for me and my cane. But now more than ever, I wanted to go up there, so I tried the first step. My legs wobbled. This was *not* going to be easy, but I was determined to do it.

Finally, I reached the top. The large open space before me was dark, except for the daylight coming from an oval window in the middle of the expanse. I could tell by its immensity that the attic spanned the entire length and breadth of the house. Searching for whatever Celia wanted me to find was going to be like looking for a needle in the proverbial haystack.

I wiped a trickle of sweat off my brow, wondering why she hadn't given me an indication about where to look. But then, Celia was often vague, dropping hints and little suggestions without ever really coming out and saying what was on her mind. I assumed this must be due to her position of servitude. Maids were often seen, but seldom heard. Or at least, isn't that the way it was said to be?

I glanced around my general area, knowing that if I wanted to do any searching, I'd need some light. I ran my hand over the wall and found a switch. I flipped it, expecting the attic to come to life before me. Nothing happened. I flipped it back down, then up again. Still nothing.

"Damn," I said, leaning against the wall. *What now? Get someone to change the bulbs before I can see what's up here?* "Shit!" I backed down the steep steps very slowly. I was turning to close the door when I saw a silver tube-like object on the floor by the wall, which I hadn't noticed on my way in. *Because it wasn't there,* I thought. *Thank you, Celia.* I reached down and picked it up, even though I knew I would need a brief respite before reinitializing my ascent—my hangover didn't mesh well with climbing steep stairs.

I flicked the flashlight on to make sure it worked, while wondering what Celia wanted me to find so badly that she would follow me and have a flashlight ready for use. *Must be something pretty important.* Or did she, like me, merely love a good mystery? Even if she was just watching someone else figure it out, since she obviously already had.

I finally reached the top again and turned the flashlight on. The narrow beam skimmed over old furniture and clothes. What a task I had before me! I hoped whatever I was searching for was big, or else I'd never find it up here. *Unless my benefactor has left me a trail to follow,* I thought.

"Come along, Watson," I said to my cane. "The game is afoot."

I followed a narrow path that appeared to meander around the expanse of the attic, providing access for future storage and retrieval. Taking my time, I scanned both sides of the path with my flashlight, searching for some sort of clue amongst the hodgepodge of dusty old furniture, racks of clothes, and cardboard boxes. In the midst of this, I was a bit surprised to find a few tailors' mannequins decked out in various ensembles—some of the clothes apparently dating back to the Civil War era, considering their styles.

I made my way over to a mannequin clad in a beautiful, dark blue gown, which I assumed had belonged to one of my ancestors. *A true Southern belle*, I thought, touching the hoop skirt. *How did they manage to get around in these things?* I mused, lifting up the skirt to look underneath. *Jesus, look at all that wasted material. She coulda made two skirts with all that cloth.*

Beside this was a dingy white lace dress, complete with a veil draped across the headless knob of the mannequin. *Someone's wedding dress?* Perhaps this wouldn't be such an awful task after all. Being up here surrounded by history was quite intriguing in itself. I could definitely let my imagination run wild, conjuring up all sorts of images concerning the people who might have worn these clothes. Panning the flashlight around, I got so caught up in imagining what they must have been like, I almost forgot what I had come for. Then again, I didn't know what the hell I was looking for.

Sitting down on the stool to a dressing table, I fanned the light around hoping something—anything—would catch my eye. The beam of light skimmed over a collection of large wooden picture frames propped up against a headboard. *If nothing else, this could prove interesting,* I thought. Maybe I would get a chance to see my ancestors, instead of merely imagining what they had looked like.

Finding little else as appealing, I made my way over to the stack and bent down to admire the first portrait. It was a distinguished Southern gentleman. My, but he did look proud in his gray outfit and top hat. His light brown eyes twinkled and his facial expression bore only a hint of a smile, as if he were too proud for that. I wondered who he was. Was this the first owner of Shady Grove, whose headstone I'd seen, or was he someone from a more recent generation? I looked for a nameplate on the frame, to no avail. *Silly!* I thought. *Who needs nameplates on family portraits? They only use those in movies.*

Noticing an old trunk near the portraits, and feeling a bit tired, I took a seat. *This is conveniently placed*, I mused, reaching out to move the first portrait aside. A slight chill ran down my spine at the thought that I wasn't the first to do this very same thing. *Silly-willy, now why should that scare you? Jesus, you're immature. You watched too many horror movies as a kid.*

I pulled portrait after portrait from the stack for closer inspection. Young children, old men, old women, young men and young women—dressed in clothes from the nineteenth and twentieth centuries—had all been immortalized on canvas. My ancestral history was unfolding before me and I enjoyed every minute of it, even if I didn't know a single one of their names.

Finally, I reached a familiar face: Vivian. I pulled the portrait out. Her blue eyes seemed sad in this one. Or was it just the artist's interpretation? Funny how a photograph could catch a person within one unique frame of time and preserve that expression for all time to come, making others who saw it assume the person was always that happy or sad, as the case might be. But an artist, on the other hand, saw the person for a longer length of time; and in their interpretation, they added things a camera wouldn't pick up in that split-second interval. I scanned the portrait again, recognizing the vague likeness to Sara's features in the flawless face. I quickly put it back. I didn't feel like crying again this morning. Besides, I had no brandy to drown my tears in.

The next one I came to was my mother. Her blue eyes twinkled and a smile spread across her lovely face, emphasizing the dimples on each cheek. I pulled it out slowly, unable to control my own smile, because she looked so very lovely. When I propped it up in front of me, I was shocked at the low-cut style of her blue dress, her bosom pushed up to tantalize the eye like all the other

Southern belles that had gone before her. Upon closer inspection, I realized she was wearing the dark blue gown I had previously admired.

Was that dress hers? I wondered. *And why had she never mentioned this portrait? Why had she left it?* Then I remembered Celia telling me how my mother and father had left so suddenly that they left many possessions behind. I was intrigued. Was Celia leading me to some clue as to why they had departed? If so, what could this possibly have to do with Sara? I stared at the portrait, wishing my mother were here to clear up all my questions.

When I got up and started to put the portrait back, the others in the stack had shifted forward, and staring me in the face was one of Ashley. I put down my mother's and pulled this one out, unable to resist though I knew it would only bring me grief. Sara's sad green eyes stared back at me from the face of a preadolescent girl, no older than eleven or twelve. Yet there was more than sadness in these eyes; they had a haunted, troubled look about them. I wondered what could have caused her to look that way. Why were these eyes filled with such turmoil? The thought of Sara's eyes having this same look as she brushed by me on the day she walked out of my life filled me with a profound sadness and an intense yearning. I wanted her back, dammit! I didn't care if we were cousins; I loved her and I wanted to be with her.

I traced my fingers over the immortalized face of the young girl who was, in essence, a stranger to me. I couldn't help but wonder if she was still a stranger to Sara. Had she regained her memories after the initial shock the other day? This was the preferred cinematic method for overcoming amnesia, except for getting hit over the head or some other such outrageous notion. But then, this wasn't a movie. This was life, and all too real.

I hastily put the portrait back, feeling the tears welling up in my eyes. Then I picked up my mother's and tried to replace it between Ashley's and another one, but it wouldn't go back in place. Something was in the way.

"Damn," I said, looking behind the picture to see what was holding it off the floor. On the back of my mother's portrait, I found a loose staple that was striking the frame behind it. As I leaned over to adjust the frame, I noticed writing on the back of my mother's picture. Using the flashlight, I illuminated the words: To the most beautiful princess in the world, Brandon.

His pet name for me had been his pet name for her! I sat back down on the trunk so hard it jarred my teeth. Had this portrait been a present from him? Is that why she'd left it behind? Was Brandon's infatuation part of the reason they'd left? Had my father

read this and gotten jealous? Or had there possibly been more to
it?

Just then, I heard a noise from the other end of the attic.
Quickly swinging the light in the direction of the east wing, I got
to my feet in order to obtain a better view. Nothing moved. *Rats,* I
surmised. *Yuck!* Shivering at the thought of them running over
my feet, I quickly checked my immediate vicinity. Relief flooded
through me when I found no sign of any furry rodents. Although I
wasn't enamored with the idea of rats running around up here
with me, I figured I might as well see the rest of the attic while I
had the chance.

Mustering my courage, I continued down the path to the far
end of the east wing and then crossed over to the other side of the
house, which put me over what had been Sara's room. This side
had no sitting room, only a bedroom, so it was much smaller. I
ambled down its small path, wondering how much money lay up
here wasting away. There were boxes neatly arranged on the outside wall, containing God only knew what. And on the opposite
side of the path, fine antique furniture that must have been worth
a fortune sat covered in a thick layer of dust. I stopped and ran my
hand over one of the dressers, which was still in very good condition. Out of sheer curiosity, I opened one of the drawers to find
clothes still inside it. *Did this family keep everything?* I wondered,
then looked through several other drawers. If was as if time had
stood still here; every drawer was packed with some woman's
neatly arranged clothing. *What a strange thing to do,* I thought.
Why save these clothes? And whose are they, anyway? The style
appeared to be from the latter part of the twentieth century, the
seventies most likely. Did these belong to Vivian? Or perhaps even
my mother? Had she left these behind, as well? *No, wait... If
Mother had left her things, they would have been in my room,
wouldn't they?*

To distract myself, I turned my attention to another dresser
and opened its drawers. These were empty, as I would have
expected. And so were the next chest of drawers, as well as an old
blanket trunk. Although not a major discovery, or anywhere near
what I thought I was looking for, this did puzzle me.

"Celia's right about secrets. This attic is a world of mystery,"
I mumbled, scanning around me, wondering where the answers to
these secrets might lie.

When the beam of light struck something white—partially
concealed behind the dresser containing the clothes—I moved
closer to investigate. The object turned out to be a mattress, lying
flat on the floor, its exterior still clad in white sheets.

"Oh, now this is just *too* much," I murmured. "The clothes I can understand, but who in this world would leave white sheets on a mattress they'd moved..." My voice trailed off as my mind began pondering the rumpled condition of the sheets and the smears of dirt marring their otherwise clean surface. Celia had said that Ashley spent time up here, so was this Ashley's doing? *Maybe, but...the sheets would surely be covered in dust after five years' time, wouldn't they?* I moved in for a closer look. Although there were smears of dust and dirt, most likely from someone lying on the mattress with their shoes on, the sheets weren't covered in dust. It was pretty apparent someone had been here recently, for even the dust on the floor had been disturbed.

"Jason," I surmised, wondering what he did up here. The beam of light swept over a small lantern on the far side of the mattress, near the head. "Aha, I bet I know." I smiled, feeling certain that if I searched beneath that side of the mattress, I'd find a stash of nudie magazines.

Having no intention of doing so, I continued looking around. Coming across a pile of dusty, dingy sheets crammed between the dresser and a chest of drawers, I switched mental gears once again. The condition of these linens was what I would have expected to find if this had been where Ashley spent her time. Why here, though? I understood why Jason, being a boy, would come up here, but not Ashley. What did she have to hide? *Or was she hiding from something or...someone, namely Brandon? I could certainly understand the desire for privacy, if he treated her like he did me. And perhaps Jason wouldn't mind if I used this as my own hideout,* I mused, availing myself of the comfortable seat it offered. *Brandon would never think of looking for me here.*

"Damn it, Faith," I chided out loud, and flopped back on the mattress. "You're thinking like a child again. Grow up. You know you can't stay here forever, waiting for Sara to return."

And yet, what awaited me out there without her was frightening. I had only been on my own when I was away at college. But then, at college you're seldom really alone. There was always someone around. You were independent, but only to a certain degree. If I left this house and moved out on my own, I would be *all* alone. And I didn't want to be all alone, dammit, I wanted to be with Sara.

Tears threatening, I rolled over on my side—flashlight still in hand—and snuggled up to the pillow near my head. It felt good to have something to hold on to, even if it was just a musty old pillow. "Sara, please come back to me," I whined. "I love you."

For a moment, I thought my mind was playing tricks on me,

or at least my olfactory senses were, because I caught a whiff of her perfume. It was faint, but I knew the scent very well. I lifted my head and sniffed the air like a dog that's just caught the scent of game, and immediately felt absolutely stupid for doing so. I had obviously imagined it because I wanted to be with her so badly.

What the hell am I doing? I questioned. My head fell back against the pillow. *I'll never find what Celia wanted me to because I have no idea where to start looking, much less what in blue blazes I'm supposed to be looking for!* "This is utterly stupid!" I said aloud, striking the mattress with the butt of the flashlight and burying my face in the pillow.

Catching another whiff of her perfume, my nose again went on the alert. *Where the devil is this coming from? Is it on my clothes?* I sniffed around my shoulder area. *Not on that side*, I surmised. *And these clothes have been washed since...* My nose brushed against the pillow. "Damn!" I cursed, realizing the scent was coming from the musty object in my arms. "You're here, aren't you? Yes, by God, you are!" I added, answering my own question when my nose found the exact spot that retained her sweet scent.

Sara...here? Why? What was she doing? Why hadn't she come to see me? Was she up here now, hiding from me?

I sat up abruptly, calling out, "Sara? Sara, I know you're here. You might as well come out." There was no response. "Sara, please talk to me." I grabbed my cane and scrambled to my feet. "Dammit, Sara, I love you! I don't care about anything else. I don't care if we're cousins. I'm not ashamed of what we did," I panned the light beyond my general area, unsure of whether she was even in the vicinity, but wanting her to hear me out. "If-if you're ashamed, well...I can understand that, but at least talk to me. Please!" The last word was a near shout. Only then did I realize that I could more than likely be heard from below. "Shit," I muttered, cursing my own stupidity.

Making my way along the path again, I swept the light from side to side, hoping against all hope to catch sight of her lovely face. "Damn, you're a stubborn woman," I mumbled, disappointment flowing through me as I moved closer and closer to the west wing and the attic entrance. "Okay, fine, if that's the way you want it. I'll leave you to...whatever the hell it is you're doing up here." With that I turned for one last scan of the attic, and then made my way slowly down the stairs, my hopes sinking with each step.

Setting the flashlight down on the inside of the doorway, for further exploration at another time, I was about to open the door when Brandon's voice drifted down the hall.

"...is she, Celia? This morning she had a headache, and I assumed she would stay in bed most of the day."

"I dunno know, sir," Celia responded from close by. "Perhaps she went for a walk."

Nothing else was said. Then I heard footsteps going down the hallway. I knew I had to get out of there, and fast. Peeking out, I noticed the door to Jason's room a few doors down the hall was open. I assumed Celia was inside cleaning up. I didn't see hide or hair of Brandon. The door to his room, down the hall from Jason's and closer to the stairs, appeared to be closed.

Quietly I made my way down to Jason's room, but Celia was nowhere in sight either. Feeling confused, I turned to go out the door as Celia entered. "Ooo!" she screeched, and nearly dropped the bed linens in her arms. "Mum, ya nearly scared me outta ma wits."

"I'm sorry," I apologized "but I was looking for you. Where's Brandon?"

"I believe he's outside, mum, looking for you," she informed me.

"Which door did he go out?" I asked, wondering how I could explain how we had missed one another.

"I don't rightly know. I wuz—"

I patted her on the arm. "Thanks anyway. Oh, and thanks for the flashlight, too."

"Flashlight?" she asked, a peculiar look on her face.

"Yes, but you don't have to own up to it." I patted her arm again. "Just answer me this, how did you know she was here?"

Celia turned away, placing the linens on a chest by the foot of the bed. "Strange sounds at night, mum. Things...disappearin'." She unfurled the bottom sheet with a crisp snap.

"What kinds of things?"

"Food, mum. An'...linens," she replied, smoothing the fitted arc over one corner.

So that's where the white sheets came from, I thought, but said, "How long has she been here?" I couldn't help but think of how Sara had conveniently shown up the very day Dr. Rosemund released me from his care and Brandon was ready to let her go.

Celia shrugged, continuing with her task. "Can't say for sure, mum. I-I think I said enough, already."

"Why? Because she doesn't want to see me?"

"I dunno nuthin' 'bout nuthin' like that. I haven't seen her." After smoothing the fitted sheet, she then secured it over the final corner. "I just know that ghosts don't eat chicken, or...steal sheets."

I couldn't help but smile, yet tried to keep the mirth out of my voice as I asked, "Ghosts? You mean this house has ghosts?"

"Didn't say that either, mum." She reached for the top sheet and unfurled it with a snap of her wrist. " Beggin' your pardon, mum, I think I should be about me work."

I shook my head, dislodging the otherworldly thoughts. I wasn't worried about ghosts, it was the living I was hot on the trail of. And also hiding from.

I proceeded down to my room and changed into my bathing suit. Swimming was the only thing I could think of doing to work off this pent-up energy...and hopefully furnish myself with an excuse for not meeting up with Brandon. There was no way I was going to let him know that Sara was here. I would say I went for a walk, came up the back stairs, and changed for my exercise. *Might just work*, I thought. *I'll deal with Sara later.*

Upon entering the heated pool, I found the water was so warm that I decided against exercise. I'd already had my share of that with the stairs and exploring the attic. Instead, I lay back in the water and relaxed. Only occasionally did I move my arms and legs to keep myself afloat. Staring up at the attic, I again wondered: *What's she doing here?*

Was she trying to torment me with her presence? *No, that didn't sound like Sara.* Keeping an eye on me, perhaps? *But why? And if so, why hadn't she made her presence known to me?* Then again, maybe her reason for being here had nothing whatsoever to do with me. Had she remembered her past? Was she indeed Ashley? Every indication seemed to suggest as much.

So, if she's Ashley, I mused, *then that means Tom had to find her after the accident.* But how could that have happened? How would he even know she was missing unless... Had he somehow been involved in the accident? Not directly, but inadvertently? If Ashley was his daughter, had he tried to make contact? Confront her even? Did Brandon know? Had *she* possibly confronted Brandon the night of the accident? That was certainly possible, wasn't it? I sighed heavily; the questions were endless.

And if Tom had found Ashley, I speculated, my analytical mind changing gears, *how did he manage to palm her off as Sara Bennington?* Were there two Sara Benningtons now, with the same social security number, birth certificate? Or had he falsified these documents? *Good Lord, what a complicated situation!* Was it even plausible that these things could have happened?

Sara's presence in the attic suggested it was. Why else would she return unless she knew she was Ashley? Then again, if all this were true, why hide? Why not come out with the truth and be welcomed back into the bosom of her family? *Because she wouldn't be welcomed with open arms,* I surmised. *Not with the way Brandon feels about her now! Oh, what a tangled web of confusion! What, if anything, could I possibly do to unravel this perplexing mess? How do I get Sara to at least talk to me? I have to know what she remembers. I have to—*

"Princess!" Brandon boomed. I nearly went under as his voice seared through my thoughts. "Where have you been?" Anger tinged his tone.

"Wh-what do you...mean?" I asked, spurting water.

"I've been searching the grounds for you. You were not here a minute ago."

"Well, I don't have my watch on, but I'm sure I've been here longer than that. Why were you searching for me, anyway?" I queried, turning the tables on him. "I'm not a child. I'm not gonna wander off and get lost."

"Well, yes, I know that. I just... I wanted to see if you were all right," he explained, calming down considerably. "After your hangover this morning, I mean."

"I'm fine. I'm exercising. The doctor has released me, ya know, and I can pretty much take care of myself." *As Sara's leaving proves,* I thought, but said, "And I am a grown woman, after all."

"Yes," he remarked, his gaze falling to my chest. "I can see that. I guess I'm just being overprotective...of my princess."

"A bit," I agreed, turning away from his stares.

"I'll join you," he stated, as I swam away slowly. I didn't offer a response. I wasn't sure I wanted him in the pool with me. At least, not with the way he was looking at me.

He left and came back a few minutes later, wearing an outdated pair of swimming trunks and a short black robe. His pale muscular legs covered in dark brown curly hair reminded me of my father's. He removed the robe, revealing a white chest untouched by the sun, the dark hairs sprinkled with gray. Walking proudly over to the diving board, he dove in. *Not bad for a man his age*, I thought. *Perhaps this could be okay, if he'd act like a father.*

I lost him in the water, then suddenly he popped up beside me. "Didn't think the old man could still do it, did you?" He slicked back his thinning brown hair. "I was on the swim team in college," he announced proudly.

"I didn't know that."

"There's a lot you don't know," he remarked, gazing into my

eyes. "Especially about men." The look in those dark depths frightened me. It seemed he was insinuating something I knew I didn't want to hear. "You've spent far too much time with...*her*. I dare say you don't know anything about men, do you?"

"Enough," I responded, turning from his stares and moving away.

"Oh, so you've made love with a man?" He was following me.

"Uh...no, I mean, we never went *that* far," I answered honestly and knew immediately I should've lied.

"Then you don't know," he maintained, coming closer. I quickly waded away, but still he followed. "You are quite attractive, Princess, even now. And I'm sure the surgery will only enhance your natural beauty. Why, only last night, one of those young men from the party, Robert, I believe his name was, asked if he might call on you sometime. Of course, I told him it would have to be your decision, but I did give him my blessing to ask you."

The thought that he was pushing me to date a man in the hope I would forget Sara made me angry.

"He comes from a fine family, well bred, old money. He'd be quite a catch for a young lady like yourself. Could be just what you need."

That did it. Now he was telling me who and what I needed. This enraged me. "Do you really think *that* would change things?" I asked disdainfully.

"Of course. I've already consulted several psychiatrists, and they all say you could definitely use a man in your life, especially since you've never been with one before."

"Oh, and sex with a man, that'll cure me, right?"

"Why are you so angry, Princess? Are you afraid it's true?"

"No," I answered evenly, trying to control my ire. "Frankly, I detest your interference in my life." I spun around to face him. "If I want a man, I'll pick my own, thank you very much. And if I want a woman, I'll make that choice myself, as well."

"Princess, don't say that!" he scolded. "You're not one of those...queers! You're simply a naïve and vulnerable child. You were seduced by that-that filthy whore. Women like her would lie down with anyone just to get their perverted kicks."

I glared at him, my bottom lip quivering as I thought of how much I'd like to slap him. I turned away to avoid doing just that.

"Princess," he said, more calmly now, wrapping his arms around my waist, "if only you knew the joys a man and a woman share, the ecstasy of their bodies joining together the way God planned." He pressed the lower part of his body against my backside. "Once you experience the passion of a man...a real man, you'll forget all this nonsense."

I felt his passion growing even as he spoke, and was suddenly afraid of what he might do next. I tried pulling away from him without actually physically lashing out, but it was to no avail; he was too strong.

"God made man stronger," he persisted, as if reading my mind, "so that he might overpower a woman. Men were meant to take women in this fashion and show them what true ecstasy is all about. You'll never find it any other way."

"That's not love!" I exclaimed, struggling against him.

"Love? What would you know about love?" he asked as he finally released me. "True love can only exist between a man and a woman."

"You're wrong!" I snapped, tears filling my eyes.

"So, you think you've experienced love with *her?*" he asked derisively. "Ha! That was just the lust of a whore who gets a thrill out of seducing innocent and helpless children like you. She could *never* have shown you love. What she did to you was...a perversion, an abomination unto the Lord."

Oh great, now he's dragging God into it, I thought, when I had never known him to set foot inside a church in all the time I had been at Shady Grove. I swam away from him as fast as I could. I didn't want to listen to any more of his accusations, and especially his sanctimonious bullshit; it felt sacrilegious.

"You'll see, Princess," he called after me. "A man can satisfy your needs and desires in ways *she* never could. Women were made for men, made from one of his ribs. God put woman here for man to protect and to bear his children. Trust me, Princess, I really do know what's best for you."

I pulled myself out of the pool by using the drainage trough. And after stumbling over to my cane, I got away from there as fast as I could, leaving a trail of water behind me. At that moment, I never wanted to see him again. I'd leave if I had to, and live by myself.

While climbing the stairs, I couldn't help but think of my mother. If Brandon had behaved in the same manner with her, I could see why she and my father would have left so abruptly. Matter of fact, I had a good mind to pack what few things I would need and get the hell out of there myself.

Once inside my room, I closed and locked the door, then quickly changed out of my wet bathing suit. A few minutes later, there was a knock at the door. I was determined not to answer it. I didn't want any part of him right now.

"Miss Faith, lunch is ready," Celia said. I went over and unlocked the door for her, then relocked it once she was inside. "Is there sumthin' wrong, mum?" she asked, placing the tray on the table.

I wanted to tell her the whole sordid tale, but instead merely replied, "No. I just...prefer a bit more privacy these days."

"Begging your pardon, mum, but I overheard...out at the pool. Be careful, mum. Men can be...very sensitive 'bout this issue."

"What do you mean, be careful?"

"Men have sensitive egos, mum. A...woman lover...threatens that. And men...do strange things when they feel threatened."

"I don't understand. He's my uncle, not my boyfriend, so why should he feel threatened?"

"He's still a man. Don't seem to matter much what relation they are ta ya. Another man don' pose a threat like a woman duz; I've seen it before, mum, believe me. Almost all men feel threatened by this; sum more'n others. Your uncle, he's a proud man. And he has no wife ta...soothe his battered pride. So please, mum, don't be throwing caution to the winds."

"Caution to the wind," I murmured, moving over to the bed. "I wasn't aware I was doing so. I guess I just don't understand much about men and their egos." I sat down, considering her warning. The inevitable question I had yet to vocalize hung in the air between us. Soon, however, my curiosity got the better of me. "Not meaning to be nosy, Celia, but...how is it you know so much about men and their egos where...*this* is concerned?"

"Well, I..." She paused, pushing the table over to me. "'Twas me sister, mum. She wuz like you." Our gazes met and I arched one eyebrow, waiting for her to continue. "'Tis a long story, mum."

"I've got nothing but time," I said softly.

"We-ell, mum...me sister had herself a suitor, ya see. Nice young man, he wuz, but...she met an older woman and..." She paused again, glancing away.

I patted the bed beside me. Obviously hearing this gesture, she looked at the bed and then up at me. After moving around the table, she took the proffered seat. "Well, me mum and dad found out what they wuz up ta and...oh my, me dad, God rest his soul, he near tore the roof off the house, he did. He also did a very bad thing." She shook her head sadly, staring at the floor. "He told her suitor 'bout it all and...suggested it might be a good thing if he...well, showed her what men wuz about, ya know." She paused and cleared her throat. "And Marcus...he...well, he took me...poor sister by force." She hung her head sadly.

"Celia, I'm sorry, I didn't mean to stir up..."

She waved my apology away as she got to her feet. "It's all right, mum. I think it's best I told ya."

"Are you trying to say that you think Brandon will...try something like that?" I knew the instant the words left my mouth how close I felt he'd come to doing just that.

Celia arched one gray eyebrow, as if she were thinking the same thing. "I didn't *say* that, mum," she emphasized. "What I said wuz be careful and don't injure his pride."

"His pride?" I asked scornfully. "What about mine? What about how I feel when he calls Sara a whore who would lie down with anyone just for kicks? What am I supposed to do, just stand there and *take* it?" I knew my anger was showing. "I'm sorry, Celia, I'm not mad at you," I apologized. "I appreciate you sharing this story with me, I do. And I can see where you're coming from, I just—"

"No apologies necessary, mum," she interrupted. "I understand your anger. Just know...it's still a man's world. And we women, we do what we must to survive. And sometimes that means tiptoeing 'round a man's ego."

I shook my head sadly. "It shouldn't be that way."

"No, mum, it shouldn't," she agreed. "But that's still the way of things."

I stared down at the floor.

"Well, I'll be leavin' ya to your lunch now." She moved toward the door.

"Celia?" I called after her. "If you don't mind my asking, what happened to your sister?"

She paused with her hand on the knob. "Wull, she-she ran off is what she did, mum. Never laid eyes on me mum and dad again."

"I'm sorry that happened," I offered, feeling relieved to know her sister had survived the attack upon her person.

"So am I, mum," she said sadly, opening the door. "So am I."

After she left, I pushed the table away; I had lost my appetite. I got up and locked the door, then walked over to the window, gazing out at the great expanse of land behind the mansion. The trees were losing their leaves, withdrawing their sap and preparing themselves for the cruel winter weather ahead. Was I to be like them and withdraw from the spiteful bite of Brandon's words, go along with all he said just so his precious pride would not be damaged?

I heard a bump that came from the vicinity of my sitting room and braced myself, waiting for Brandon's knock. None came. Yet there was another noise that sounded like the squeak of a hinge. I wanted to run over to the secret door and snatch it open to see if Sara was in there. But instead, I merely stared at the place on the wall where I knew the door was. She was obviously using it again, but why? To what end? What was she even doing back here? Did she merely want to be near me? If so, why not come out in the open? Was she afraid of how I might feel about her now? It seemed it was up to me to make the first move, since she was hiding behind walls and in attics. Noticing my lunch on the table, I thought this just might be the bait I needed to lure her out.

I walked over to the bed and sat down. "Food's getting cold," I said aloud. "Looks good, too." There was no response. "Plenty for two. And you know I don't like eating alone." I waited with bated breath. "All right, I guess it'll just go to waste."

No response still. *Must have been leaving*, I thought with a heavy sigh. But I would give it one more try. I got up and walked over to the secret door. "I...love you, Sara. To me, you're not my cousin. You're not Ashley. You'll always be...*my* Sara."

I was very tempted to push the door open, but couldn't bring myself to do it. I didn't want to force her out if she didn't want to see me. I'd give her time to come to me.

Having no appetite, I hardly touched my lunch. All I could do was stare at that secret door, hoping she would come through it. Finally tired of waiting, I took the apple off my tray and went over to the door. I pushed on it slowly; nothing moved inside. Opening it all the way, I found it empty. My heart sank. Had I imagined the squeaking hinge? I placed the apple on the floor of the closet and closed the door.

Trying to save Celia a few steps, I carried the tray back down to the kitchen. I should've known it was a bad idea, for on my way back up, at the top of the stairs, I ran into Brandon.

"Oh, Princess, there you are. Please forgive me," he apologized, drawing near. "I lost my head for a moment out there. I truly didn't mean to hurt your feelings."

I didn't dignify this with a response, but merely turned and headed back down the stairs.

He followed. "Princess, please, I'm truly sorry. Please forgive me. I never intended to...say all those things. Believe me. It just makes me so angry when I think of how...she used you."

I stopped and stared at him. *Used me?* I thought.

"She did, you know," he maintained, as if reading my expression. "She used you, then cast you aside when she got ready to leave, didn't she? Princess, I can see you're hurting. I realize you probably felt she loved you, and that...you loved her." He frowned as if the words left a bad taste in his mouth and then continued. "But you know now it wasn't real, don't you? I mean, look around you, she's gone. And all she left you was a note. Dear Jill," he added, a solemn expression on his face.

I turned away and took another step down the stairs.

"Princess, please. I'd hate myself if I thought I had hurt you so much that you'd never forgive me. I wasn't considerate of your feelings, and...I'm truly sorry for that. I'm...an old man. I've forgotten what it feels like to be young and naïve and vulnerable. I've forgotten how these first...encounters can be. They can seem magical, I know. I was just so angry, Princess. Please, say you forgive me."

He rambled on and on, apologizing over and over, but my heart was very reluctant to give in. His words had cut deep, and I knew that I'd finally seen through his facade. Still, my mind kept telling me I should say that I forgave him, whether I did or not. After all, I didn't need him following me around apologizing and trying to make it up to me. I needed him to think everything was okay, so he'd go on about his business and let me get on with mine. Mine being getting Sara to at least talk to me.

"Okay," I finally relented. "I...I forgive you." The words had not come easily.

"Thank you, Princess, I needed to know that." He reached out, taking my hand. My insides turned cold at his touch. "By the way, where were you going?"

"Oh...I...I thought I'd...do some reading," I lied.

"That's good. I'll see you to the library."

"No, that...that won't be necessary. I mean, you probably have more important things to do." I bit my lip, knowing I had said the wrong thing but unable to take it back.

"Nothing is more important than you, Princess." He offered me his arm. "I'll escort you the rest of the way down. Perhaps I'll even do some reading myself."

Oh what a tangled web we weave, I thought. Now I might possibly be trapped in the library with him for the rest of the afternoon.

Which, to my utter dismay, is exactly what happened.

Chapter
17

I wandered around the library, taking my time scanning the titles, hoping he'd get bored and leave. He did seem to get bored, but didn't leave. Instead, he pulled out a photo album and sat down on the sofa with it. A few seconds later, he chuckled to himself, which I presumed was supposed to make me curious. It did, of course, but I didn't rush over to him to see what was so amusing, as I believe he wanted me to.

"Princess, come over here. Let me show you something."

It appeared I was stuck here for the duration. *Might as well make the best of it.* Reluctantly, I ambled over. He showed me an old snapshot of my mother and father, obviously clowning around: she had her eyes crossed, and he had his fingers in his mouth, pulling the sides apart in a grotesque grin. I had never seen any pictures from this time period in their lives. All of their photos or snapshots were taken after they left Shady Grove. And by then, my mother was pregnant with me.

We spent quite a long time looking at one photo album after another. There were lots of pictures of my mother in the first two, some of which appeared to have been taken without her knowledge. Or at least, she wasn't looking at the camera. I could only guess at who the photographer had been.

There were no pictures of Ashley or Vivian, as I would have expected, yet many sheets of partially filled or blank pages suggested there had been. When I inquired about this, he explained that he found it too painful to look at their pictures, so he'd removed them.

Moving on to another album, he showed me photographs of my ancestors, at least those who had lived after the invention of the camera. Brandon named each and every one, putting names to some of the faces I had seen in the attic, as well as offering a short narrative on each. From this, I learned that there were some members of the family who had moved away from Georgia, which meant I had distant relatives in various places. It also seemed that the family—especially our particular branch, which had stayed with the old homestead—had a knack for dying, by various means, before the age of fifty. To which, Brandon added that he must be doing something right, because he was fifty-two already.

I also learned something else no one had made mention of: Brandon and my father had different mothers. He showed me the only picture he had of his biological mother, which was a faded snapshot. Then he explained how she had died during childbirth, that fact seemingly being something he felt a twinge of guilt over; for he moved on rather quickly, showing me *my* grandmother, who he claimed was the only mother he had ever truly known. And of course, my grandfather, whom he resembled a lot, as did my own father. It appeared the Neilson genes were quite dominant. *Except when they tangled with my mother's*, I thought.

When he came upon a recent picture of Jason, he started bragging, repeating the plans he had for his son's education and life.

Then, without preamble, he closed the album and looked up at me. "As soon as you have your surgery, I'll arrange a sitting with the best photographer and the best artist, so that your beauty can be preserved for future generations."

I offered no objections, because I knew it would be futile. Besides, all I could think to say was, *I don't want to be preserved like a jar of peaches.* And I didn't think that would go over well. When he started on my future, however, talking about changing my major to business, and extending my class load from twelve semester hours—which had been my choice, so that I could work and help pay for my miscellaneous expenses instead of having my parents shell out for everything—to fifteen or even eighteen, I had to say something.

"I think that should be my decision," I asserted.

"Oh, of course. I was merely suggesting this because a lot of things have changed for you."

"Indeed," I agreed. "And speaking of change... I know you mean well, and I don't propose to handle *all* my inheritance, at least not my father's share of the business, but...I'd like to handle my own finances from now on."

He merely stared down at his hands, intertwined on top of the photo album.

"I appreciate all you've done for me," I continued, "but I've depended on you far too long. I can get around better now, and I think I should start taking on more responsibility." I was trying to ease into saying what I wanted, in terms he would understand and offer little objection to. "As you've pointed out, I am a Neilson, and I have the same pride you do. I'd like to be...more independent. You can understand that, can't you?"

He sighed heavily and slowly got up from the sofa. Turning to me with a sly smirk on his face, he said, "Yes, you are a Neilson, through and through. Your father taught you well. Raymond always told us never to depend on anyone but ourselves. So, yes, I do understand." He shoved his hands in his pockets as he walked over to the fireplace.

"Your inheritance from your father was placed in a savings account and a small checking account for you. It hasn't been touched. I...I was waiting for you to...inquire about it. I didn't realize it would be so soon, however. But, as you say, you have your pride. I can sure see that. I'll...I'll bring your passbook and checkbook up tonight, if you like. Just promise me one thing?"

"That depends on what the promise is."

He quickly turned to face me and smiled, his voice softening. "That's your mother talking. She was always careful about what kind of promises she made. You're quite a unique combination of the two." He cleared his throat. "Just promise me you won't spend it on trivial things."

"What do you consider trivial?"

"Perhaps you *could* handle business affairs," he commented with a wry smile. "You don't agree to anything until you have all the facts, right?" I nodded. "Well, trivial is expensive clothes you don't need, lending to people you don't know and some you do." He paused, seemingly for effect. "And buying an outrageously expensive car for its looks."

"Anything else?"

He hesitated a moment. "Just don't throw the money away. My advice is to invest it. Let it work for you."

"Well, I can tell you now that I won't be buying a lot of expensive things, because I want what little there is to last. And I assume from what you said that my allowance came from you, not from my own money, but why?"

He glanced down at the floor. "It was all left to you in his will, I couldn't touch it."

"Oh, well then, I'll reimburse you for my allowance and pay you back in installments for all the other expenses you had to incur on my behalf." He chuckled as if I had said something quite funny, but I didn't get it. "I'm sorry if paying in installments seems funny to you, but I'd like to keep some for a rainy day. I mean, I know there's not much, but—"

"Oh, quite the contrary," he corrected. "Your father was obviously more...astute than either of us realized. You have over a hundred thousand dollars in your savings account and several thousand in checking. Plus, your father invested in stocks, computer stocks, no less. All totaled, including life insurance policies—excluding the house, of course—your inheritance was over four hundred thousand dollars."

"What?"

"Yes, Princess, your father was rather successful with his writing, although he shunned the limelight, which I'll never understand. He had the most beautiful woman in the world to share it with," he remarked, turning toward the fire. "He had everything, and yet he chose to live in that small town in Tennessee."

"He probably had his reasons," I commented, thinking of how he had labored over each novel.

Perhaps that small town was his inspiration, I mused. Its quiet streets and friendly people, a place he could retreat to and let his imagination run wild. Although he wrote adventure novels, I knew he penned them from the lives of some of the people around him, as well as from his own heart. Many times had I watched him intently listen to some of the old men in town while they recounted the adventures they'd had, and some they had missed out on experiencing. This, coupled with his imagination, would turn into a novel. Within those pages lay the worlds he created for himself and others who craved adventure. A tear came to my eye as I thought about him and the wonderful talent that so many people would surely miss.

"'Scuse me, sir," said Celia, interrupting my quiet thoughts. "Dinner is served. Will ya be dining at the table, mum, or—"

"Yes," Brandon answered, before Celia even finished her question.

I didn't object to eating with him, for I hoped he'd eventually become bored with me. Unfortunately, this didn't happen until around ten o'clock. And then I knew a glass of milk would soon bring him back. I undressed and got ready for bed, then waited for the goodnight ritual. He returned a while later with the milk, my passbook, and checkbook. Then he gave me his usual lingering kiss on the cheek, telling me in a soft, sensual voice how much like my mother I was.

After he left, I lay in bed pondering the question of how I was going to get Sara to talk to me. I didn't want to force the issue by blundering around the house looking for her, at least not yet. I knew it could prove fruitless, and might make her presence known to the rest of the household. No, I had to be subtle and cunning and lure her to me. But how? She was no moth, and I certainly wasn't a flame; but somehow I had to let *her* know that I knew she was here and wanted to talk to her.

I stared up at the ceiling, wondering where she was at this moment. Was she sitting up there on her makeshift bed? Or was she close by...in the closet, perhaps? My eyes strayed over to the secret door. I longed to go over there and throw it open, but knew that wouldn't be wise. Remembering the apple I had previously left inside, I was quite curious as to whether it was still there. But, alas, that could wait until morning. If she was there, she obviously didn't want me to know about it.

"Goodnight, Sara," I said aloud as I turned off the lamp. At that moment, I wished more than anything I would hear a response.

The first thing I did the next morning—after cutting off the alarm on my recently purchased bedside clock—was open the secret door. The apple was there, just as I had left it. I sadly closed the door and ambled into the bathroom.

Celia brought me breakfast as usual, eyeing me curiously, as if inquiring as to whether I'd had contact with Sara. "She's a stubborn woman," I finally voiced.

"Persistence has its rewards, mum."

"Perhaps, but I don't think so in this case. I don't think she came back because of me; I think I'm what's keeping her hidden."

"Begging pardon, mum, but...I disagree," she said, pushing the table over to the bed.

"Why is that?"

"I...I didn't know ya wuz in the library yesterday, so I came up here, 'cuz I'd forgotten ta ask if ya had any request for dinner and—"

"You saw her?" I inquired excitedly.

She glanced down at the floor, as she backed away. "Yes, mum, that I did."

"Where was she? In here? What was she doing?"

"She wuz...standing 'bout here and..." She paused, moving over to the end of the bed.

"And?"

She shook her head. "Just...looking, mum," she replied, as if a bit embarrassed.

"Looking at what?" She had me on pins and needles now. What had Sara been looking at?

She dropped her eyes. "At the bed."

"I don't understand. Why do you act embarrassed about this?" I couldn't understand the big deal about looking at the bed.

"I...I felt I wuz...watching a private moment, mum," she replied, her cheeks flushing bright pink.

"Oh...oh, I see. Umm...thank you...thanks for everything, Celia."

"Yes, mum," she said, then turned and exited the room.

So, according to Celia, Sara must still feel something. But Celia also could have been mistaken about the reason she was looking at the bed. *Was she remembering with longing, or with regret?* Then again, I couldn't take the chance that it was not the former. There had to be some way to get to her.

I sighed heavily and turned on the stereo via the remote, setting it to "tuner" and the radio station that played easy listening music. Nibbling on my breakfast of sausage, eggs, toast, grits, and juice, while the morning disc jockey joked with his cohort, I pondered what I should do. Several ideas ran through my head, but none seemed plausible since I did not want to run the risk of exposing Sara.

A few seconds later, the chatter of the disc jockeys ended and a slow love song—one Sara and I had liked—began playing. "Oh, great," I said aloud. "Just what I need to start the day off right: tears in my grits."

I'd picked up the remote to change the station when I heard a faint bump overhead. *Not rats this time,* I thought, staring at the ceiling. Then suddenly it hit me: if I could hear her, she could hear me. Well, perhaps not me, but something I wanted her to hear, something with which to bait my trap. At least I hoped and prayed it would be bait and not a repellent.

Instead of changing stations, I turned up the volume. Having yet another flash of inspiration, I turned on the CD player, knowing there was a soundtrack album from a movie inside. I'd seen the video for the song and wanted to see the movie. Sara had promised to rent it for me as soon as it came out. In the meantime, however, she had bought the CD, and I had fallen in love with two of the songs. I programmed those two into the CD player, set it to "repeat disc," and as soon as the song ended on the radio, I switched to the CD.

The two songs I had chosen—the first in essence saying, "Without you in my life, I have nothing to live for," and the other, about a woman's desire to run into her lover's arms, and asking the question, if she did, would her lover run away—repeated three times before Brandon showed up.

He didn't knock, or if he did, I didn't hear him. He came in with an angry look on his face, and went straight to the stereo. "Princess, why is this so loud?" he shouted, turning the volume down. "I can hear this downstairs."

"Sorry," I apologized. "I didn't realize."

He looked at me curiously. "Are you all right? You aren't even dressed yet."

"I'm fine." I was miffed at his intrusion, however. "I was about to do just that. So, if you'll excuse me."

"Of course. Then we'll take our morning walk." He glanced down at his watch. "Shall we say eleven-fifteen, then?"

I took a quick peek at the clock. "Fine," I answered, agreeing merely to get rid of him.

From eleven-fifteen onwards, he stuck to me like glue, following me around and lavishing me with attention as if he were a suitor. Or at least, I felt like the pursued. His caresses made me quite nervous, and I was constantly forced to shy away, as best I could.

After dinner that evening, I suggested putting a puzzle together, thinking this would surely bore him. But, no, he stayed until after ten and as usual, was back a few minutes later with a glass of milk. While bending down and kissing me goodnight, his lips touched so close to my own, I nearly gasped. He merely pulled back, smiled, and turned to exit the room as if nothing was amiss. I tried to pass it off as just a mistake. *Did I perhaps flinch and cause this?* I didn't think so.

These thoughts, however, were soon relegated to the back burner, for I had more important things to think about: namely, Sara. The next day was Monday, so Brandon would go back to work, or at least I hoped he wouldn't take any unscheduled time off. In the morning, I would bait my trap once again, and if she didn't take it this time, I was going to flush her out personally.

The next morning, I played the CD from the day before over and over again, until I was sick and tired of hearing it. After lunch, I was on my way to the attic.

Slipping inside the door, I glanced back to make sure no one was nearby. Brandon hired outside help to come in and clean the unused rooms once a month, and I couldn't remember when they were due. Nearly tripping over the flashlight I'd left there on my previous visit, I reached down and picked it up before it fell over. Turning it on, I ascended the stairs as quietly as I could.

Once I'd made it to the rear section of the west wing, I proceeded slowly down the small path, trying to make as little noise as possible just in case anyone was below. Along the way, I kept the flashlight trained ahead of me on my destination—the dresser behind which I suspected she was hidden. As I neared it, my heartbeat increased, drowning out any other sounds. I swung the flashlight over behind the dresser, spotlighting the mattress.

To my utter dismay, it was empty. "Damn," I said quietly, leaning up against the dresser.

"You shouldn't be here," declared a voice from behind me. Naturally, I gasped and quickly swung the flashlight around, the bright beam catching Sara in the face. She put her hand up to shield her eyes. "Please, Faith."

I swiftly lowered it, holding it by my side while scrutinizing her attire. I had half expected her to be disheveled and dirty after hiding up here for at least two days, but she was neither. Wearing a clean white sweatshirt and a pair of tight blue jeans, her hair recently brushed, she smelled wonderful.

"Go back to your room, Faith," she ordered, turning to walk away.

"No, Sara. You can't get rid of me that easily." I reached out and grabbed her arm.

"Faith, don't, please," she muttered, looking down at my hand on her arm. "Go back downstairs; you shouldn't be up here."

"Why are *you* here?" I obligingly let go of her. "Don't tell me you didn't want me to find you. You provided this flashlight." I was guessing about the flashlight since Celia hadn't appeared to know anything about it.

"I didn't want you to find me, but...I couldn't have you blundering around up here in the dark, now could I? Because I know you would've."

"What are you doing here?" I persisted.

"Looking for answers, I suppose. Someone put this," she paused as she reached over to one of the dresser drawers and opened it, withdrawing a book with a flowered cover, "in with my things. I found it when I got back *that* day." She was obviously referring to the Saturday when my curiosity had caused all this misery.

"What is it?"

"Ashley's...my diary," she corrected herself.

I braced myself against the dresser, feeling disappointed. "Well, what did it say that brought you back, because obviously you didn't come back because of me."

She lowered her eyes and stared at the book in her hands. "I don't really know. It's odd. I'm writing about things that make no sense. Trees...walls...animals with ugly faces. I don't know what it's about. I came back hoping I'd remember something."

I bit my lip. She had ignored my reference about her obviously not coming back for me. I could only conclude it was a true statement, her silence signifying agreement. "How long...have you been here?" I asked, trying not to let my damaged feelings show.

"Several days," she replied, glancing up at me.

"You've obviously been doing well for yourself," I remarked, looking her up and down.

She nodded, her gaze leaving mine. "I found some clothes. And I got into one of the bedrooms. I'm afraid I used some of your soap and shampoo."

Who gives a shit about soap and shampoo? I thought. "Why didn't you come to me? Maybe I could help." I sighed heavily, knowing she'd turn me down.

"I... No, it..." She glanced up at me and her eyes held that oh-so-soft expression I had come to love. "No, I need to do this alone." She looked away.

Her expression suggested Celia had been right. Sara was trying to hide her feelings, just as she'd been trying to hide her presence. I was on to her now. I took a step forward. "I don't care if we're cousins, Sara."

"I do, Faith," she retorted, holding up a finger in warning and backing away. "Don't do this to me. I feel dirty and...and disgusting."

"I don't." Her eyes narrowed in disbelief. "I don't believe we are cousins, Sara. At least, not by blood."

"It's Ashley," she corrected.

"No," I countered, taking another step forward. "You will always be Sara to me. Ashley died in that car crash five years ago. *You* are Sara."

"No, Faith. Sara Bennington died a day or two after *her* car crash."

"How did you—"

"The detective. He checked out the hospital where she was admitted," she explained. "I was listed as a transfer at the last hospital I was in." A frown contorted her features. "I had been moved from a smaller place north of Atlanta, where I'd been listed as a Jane Doe. An apparent victim of a hit-and-run, I was supposedly brought in by a good Samaritan who conveniently vanished in the E.R." She let that sink in before continuing. "I vaguely remember regaining consciousness in the first hospital and not knowing who I was or what had happened." She frowned, seemingly at the memory.

"Once stabilized, I was moved to a larger hospital, with better facilities for reconstructive surgery and physical therapy. That's when Tom showed up, claiming to be my father and...that I was Sara." She scratched her head and sighed heavily. "I still don't know how he pulled it all off. I assume the hospital was just glad someone showed up to foot the bill. It's the only sense I can make out of the situation." She paused once again. "The detective's still checking on the police reports about Jane Doe and the supposed hit-and-run. My gut tells me that Tom was the good Samaritan. And if so, there's no telling what cock-and-bull story he fed the authorities. I'm sure it wasn't the same one he spoon-fed me."

We both fell silent. There could be no more denial. She was Ashley.

"I'm Brandon's daughter, Faith, and we both know it," she stated, finally breaking the silence.

"If so, then why did Tom do all that? Why leave you everything in his will?"

"He was probably crazy. Who knows?" I could hear the frustration in her voice.

"I don't think so. What if you are Tom's daughter? It's possible, ya know. Remember the birth date I saw on those papers of his? It would make sense now if you're Ashley, because she..." Realizing my mistake, I paused, before correcting myself. "I mean, *you* would only be twenty-seven, not thirty-two. That would make Tom at least...seventeen or eighteen when you were born."

One eyebrow arched skyward, as if she were considering the logic of my argument. "But there's no proof, Faith. No proof at all. The only person who could've answered that question died over fourteen years ago," she proclaimed, obviously referring to Vivian. "At best, it would be wishful thinking. And I'd never be sure, I'd always have that doubt in the back of my mind."

So, she was admitting she still cared. The only thing standing in her way was the thought that we were cousins. "If we could prove you're Tom's daughter," I paused, and took another step forward, "would you come back to me?"

"Don't do this to me, Faith," she muttered, turning away.

"All right, I won't pressure you." I obligingly stepped back and regrouped. "Ya know, I half expected to come up here and find you missed me as much as I missed you. Then I'd tell you it didn't matter to me, and we'd ride off into the sunset together."

"I'm sorry, but this isn't a movie," she responded ruefully. "And even if it were, sweetheart, the princess never rides off into the sunset with the heroine."

"In this one she will. Just as soon as we can prove you're not my cousin. Which I hope we'll do soon, because I don't know how much longer I can stay here."

"What? Why not?"

"Brandon knows. He read your letter."

"Oh, good God!" she hissed, running her fingers through her hair. "What did he say?"

"What didn't he say is more like it? And, he's acting...strangely."

"How?" She sounded quite concerned now.

Making myself at home on the mattress, I told her an edited version of the incident in the pool. I even passed on Celia's warning to be careful and her story about what had happened to her sister. After I'd finished, Sara came closer and propped herself up on the dresser. She stared into the darkness of the attic, seemingly contemplating all this new information.

"Perhaps it *would* be better if you left," she said evenly. "I've never wholly trusted him where you're concerned. And don't ask me why, because I don't know. I just believe you *should* leave."

She didn't know how badly those words wounded me. Still, I managed to say, "Not until you come with me."

"I can't, Faith. I have to find out who I am. I have to remember. This book was given to me for a reason."

"I can imagine who'd do that." She glanced up at me. "Celia knows who you are, and she's the one who sent me up here to begin with."

"She knows *everything?*"

"Yes. And I think she knows more than she's letting on about all this stuff. You know how she is, never comes out and directly tells you anything, just offers vague hints. But I don't believe you're Brandon's daughter, because I asked her about it and she said she 'couldn't rightly say.' She did, however, admit that Tom and Vivian were close."

"That still doesn't prove—"

"Yes, but, Sara, he must've thought you were his. He left you everything he had in this world. He has a stable named the Vivian Leigh—not after a movie star, but after your mother, I'd bet. And what was the other one, Marie's what?"

"Marie's Pride," she said slowly, as if considering this could possibly be named after her: Ashley Marie. "But why lie to me? Why not tell me the truth?"

"*That* I don't know. Perhaps he was afraid you'd want to come back here and...he'd lose you or something, I dunno. Seems he sure went to a helluva lot of trouble to give you another identity. You're sure he didn't leave you anything in writing?"

"If he did, it wasn't where I would find it right off. I did find some more old photographs of a little girl on horseback, like the other one. But it could be anyone—a niece, a neighbor's kid—"

"Or you," I interrupted. "You were a cute little girl, who grew into a beautiful woman."

She shook her head and turned away, nibbling at her lip. "I think he wanted to get even with Brandon for firing him by taking his daughter away; or maybe he just needed an heir to leave his things to, instead of letting the state get everything. Ah, who the hell knows?" She ran her fingers through her hair again, in apparent exasperation.

"Pretty expensive and complicated revenge, wouldn't you say? As for an heir, there was always the possibility you'd regain your memory. Besides, if he'd wanted revenge against Brandon, why leave everything he had to *Brandon's* daughter?" She glanced over at me and continued nibbling on her bottom lip. Her eyes said she knew what the truth was, she was just afraid to accept it. "If you really believe you're Brandon's daughter, why not tell him who you are, instead of hiding up here?"

"I dunno, I just...don't know." She ran her fingers through her hair. "He...he gives me the creeps, to be honest," she said at length. "When he's around, I-I feel trapped. I want to get away from him before I...suffocate or somethin'."

I wanted to ask: *So why come back to his house?* Yet, listening to her and seeing the look in her eyes, I thought she might be on the verge of remembering something. Something that obviously wasn't pleasant. And she was fighting it because she didn't *want* to know. I could only hope her answer to my unvoiced question would have been: *Because I wanted to be near you.*

Not wanting to risk pouring salt in my own open wound, I changed the subject. "Let me see the book," I suggested, afraid she'd soon ask me to leave again, and this time I'd feel obligated to comply.

She handed it to me hesitantly. It was not a cheap diary, but one of the expensive kind you find in bookstores: unlined pages, gilded around the edges. I opened it and began reading. The handwriting on the first couple of pages was far from neat, and in several places nearly illegible. Yet I could make out that the rather short story recorded there was about a baby bird, one who had been orphaned by its mother's death. A death the baby bird felt responsible for, because its mother was trying to remove it from harm's way when she was attacked herself. In the baby bird's panic, it somehow caused itself and its mother to be thrown from the nest. Sensing the mother's death, the unnamed attacker then flew away. The baby bird was left alone in a hostile environment she knew nothing about. She wandered aimlessly through the dark, silent forest. Unable to fly, she knew she was easy prey for other animals, like the unnamed attacker.

The next entry was in a different handwriting, much more legible and neater in appearance, as if written by someone older. The passage started with a bricklayer and a structure he was building. He labored carefully on the walls, laying each brick cautiously and with great care, so the fortress would be impenetrable. He wanted to be sure the walls would stand up against the storm he knew would soon come. He worried whether it would hold back the torrential winds he foresaw with this storm. Finally, when he was finished, he sat back and marveled at his magnificent accomplishment. It was a fine structure that he knew would stand up against any onslaught.

When the storm finally came, and the rain began to fall, he realized he'd forgotten one crucial part of his structure: a roof. He'd been so concerned with his walls surviving the wind that he had completely overlooked the element of rain. Now it was too late. The rain was pouring into his structure. Then another fatal mistake soon made itself apparent: he'd left himself no means of escape, except climbing over the walls. As he tried to scale them, he fell back down; his walls were so neatly and carefully arranged that there was no purchase by which to ascend them. They had become as slippery as ice in the rain. He was now trapped in a prison of his own making. His refuge against the storm was a double-edged sword: not only did it keep things out, it kept things in, as well. His safe haven had become his tomb.

After reading this, I got the impression this wasn't just a story she had made up. It was much more than that. "You don't understand any of this?" I asked, closing the book.

"No. Why would I write about birds and...making walls? They're just stories. I don't understand why Celia put the diary with my things. Maybe she grabbed the wrong book or something."

"They're stories for your eyes only," I offered. "I assume you wrote these this way so that if anyone else found the book, they wouldn't understand what you were talking about."

"Well, I did a good job, because I sure don't understand it."

"I'm assuming you wrote them as metaphors, so to speak."

"Metaphors? What do you mean?"

"Okay, for instance, let's say I wanted to write about...um, what happened yesterday in the pool, but was afraid someone else might find it. I would disguise the characters in the real drama so that only I knew what it meant." She frowned. "Hmm, well, perhaps I'd use an...octopus, say, to represent Brandon, and...a crab to represent me, ya following me?" She nodded. "All right, let's see... I might write something like: the little crab felt defenseless and helpless within the octopus' strong grasp."

Her eyes narrowed. I'd forgotten I hadn't told her about him grabbing me around the waist and holding me. I'd merely told her what he'd said, and that he'd followed me around the pool.

"He had his arms around you?" she questioned. "You didn't mention that before."

"I...uh...I didn't feel, well...it was nothing, really."

"The crab felt helpless and defenseless...sounds like something to me," she asserted, dropping to her haunches in front of me. "He didn't...try anything, did he, Faith?"

"Oh, of course not," I answered. "He...well, you know how I am. You had to hold me down to get me to listen." I knew I'd blundered as soon as the words slipped past my lips. Unable to recall them, I held my breath waiting for her reaction.

"Yes, I...I remember that well," she said softly, reaching toward me.

Oh, how I had been waiting for this moment. My hand moved toward her face, and she pulled back.

"No, Faith, don't. I-I only wanted the book," she explained.

My heart sank to my toes. I hastily lowered my gaze and handed over the slim volume, then turned away and bit my lower lip. I wanted to feel her touch so badly, but she was turning me away again.

"I'm sorry," she muttered, as she got to her feet. "I... You should be getting back. And..." She paused, extending her hand to me. I gazed up at her, tears welling up in my eyes. She stared down at me for several moments. Slowly I offered her my hand. She swallowed audibly, shut her eyes, and released a heavy sigh. "You should leave here, Faith," she added, pulling me to my feet.

"I'm not leaving without you."

Her gaze met mine, her eyes darting back and forth. "Don't come here again. It's...it's too dangerous for you."

"The world is a dangerous place, Sara." I held onto her hand, not allowing her to pull away. "For crabs...baby birds...their mothers, and...even those who think themselves hidden away and protected from all of life's storms."

"Damn you, Faith. Why can't you just...just do as I say?" She made a rather lame attempt to pull away from me.

"Because I love you too damn much! And I don't wanna lose you." I took a step forward, which put me mere inches from her face. "I...I set you free, Sara, like the saying. If you love something, set it free. If it comes back, it's yours forever. If it doesn't, it never was to begin with, or...something like that." She looked at me. "Well, you did come back." Of course she'd made it plain she hadn't come back for me, but I didn't want to think about that right now. "And I know you love me," I babbled on, well aware I was throwing caution to the wind, yet feeling this was the truth. "I can see it in your eyes." I still held her gaze. That was a good sign. "It's written all over your beautiful face, right this very moment."

"Faith, please." She turned away.

"I love you, Sara," I whispered, as I reluctantly let go of her hand and started by her.

She touched my arm as she cleared her throat. "I'll...see you safely down the stairs."

I started to object, but the warmth of her touch caused me to rethink this and swallow my pride. "Thank you," I said instead.

We walked slowly over to the stairs, as quietly as possible. She went down the first couple and motioned for me to follow. I started down them while she looked on, watching each step I took. I knew this because she even steadied me once by putting her hands on my behind. No one, not even Sara herself, could make me believe this woman did not care for me. I felt it would only be a matter of time before she came back around to her old self again. And no matter which name she chose to go by, she'd always be Sara to me.

When we got to the bottom, she stepped back against the stairwell so I could get past her. We stared at each other for a moment, and then she motioned with her head. "Go on, Faith," she murmured.

"I'll go back to my room, Sara, but I'm not going anywhere without you."

She ran her fingers through her hair yet again. "Why do you have to make this so difficult?" she grumbled.

I reached out and did touch her face this time. She couldn't run from me any longer; she was trapped between my body and the stairs. I wanted to kiss her so badly I could almost taste her sweet lips against mine. I quelled this urge, however, and merely brushed her hair out of her eyes and caressed the side of her face, all the while wishing I could grab her, shake her, and make her see reason.

Turning, I quietly exited the stairwell.

The afternoon was dreary and cool, the temperature dropping rapidly toward evening, or so I surmised from my seat by the win-

dow. The puzzle on the table before me was filling in at an excruciatingly slow pace. My mind wandered off at every opportunity.
Until time for Brandon to come home, I had held out hope that
Sara would show up, saying she'd had a change of heart, change of
mind. Disappointment seeped into my bones like a damp chill.
After dinner, I was forced to break out sweatpants, sweatshirt, and
fuzzy booties. Winter was definitely just around the corner.

Needless to say, Brandon was not impressed with my cozy,
warm attire. He didn't say so, but his expressions told the tale. I
couldn't have cared less, however. Despite my being an affront to
his impeccable sensibilities, he sat with me, searching for piece
after piece in the quest to solve the picture puzzle. He left only
long enough to bring me a special treat: hot cocoa.

I had never been especially fond of hot chocolate—or cocoa,
as he corrected me—but I was not so ungrateful as to refuse his
special treat. Besides, it was tasty, quite sweet, and most of all,
hot. It seemed to warm my emotional and weather-chilled insides.
At times like these, it was all too easy to feel an almost daughterly
affection toward him. I had to remind myself that this was the
same man who had held me and rubbed himself against me in the
pool not so long ago. Remembering Celia's warning about men
and their egos, I found myself wondering if *I* had somehow
prompted that sort of behavior from him just by virtue of my
"preferences" alone, much less saying so to his face. It had always
seemed somehow easier to make an attempt at forgiveness if I
shared at least some of the blame.

Soon I was too sleepy to concentrate on the puzzle. Obviously sensing my somnolent condition, Brandon called it an
evening, kissed me goodnight, and graciously left without hesitation. I could only assume the hot chocolate had a similar effect on
him as well.

My last thought before my head touched the pillow was of
Sara: *Tomorrow she'll come to me. I just know she will.*

Chapter
18

The alarm clock went off at 9:30. I groggily reached over and turned it off, then floated back to la la land. The next thing I knew, Celia was knocking on my door.

"Come in," I grumbled.

She entered with the usual breakfast tray and put it on the table, then pushed it over to me. By this time, I normally had the head of the bed raised and had already paid my morning visit to the bathroom. Today, I had accomplished neither.

"Are ya all right, mum?" Celia asked, as I struggled to focus my sleep-heavy eyes.

"Umm...yes. Must be...the weather," I replied groggily, offering both of us an explanation for my seeming stupor. "Cold, rainy weather...all I wanna do is sleep."

"Oh?" she expressed, seemingly asking for more information on the subject. "Are ya ready for breakfus', or..." She glanced around the room as if she were looking for something, or possibly someone, "should I bring it back later?" I wiped my eyes, which were finally beginning to focus. "Should I bring another tray, mum?" she added quietly.

"Huh? What? Why would I need anoth—" I paused when she cut her eyes over to the other side of the bed. I followed her gaze, finding an obvious indention in the pillow beside mine. *Had Sara come in while I was sleeping?* I wondered. I glanced back at Celia and wiped my eyes again. "I, uh...no, don't bring another tray. If she won't stay, then she shouldn't eat, hmm?"

Celia flushed red as a beet.

"Oh, I'm sorry," I apologized. "I...I'm so dizzy-headed," I explained, starting to rise. That's when I felt something was amiss in another area. I lifted up the covers, knowing what I would find.

"Oh, Celia, I'm sorry, but I believe I had *more* than one visitor last night."

"Oh, think nuthin' of it, mum. That's just one of the burdens of being a lady. Here, let me help ya up, and..." She grabbed hold of me as I almost fell backward. "Oh my, so sorry, mum."

"I always heard my mother complain about her balance being off during this time of the month, but this is the first time it's affected me. I have to say, I don't like it very much."

"Yes, mum. The things we women go through. It's a wonder we don't die 'fore the men."

"Can you help me into the bathroom, too, Celia? I'm...a bit dizzy this morning."

"Oh, of course, mum."

"If Sara had stayed around, then you wouldn't have to do this. Guess she thought no one would notice she'd laid her head on the pillow, hmm?" Celia glanced up at me as she helped me to the bathroom. I knew what she was thinking. "No, I didn't even know she was there. I think she likes sneaking in here thinking it will be her secret." She helped me to the toilet, then backed away and stared at the ceiling as I did what needed to be done. "And speaking of secrets, you know some you aren't telling, don't you?" I inquired.

She offered no response, so I decided to make my question more specific.

"Okay, how about this? Brandon isn't her father, is he?" I asked as she helped me over to the bathtub, where I sat down on the side. "Is he, Celia?"

"I don't like ta speak about things I'm not sure of, mum," she replied, straightening up and avoiding my gaze.

"Tom was sure, wasn't he? He and Vivian were having an affair, weren't they? And he thought Ashley was his daughter," I concluded, hoping she'd give an indication, one way or another.

"I've always kept me mouth shut 'bout them things." She paused and sighed heavily. "But they're gone from this world, God rest their souls." She gazed heavenward. "An' I see ya won't be satisfied with nuthin' but the truth." She arched one gray eyebrow. "So, yes, mum, they wuz having a luv affair. Tom wuz head over heels in luv with her."

"And Vivian?"

"Oh, she luvved him, there was little doubt about that. But she wouldn't leave Mr. Neilson. See, Tom wuz poor, didn't have much in this world but the clothes on his back and...how could he very well ask her ta leave all this and come away with him?"

"So, she is his? Sara, I mean Ashley, is Tom's daughter?" I

turned on the water for my bath.

"I 'spect only Miss Vivian could say for sure, but...she's got young Tom's coloring...and his green eyes."

Aha, so that's where the green eyes came from. "And I bet his eyes changed color, didn't they?" I was on the trail of proof to offer Sara.

"Changed color?" she mused. "Wull...yes, now that ya mention it, mum, indeed they did. Strange thing that wuz ta watch, I have ta say."

"Tom left after Vivian's death, right?"

"Wull..." She paused and cleared her throat. "Actually, mum, he left a'fore then. Stayed gone 'bout two years a'fore he came back with his pockets a-jingling with money. Said he'd had a grand streak of luck out in Kentucky betting on the horses."

"Oh, so I assume he left and made some money so he could take care of Vivian, hmm?"

"Yes, mum, I believe he thought so. But I think it just put too much strain on Miss Vivian, once he came back. She wuzn't a strong-willed woman. Not like your muther, mum. No. And Miss Ashley...she inherited a bit of that weakness a'heart from her muther, I think."

I raised my eyebrows. *Sara? Weak?* I thought.

"Oh, now, she wuz a rebellious sort," she added, obviously answering my unvoiced question. "Yes, she wuz that at times. Especially after Tom left. But she wuz fragile in here." She tapped her chest. "It came in spurts, mum. She wuz never rebellious for long. It'd just flare up from time ta time."

"You said after Tom left? Why would that affect her?"

"She wuz a happy child, until he left for good. He spent lotsa time with her, he did. Bought that wild horse for her. They wuz the only ones who could ride it; strangest horse I ever did see. Why, Mr. Neilson, he couldn't even go near it without it raising the roof down there."

"You know a good bit about what goes on around here, don't you?" I asked softly.

Her cheeks flushed. "Servants notice things, yes, mum."

"You know what happened the night Vivian died, too, don't you?" I pressed. She didn't offer an immediate response, so I added, "Sara, I mean Ashley, didn't shoot her, did she?"

"No, mum!" she answered hastily. "Why, wherever did ya hear a thing like that? Miss Ash— She don't believe that, does she, mum?"

"Jason overhead you talking about it, and he told me. I can't remember telling Sara, but I might have. She hasn't mentioned it."

"Oh, wull, mum, *I* never believed Miss Ashley wuz capable of doing that. No, she loved her muther. But...she wuz there that night, by the missus...the gun in her hand. Poor thing wuz standing there screaming...blood all over her hands." She shivered.

"So it was covered up?"

"Yes, mum." She sighed heavily. "Mr. Neilson, he didn't want ta see Miss Ashley put in jail. Who would, a young thing like that? So, we all went along with whatever he said and didn't breathe a word 'bout her holdin' the gun. Shame of it wuz, she's sent away, anyhow. Seemed her mind...just snapped."

"Is that all you saw that night?"

"Yes, mum, I put the missus' suitcase away an' tried to forget."

"Suitcase?"

Her eyes flitted around the room. "Um...yes, mum. Miss Vivian, she wuz going sumwhere that night," she whispered, looking down at the hands now fidgeting with one another. "Mr. Neilson, he ordered me ta unpack her suitcase and put things away a'fore the law got here."

"Wait a minute, lemme get this straight. Vivian had a suitcase packed and was ready to go off with...Tom, I presume?"

"I dunno where she wuz going, mum, but you can see why Master Jason overheard us saying Miss Ashley might've had a hand in it."

"Because her mother was leaving her, is that the assumption?" I wondered if this might be the reason Sara didn't want to believe she was Tom Randall's daughter. Had Ashley known Vivian was leaving with him? Leaving her with Brandon perhaps? And had she stopped her mother from doing so? Did Sara know this on some unconscious level? I realized I was thinking about the same person as two separate entities, but to me, they were. Especially since Sara had no memory of being Ashley.

"We all knew Miss Ashley doted on her muther, mum," Celia answered. "Her and Mr. Neilson, they weren't close a'tall. Fact is, Miss Ashley often hid from him, up there." She nodded toward the ceiling.

"Why?" I asked, turning off the water.

"Don' rightly know, mum. Miss Ashley confided in no one but her muther and Tom. And when they wuz gone, wull, she didn't talk much ta anyone."

The baby bird alone in the forest, I thought. "What do you think really happened to Vivian, Celia?"

"Oh, mum, I wouldn't even want ta speculate. No, not me, mum. Do no one any good. That's what we all agreed at the time:

putting Miss Ashley in jail, it wouldn't bring Miss Vivian back."
She shook her head.

"So there was only Vivian and Ashley on the stairs, right?"

"I suppose, mum," she answered a bit hesitantly. "A'course, by the time we servants got there, Mr. Neilson wuz already trying ta calm his daughter."

"Trying to calm her? Why, was she hysterical or something?"

"Oh, yes, mum. Like I said, she wuz screaming sumthin' awful. And when Mr. Neilson reached for the gun, she threatened him with it." This raised my eyebrows. "Said she'd kill him, she did," Celia added, as if she thought I didn't believe her. She glanced down at the floor. "But I don't think she coulda'," she added in a softer tone.

"How'd he get the gun from her?"

"Wull, he smooth talked her for a while. An' when she calmed down, he snatched the gun away from her. Fainted dead away, she did, right there beside her muther." She shook her head.

"You said the police were called. What did Ashley say happened?"

"She never said anything, mum. Not 'til the day she die—I mean, she's never said," she corrected herself. "Her mind, mum, it snapped. Poor child, never said another word a'fore they took her away ta hospital." She was shaking her head, a rueful expression on her face.

"How was she when she came back?" I asked, pulling off my top.

Celia immediately turned away, as if embarrassed. "Very withdrawn, I guess ya would say. Never spoke ta anyone. 'Cept, a'course, Master Jason."

"She didn't have any friends?"

"Not 'til college, mum. She brought a few young women home then, as I recall."

"Young women? Was she..."

She nodded even before I finished. "I 'spect so, mum. The few I met were...not so ladylike, if ya know what I mean. 'Course, few are. Not like girls in my day."

"Did Brandon know?"

"I dunno, mum; they wuz so seldom together. Mainly went their separate ways after she went off ta college. That's when she got real rebellious. Seldom had a civil word for one another in them days. Even had a big row the night she had her accident, so I wuz told. Sammy said she tore outta here like the devil himself wuz hot on her heels."

"Oh, really?" This was interesting news, which fit perfectly with my thinking on what might have happened that night and why Tom had more than likely been close by at the time of Ashley's accident in order to find her. I pulled down my pajama bottoms. "What was the row about? Do you know?"

She turned to look over at me, then twisted back around in a flash. "No, mum, no I don't know what it was about. I-I should leave ya ta your bath, now. I have me chores ta do. Take care a'those linens for ya," she rambled on, as if embarrassed about something. I assumed this concerned revealing so much about Ashley and Brandon's relationship. "Want I should take your breakfus' down and keep it warm, mum?" she inquired.

"No, that's all right. If my visitor comes back, she might want something to eat."

"Will ya be needing me ta cum' back an'...help ya outta the bath?" she asked, her tone suggesting she hoped her services would not be required.

"No, thank you. I'm sure I'll be able to manage."

"Yes, mum." She closed the door behind her on her way out.

I was eager to tell Sara what I had learned, which was a lot. Celia was a veritable fountain of information—once you got the water running, that is. After eating part of my cold breakfast, I started out for the attic, but things were definitely not right in my head. I was almost too light-headed to walk, much less climb stairs. I turned around halfway down the hall and made my way back to my room. I would just have to lure her to me.

I sat down on the bed and turned on the stereo, programming the same songs as before. I turned up the volume and hoped that my invitation would be accepted. On the tenth repeat, I was growing tired of it myself and had already moved over to her chair, feeling disheartened that she hadn't responded. I was gazing out the window with my finger on the button to stop the player when I caught movement out of the corner of my eye.

"Please!" Sara shouted, as she shut the door behind her. "I don't think I can take hearing it again."

I pressed the button, stopping the music while never taking my eyes off her. She looked wonderful, neatly dressed in a pair of tight jeans and a white button-up shirt; her hair had been recently brushed, hanging long and flowing over her shoulders. God, how I wanted to run my fingers through it.

I started to get up, but she shook her head. "No, Faith, don't. Just...stay right there. It'll be easier that way."

For whom? I wanted to ask.

"I assume you wanted me," she said, toeing the carpet with her tennis shoe.

I couldn't resist. "You'll never know how much."

She sighed heavily and looked up at the ceiling. "This is hard enough, Faith, don't make it any harder. What do you want?"

I cleared my throat, for I'd almost said *You.* "I have a lot of things to tell you," I answered instead.

She glanced over at me. "About what?"

"I've been talking to Celia. We had a very informative little chat. Did you know you used to like Tom? That he got a horse for you, one that only you and he could ride? And that you have his skin tone and his eyes?"

She leaned her head back against the door. "You're not just telling me this, are you?"

"You think I'd lie to you about *this?* Then we'll call Celia up here and ask her," I declared, getting up out of the chair, headed for the phone.

"No, Faith, I...I believe you," she affirmed. "Don't...don't bother her."

"You want to sit down and listen to a few other things, or do you have a busy schedule today?"

"I'll listen...from here."

"Afraid I'll bite?" I asked sarcastically as I sat down on the bed.

"Frankly, yes," she admitted, still digging at the carpet with one foot.

There was a long silence between us as I sensed my new information changed nothing. Then I relayed the rest of what Celia had told me.

"Doesn't say much for my mother's character, does it?" she asked.

"Well, we don't know the whole story and...probably never will. But I should think that if Brandon fell in love with my mother, Vivian probably wasn't the first to stray."

She sighed heavily. "Where are you going when you leave here?" she questioned, deliberately changing the subject.

"Well, first I want you to go with me to Jackson Falls." I picked at a piece of fluff on the bedspread, assuming she would object. "I need to settle things there."

"Where then?" she prodded, without even looking my way.

"I dunno. We...haven't discussed it. Oh, but I have my inheritance now. Brandon gave me the savings account passbook and the checkbook. It's all mine. It came from my father. None of it's his. I intend to pay him back for all this, too." I was referring to the stereo, clothes, physical therapy equipment, etc.

"Tell me about Jackson Falls," she requested, finally looking over at me. "Would you like to go back there to live?"

"I don't believe *we'll* be able to. There probably aren't a lot of jobs for a private duty physical therapist. At least, not like what you're used to. And we'll need to be near a college so I can finish my education."

"You keep saying 'we.' I asked about you."

"I...I don't want to even consider life without you, Sara."

She sighed again even more heavily. "I'd be no good for you, Faith. I... Everything is just too messed up."

"Are you saying that we can't fix whatever is messed up?"

She ran her fingers through her hair. "Why don't you just go back to Jackson Falls and forget about all this?"

"I can't, can't you see that?" I got up from the bed and started toward her. "Didn't you listen to the song? Without you, Sara, I have nothing, absolutely nothing. I love you, and I'm not leaving here without you."

"Faith, please, I told you, don't." Her right hand fumbled with the doorknob as if she was going to leave.

"You gonna run again, Sara?" I took a step forward. "You gonna spend your life running from me?" I pressed, taking several more steps in her direction. "Because I'll follow you, Sara. I'll follow you to the ends of the earth, if I have to," I promised. "'Cause I know you love me. It's there in your eyes, and it's written all over your face," I added, covering the remaining distance between us while watching her grip the knob but not make any attempt to actually open the door.

"What if Celia is wrong?" she asked quietly. "What then?"

"I'll still love you just the same. I can't change what I feel." I reached out to touch her face.

"Faith, please," she objected, turning away. "I'm begging you."

"No, Sara, *I'm begging you.* Don't run from me, please! I need you, I want you, and I love you." I let go of the cane and placed both hands on the door, one on either side of her head. She merely continued to stare at the floor. I leaned over closer to her face and placed a kiss on her cheek. "Come back to me, Sara. I need you so much," I whispered, nuzzling my face against the side of hers. God, she smelled wonderful.

"Faith, please, you'll...you'll only end up hating me if—"

"I believe you said something similar once before," I interrupted. "And that time I ended up falling in love with you." I whispered this in her ear. "Head over heels, as I recall." I placed a kiss on her neck.

"Dammit, Faith!" she hissed softly. "You're always so persistent." She placed her hands on my waist. "But I can't let you do this. You'd be throwing your life away on me, cousin or not," she added, gently pushing me away.

I bounced right back. "You *are* my life, Sara, you know that." I kissed her cheek.

"Oh, you're so blasted stubborn," she said softly, finally facing me.

"Yes, but you wouldn't want me any other way." I placed a light kiss on her lips and then eased back, watching her eyes dart back and forth, searching mine. "I love you, Sara, with all my heart."

She hesitated a moment, then suddenly pulled me to her and pressed her lips to mine. "Damn...you...Faith," she mumbled around her kisses. "I...love...you...too." Except for a few moans, she fell silent for several moments. "Faith, no," she objected, hearing me lock the door. "I can't stay. I shouldn't stay. Faith...don't..."

"Yes, you can, and you should. I've missed you."

I didn't give any thought to the other visitor I'd had the night before, until we were on the bed. "Uh-uh," I objected, stilling her hand. "It's...*that* time."

She hesitated a moment, her eyes staring accusingly into mine. "You mean you get what you want, but I can't?"

"Um-hmm, that's about the size of it," I agreed, unzipping her pants. "I know you've encountered this before."

"Not with you," she countered, gazing into my eyes as if I were somehow different. As my hand slid inside her pants, she groaned, "Awww, sweetie, I've missed you."

"Celia, put a hold on lunch, please," I said into the phone. "And would ya be a doll and buzz me when Brandon gets home?" I ran my fingers through Sara's hair. "Oh no, I don't want to see him; just let me know when he gets here. Thanks, Celia."

"Pretty chummy with Celia these days, aren't we?"

"You left me all alone, I had to have someone to talk to. Besides, isn't it nice to know we don't have to hide things from her? Oh, no you don't... I *told* you—"

"Let's go take a shower then." She wiggled her eyebrows up and down and moved her hand up the inside of my thigh.

"For someone I had to practically drag into this bed, you sure are eager now."

"You're the one that put the lighter fluid on the charcoal and struck the match, so don't be complaining 'bout the fire you started, hmm? Come on."

"I think you'd better order that lunch now," she suggested. "Or else I won't get anything to eat again until after they all go to bed."

"Have you been starving up there?" I teased, running my finger around her lips.

"Um-hmm, in more ways than one."

Celia left the tray in the sitting room. Sara sneaked out and got it, then tore into it like she really was starving. "Want me to ask her to leave a tray for you tonight?" I inquired.

"No, that would be too obvious. But you could save me some of yours."

"Should I bring it—"

"No, too dangerous for you. I'll come get it."

"Good."

"Uh-uh. I know what you're thinking; I can see your wheels turning. No, I can't stay the night."

"Why not?" I moved my hand over her back. "You've done it before."

"Yeah, well, at least before we would've been able to make up some excuse if he happened to find us. Now... Whew... Uh-uh."

"Let's leave tomorrow, then."

"What are you gonna do, just leave while he's at work?" she questioned, frowning.

"That would be kind of... rude, don't you think? Making him worry like that."

"Might be for the best, though. I'd hate to see the scene he'd create over you leaving with me."

"You may have a point there," I acknowledged, knowing how he felt about her. "I guess I could move my stuff out while he's at work, then come back, pay him off, and say goodbye."

"Or handle the rest via long distance. I don't like the idea of either of us coming back here once he knows you're leaving with me."

"Why? What can he possibly do? I am an adult, you know."

She shook her head. "I don't know. I just...I don't like the idea." She paused briefly. "Are you sure about this? I mean, you know I'm not good with commitments."

"I'll take my chances," I responded, laying my head against her back and putting my arms around her waist. "Are you...satisfied with what you've found out, about the diary and all?"

"I suppose. I don't think my memory is ever coming back, though. Maybe it's better if it doesn't. When I try to concentrate on these little fragments, I get this awful...foreboding feeling. As if part of my mind is saying, 'You don't wanna know.'"

"Maybe it's that part of you who wants to remain Sara Bennington."

"Yeah, I-I think I do want to remain Sara Bennington." She rubbed her hand over my arm around her waist. "I know I liked her much better with you. Finding out about being Ashley has only been painful, and to tell you the truth, I don't think I'd want to be *his* daughter, even if he did accept me." I assumed she was referring to Brandon.

"Then there's nothing for either of us here anymore, is there?"

"I thought my memories might be here, but I suppose those would be better left in the past," she agreed.

"I beg your pardon. I have a very nice memory of the first time we made love, right here on this very bed," I rebutted teasingly.

"Umm, too bad we can't take the bed with us, hmm?"

"That's an idea. We could take the frame and mattress...leave the canopy part. I could buy it from Brandon and have it—"

She put her finger to my lips. "Why don't we just buy our own bed, hmm? Start over fresh? And the first thing we do is break in the bed."

"Sounds good to me," I acknowledged, and hugged her tightly.

"Oh, and that reminds me, I never did get to tell you much about my trip to Columbus."

"No, you didn't. How was it?"

"The place is beautiful, Faith. It's nothing like this, of course. Only a two-story brick house with maybe ten, twelve rooms at most in the whole house."

"That still sounds big."

"Well, it's not, not really. Anyway, the best part is the pond out behind the house. It has this gazebo built out over the water, with a swing, and there's ducks and... Oh, you'd just have to see it. It's really...charming," she said as she turned to face me, her expression changing from very happy to somber in an instant. "Um...since we're...leaving and all, I..." She turned away for a moment and nibbled her lower lip. Then she slowly moved the table away from her and turned around again. "Faith...I..." She paused, reaching down and taking my hands in hers. "I want you to come live with me there." She spat the words out very rapidly.

I was a bit taken aback. This sounded a lot like a proposal. It seemed things had changed a great deal in the last couple of hours. "Are you proposing..." I paused, for I couldn't say marriage. "...making a commitment?"

She nodded as she brought my left hand up to her face and kissed the palm. "Yes, I suppose I am." She gazed into my eyes.

I didn't want to ask this, but I felt I had to. "Are you sure?"

"Yes, yes, I am. I...I came back here that Saturday to tell you all about the place and...because I didn't like being without you. I wanted you with me that day. And I...well, I knew I wanted you with me always." She kissed my palm again. "I know it seems sudden, and it sounds odd since only a short while ago I acted as if I didn't even want you touching me, but I had to know for sure that you wanted *me*, no matter who I was or what I'd done in the pa—"

I silenced her by putting my finger to her lips. "I've been waiting a long time for this." I reached out and pulled her close, tears welling up in my eyes. I kissed her on the neck and whispered softly, "I told you I'd follow you to the ends of the earth, and I meant it. Wherever you are, that's where I want to be."

"Oh, Faith." She eased back, "I do love you so." Our lips met in another passionate encounter.

I lay back on the bed, taking her with me. We languished in each other's arms for quite a while before hunger urged her back to the mundane business of providing real sustenance for her body.

"I'm so happy, Sara," I affirmed, holding onto her once again while she attacked the now cold food. "You just don't know how it hurt when he told me you'd agreed I was well enough not to need your services."

"I never said that, Faith," she mumbled around a piece of bread. "He let me go that night."

"But he said you agreed with Dr. Rosemund that I was well enough to be released."

"Released?" She looked over her shoulder at me. "Has Dr. Rosemund been out here lately?" I shook my head. "Then I'm pretty sure he hasn't released you." Her eyes darted back and forth as she stared down at the tray. "I wonder why Brandon would tell you that?" she murmured. "He didn't say he was changing doctors?"

I shook my head. I wasn't interested in Dr. Rosemund or any other doctor. "How come your letter said, 'I'm sorry, but I can't stay here any longer?' You made it sound like it was your choice."

"Well, I was planning on leaving, only not *that* night. I came back as I was scheduled to, remember?" I nodded. She hadn't been due back from Columbus until Monday afternoon. "Well, Brandon was waiting for me when I walked in the door on Monday. He handed me my walking papers, which shot the way I had planned to say goodbye to hell and back," she grumbled. "Didn't I say I wanted to say goodbye, but I just couldn't face you?" I nodded.

"You know, I...I sat right here on the bed and wrote that while I watched you sleeping. And God, how I hated to leave you, but...there was nothing I could do. I kept hoping you'd wake up, because I couldn't bring myself to wake you, you looked so peaceful."

"Why not?"

"Guilt. I felt so ashamed of what I had done to you. I had always dreaded the thought of hurting you by not being able to commit to a relationship, but I never dreamed I'd ever hurt you *this* way. And knowing how ashamed I felt, I assumed you had to be feeling...just awful! So I figured maybe it was for the best, you know? And I had myself pretty well convinced I was acting in your best interest, until—"

"Until today?" I interjected.

"No, yesterday in the attic. You sure know how to wear down a person's resistance."

"I know something else I'd like to wear down, or more accurately, tear down. And that's all these lies that Brandon—"

"Shh," she said, rubbing my arm wrapped around her waist. "It doesn't matter now, sweetheart, we'll be leaving tomorrow." She brought my right hand to her mouth and planted a kiss on my fingers. Then she returned her attention to the food on the tray.

"You like watching me sleep, don't you?" I asked, kissing her on the shoulder, remembering the indention in the pillow this morning.

She shrugged. "What can I say, you're pretty when you're asleep." I popped her on the belly lightly. "Oops, I didn't mean you weren't pretty all the time, it's just..."

"How did you sneak back in without being seen?" I inquired.

"Oh, that was easy. You know they all have Tuesday nights off," she was referring to the servants, "and I knew Brandon would more than likely be up here with you, so it was just a matter of—" The phone rang, silencing her.

I snatched it up promptly. "Yes," I said, into the receiver. "Thanks so much, Celia." I put the phone down. "Get your clothes on, Brandon's coming up the drive."

"So early? Gee whiz. He would pick today of all days. Oh well..." She kissed me long and hard. "See you later. Remember to save me some dinner. Put it in there." She motioned toward the closet.

"Have you been in there a lot?"

She merely looked at me. "The apple was tempting. I eventually ate it. I just didn't want you to know I was here, *then*."

"Why'd you show yourself in the attic yesterday?"

"Because if I hadn't, you'd have alerted the whole damn house, and I couldn't have that, now could I?" She zipped up her jeans. "Gimme one more of those French fries," she asked, reaching over to the tray.

"Ah-ah-ah," I said, popping her hand. "Either I feed you or I dress you, take your pick."

"Feed me, and make it quick."

I stuffed two French fries in her mouth while she slipped her shirt on and buttoned it. Then she sat down on the bed and put her shoes on while I fed her the rest.

"Umm, I like feeding you. Come back tonight and let me do this again."

"Oh no," she objected, shaking her finger. "I know you, you'll have me hungering for more than food." I arched both eyebrows and chuckled. She leaned over and gave me a quick kiss. "Hadn't you better get dressed, too?"

"I will. He won't come up here first. 'Course, if he does, the door's locked. Be sure to lock it on your way out." As she set the door to lock behind her, I said, "Sara, I love you."

"I love you, too, Faith, especially for your stubborn, persistent streak. I love the way you wear down my resistance."

"Come back and I'll do a little more...*wearing* on that *resistance* of yours."

"I bet you will." She arched an eyebrow, and then was gone.

Chapter
19

Although Brandon arrived home around two, he didn't come up until right before dinner to escort me downstairs. When we paused at the stairs, I glanced down the corridor at the attic door and smiled, knowing that Sara was up there somewhere. Brandon, of course, thought I was smiling at him, and began his usual chatter about his business. I heard him, but my mind was elsewhere.

After dinner he escorted me into the library, saying he had something he wanted to discuss with me. I didn't really want to talk to him, but knew I should humor him. And besides, it at least kept him downstairs, where he was less likely to hear Sara if she moved around.

He offered me a drink this time. I hadn't had anything since the night of the party, so I decided, why not? It seemed he had something important to tell me, and I might as well have a drink to wash it down with. Especially if it was bad news or another lie. Hopefully, it would be the last of these I'd have to listen to.

He left the room for a short while and returned with two glasses of champagne. He handed me one, then sat down on the sofa beside me. "I'd like to propose a toast," he said, raising his glass. "To you, Faith, my beautiful niece, may you make your family proud by being the first psychologist in the Neilson family."

Oh, so this was his announcement. He had accepted my own choice of professions. "Thank you, Brandon." We touched glasses.

"And that's not all," he declared, as I took a sip of my champagne. "I've seen to it that you will be enrolled at the University of Georgia next semester."

"Next semester?" I asked, quite shocked at this revelation. "I wasn't planning on starting until the summer session. I assume it'll take that long before I'll be walking and looking normal after the plastic surgery."

"I've already arranged the appointment for your surgery with the best plastic surgeon in town. He says you should be home in three days, maybe less. And your records are being transferred here. You can start back to college in January."

My records are easily transferred, but not my clothes and other belongings, I mused. And yet, I said, "Well, Brandon, I-I appreciate the thought and all the trouble you went to, but...I haven't decided what I'm going to do. First, I need to go home. After that—"

"Home? Your home is here, where your family is, Princess. Jason and I are the only family you have left. I can take care of all of your affairs up there. Selling the house and—"

"Having my clothes and some of my things sent here?" I queried, interrupting him.

He looked at me rather strangely. "Your things were here. I thought you already received your clothes months ago."

"No, you haven't said anything about—"

"I distinctly remember telling Miss Bennington, because I...I didn't want to tell you. I do so hate to see you sad, and I knew how this would affect you."

"You told Sara?"

"Yes, Princess, I thought you had already gone through those things and picked out what you wanted. I had one of those rescue organizations come by and pick up the boxes Miss Bennington said you didn't want anymore."

"What?" I asked, quite perplexed now.

"You never saw any of your things, did you? That woman!" he fumed.

"Wait, my things were here and...they were given to a rescue organization? Even my stereo?"

"I suppose. I didn't look in the boxes; I merely went on her word. I'm sorry, Princess, I never should have trusted her. That was my mistake, ever trusting *that* woman."

"I never saw those things. Why weren't they brought to my room?"

"I had them put in the attic until you found time to go through them. They would only have cluttered up your room."

The attic? Just the fact that he had mentioned it sent a chill through me. And it also made me quite suspicious. *Had there ever been anything of mine in the attic?* Surely if he had informed Sara, she would have told me. She knew how I felt about my old clothes. Sara wouldn't do this to me. And come to think of it, I'd never known Brandon to let Sara handle anything that wasn't unmistakably her job, especially not family matters.

"Princess," he said, pulling me back to reality.

"Uh, yeah?"

"I'm sorry about this, Princess, but, well, as you see, I did do my part. And I can contact a good real estate agent, and—"

"Real estate agent?" I interrupted.

"Why, yes, to sell the house and—"

"No. No, that won't be necessary. I'm not sure I will be selling the house. I—"

"What?" He asked sharply.

"At least not right now," I added, thinking of how Sara and I might stay there a while during our trip. My mind then wandered back to my things. How much had been given away? And more importantly, why? Was he just making this up to try and turn me against Sara?

"All right," he agreed sweetly. "We can do that soon enough. But we have to start thinking of your future now. You can't stay behind these walls forever."

"I am thinking of my future, and *I* haven't decided exactly what I want to do. Don't get me wrong, I appreciate everything you've done for me. You've been very kind to take me in like this and cover all my expenses and... Well, perhaps the best way to repay you for everything, all the bills, et cetera, would be to turn over my interest in the company to you."

"What? Part of your holdings in Neilson?" he questioned incredulously.

"Yes." I wanted to add, *My father never wanted any part of it, so why should I?* I literally held my tongue with my teeth.

"No," he objected and turned away. "We are family, Princess. I will not have you repaying me for any of this."

"But I must, Brandon. I don't want to leave here feeling indebted to you."

"Leave here?" He flinched and turned toward me abruptly, as if I'd just pricked him.

The proverbial cat was out of the bag now. The bridge I had laid a course to cross tomorrow—via long distance, as Sara advised—yawned before me now. Why I was afraid to tell him this, I didn't know. Was this due to Sara's warnings that it wouldn't be easy to get away from him? But what could he do, short of physical violence? And why should I fear that? He'd never exhibited any signs of that kind of behavior.

I decided to go with the flow, albeit treading lightly, and see what happened. "Yes, I told you once before that I wouldn't be staying indefinitely."

"But you *have* to stay here, we're your family, Princess. And you need to be with family. Where else would you go? Where else could you find anything better than Shady Grove?" He set his empty glass down rather hard on the table in front of him.

Standing up, he shoved his hands deep into his pockets. Something inside made a jingling sound, which he stifled. "I just can't see you leaving, Princess," he continued in a softer tone. "Aren't you happy here? I've...I've tried to give you everything you wanted, everything you asked for. But obviously," he paused and walked around behind the sofa, "obviously I didn't. Just tell me what you want, Princess. I'll give you anything...anything within my power, of course.

"Do you want more parties?" he questioned. "More freedom to come and go? I'll hire another driver and put the other limo at your disposal. It should be yours, anyway; it was your father's. Oh, and I'll have it updated, of course, with every modern convenience you might want. You can use it to go back and forth to college. You'd never have to worry about the traffic or anything of that nature.

"You can even have your own parties," he went on, his voice getting that excited I-have-great-plans-for-you tone, as he put his hands on my shoulders. "We'll invite more suitable guests. Yes, yes, that's it. You'll be making new friends at college and meeting plenty of nice young men. I'm sure you'll have so many flocking around you that I'll have to lock the gates to even be able to spend any time with you. Oh yes, can't you see, it could be so wonderful, Princess."

For whom? I wanted to ask, but refrained, and took another sip of champagne. I stared at the glass, sensing an odd odor, as if it hadn't been cleaned properly.

I could feel his strong hands on my shoulders applying enough pressure to keep me from rising up to set the glass down. This was a bit disconcerting. "Brandon, I—"

"I need you, Marion," he proclaimed, gripping my shoulders a bit harder, obviously unaware of calling me by my mother's name. I rolled my eyes skyward. I knew he was off on his spree with my mother's memory. "This place needs a woman's touch. Things are so drab. Before you came, I dreaded coming home to this big lonely house. But now that you're...here, it's so different. I feel alive again. You're like a ray of sunshine in my dark and dreary life, Princess."

Listening to the tone of his voice, I started to feel sorry for him. I hadn't given much thought to how lonely he must be. I had only seen the cheerful side of his personality, the one that spoke of

his business as if it fulfilled him wholly. Only when he talked of
my mother did he seem lonely. And I knew all too well that he was
thinking of her now.

"Stay with me. You'll see, I'll make all your dreams come
true." His voice again took on that excited tone. "After you finish
college, we'll go on trips. Yes, we'll see the world. I can take you
to all the wonderful places I've been. And they'll be so much more
special then, with you by my side." His voice lowered an octave to
a soft, soothing tone as he placed one hand on the side of my head
and slowly stroked my hair. "Then you'll be ready to settle down
with...the man of your choice. And I'll have your mother and
father's whole suite redecorated for you. We can make one room a
nursery. Perhaps even the one across the hall. Yes, of course.
Doesn't that sound wonderful?"

This proposal of his was not one I fancied. It was nowhere
near my dream. While I might once have wanted to stay at Shady
Grove—it had been my home for many months now, and I knew
I'd miss Celia and the servants I had gotten to know—I did *not*
want him planning my life. Especially concerning marriage,
because I had my own ideas on who I wanted to spend the rest of
my life with. And *we* had already made *our* plans.

"Brandon, what if my choice is a woman?" I questioned, to
see what he would say.

"Oh, good God almighty, Faith!" He quickly removed his
hands. "I told you all you need is a good man, and—"

"But I don't *want* a man," I objected.

"Utter nonsense," he said disgustedly, walking down the
length of the sofa. "You'll get over this, you'll see."

"Brandon, if I can't be myself here, I can't stay."

He turned and shot me an angry look from the end of the
sofa. "*She* did this to you! Put these ideas in your head and turned
you against me. From the very first time you opened your eyes,
she did nothing but come between us. And now I know why! I
should have fired that disgusting bitch the very first time she disagreed with me," he pronounced angrily as he began pacing the
floor.

"And that was over your mother, you know," he continued.
"Yes, they both advised me not to tell you. No, it will upset her,
they said. But I wanted to, Princess. And I wanted to fire her then
and there. But no, Dr. Rosemund said she was an excellent therapist. Always got results with her patients. She got results, all right.
And I doubt you're the first patient she's seduced, either."

"This is not her fault, Brandon. None of it," I defended,
knowing he was lying about not telling me about my mother.

"Sara didn't seduce me, I seduced her."

He turned and glared at me. For some reason, I felt unafraid of his anger now.

"Oh yes, it was me, not her," I went on. "And she is not the cause of me wanting to leave. The reason I can't stay is because *you* can't accept me for who I am."

"Who you are?" he huffed. "You have no idea who you are, and that's the damn problem. You want me to accept this-this perversion, when I know your mother wouldn't!"

That stung, because I wasn't sure how she'd react. "She'd want me to be happy," I finally said, running my finger around the rim of my glass.

"Happy?" he asked, as he abruptly stopped pacing. "How could you possibly be happy with another woman?"

"I *was* happy with Sara."

He glared at me again and shoved his hands in his pockets. Whatever was inside jingled. "That cannot be happiness. Women were made for men, *not* for each other. You can plainly see that, Princess, can't you?" His tone was almost beseeching. When I offered no response, his tone changed once again. "No. No, I can't accept it, and I won't! I will not sit idly by and watch while you throw your life away because some...perverted whore turned your young head. No, we'll just have to fix this!"

Fix it? I felt heat rush to my cheeks. "And just how do you propose to do that?" I asked contemptuously in response to his overall demeanor, which seemed to suggest he, above everyone else, had the answer to everything.

"I'll hire the best doctors money can buy. You'll see, they'll know what to do to make you normal again. They'll know how to undo what that-that beast did to you."

I could feel the rage building inside me as the word "beast" echoed in my ears. I set my glass down on the table hard, sending some of the half-full remains dribbling over the side. I abruptly stood up to protest this insult, and then the room started to spin. I sat back down, hard. I could hear Celia's warning concerning his ego echoing in my mind: *"Be careful, mum, be careful."*

"She's a sick-minded woman to seduce such a child." He continued with his tirade, oblivious to my plight. "She took advantage of you is what she did. Doesn't matter who made the first move. She precipitated it. I should have seen through her when she had you putting your arms all over her out there in that pool. Such a sick, disgusting excuse for a human being; all her kind should be destroyed!"

Damn his infernal ego! I thought. He had no respect for my feelings, so why should I have any for his? I rose up slower this time and made it to my feet. "She's not a sick beast!" I shouted. "Nor a perverted whore. When you start calling names, you'd best look inside your own heart, uncle, because that was a *disgusting* display you put on out there in the pool. Now that's perversion. Rubbing yourself against your own niece. *She* never had to hold me like that."

At this point, I was saying anything that came into my head in order to strike back at him. I was on my own tirade and out for blood. "I don't doubt you'd want to keep me here for some perverted reason or another. If you need another woman around here, *find* yourself one. Or is that too difficult?" I didn't give him time to offer a response. "Of course it is, isn't it? No one compares to my mother, do they? That's why you never married again, because no one could fill her shoes, could they?"

He didn't answer, but merely turned his back to me and faced the fire.

I knew I'd hit pay dirt and kept digging. "Is that the reason you want me to stay here, because I remind you so much of her? You don't want *me* here, Brandon, you want *her!* You want a memory you could never have!" He gave a quick glance over his shoulder as if he might say something, but didn't. "Or did you?" I questioned, wondering if this was what he had wanted to say.

He spun around on his heel to face me with a look of utter surprise on his face.

"You did, didn't you?" I accused. "You had an affair with your brother's wife, didn't you?"

His eyes narrowed until they were no more than tiny slits. I could still see the anger and guilt written all over his face. I'd truly hit a nerve and I knew it. He was bleeding inside, just as he'd made me bleed.

"How dare you smear your mother's good name!" he growled, moving toward me, his dark eyes shooting daggers. "She was never anything but faithful to your father. She was extremely loyal."

"And you, were you loyal to your brother? Or did you lust after his wife so much that you drove him from his own home?"

Before I even saw it coming, he'd slapped me across the face with the back of his hand. I stumbled backward, my head reeling. The only thing that saved me from hitting the floor was a chair close to the sofa, into which I stumbled. I looked up at him, my vision a bit blurry for a moment and my lips stinging from the blow. The coppery taste of blood shocked my foggy brain into alertness. I reached up to my lips to see what other damage had been caused by the severity of his blow. Removing my hand, I found blood coating my index finger. I scrambled to my feet, my head still spinning, then wove my way to the door and eventually, the stairs. The taste of my own blood combined with the dizziness made me feel nauseous. I paused at the foot of the stairs, afraid I was going to be sick.

"Marion," he called from behind me. "I'm sorry, I didn't mean it. I...I lost my temper, darling."

Darling, my ass! I thought, and started climbing the stairs as fast as I could. *If only I can reach my room, I'll be safe.*

"Marion, Marion, please," he called from the foot of the stairs.

"I'm *not* Marion!" I shouted from the second floor landing. "And stay away from me! I never want to see you again!"

As I started off down the hall, I heard him coming up the stairs. I increased my pace, knowing he was getting closer with each long stride. All I could think about was getting to my room and locking the door. I tried for more speed, but my head was truly reeling now and I couldn't focus on anything. I was moving on pure instinct and adrenaline, reaching out to the walls for support.

I made it to the door to my sitting room just moments ahead of him. Slipping around the door, I slammed it behind me, then backed up against it and locked it.

"Princess... Princess, don't do this. Let me explain!" He turned the knob.

"Go away, Brandon." I moved away from the door. "I don't ever want to see you again."

"Princess, please don't say that. I...you made me mad with what you said and I...I really didn't mean to strike you. I...I lost my head. Please, Princess..."

"Just *go away*," I yelled over my shoulder, as I went into my bedroom and locked those doors behind me also.

My heart was beating ninety to nothing, my head pounding; it was hard just keeping my balance. I leaned back against the door to rest for a moment. I could feel the blood coursing through my veins, providing the necessary elements to keep moving. I reached up and touched my lip again; it was still bleeding in the corner.

"Damn him!" I straightened up and started over to the bed.

I turned quickly as something jingled outside the door. I heard a sickening click and then saw a sobering turn of the knob. The door opened with a spine-tingling squeak of the hinges.

"Princess, please forgive me, I didn't mean to hurt you," he maintained, closing the doors behind him.

"What the hell are you doing with a key to my room?" I

screeched, taking a step back.

His right hand stayed behind his back for several moments. "Why, I have a key to every room, Princess," he stated calmly. "It is my house, after all."

"You carry them all with you?" I was getting scared now, and started backing up in the direction of the phone on the nightstand. I wasn't sure who I was going to call: Celia or 911. What would I say to the 911 dispatcher? My uncle is in my room, come arrest him? What would I say to Celia? I had no idea. I just wanted someone to know what was going on up here. And I was hopeful that the mere threat of me calling someone would be enough to make him leave.

"What are you doing?" he asked, moving toward me.

"I want you out of my room," I responded, reaching for the phone and wishing like hell I could call the attic.

I had the receiver to my ear when he lunged for me and snatched it out of my hand. "Wouldn't do you any good," he growled, slamming the receiver back in the cradle. "They all have Tuesday nights off, remember?" He ripped the phone cord out of the wall. "Even Celia has a friend she visits." He snatched the other end of the cord out of the base. Receiver and cradle hit the floor with a whack and a jingle of the ringer.

"What the hell are you doing?" I exclaimed, taking a step back. "You're scaring me!" That was an understatement.

"Scaring you?" he asked, his eyes glassy and wild looking as he started toward me with the phone cord in his hand. "Oh well, we wouldn't want that now, would we?" A devilish smirk spread across his lips.

"Brandon, stop!" I pleaded, unsure of what he planned to do. I felt the bed touch the backs of my legs. *Not good!* I started crab walking down the side of the bed.

His gaze fell on the turned-back comforter and sheets. "Had yourself a fine time in here today, didn't you?"

"Wha..."

"Oh yeah, I heard it all. After the fact, that is." He was winding the phone cord around his left hand. "Your whore's been staying in the attic, hasn't she?" He arched his eyebrows suggestively. "Well, not anymore. Oh no, I expect she has a quaint little cell in the county jail by now."

Jail? Sara? "What are you talking about?" I feigned innocence while rounding the end of the bed, never taking my eyes off him. My plan was to get to the open bathroom door. Surely he wouldn't have a key to that.

Reaching beneath the canopy top, he felt around, then produced a small round object that looked like a magnet. "I put it here last night, after you went to sleep," he explained, as if answering the unvoiced question on my face. "Food missing, strange noises in the attic; she should have covered her tracks better." He smiled slyly and slipped the bug into his pocket, then started toward me again. "Let's see, now how did that go? Oh yes: 'You're the one that put the lighter fluid on the charcoal and stuck the match, so don't be complaining about the fire.'" His tone was high-pitched, apparently mocking Sara.

"Oh, God," I gasped, realizing he had indeed heard us.

"Yes, quite a tape I have in my study. Hot stuff, little Princess. Frankly, I didn't know you had it in you."

I suddenly felt very sick, knowing he had listened to us making love. "That was a sick thing to do," I hissed, taking one excruciatingly slow backward step at a time down the end of the bed, toward the bathroom. "Placing a bug in my room as if you were some sort of spy."

"I had to find out what you were up to. I got more than I bargained for, I'll grant you." That devilish grin was back. "Too bad it wasn't a video camera. I could let you watch yourself on TV. How would you like that, hmm?" Both eyebrows arched suggestively. "Watching yourself and your whore fuck each other's brains out, hmm? Oh, I'm sorry, excuse me, Princess, you prefer to call it 'making love,' don't you?"

I did feel sick now. "Brandon, stop this right now!" I pleaded, as he kept moving closer, the look in his eyes becoming more frightening with each step. I didn't dare turn my back on him in order to run for the door because I knew he'd be on top of me before I could get the door closed. "I don't know what you're so upset about. We're leaving, like I said. I mean, you heard that too, right? You'll get your money back for all of this, I promise. Matter of fact, I'll-I'll write you a check, right now. And I'll sign over my interest in the company. I don't want anything to do with it." I was saying anything that came into my head, all of which I was willing to do at that point to get away from him. "It'll all be yours. Just-just go downstairs and draw up the paperwork, and I'll sign it, I promise. And then I'll be out of here and out of your life. You'll never have to lay eyes on me again."

"Oh no, Princess, that's not exactly what *I* had in mind. You see, you don't need to sign anything over to me, 'cause you're not going anywhere."

His statement hadn't even registered in my brain when he lunged for me. I screamed and stumbled backward. His arms wrapped around me tightly, pinning mine to my sides before I could even voice another protest.

"It didn't have to be this way, Princess," he asserted, staring down at me. He didn't look so angry now, only determined. "I gave you ample chances to accept my offer. It could've been so wonderful." He leaned over as if to kiss me, and I turned my head away. "I had such grand plans for the two of us." He rubbed his face against the side of mine. "But you just wouldn't listen. *Why* wouldn't you listen?" His voice had taken on a softer tone now. "All I ever wanted was to love you, take care of you, keep you here with me. I would've given you everything. Everything your heart desired." His lips pressed against the side of my neck, and his hold loosened slightly.

I found myself able to move my right arm and jabbed the head of my cane into his groin.

"Oof!" he gasped, his grip loosening even more. I tried to pull away. "Oh no, you don't!" He spun me around so that my back was to him and tightened his grip. "Ungh!" he groaned, "You're a little fighter, aren't you?"

"Lemme go!" I growled.

"Never!" he hissed in my ear. "You're not going anywhere, Princess!" He jerked me off my feet and turned around, starting back toward the bed. "No one's ever going to leave me again!"

It finally registered in my brain that he was more than likely planning to kill me. For a fleeting moment, I couldn't accept this as being real. *Kill me? Why? It doesn't make sense. Brandon's not a killer.* And then it hit me, full in the face: Vivian died here—a supposed suicide; my mother and father had left here hurriedly, leaving things behind. *"No one's ever gonna leave me again,"* he'd just said. Adrenaline surged through my body. I kicked and screamed and somehow managed to hit him in the shin.

"Ow!" he cried out, then shoved me onto the bed face first. His body weight crashed down on me, knocking the wind out of my sails. "And give me that thing," he growled, his voice sounding like a 45 record being played at 78 speed for several moments. He stripped the cane from my grasp. "I thought you'd be pretty sleepy by now. But obviously I didn't use enough tonight for what little you drank."

I heard the cane slam against the wall behind us. And strangely enough, under the circumstances, I worried about it being broken, because it was something Sara had given me.

"I don't like fighting, you know," he continued, scrambling to get my arms over my head as I struggled against him. "No, never have liked it." He grunted, holding me down with his body and tying my wrists together with the phone cord. "I much prefer my women quiet and subdued." He grabbed hold of my legs and flipped me over on my back. I tried to kick out at him, but he was too strong. He moved quickly between my legs, making them useless as weapons. "Last night I did it right, though," he went on, using his body weight once again to hold me down. "You didn't fight me *at all*."

My heart sank to my feet at the thought of him doing anything to me.

"You must have known," he said, unbuckling his belt. "You bled like a true virgin. So, I guess she didn't do much damage, did she?" he smirked.

I suddenly felt faint at the thought of him taking advantage of me while I slept.

"Just for the record, you would've enjoyed it. I did." He chuckled. "But tonight you'll get to savor it. Oh yes, every precious moment, Princess, 'cause it's just you and me in this big old empty house," he gloated, unzipping his fly.

I put all my strength into bringing my arms forward and ramming them upside his head. He grimaced, but quickly had control of me again.

"Damn, you're a little fighter," he growled, and reached down, pulling his belt off with one hand, then looping it through the telephone cord around my wrists. "Fix you," he proclaimed with a grunt as he buckled the belt around the closest bedpost.

"Why are you doing this?" I asked, close to tears. I was still having a hard time accepting this behavior from him. For someone who wanted to be a psychologist, why had I not seen this coming?

"Why?" he mimicked, grabbing my blouse and ripping it open. Buttons popped off in all directions. "'Cause it's pretty obvious now that you're no better than that whore you spread your legs for. I tried to reason with you. Make you see the error of your ways, but nooo, you insist on being a pervert! And so, if you can spread your legs for her, you can damn well do it for me!" He reached down to the waistband of my jeans. "Tsk-tsk, pants are not very becoming on you, Princess. These are men's clothes." He pried the fabric off around the button and snatched the zipper down. Reaching around me, he grabbed hold of my jeans from behind; his fingernails raked over my skin in an attempt to pull them down. "Damn, these are tight!" Snatching downward, his fingernails clawed my backside as he freed the jeans from my hips, taking my underwear with them.

I screamed, though it was a feeble attempt and sounded more like a squawk. I was helpless and I knew it. He had complete control, and all I could do was watch as he lifted my bra and pulled it up over my breasts.

"Oh yes, you are beautiful," he declared, licking his lips. "Just like your mother."

I did manage to get out a scream this time, realizing he had probably done this same thing to her. He quickly covered my mouth with his own, applying pressure to the cut where he had hit me. His tongue went so far down my throat I thought I would gag on it. I clamped down with my teeth.

"Ow-w-w!" he cried out and jerked back. "God...damn you...you fucking little queer!" He grabbed his mouth; his hand came away with a spot of blood on it. "You'll pay for this!" He backhanded me across the face. Pain shot through my skull. "Like it rough, huh? Okay, I'll give you rough." He grabbed hold of my breast and squeezed the nipple.

I screamed as stinging sensations shot through my body. He quickly covered the throbbing nub with his mouth and squeezed it between his teeth. I screamed again in sheer agony. I'd never felt such excruciating pain in my life.

I felt him fumbling with his pants now, his breathing becoming heavier as if he were enjoying this. I prayed I would faint or something, anything so I wouldn't have to consciously endure what I knew was about to happen.

"Get off her, you bloody bastard!" exclaimed an angry voice behind him.

His head came up quickly and he turned, looking over his shoulder. "What the hell? You're supposed to be *in jail*."

"Am I now?" Sara retorted. "Doesn't look that way to me," she taunted, moving slowly into the room. Her hair was in disarray, white shirt speckled with dirt. "I believe I told you to get off her," she growled, producing a small-caliber silver pistol and aiming it at his back.

He glanced from the gun to her. "You wouldn't dare," he hissed, even though he did make a move to get up.

"Slow and easy," she directed, the gun trained on him as she cautiously moved around to the other side of the bed. "Make one false move, and I swear to God I'll put a bullet in you!" He paused in his movements and glared at her. "If I were you I wouldn't take the chance that I might not use this, because I'm crazy, remember? Spent three years on a nut ward."

"I don't doubt that!" he spat, slowly pushing himself up off the bed and ignoring Sara's reference to being Ashley.

Not wanting to be anywhere near him any longer, I squirmed backward across the bed toward Sara while he reached down for his pants.

"No! Let 'em drop," she instructed, motioning with the gun.

"What?" he asked incredulously.

"You heard me, let 'em drop...to the floor!" she ordered. He reluctantly let go of his pants and then started to cross his arms. "Oh no, let's see your equipment. What you wanted to use on her. Pull those boxer shorts down, too!" She motioned again with the gun.

"Oh, so that's what this is all about? You wanted to join the fun?" he goaded.

"Fuck you!" she retorted. "Pull 'em down, now!" The gun was leveled at his groin area now, and he reluctantly complied. "Hmph. That's the ugliest damn thing I've ever seen," she commented. He quickly covered himself with one hand and the tail of his shirt. "And the smallest," she added. "What's the matter, guns don't excite you?" He gritted his teeth and growled. "Come on, motherfucker," she taunted, "Gimme an excuse to send you straight to hell!"

"Sara, no," I admonished.

"Shut up, Faith. This is between me and..." She paused for several heartbeats, just staring at him. "Mister Rockhard, wasn't it?" His eyes widened, answering for him. "Oh yeah, I remember the story now. Didn't think I would, did ya?" She was obviously answering the unvoiced question on his face. "Oh yes, Mister Rockhard and his motorcar. How could I possibly forget?" The anger in her voice intensified with each word. "Mr. Rockhard needs to find a garage in which to park his motorcar, and mine's the *best* garage in town, isn't that the way it went? Fuck you, ya slimy bastard, I oughta blow you to hell and—"

"Sara, please don't!"

"Can't be," Brandon murmured, staring at Sara in utter disbelief. He obviously hadn't listened to the entire tape. "Those eyes... But they said there was no way you could have survived the—"

"Oh, but I did," she interrupted. "Aren't you happy to see me...*Father?*" she asked derisively.

"What... How..." Disbelief was swiftly giving way to acceptance. "But why didn't you come back home?" he whined, as if talking to a child who had merely run away. "Where have you been all this time?" Acceptance had apparently turned to anger. "And why did you deceive me this way?"

"Come home?" she scoffed. "To what? So you could continue doing *this* to me?" She glanced down at me for the first time. "Oh, my God, you sick bastard! You just had to hit her, didn't you? Ooh, I oughta waste your ass right here and now!"

"Sara, please don't do something we'll both regret. Get me

loose," I suggested, trying to distract her before she put a bullet in him and ruined both our lives.

He glanced down at me. "You should listen to your cous—" He stopped in mid-sentence, his gaze alighting on my right arm. His brow contorted into a frown as he stared at it. I had no idea what he was looking at. Bruises, perhaps? Was he suddenly feeling remorse?

"Take your ass over there to that chair, slow and easy," Sara directed, causing his attention to shift. He looked from her to me. "Do it!" she reiterated, motioning to the chair by the window. "Oh no, you don't," she added, when he made a move to pull his pants up. "Leave 'em just like that."

"I can't walk like this," he complained, covering his genitals again.

"That's the whole point, asshole! You didn't think I really wanted to see that thing, did you?" she scoffed, emitting a cynical chuckle. "Knowing you, you probably did, though." Her upper lip curled in disgust, eyebrows drawn together as she waved the gun toward the chair again. "What is that anyway, a birth defect or something?"

Apparently having lost some of his bravado, Brandon grumbled something that sounded like "botched circumcision" as he shuffled over to the chair with a semblance of a beaten man. Although I hadn't seen what they were referring to—nor did I care to—for a fleeting moment, I felt a twinge of sympathy for him. When he sat down in the chair, Sara turned her attention to me, the gun still trained on him. "I'm sorry it took so long." She glanced back at him occasionally while her left hand worked on the telephone cord. "I'm so sorry, sweetheart, look at your poor lip," she added, gazing down at me while loosening the bonds.

I caught movement out of the corner of my eye. "Sara!"

"Sit your fucking ass down, pervert!" she exclaimed, pointing the gun at his head.

"That's the pot calling the kettle black," he remarked, easing back down in the chair.

"Get out of here, Faith," she ordered, removing the cord from my wrists and tossing it aside. "Go downstairs and wait for me."

"I'm not leaving this room without you," I countered, sitting up in the bed and moving toward the side.

"Touching," Brandon mumbled.

"Fuck you!" Sara hissed.

"Look who's talking about fucking," he said evenly, as he stared at me. "You're *both* perverted whores—you fucked your *cousin*."

"You have the audacity to call us perverts, when you raped your own daughter?" she shot back.

"How did you..." He glanced up at Sara and then down at me. His eyes darted back and forth wildly.

"Incest, Brandon, that's what it's called. I wonder what your well-to-do friends will think of that when it hits the papers."

"You have no proof!" he scoffed. "No one will ever believe you. I'll tell them it's all lies," he declared, seemingly trying to maintain his composure.

"Ahh, but you won't be here," she said in a sinister voice. "Dead men tell no tales."

His eyes grew wide. "You wouldn't." I could tell he was uncertain. So was I.

"Oh, wouldn't I? According to the servants, I killed my mother," she responded. "And threatened to kill you. But obviously I never carried through on that, did I? Now, well, I have a second chance, don't I?"

"You'd never get away with it; they'd catch you and fry you in the electric chair."

"They didn't fry me last time, when I killed my mother, so what makes you think they'll do so this time, hmm? Especially considering my history. No, I think I could get off on an insanity defense. Hell, it'd be worth spending a few more years in the nuthouse to get rid of you!" She aimed the gun at his head.

"Sara, no!" I exclaimed, afraid that she had regained her memory and was really going to kill him.

"Why the hell not, Faith? He was gonna kill you, wasn't he? He said no one would ever leave him again." She recounted his earlier statement. "And I've already murdered my mother, so why not my father, too? Hmm? Or," she paused, her eyes lighting up, "I could give those psychiatrists something to sink their teeth into." She lowered the gun, leveling it at his groin. "What do you think? Take away your weapon of choice, hmm? That might be even better than killing you outright. Fit right in with the insanity defense. Looks like it'll work for that Bobbitt woman, don't see why it wouldn't work for me. Only I doubt they'd be able to find enough of yours to sew it back on."

He swallowed hard as she took a step toward him. "You didn't do it," he murmured.

"What? What was that?" she questioned. "I don't think I heard you."

"I said, you didn't...kill your mother," he answered, sounding as if someone had let all the air out of his balloon. He propped his elbows on his bare legs and hung his head.

"Oh, really? Then how'd I get the gun in my hands, huh?" He offered no response. "How?" she demanded.

"I-I panicked," he mumbled.

"You what?"

"Panicked. I was scared, all right?" he shouted.

"Because you killed her, didn't you?" she shot back. "You killed her because she was leaving you for Tom Randall, right?" He looked up quickly, surprise written all over his face. "Oh, I know about Tom," she continued, answering the unspoken question on his face. "She was leaving you and taking me with her, because I'm not your daughter, I'm Tom's, right? She knew better than to trust you with a little girl, didn't she?" He just stared at the floor. "Didn't she?"

"She was...crazy. She actually thought I'd let her leave here with my child," he grumbled. "No one takes my child away from me," he stated.

"You're saying I *am* your daughter?" Sara's voice held a note of disappointment.

"No, *you're* not my child," he confirmed. "Jason's my only heir. And she thought she was going to take him away from me. No one takes *anything* away from me!" he asserted.

I glanced up at Sara. "And so you killed her, didn't you?" she accused. He shook his head. "Didn't you?" she screamed, and fired the gun at his feet. The sound was horrendously loud. He cringed, covering his groin. I jumped, but Sara didn't even seem to flinch. Instead, she smiled.

"All right, goddamn it. Yes, but...I didn't mean to," he confessed. "It-it was an accident. I didn't mean for the gun to go off. You...you hit my hand and-and it was a just a freak accident!" He placed his head in his hands, as if he were about to cry. "If only she'd never pulled that gun on me." He shook his head ruefully.

Sara glanced down at me briefly. "So you were gonna frame me, weren't you?" she further accused, obviously referring to how the gun got in her hand that night.

"I-I decided against it, later."

"When? After I threatened to *kill* your ass?"

"I couldn't bear to see you in jail," he mumbled.

"How touching," she commented, mimicking his previous remark, disdain dripping from each word. "Truth is, you decided against it not to save me, as you say, but to save *your good name*. A suicide was much less *scandalous* than a murder, wasn't it? And besides, if I was involved in the shooting and they questioned me long enough, I might've told them the truth, right? And they *might've* believed me. So, what did you do to keep me quiet, Brandon?"

"You were in shock."

"Why did they keep me for three years, if it was only shock?"

"You wouldn't respond to treatment."

"Bullshit! What did you do, keep me doped up with these?" she asked, producing a bottle of pills from the waistband of her jeans. "Tranquilizers, aren't they, Brandon?" She glanced at the bottle. "No label. Must pay some pharmacist a shitload of money to get you these without a prescription. And you've been giving them to her, haven't you?" She tossed them on the bed. "A little every night in a glass of milk, gradually getting her used to it so she doesn't suspect anything, and then, one night you up the dose and," she snapped her fingers, "she's out like a light and putty in your hands, right? What happened tonight? Was she too smart for you? Didn't drink what you gave her?" She paused, aiming the gun at his head again, and went right back to her original question. "Why the hell did they keep me in the hospital so long, Brandon? Tell me, goddammit!"

"You were...suicidal. Every time they set a date for you to come home, you'd try to kill yourself, or...threaten to kill me."

"And we both know why I didn't want to come back here, don't we?" she hissed, backing up toward the bed.

"Oh, Sara," I said, and put my arms around her waist. I knew he'd done the same thing to her that he claimed he'd done to me the previous night: violated her without her knowledge. I couldn't imagine how many times he might have done so to her.

"So how did I end up back here, hmm?" she further interrogated. "What? Did I suddenly have a change of heart? Hmm? And why don't I have memories of all this? Huh, why? Tell me, dammit!"

"Shock treatments," he answered.

I gasped. "Oh no, Sara."

"Well, that explains a lot." She sounded tired now. "Shock treatments, head injuries, amnesia... No wonder I have Swiss cheese for memories." Reaching back, she put her left arm around my shoulder. "You all right?" she inquired softly.

"Yeah, I'm okay. Let's...let's just get out of here," I whined, laying my head against her body.

"Yeah," she agreed, the arm around my shoulder moving down my back, her hand going underneath my arm in order to help me to my feet. "I think we've got enough on Mr. Fancypants here that he won't be standing in our way anymore."

"You sick bitches," Brandon growled, getting up from his chair. "I've had all I'm going to take of this!"

"Oh, sit down, asshole," she grumbled. The gun in her hand was still pointed at him, but not at his head. Sara seemed to have lost some of her steam.

He glanced at the gun, as if sensing it no longer held an immediate threat. "You going to use that thing? Go ahead. Shoot me, bitch!" She offered no response, even as he reached down to pull up his pants. "I'm calling the police," he declared.

"Don't bother, they're already on their way," she announced.

"What?" This seemed to take him by surprise. "We-ell, no one will believe a word of this, anyway," he asserted. "I'm having both of you put in jail. Homosexuality is still against the law in Georgia, or didn't you know that?" He was looking at me.

"Celia, you wanna step in here with that tape recorder?" Sara requested. "Let's show Mister Fancypants just what kind of proof we have, hmm?"

Celia walked out of the bathroom with a small black rectangular box in her hand.

Brandon's mouth dropped open. "C-Cel-ia!" He stammered. "Why aren't you... That's mine!" he proclaimed, obviously referring to the tape recorder and seemingly trying to regain some sense of control and dignity in this situation. "You know you're fired if you don't give me that, don't you?" Maintaining eye contact with her, he discreetly zipped up his pants. "You'll never be able to get work in any other fine home in this city. You'll be out on the streets, homeless. And at your age, Celia, you know you won't last a month."

I could hardly believe he was attempting to hold sway over her after all he had admitted to moments before.

"Sod ya, ya bloody bastard!" Celia retorted, with an unmistakable growl to her normally calm voice.

Sara immediately looked over at her, as did I, for neither one of us could believe the Celia we knew and loved had said this. Sensing Sara's lapse, Brandon made a mad dash for her.

"Miss Sara!" Celia cried out, but it was too late.

Brandon plowed into Sara and they pushed me back on the bed, knocking the air out of my lungs. Sara kicked and squirmed and they rolled off me onto their sides, struggling for control of the gun. Brandon grabbed her by the throat with one hand, and the gun went off between them. Sara flinched and gasped for breath while he continued to choke her.

"Oh, God!" I cried, and looked up in time to see Celia bring my cane down across Brandon's head. There was a sickening thud and then he went limp, blood oozing from his temple.

"Sara...Sara!" I rolled her over on her back. The front of her shirt bore a large crimson stain. Tears sprang from my eyes, spilling down my cheeks. "Oh, God, no!" I blubbered.

"Fa-aith," she said softly, reaching up and touching my face with her bloody hand.

Chapter
20

We were sitting in the visitors' waiting room of the county hospital's intensive care unit when I finally asked of my companion, "How did Sara find out that Brandon knew she was in the attic?"

Celia looked up at me, a sly smile forming on her face, which answered my question.

"Uh-huh," I acknowledged. "And need I ask how she got back in the house last night?"

"I doubt she ever left, mum." She fidgeted with her hands in her lap, as if she found them quite interesting.

"You want to elaborate on that for me?" I requested, when she offered nothing further.

"Well, mum," she glanced up, "I 'spect she hid in the tunnel when the deputies wuz searching the house an' attic."

"Deputies? I never heard anyone in the house."

"They's very quiet. Mister Neilson didn't want 'em ta alert ya, mum. Said it would upset ya ta know she wuz lurking about."

"Uh-huh. And this tunnel?" I prodded.

"Yes, mum. Underneath the house, there's a tunnel leading to the back gate, or so I wuz told."

"Who told you that?"

"Miss Ashley."

"So Sara already knew about this?"

"No, mum, I had to show her."

"And how do you get to the tunnel?" I queried.

"There's an entrance in the hallway of the servants' quarters. That wuz another a' Miss Ashley's hiding places."

"I see." My mind was awhirl with questions, switching tracks often. "And so, how come you didn't go see your friend tonight?" I probed. She cut her eyes over at me. "Brandon told me you had a friend."

"That's a bit of a long story, that is."

I held out my hands palms up. "I'm not going anywhere."

"Wull, ya see, I wuz going out as usual, but...me ride didn't show up. So, I cum back in the house and called my friend. That's when I found out," she paused and sighed, " me...friend's granddaughter, who wuz ta pick me up, she'd been trotted off ta jail."

"Jail?" I repeated. Celia merely nodded and hung her head as if embarrassed. "I hope she's not in any serious trouble."

"Oh no, mum, mistake's all it wuz. She...happened to look like sumone they wuz looking for. She's home now, safe and sound."

That's who Celia was calling a while back, I thought, remembering her standing at a pay phone in the hospital's cafeteria area. "So you were in the house the whole time?"

"Most a' the time, yes, mum. I stayed in me room until I heard you two quarreling an' you storming up the stairs. That's when I knew for sure sumthin' wuz bad wrong."

"Knew for sure?"

"Yes, mum. I heard Himself fixing the drinks." She nodded toward the hall and the room beyond, as if she didn't want to say Brandon's name. "T'wuz no reason ta use a spoon for champagne, but I know I heard him mixing sumthin'. And later I spied the spoon an' pill bottle. That's when I started thinking 'bout Miss Ashley, and...your bed linens."

"Excuse me? My bed linens?" I couldn't imagine what my sheets had to do with Ashley, unless Celia was referring to Sara. But what could that possibly have to do with Brandon and a pill bottle?

"Wull, yes, mum, when I changed your linens this morning...Wull, it's more like yesterdee now, isn't it?" She glanced down at her watch. "Anyhoo, when I gathered 'em up ta launder, his cologne wuz on 'em; and I didn't think that wuz right. Then you being so dizzy an' all... I happened to recall Miss Ashley wuz like that sumtimes. An' those mornings, she wuz ill as a hornet, she wuz. Them's the times she'd hide from him."

I nodded in understanding. That explained Sara's sense of foreboding concerning glasses of milk. And why Ashley hid from Brandon in the attic and in the tunnel. "So, how did you find Sara and know to bring a tape recorder?"

"Well, mum, the recorder wuz easy. I'd seen it before. He uses it for recording notes ta himself, he duz. So, after you went tearing off upstairs, I went into his office and took it, thinking I'd carry it

with me when I checked on you, just in case sumthin' happened,
mind you. I mean, I watch the telly, too, and I know how the bad
ones always say ya can't prove nuthin'." She glanced back down at
her hands, then up at me, as if questioning whether I wanted her
to continue.

"Go on."

"Wull, the sitting room door wuz locked, and I didn't have a
key ta your room with me, but I did have Miss Ashley's, sooo... I
let ma'self in that way." She glanced down at her hands again and
clasped them together, fidgeting in her seat. "I-I'm as sorry 's I
can be, mum, 'bout not coming in sooner, but," she shook her
head slowly, "I've never been much of a fighter. And I-I wuz
scared of him, I wuz. I mean, I knew there wuz no one else about
but me and you, an' I had nuthin' to...defend us with—"

"It's all right, Celia," I interjected. "You don't have to apologize. I'm just glad you were there."

"But I'm ashamed, mum, cuz I wuzn't much help."

"Yes, you were. You got most everything on tape, especially
the last part, which was the most important anyway...to clear
Sara." I watched a nurse coming out of Brandon's room. She
smiled sweetly and headed off down the hall. "So, how did Sara
get your gun?" I asked quietly.

She glanced around us before answering, "Wull, like I said, I
had nuthin' to defend us with—*'cept* me gun that wuz downstairs.
So I left the tape recorder in the loo by the sink, an' wuz headed
down the hall when I met Miss Ash—I mean, Miss Sara. She wuz
cumin' up the back stairs, an' I told her what wuz happenin'."

"Ah, so Sara went down and got your gun, I presume?"

She looked past me as she nodded. "There's 'em two detectives again, mum. I-I think I'll go get sumthin' ta drink. Would
you care for sumthin'?"

"No, thank you, Celia. Oh, but when you speak to your
friend, tell him I'm sorry his granddaughter was arrested." Celia's
mouth dropped open. She hadn't told me that the young woman
had been taken to jail instead of Sara, but I'd put two and two
together and come up with what I thought was four. At least it
sounded quite plausible, since Brandon seemed certain Sara was
in jail. "She looks a bit like Sara?" I queried.

"Dark hair, yes, mum. An' what with that fancy car of hers...
Just had ta have one like Miss Ashley. She used ta look up ta her,
she did."

"Well, tell him, and her, that I'm truly sorry for all the trouble we've caused. I'm sure after all this is over, I can make some
sort of...monetary restitution." I knew I sounded like Brandon,

but how else could I make up for such a thing?

"Yes, mum," Celia agreed. I saw her get up, but my mind was on other things—mainly what those two cops standing in the hall conversing wanted now. They'd already questioned all of us—with the exception of Brandon—several times. They'd even come back to question Sara again, taking her down the hall only a short while ago. "My friend," Celia added, still standing beside me, "weren't no man, mum."

I turned and looked up at her. There was a smile on her face. "What, Celia? I'm sorry?" From her smile, I thought that I had missed something.

"My friend, weren't no man, mum," she whispered. "An' truth be told, 'twuz *my* granddaughter."

I was quite taken aback and it took me a moment to digest this new information. "Why, Celia, I didn't know you'd been married."

"Never wuz." She gazed down at me, the smile still in place, her head cocked to one side as if she were trying to communicate more than she was willing to put into words. "An' I never had a sister, only bruthers," she added, then turned and walked away.

It took me a moment to put what she'd just told me into context, and then I couldn't help but smile, too. Celia had told me her own true story: *she* was the one who'd suffered the rape, then run off to America. I could only assume she'd also borne a child from that assault and now had a granddaughter.

"What are you smiling about?" I flinched when Sara spoke. Being preoccupied with Celia, I hadn't noticed her coming down the hall. "Those detectives are gonna get the wrong idea," she added, slipping into the chair next to me.

The smile faded. "So, what did they say this time?"

"Still want to know about the gun."

"And?"

"Like I said, I found it in a trunk in the attic."

"Don't bullshit *me*, Sara. I know its Celia's. Why didn't you just tell 'em the truth?"

"And drag the ol' girl in deeper than she already is?" she whispered. "No way. Besides, she'd already told me the damn thing wasn't registered. And that's why Tweedledee and Tweedledum are back." She turned and smiled at the detectives as they approached.

"Any change in his condition, ma'am?" the taller one named Levi asked, directing his question at me.

I shook my head. "Not that I know of."

The two detectives looked at each other. "We might be wanting to talk to both of you again, so don't leave town."

Sara and I nodded simultaneously. The shorter detective, Jun-ior, who had been looking us over carefully, then glanced from me to Sara rather quickly and shook his head.

"Come on, Junior," Levi said, "Ain't nothin' else here for us until Mr. Neilson comes around. We'll be in touch, ma'am and, uh...ma'am." He nodded at each of us.

Sara and I both returned the gesture and watched them walk away. About halfway down the hall, Junior glanced back. He shook his head in disbelief, then turned around and continued on his way. I knew the look he gave us had nothing to do with the case as such. The tape recorder told it all, or almost all of it. There was a blank space when Celia moved from the sitting room into Ashley's old room, but she'd left the recorder running, so it was evident what she'd done. Then there was the testimony of Celia—a long-time, devoted employee no less—the phone cord, the champagne, which was being tested, my face, and the bruises on my arms. All the evidence added up to the fact that we were telling the truth.

What Junior was shaking his head about concerned the tape revealing that Sara and I were lovers and had once thought we were cousins. One was bad enough for poor Junior, but when he'd heard the cousin part, he'd started shaking his head, and he hadn't stopped in the four-hour time span during which they'd interro-gated us. He would do it each time he saw us together. One time when he thought I wasn't listening, I overheard him tell another uniformed officer, "And they're both damn good looking, too. Ain't like no dykes I ever seen before." At that moment I had wanted to say, "*We don't all wear leather jackets and ride Harley Davidsons, but I'm thinking about getting me one of each so I'll be more easily recognized.*"

"I think he's got a crush on you," Sara teased.

I swung my eyes in her direction, trying to avoid looking at the big red stain on her shirt, but failing miserably. "You were lucky. You don't know how I felt when I turned you over and...saw *that.*"

"Took me a little while to realize it wasn't mine, too," she admitted.

"Why'd you flinch like that?"

"Scared the hell outta me. I mean, I knew one of us was prob-ably shot, and I assumed since he was still choking me, it must be me and I just hadn't felt any pain."

The light outside Brandon's room started flashing.

"Uh-oh," Sara commented. "Those detectives might be back

sooner than they expected. And this time they'll be investigating a homicide."

Several nurses came flying down the hall and disappeared into Brandon's room. The doctor was soon hot on their heels. A few seconds later, an intern came tearing down the hall with a crash cart—the machine I'd seen used on TV whenever some character's heart had stopped beating. I could almost imagine what the scene in his room must be like.

They stayed a good while before the doctor finally came out. "Miss Neilson," she began, "your uncle has suffered a massive coronary. I wish I could tell you he will pull through, but honestly, I can't say that with any assurance. He's lost a lot of blood and... Well, we thought we had him stabilized, until this." She shook her head as her eyes strayed over to Sara and she surveyed her attire. "He's asking for you, Miss Neilson," she said, glancing back at me. "The nurse will let you know when you can go in, but I must ask that you not upset him. He seems upset enough as it is." Her eyes strayed back over to Sara. "You were lucky, Sara. That could have been you lying in there."

"I know."

"Let's just be thankful it isn't." She glanced over at me, nodded, then turned and walked away, her white lab coat fanning out behind her.

I cut my eyes over at Sara and found her already looking at me. "It was a long time ago, Faith," she explained. I continued to stare at her, my expression unchanged. "It was only a short fling and *she* ended it. Is that what you wanna hear?"

"No, not unless it's the truth."

"Go ask her then."

"One of the few?" I inquired.

"No, actually, come to think of it, there were several who didn't fall *madly* in love with me."

I merely raised one eyebrow.

"'Scuse me, mum," said Celia, who had quietly rejoined us. "Wuz that Mr. Neilson's doctor I saw just now?"

I nodded and glanced down at my hands intertwined in my lap. I knew this would not be good news to Celia, because she felt very guilty about hitting him over the head when he had already been shot in the stomach. "Brandon's had a heart attack," I explained.

"Oh no, mum," she gasped, her hand going to her gaping mouth as she backed up into the chair on the other side of me. "Will he..." She let the question hang there.

"I don't know, but I don't think the doctor is all that hopeful."

I sounded crass, even to my own ears.

"Oh, mum, I shouldn'a hit him so hard."

"He was choking me," Sara spoke up. "And that's all you saw. How could you know which one of us was shot? Besides, the head wound was minor. You merely saved me and him a lot more pain."

I was a bit shocked at Sara's bluntness. I thought she should have some feeling for him, but obviously she didn't. Of course, *I* wasn't going to win any awards for Niece of the Year.

"Yes, mum," Celia finally agreed. "Oh, Master Jason, mum?"

"Good Lord, Celia, I'd completely forgotten about him in all this."

"I'll take care of it," she assured, and patted my arm as she got up and left again.

I glanced over at Sara, who in turn was looking at me. "The old girl doesn't know it, but she may have saved my life." She reached up and rubbed her bruised neck. "I don't think Brandon knew he was shot. Or at least it didn't affect his strength right away, 'cause he was still trying to get the gun and choking the shit outta me."

There was a long silence between us, and then I asked, "Sara, do you have your memory back?"

She sighed heavily. "Bits and pieces. They don't really mount up to much more than before."

"Then how did you know about all that stuff? I mean, you asked some pretty *pointed* questions. It sounded as if—"

"I know. I did remember that one thing, about...Mr. Rock-hard." She cleared her throat and frowned. "It just suddenly...leaped into my mind and...nearly blew me away, actually."

"He really said that to you?" I asked, instead of the question on the end of my tongue: *He raped you, too?*

"I don't think he thought I'd remember after he doctored the milk. But..." She shook her head, as if removing those thoughts. "As for the rest, remember that diary? Well, on the back inside cover, there was a small rip in the fabric. Inside was a key, a key to one of the trunks in the attic."

"How'd you know that?"

"I didn't. I just took the key and tried it in the first available lock I saw, which was on this old trunk nearby. Convenient, huh?"

"Sounds like you made it up."

"But I didn't. It really happened that way. You know they say life is sometimes stranger than fiction."

I nodded, thinking how our lives had seemingly been turned into fiction the past few hours. "So what did you find?"

"Another diary. The real one: no metaphors. That's where I

got most of the story. The part about my mother's death, well...I guessed at that. I mean, from what you told me, and what I had written in the diary—which wasn't much more than fragmented memories, like my whole past is now—I put two and two together and threw it at him to see what he'd toss back." She sighed heavily and crossed her arms over her stomach.

"Do you believe the part about you hitting the gun?"

She shrugged. "It would seem from that story about the baby bird that I felt responsible, somehow, but...I don't know. I'm afraid I never will know exactly what happened, unless he pulls through and decides to spill his guts. And I'm sure it'll be a cold day in hell before he does that. I'm surprised he revealed all that he did." She paused for several moments and ran her fingers through her hair. "I expect there're a lotta things I'll never really understand. Like, how did Tom find me after the accident? How'd he get me to a hospital without anyone noticing or suspecting who I might be? How'd he know to use Sara Bennington's name? How'd he... Aw, damn, there's just so many things that..." She let the sentence hang there as she shook her head sadly and ran her fingers through her hair once again.

I nodded in understanding. The door to Brandon's room opened. "So where did you hide when the cops came looking for you?" I wanted to hear Sara's version of the evening's events.

She sighed heavily, as if she were about to launch into a long spiel.

"Miss Neilson?" called one of the nurses, making eye contact with me from the hallway. She waited until she got closer to finish. "Your father wants to see you."

I glanced over at Sara, then back at the nurse. "He's my uncle," I corrected. "He was *her* father."

She looked from me to Sara, quite puzzled. "Oh, I'm sorry. Well, he's asking for his daughter Faith. I thought you were Faith."

"I am, but I'm not his daughter. Sara is."

"Oh, well, perhaps he's asking for both of you, then."

"Not likely," Sara mumbled.

"Please, don't upset him," the nurse cautioned. "He's groggy, and maybe even a bit incoherent, but he's insisting on seeing you, so..."

"We understand," Sara confirmed, helping me to my feet. "We'll just go along with whatever he says."

"That'll probably be best. Now, stay only a few minutes. If you need me, I'll be right outside the door."

"Believe me, we'll stay no longer than we have to," Sara murmured as she escorted me across the hall.

Brandon was hooked up to an assortment of different machines. The most prominent one had a monitor that showed a beeping, flashing heart and the arcing blue line that moved to the rhythm of his heartbeat. How many times had I seen that blue line on TV as it went flat when a character died? But this was not the movies, and Brandon was no actor who could get up out of bed when the scene was over.

I glanced over at Sara, who was watching me intently. "I doubt he wants to see me," she whispered. "I'll stay here. Go on over."

"But she said he was asking for his daughter."

"I'm *not* his daughter, Faith. Now go on."

I frowned at her as Brandon began mumbling, "Daughter...want Faith," as if talking to someone else in the room.

I turned back to Sara. He wanted us both. She waved me on, mouthing, "One at a time. Go on."

I proceeded over to his bedside. He was very pale and looked ten years older. It was hard to believe that this man had been the one to attack me a mere six hours ago. He hardly looked strong enough to swat a fly.

"Nurse," he said, as he swallowed hard. "Please...my daughter...Faith must..."

"I'm here, Brandon," I said softly.

His eyes fluttered open for only a brief moment. He swallowed hard, frowned, and they fluttered open again with obvious effort. "Princess," he said weakly. His eyes seemed to roll back in his head.

I gasped. I thought he was going to die right then and there. Then I realized the heart monitor wasn't flatlining, and breathed a sigh of relief.

"Princess." He swallowed hard again and his tongue snaked out, wetting his lips. I vividly remembered biting down on that tongue, which was almost gagging me at the time. "So sorry...Princess. I...I didn't know... Sh-she never... I sw-swear...never knew..."

Never knew what? I wondered. I stared down at him, waiting for more. What didn't he know? Did he even know what he was talking about?

"I...I don't understand," I finally expressed, realizing he wasn't going to say anything more.

"My daughter...beautiful daugh-ter..."

"Sar—um, Ashley's here, Brandon. Do you want to—"

"No! Not mine!" he stated emphatically, shaking his head

back and forth. The line on the monitor began jumping erratically. "Not m-mine...n-not mine!"

"Calm him down, Faith," Sara admonished. "Say anything, just calm him down."

"Brandon...Uncle Brandon, listen to me, it's...it's all right," I soothed, touching his arm. "It's all right now, none of this matters." I was lying through my teeth. "Just...you just get well and...we'll...have you back at Shady Grove in no time."

I watched the line on the monitor slowly return to normal, as did the sounds of the room. The rhythmic bip, bip, bip, the sighing of the IV machine, and Brandon's raspy breathing created an off-beat trio. I sensed the same type of trio had played in this room, and others like it, many times before, with the patient's heartbeat the conductor and composer.

"Faith...Princess?"

"Yes, Brandon, I'm right here," I said, gently squeezing his right hand.

"I...I didn't know." He paused as he reached over with his left hand and touched his right arm where the two IV tubes were taped together.

"What's wrong?" I asked, a bit concerned. "Is your IV..."

"I swear." He patted his arm.

"Brandon, I don't understand. Is something wrong with the IV in your arm?" His eyes grew wide as he kept tapping it. My first thought was something I'd heard on TV about air bubbles in IV lines—straight to the heart, kills the patient. "Sara, get the nurse!"

"Princess, for...give...m-me. God...forgive me," he uttered in a whispery voice, the heart monitor beginning its erratic display once again.

The nurse came rushing in. "Please leave, Miss Neilson," she ordered.

"He...he has my hand," I explained, feeling the pain as he apparently gripped it with all the strength he had left. He continued staring at me with those wide, scary eyes. "He was hitting his arm near the IV. Could that mean—"

She pushed me to one side and hastily checked his IV, but Brandon still clutched my hand.

"Please, Miss Neilson," she said, having to go around me.

I propped my cane on the side of the bed and reached over to break his grip. He squeezed tighter and moaned. I looked up at him. What did he want from me? Did he want me to say I forgave him? How could I do so in all honesty, after what he'd done?

"Miss Neilson, I must insist."

"I'm trying, but—" His grip suddenly relaxed and I took a step backward, absorbing the momentum of my previous attempts to break loose. Sara was behind me in an instant.

Then everything seemed to happen all at once: the heart monitor flatlined; people dressed in white streamed through the door. Sara and I were caught in the melee and forced into a corner. I was quite mesmerized by the whole scene unfolding before me as they prepared to resuscitate him once again.

"Come with me, sweetheart," Sara urged softly, when the path to the door was clear. She led me out into the hall. "What was all that about?" she asked.

"I...I don't know. Maybe...maybe he was delirious, but my God he was still strong, right up until..." I couldn't finish, but shook my head sadly.

I had wanted to hurt him with words and make him bleed inside, just as I had over his cruel words to me. I had never wished him dead, though.

Regardless, on November 14, Brandon Jason Neilson passed from this earthly realm, leaving Jason with only a cousin and a half-sister for family.

It was no easy task breaking the news to Jason, who had immediately come home from school when Celia called, but actually, it took only an hour to tell it all and answer his few questions. Strangely enough, he accepted it all, seemingly as a matter of course. The only parts that seemed to disturb him were finding out Sara was his sister Ashley—he had felt something for her, but not recognized her as such—and Brandon's attempt to rape me. No one but Celia and I knew about him violating me the previous night, and since neither of us had any proof, we decided that it was best to let sleeping dogs lie. Especially in light of how I knew Sara would feel about this incident.

Returning from the funeral at Shady Grove, where Brandon was interred in the family cemetery, I held Jason's hand while he stared out the window. So far, I hadn't seen him shed one tear over his father's death. I could only assume he had shed plenty when he was alone.

Nearing the mansion, Jason patted my arm and then removed his hand from mine. He opened the door for me like a true gentleman, while Sara eased out the other side, preferring to open her own door. As Jason closed the door, I put my cane in my left hand and reached up to wipe my eyes. I saw his gaze linger on my arm and a puzzled look come over his face.

"What's wrong?" I inquired, switching the cane back to my right hand.

"Is that a birthmark on the back of your arm?"

I smiled. He was the first one to recognize it for what it was. Most people assumed it was a bruise. "Yes, it is."

"Can I see it?" he asked.

I shrugged. "Sure." The cane changed hands again, then I bent my right arm at the elbow and turned it slightly so he could get a better look. The mark wasn't that noticeable.

"Funny, I have one just like that," he said, and started to roll up his sleeve, but found he couldn't because of his jacket. "Oh well, I can't show you now, but Father always said it came from the Wyndam side of the family." He shrugged, as if dismissing his line of thought. Then he glanced up at Sara, who was extending her arm to me for support, even though I didn't really need it. "I'll still think of you as my sister, even though I know you don't remember me," he said ruefully. I saw tears well up in his eyes for the first time. "I know you can't stay, but I sure wish you would." With that said, he immediately took off around the front of the car and dashed up the steps into the house.

Sara turned to me. "You told him we were moving to Columbus?"

"He asked where we'd be living. I told him he could come stay with us during holidays and summer vacation."

"What did he say?"

"Seemed to like the idea. I'll have to talk it over with the lawyer; he'll be his guardian now."

Sara merely grunted. We'd already asked about the possibility of Sara proving she was Ashley in order to be Jason's guardian, but the lawyer had made it plain that Brandon's will was specific concerning the lawyer filling that role. This particular lawyer evidently did not care to forgo monetary gain despite Jason's desires or best interests.

"He also...knows," I added, to head off any worries she might have about him coming to visit us.

"Knows what?" she asked with a frown.

"His room overlooks the pool."

"Oh, you mean he saw me and you?"

"Um-hmm."

"And he never said a word?"

"He said it made me happy, so he wasn't about to ruin it for me. He knew Brandon would go through the roof."

"Thoughtful kid," she said, as we started up the steps. "Wish I could remember him, but... Oh well, maybe one day." She paused briefly. "What was that about your birthmark?"

"Oh, he has one like it. He said Brandon told him it came

from his mother."

"Not my mother?" She frowned.

"No, of course not, silly. Brandon's mother."

"That's a relief. For a moment there I thought you were gonna tell me we're sisters." We both snickered at the absurdity of that thought. "So, your grandmother had the same birthmark, hmm?"

"Well no, Brandon's mother... Ya see, Brandon and my father had different—" I stopped in mid-sentence as the truth behind Jason's innocent remark finally hit home like a ton of bricks. "Oh, my God!" My legs started to tremble.

"Faith, what's wrong?" Sara asked, grabbing me around the waist.

The scene in Brandon's hospital room played out before my eyes. Brandon had said: "I didn't know. I swear, I never knew." And he'd been tapping his arm, obviously trying to tell me something. Then I reviewed the scene in my bedroom that fateful night when he had been staring at my arm.

"Oh no. Oh, God, no!" I hissed, the world starting to spin before my eyes.

"Faith, what the hell is it?" Sara demanded.

I swallowed hard, feeling my knees start to buckle. "Brandon...Oh, God, Sara..." I could hardly force the words out. "He was *my* father!" The world around me faded from view.

Epilogue

Once the investigation was wrapped up—kept quiet actually, to avoid sullying Brandon's good name—and we were able to leave town, Sara and I drove to Jackson Falls. Everything was pretty much as we had left it, except for my belongings. I discovered that Brandon had contacted the lawyer my father had left in charge of his affairs, and tried to bribe him into allowing him to sell the house and all our belongings on my behalf. Although the lawyer, Mr. Gorman, had found a way to have my personal belongings shipped to me at Shady Grove, there was nothing either one could do about the house without my signature.

After boxing up the personal items I wanted to keep, and any and all family memorabilia, I put the house up for sale. The memories I wanted to take with me into my new life were shipped to my new home in Columbus: the Vivian Leigh.

I also learned that the producers in Hollywood had been trying to get in touch with me all along concerning the rights to my father's novel, but Brandon had put them off by claiming I wasn't well enough to make any decisions concerning the contract they were offering. This was something I intended to take care of as soon as possible, as it would put me more on a par with Sara as far as our finances were concerned. After all, we Neilsons are an independent lot. First, however, I needed to take care of my mental and emotional state. Actually, we both did.

Having similar though separate concerns—Sara's Swiss cheese memory, for one, as well as the decision she needed to make concerning whether to remain Sara Bennington or go through the hassle of trying to prove herself to be Ashley Neilson—we had decided it best to consult different therapists so as not to cloud any issues. Sara was doing better at psychotherapy than I, confidently making the decision to remain Sara, since she didn't seem to be making much headway as far as regaining her

memory of being Ashley was concerned. I suspected her inability
to remember was due in part to the fact that she didn't truly want
to.

I thought this might be for the best, because I was having my
own share of problems due to remembering far too much, in vivid
detail. Not only was I dealing with all the complicated and perplexing issues of that final night with Brandon and its world-alter-
ing revelations, but I was also faced with unresolved issues over
the death of my parents and the plane crash, which had surfaced
during therapy. These latter issues would remain unresolved, or so
the therapist contended, until I was ready to hop on a plane again.

Jason came to visit at Thanksgiving. He had returned to
school right after the funeral, and his life had gone on much as
before. He appeared to be doing fine, and seemed especially glad
to see Celia happily ensconced in our home, going about her usual
duties. He even returned and spent the Christmas holidays with
us. And although Sara still did not remember him, they got along
famously.

The last hurdle in my recovery—the cane having gone the way
of the walker, a week or so before Christmas—was to get back on
the horse that had thrown me. This was going to be harder than it
sounded, but at least I had the woman I loved and intended to
spend the rest of my life with by my side. We would face this challenge together and prevail, just like we had all the previous ones.

"I've never been to California," Sara commented absently as
we sat waiting for our flight to be called.

"Neither have I," I responded ruefully, somewhat distracted
by the scene unfolding before me. A young man in baggy jeans,
floppy T-shirt, and Braves baseball cap had nearly run into a little
old lady carrying a heavy bag, because she had abruptly stopped
in front of him.

"Faith, I'm sorry," Sara apologized, "I didn't think before I
said that. I—"

"It's okay." I waved her apology away, still watching as the
young man mumbled an automatic apology to the old lady, moved
on several steps, paused, and spun around on his heel. He eyed the
lady briefly and then glanced back down the concourse in the
direction he had been headed. Reaching up, he removed his cap
and scratched his head. Just then an attendant driving one of the
customer courtesy carts rounded a corner. The young man waved
his cap in the air to get the driver's attention. Once he had it, he
gestured toward the lady. The driver nodded, and the young man
returned his cap to his head and continued on his way.

"I know this is hard for you, sweetheart," Sara said as the

driver stopped the cart and asked the lady if she needed any help.

I merely nodded, still engrossed in the lady's plight. She got in on the other side as the driver took the heavy bag and loaded it on the cart. I wondered if this scene would be playing out now had the young man not nearly run over the lady and then taken the time to flag down the driver. My belief in the kindness of strangers and the caring nature of the human heart somewhat restored by this brief incident, I turned my attention back to the love of my life, who was touching my hand.

"Although I wanted to save this and surprise you later, I think I should go ahead and tell you now." Green eyes filled with love, warmth, and a tiny bit of uncertainty darted back and forth, searching mine. "I changed our travel arrangements and booked passage on a train for our return trip. I thought we'd take our time getting back and...see a bit of the country along the way." One dark brown eyebrow arched skyward and quivered.

I couldn't help but smile. "This my reward for facing my fears?" I queried.

"Maaay-be," she drawled, a sly smirk forming on her face as she leaned in closer. "Then again, maybe it's just because I want to make love on a train...cross country." Both eyebrows bounced up and down in a suggestive dance, green eyes brimming with enthusiasm and amusement.

"Oh, you." I squeezed her fingers.

"Just think about it, we can say we've made love in..." She paused briefly in thought, then gave up the calculation. "Well, however many states there are between here and California. Not many people can say that, hmm?" The eyebrows danced again.

Leave it to Sara to come up with a way to reward my efforts and make yet another hurdle a memorable occasion. I could only marvel at what our life ahead might hold in store.

I found it quite ironic, although also sad, that if not for the accident ten months before, I probably never would have met the wonderful woman beside me, much less fallen in love with her. As a matter of fact, a lot of things had to fall into place in order for our being together to come about. Sort of like the young boy and the old lady. Was it destiny at work? Or was it mere happenstance? Like most of life's perplexing and unanswered questions, I knew this, like Sara's missing memories of her childhood as Ashley, was yet another mystery I would ponder for the rest of my days.

Other titles to look for in the
coming months from
Yellow Rose Books

Red Sky At Morning
By Melissa Good

Honor Bound
By Radclyffe

Thicker Than Water
By Melissa Good

The Light Fantastic
By L.A. Tucker

Tomorrow's Promise
By Radclyffe

Twist of Fate
By Jessica Casavant

Passion's Bright Fury
By Radclyffe

Rebecca's Cove
By LJ Maas

Thy Neighbor's Wife
By Georgia Beers

Raised in a small Georgia town, Anj is a homebody at heart. She loves animals, writing and dabbling in arts and crafts—a recent obsession is the world of miniatures. Anj currently resides in a midsize city south of Atlanta with her partner of twenty years and a black and white spotted Chihuahua named Toby. *Faith* is her first novel and the first story she submitted to a publisher.

Printed in the United States
849200002B